Paws for Love

MARA WELLS

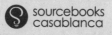

sourcebooks
casablanca

Published by Sourcebooks Casablanca, an imprint of Sourcebooks
P.O. Box 4410, Naperville, Illinois 60567-4410
(630) 961-3900
sourcebooks.com

Printed and bound in Canada.
MBP 10 9 8 7 6 5 4 3 2 1

With love to my husband, Michael Crumpton, for understanding that sometimes cleaning out the garage is important to the artistic process. Trust. Patience. Love. Twenty-one years later, we're still lucky in love.

CHAPTER 1

"Oh, Dad, it's so much worse than the trainer led us to believe." Danielle Morrow swept her chin-length bangs behind her ear and placed her hand on the heaving side of her newest foster dog—a retired racing greyhound with a broken leg the unethical trainer had claimed was from an accident while racing. Spiral fractures in various stages of healing, like the ones in the X-ray hung on the light box on the wall, showed the trainer had lied. Fractures like these only came from one thing—abuse.

"Good thing the whole nasty sport has finally been outlawed in Florida." Danielle's dad adjusted the reading glasses perched on the end of his nose and stared intently at the X-ray. After thirty years running his own veterinary clinic, Dr. Morrow was no stranger to the cruelty inflicted on animals, but he treated each case as a fresh outrage. His jaw clenched, and he ran a palm over his completely bald scalp. "Hopefully, these types of injuries will soon be a thing of the past."

"Hopefully." Danielle didn't share her father's unrelenting belief in a brighter future, not for animals and not for herself. But she was happy to be where she was at this moment—by her father's side helping a four-legged friend in need. When she'd seen this six-year-old on the Miami shelter's website and read the comments left by his supposedly heartbroken trainer, she knew he was perfect for their father-daughter approach to fostering. Her dad got the dogs healthy, and she trained them for life in a home.

If she'd once imagined working side by side with her father with her own veterinary medicine degree, well, that time was long past. Her own job, heading up Homestretch, a greyhound rescue group, kept her busy, too busy to worry about what might have been. All her worrying centered around finding these forty-mile-per-hour couch potatoes their perfect forever homes.

No doubt about it. The poor dog on the table, currently sedated, was going to be a challenge. Medical conditions and age posed obstacles to easy adoption, and this poor guy had both working against him. But he was gorgeous, long and lean like all racers, dark-gray brindle with a white chest and socks that made him look a little bit goofy.

"Might as well do his teeth while he's under." Danielle's dad broke out the necessary equipment and got to work irrigating. Care had not been the top priority wherever this dog had been held since Florida shut down the racetracks. Plaque-encrusted teeth, underfed, and the fractured leg—clearly not the dog's first—that had gotten infected, swollen, and painful to the touch.

Poor guy. Danielle's brown eyes filled with tears. She couldn't help it. No matter how many dogs she saved, it was never enough. There were always more, and if she thought too much about how many greyhounds had been put down after dog racing was banned and how many more were put down in shelters every day, she'd be unable to function. So she did what she did, one dog at a time.

She assisted her dad with the cleaning, like she'd been doing since she was shorter than the examining table, handing him tools as he asked for them, keeping her hand on the dog's side to comfort him. And herself. There was nothing more reassuring than the steady rise and fall of a dog's breath. "You're going to be okay," she whispered to the dog.

"What're you going to name this one?" Her dad removed the brace that kept the dog's mouth open in a ferocious grin that exposed every tooth.

Danielle stroked the greyhound's warm side. "I don't know. It'll come to me, though, once we get to know each other better."

Her dad busied himself cleaning up from the procedure, wiping down tools and placing them in their portable containers. "He's lucky to have you, pumpkin."

Danielle winced at her childhood nickname, which always reminded her that at a mere two inches over five feet, she'd never grown out of her baby fat. A little rounder than she'd like to be, in spite of her daily long walks with her two failed fosters, Danielle had long resigned herself to the curvy category of online shopping.

And boy was she happy that the fosters failed, because Luna and Flurry were the best roommates—cheerful, encouraging frequent exercise, and an excellent home security system. They might not love adding a third to their tight partnership, but Danielle knew they'd adjust quickly. They really were the sweetest girls, and this tough guy on the table could use a little of that sweetness.

"I'm sorry, honey." Her dad reacted to her wince with an apologetic grimace of his own. "I forget how much you hate that nickname. It's just when you were a baby, you were such a cute little butterball."

"Could be worse." Danielle smiled at her dad. She could forgive him anything after all the unconditional support he'd given her, especially during the rough years right after high school. "You could be calling me butterball."

Her dad ran a hand over the dog's protruding ribs. "Maybe we should call this one Butterball."

Danielle shook her head. She'd know the dog's name when she heard it, and Butterball was definitely not it.

Just then, the dog raised its narrow muzzle, forcing open eyelids that wanted to stay closed. He struggled to roll to his feet. The task was compounded by both the sedative that wasn't fully worn off and the pain from his injured leg.

"Relax, big guy. You'll feel like yourself again soon." Danielle tried to soothe him, but he shook off her touch, determined to stand on his own.

"We better help him." Danielle's dad motioned for her to assist him in lifting the dog off the table. "He's going to be surprised by the cast. It'll take a minute for him to get his bearings."

Toes scrabbling on the epoxy floor, the greyhound watched them warily, hackles raised. He backed up, then whipped his head around to look at the hind leg, set in a bandage cast. He growled low in his throat, putting more weight on it. When his legs went out, Danielle was there to catch him.

"You're okay now. I promise, life is about to get a whole lot better."

He snarled at her, curling one lip to show a freshly cleaned tooth. Careful to avoid his mouth, Danielle eased him to the floor. Lying on his side, he growled one last time before giving in to the sedative and closing his eyes.

"He's a fighter that one, a real soldier." Danielle's dad sprayed disinfectant on the table and rubbed it down with a paper towel.

Danielle smiled, hand trapped between the dog's side and the floor. She shifted until she was sitting on the floor, legs stretched out the length of the greyhound. "You're right, Dad. Let's call him Sarge. What do you think, Sarge? Is that what we should call you?"

Sarge's ears twitched at the sound of the name.

Danielle laughed. "I think he approves."

"It's a good pick for this one. He's a trouper." Danielle's dad squatted to give the dog a pat. "Want some help crating him?"

"I'll wait until he wakes up." Danielle stroked a hand down Sarge's back, counting the bumps on his spine and planning what dietary supplements would help speed his healing and fatten him up a bit. Not that greyhounds ever got fat, but he shouldn't have more than three spinal bumps visible, not the eight currently protruding from his back.

Danielle's dad patted her head. "He's lucky to have you."

"We're lucky to have each other."

Best man? Ridiculous. Knox Donovan suppressed a groan and rubbed the area above his leg brace, encouraging the tight muscle to calm the hell down already. Per usual, it did not listen to him, damn insubordinate thing. If only his own body listened to him the way Marines under his command had, his life would be a lot easier. But no one was under his command, not anymore.

Instead, he was stuck in an upscale bridal store getting fitted for a light-gray tuxedo. Until a year ago, he'd barely known his youngest brother, Caleb, and now he was the best man at his wedding? Unbelievable. Of course, he was sharing the so-called honor with his other brother, Lance, also standing on a raised platform in gray, stoic as the tailor got up in his business.

"You should just go to the courthouse like Carrie and I did." Lance winced when a pin got a little too close to his junk. Knox had thought Lance remarrying his ex was a big mistake, but so far, they seemed happy. Deliriously, sickeningly so.

"No way." Caleb grinned at his brother. "Riley's been working on this wedding forever. Forget disappointing Riley, her Grams would kill us if we backed out of this extravaganza. Sorry, brothers. This is how it is."

Caleb, of course, looked comfortable in his lightweight suit in a slightly darker gray than the groomsmen's outfits. Knox plucked at the too-tight seam holding his tuxedo's sleeve to the shoulder and sighed. Maybe he'd get to use this suit twice. After all, his grandfather was engaged to his ex-first-wife, a wedding in the works that would be twice as elaborate and twice as expensive as Caleb's.

All this focus on exes and weddings made Knox itchy in a way that couldn't be scratched. He'd been back in Miami Beach for over a year and still hadn't seen Danielle, his high-school sweetheart. The girl he'd left for the Marines, the girl he'd never quite gotten out of his mind, the girl he deliberately refused to look up. The past should stay in the past. But he'd really thought with all the people they had in common—his grandfather who'd adopted one of her foster dogs, for one—that they'd have crossed paths by now.

Perhaps it was because he still felt as much a stranger as when he'd arrived. His real home was the Marines, but they didn't want him anymore. Medically separated. The words choked him. The memories haunted him in his sleep. His unit was still deployed, and it killed him not to be out there with them.

Sure, his brothers had welcomed him, given him meaningful work, made him partner in their crazy scheme to renovate a gone-to-hell, fifty-five-plus retirement building into a desirable property, and he supposed that when he was around them, things were better. But he still spent his nights alone in the studio apartment he'd rented just over the causeway in Little Haiti. He lived with the hope that all the physical therapy appointments at the VA would result in a miracle. No doctor agreed with him, but he wasn't ready to admit his time in the Marines was over for good.

"Sir?" The tailor, an older man with a carefully groomed mustache straight out of a black-and-white movie, indicated that Knox should place his feet wider for easier access to the inseam.

Knox gritted his teeth and spread 'em. He'd lived through an exploding IED. He could handle a few hours getting suited up for his little brother. When this was over, though, Caleb owed him a beer. Or two. Knox pictured the bottle, frosted and cold, and waited for the sartorial torture to end.

CHAPTER 2

THE GRAND OPENING OF FUR HAVEN DOG PARK WOULD BE AN excellent opportunity to scout potential forever homes for the many dogs Homestretch volunteers fostered, including her beloved but still reluctant Sarge. Danielle had placed three dogs at the last Fur Haven event, but that was almost a year and a half ago. In that time, she'd seen Fur Haven transformed by the Donovan brothers, had even caught glimpses of both Caleb and Lance, but never Knox. Never the Donovan brother she was looking for, never the Donovan brother who'd broken her heart.

She hid the desire to see her high-school boyfriend deep down where she could pretend it didn't exist. Instead, she kept her attention in the present, marveling at the changes wrought in such a short time. Fur Haven was no longer a dressed-up empty lot or the makeshift front lawn of the old Dorothy building. No, the Donovan brothers had built a two-story parking garage on the lot where the dog park used to exist, but that hadn't been the end of the park. Instead, in some clever engineering, they'd moved the dog park to the top of the parking garage.

Like the whole neighborhood, Danielle was anxious to see the result. The Donovans had kept the parking garage roof closed until the grand opening, building up the suspense. Fur Haven had its own website where someone posted beautiful but cryptic photos of the new space to build hype. When Riley Carson contacted her about having a table at the grand opening, Danielle jumped at the chance. She didn't like to leave dogs in foster homes for too long, worried about the separation anxiety that came when they settled in and then were asked to move again.

Now, Danielle straightened photos of the dogs available

for adoption, beautiful greyhounds all of them. Retired racers and dogs used for breeding racers. So many still left to rehome. Danielle'd heard that some greyhound rescues rented vans and took groups of greyhounds out of state for adoption. Danielle wasn't that desperate yet, but she could use the boost of placing a few dogs to brighten her week—and free up some fosters to take in new dogs.

Luna and Flurry lounged under the table, already at home in their new space. Danielle always brought them with her to events. They were excellent examples of what chill companions retired racers could be. They lumbered to their feet when visitors approached, eager for a scratch behind the ears and a leg to lean on. People were often surprised at how affectionate they were, and it warmed her heart to see Flurry and Luna take on the role of breed ambassadors.

Sarge's hair bristled, but he didn't growl.

"Easy, boy." She praised him for his control with a scratch behind the ears. He'd come a long way from when she'd first brought him to her father's veterinary clinic. It'd been about a month since her dad had operated on his leg, and although much of the damage was repaired, Sarge would always walk with a limp. The broken leg would remain weaker than the others. She could tell it bothered the dog. He licked the hair above the top of his cast a lot. When the leg would unexpectedly give out, he always turned his head and perked his ears at it, as if surprised.

Beside her now, his head reached nearly as high as her hip. She rested her hand on the dome of his crown, noting the anticipatory tremble in his muscles.

"Good, Sarge. Stand at attention but don't engage. You're always ready for action, aren't you? But today you can relax and hang with me." She'd brought him today for the crowd exposure, but she didn't intend for him to leave her side. Luna and Flurry would handle charming people. Sarge's job was to stay by her side and not show any signs of aggression. The martingale collar gave her control should he decide to lunge. Greyhounds were famous for slipping collars and leashes because of their long, thin heads, so the double loop was imperative to keeping the sight hounds close by.

Luna and Flurry knew who buttered their bread, or rather, baked the dog biscuits, so Danielle didn't worry about them taking off. But she kept Sarge's leash short, her leg always in contact with him. Danielle busied herself setting up the table. She reached into one of the many tote bags she'd brought with her and pulled out the individually wrapped dog treats she'd brought to entice people to her table. She placed them in a bone-shaped bowl and then laid out more swag—Frisbees and tennis balls with the rescue's name.

"You all set?" Riley approached the table, all smiles, holding hands with her fiancé, Caleb Donovan. The two had built the first Fur Haven, and Fur Haven-in-the-Sky was their special project.

"Ready." Danielle smiled at Riley. She'd always liked her. Riley's grandmother was a long-time client of her father's, and she and Riley had been only a few years apart at Beach High. It was good to see her happy with Caleb. Danielle wondered, briefly, if Knox might attend the grand opening. Her heart pinged at the thought. Of course he wouldn't. Although he'd been in town for over a year, he hadn't bothered to look her up. Not that she expected him to. It'd been over a decade after all. Why would he think of her at all?

"The new Fur Haven is fantastic. You must be proud."

Riley's wide smile grew even wider. "We are. Caleb and I are going to be married here."

"Congratulations. It sounds perfect." Danielle could easily picture the ceremony. The park was lovely—healthy grass covered the garage roof, with a variety of palm trees and other plants strategically placed for shade and as demarcation for various parts of the park. Small and large dogs could be separated by a sliding gate that could also be left open. Agility equipment filled one corner of the park, and bone-shaped benches for owners were scattered over the rooftop.

"Thanks." Riley picked up a branded tennis ball. "Can I take this for LouLou?"

"Help yourself." Danielle swept her hand to indicate all the Homestretch dog swag on the table. She wasn't surprised when Riley scooped up a dog treat, too. Riley doted on her little poodle. "I'm sure you have a million things to take care of today."

"That we do." Caleb's easy smile reminded Danielle so much of his older brother that she had to pause and blink back old memories. "Please excuse us. We hope you find homes for all these gorgeous dogs today."

"Thanks. Me too." Danielle watched the couple leave, hand in hand, and couldn't suppress the envy that rose and colored her vision, making Caleb look even more like his brother as he walked away. It wasn't like she thought of Knox all the time, but it was hard not to with Caleb's involvement in the dog park.

Of course, she'd thought of calling Knox a few times since she'd learned he was back. It was normal to wonder about an ex, she reassured herself. Totally normal. His meddling Grandpa William had even slipped her Knox's cell number with a wink when he'd picked up his rescue greyhound from her house after she'd babysat the dog while he was on a cruise. Grandpa William'd come back glowing. She'd thought it was the sunshine, but a few weeks later, she heard he'd asked Riley's Grams to marry him. The Donovans were all falling in love. Only Knox was left. She couldn't help but wonder if he was seeing anyone. So what if he was? It was none of her business and hadn't been in over a decade.

Danielle straightened the flyers and the tablecloth with the Homestretch logo on the front. She stacked the brochures that explained how Homestretch worked—they didn't have a facility but instead used a network of coordinated foster homes— on both corners of the table and set up the science-fair board behind her with pictures of adopted greyhounds living happily ever after.

"Is that my grandfather?"

Danielle hadn't heard that voice in fifteen years, but the way her heart sped up, pounding like it would beat through her chest and launch across the table, told her exactly who it was. Knox Donovan. High-school boyfriend, first love, father of the baby she'd lost.

Words froze in her throat, the real reason she hadn't reached out to him now so obvious. How she'd cried after their last conversation. He'd said maybe it was for the best that she'd lost the baby, that they were really too young for all this. *This* being their engagement. She'd thrown the ring he'd given her at his head. He'd caught it with his quick reflexes, a move she replayed in her head over and over again for months afterward. He'd sighed and stuck it in his pocket. He'd walked away, and she'd never seen him again. The Marines? He'd rather risk his life than be with her? God, she hadn't even looked up yet and she was already a mess, all those feelings overwhelming her again, her heart beating so fast now she wouldn't need to worry about cardio for the day.

"Is it?" His voice again, strained, huskier than she remembered. He cleared his throat, something he used to do before asking a question in class. Was he nervous?

She dragged her eyes up to his. Those Donovan blues all the brothers seemed to have inherited from their grandfather, the ones she'd hoped her own child would have.

She swallowed years of unshed tears and unsaid words. "Yes, your grandfather adopted a greyhound from my rescue. Pops. Have you met him?"

Knox nodded, his military-short hair as thick as it'd been in high school. Why couldn't he be balding? When she'd thought of him these past few years, and she hated to admit that she had still thought of him, she'd imagined him balding, beer bellied, with late-onset acne. Anything to make him less attractive to her. But no, in the flesh, he was every bit as riveting as her memories painted him. Maybe more so. Damn it.

"Yeah, Pops is quite a character." Knox's gaze traveled down her body, eyes lighting with an appreciation she couldn't bear to see. "You look good, Danielle."

"Thanks." Danielle crossed her arms over her chest. She knew it wasn't true. She was a few pounds—okay to be completely honest, twelve pounds—heavier than she'd been in high school, and she hadn't been thin in high school. "You too."

He snorted like she was the one lying. But he did look good to her, tall with military-straight posture he hadn't had when they were teens. Muscles bulged from under the USMC T-shirt that stretched tight against his defined pecs.

There they stood, looking at each other. She looked. He looked back.

"Been in town long?" she finally forced out of a throat suddenly turned sand-dune dry.

Color crept up his neck, a flush that could be attributed to the warm, humid March air. "A little over a year." His color deepened, and his thousand-yard stare landed somewhere over her right shoulder. Maybe it wasn't the heat. Maybe he was realizing that in the past year, of course she'd heard he was back in town. She might not get out much between her work for the rescue and the hours she spent at her dad's clinic, but plenty of folks reported Knox sightings.

Danielle'd heard he was somehow involved with his brothers in all the changes happening at the Dorothy, in the construction of the very dog park where they currently stood. That he was living nearby while they finished the major renovation before opening up to new unit owners. She'd also heard about his leg. Though no one seemed to know the details, it was an oft-reported fact that he'd been injured on his last tour.

"Still handsome as sin." Eliza, a long-time client of her father's and a family friend, had leaned on the high reception desk at the veterinary clinic last summer, fanning herself with one hand. "Even if his injury does slow him down now." Danielle had declined to comment, merely pulling up Eliza's black Lab's file and changing the subject by asking why Eliza'd brought Lady in this time.

Danielle looked at Knox now, and injured was not the first word that popped to mind. Yes, his left leg was in an elaborate brace he wore outside a pair of molded-to-his-body jeans, but he stood straight and tall, his strong jaw clean-shaven and as stubborn looking as ever. Handsome as sin, exactly as Eliza'd reported. Older, sure, but also more developed, his face more interesting, lined as it was with new creases around his eyes and a few around his mouth. The tattoo, half-hidden by his dark-green sleeve, intrigued her. She could just make out the word *Fidelis* and wondered how far up the ink went. Her fingers itched to trace the lettering, to find out where the swooping scrolls led. Did he have others?

A cool nose to her hand reminded Danielle where she was. Dog park. Out in public. Focused on finding new foster and forever homes for the greyhound rescues she adored, not on a love forever lost in the past.

"Good girl, Luna." Danielle slid her hand down Luna's sleek neck. Danielle gave thanks every day for the dog's presence in her life. Like now, when she seemed to sense Danielle's feelings and reached out in support.

The retired racing greyhound reached twenty-five inches at the shoulder, maybe six inches less than half Danielle's height. At five foot two, Danielle was accustomed to being the shortest person around. It made her an ideal height, however, for greyhound snuggles. Luna leaned against her leg, not heavily, a gentle weight reminding Danielle she wasn't alone.

"Your dog?" Knox hadn't moved, not a single muscle twitch, during their long silence.

Danielle relaxed into the familiar conversation. "Yes, this is Luna. The typical who-saved-who? story. Ask your grandfather. I'm sure he could tell you tales about what great companions these retired racers make."

"Thought I read something about dog racing being banned in Florida." His thousand-yard gaze switched to Luna, who stretched out her muscled neck for an exploratory sniff.

"Offer her the back of your hand," Danielle instructed, feeling more stable as the conversation flowed onto predictable tracks. "And yes, it's illegal, but the industry was given a grace period to shut down, and there are thousands of dogs that need to be rehomed. Of course, some people thought they should all be put down, and that's when Homestretch got involved. We specialize in finding homes for these deserving dogs."

"Seems like this one found a good home." Knox followed her instructions, holding out his hand at dog-sniffing distance. Luna's ears perked forward, and after a brief snuffle, she levered her head so that Knox's large hand palmed the top of her long head. He visibly relaxed, shoulders losing their rigidity, and stroked his hand across the top of her head and along her spine.

"I like to think so." Danielle blocked memories of those hands stroking the skin of her own back. Flurry stretched her front legs forward in what Danielle liked to call the greyhound downward-dog position, then joined Luna in sniffing Knox's hand. "Meet Luna and Flurry."

"Hello there." Knox gave each dog one of his hands, and they took shameless advantage, angling their heads to get scratched in their favorite places. Danielle felt a twinge of envy. She'd once loved Knox's touch, too, could remember the intense thrill of being the sole focus of his attention. She shut down that line of thought. Jealous of her dogs? Ridiculous. It was simply the shock of seeing him after so long, the surrealness of their incredibly normal conversation.

"Three dogs, huh?" Knox's husky voice brought Danielle out of her thoughts. "You must live on a ranch or something."

Startled, Danielle looked down to see Sarge had joined in the attention-craving behavior, bumping his head against Knox's thigh, the one without the brace.

"No, still in my dad's guest cottage." Danielle felt strangely bereft, watching all three dogs jockey for Knox's attention.

"You're living with your father?" Knox's gaze snapped to hers. "Is he sick?"

"Healthy as a horse." Danielle busied herself realigning the perfectly aligned brochures.

"Funny, I always pictured you in one of those big houses on the bay. Your own veterinary practice. Kids." His voice dropped. "Husband."

Danielle snorted, closing her eyes against the pain of his words. No doubt he'd known her eighteen-year-old self, still able to list her biggest dreams without blinking an eye. "Things change, Knox. People change."

Knox stayed quiet for a long moment. "Don't I know it." He rubbed his left leg, right above the brace. "Still, three of these giants seems like a lot of dog for a guesthouse."

"I'm fostering this dollface." Danielle stepped around the table to reclaim Sarge. "Hoping to find him a home today." She eyed Knox from the top of his head to the tips of his scuffed all-terrain boots, sizing him up for his fitness as a potential forever home.

"Don't look at me." Knox's rigidity returned, and he snatched his hand back like the dog's fur had burned him. "I'm not in the market for a dog."

"People rarely are. But when your dog finds you, what're you going to do?" It was a statement Danielle often said to prospective adopters, and usually people smiled and agreed with her. Knox, however, was not most people. He glared at her as if she could force him to take home a dog against his will. Some things about him hadn't changed. He still didn't like to be coerced into anything.

"Homemade brownie?" She offered him a snack from the human-treat bowl.

The suspicion melted off his face, and he took the offering. She'd known he would. Knox'd always had a sweet tooth, a whole mouth full of them.

The dogs watched longingly as Knox stuffed the entire thing in his mouth in one bite.

"Here you go, Luna. Flurry." She flicked each of them a biscuit. "And one for you, too, Sarge."

"What did you call me?" Knox barked, mouth still half-full of her brownie.

"Nothing. I was talking to the dogs."

Knox chewed fast and took a hard swallow. "I heard you say 'Sarge.'"

"Yeah, the dog." Danielle set a protective palm against Sarge's head. "Knox, are you okay?" Maybe her brownie wasn't sitting right. Her baking skills were usually put to canine use. Perhaps she'd lost her touch with human food? She scanned him for signs of choking, but all she noted was a paleness around his mouth.

"Sorry." Knox shoved hands into his jeans' pockets, disappointing Luna, who was angling for more petting. "I'm a gunnery sergeant. Was a gunnery sergeant."

"I didn't know." Oh my God, did he think she'd named a dog after him? She couldn't stop the flush of heat that washed up her neck and took over her face.

"Why would you?" Knox's laugh sounded creaky, unused. "Besides, my men mostly called me Gunny."

The casual *Why would you* cut Danielle in an unexpected way. While he'd been imagining her carrying out all their dreams without him, she'd imagined him much the same—brash and bold, running off to the Marines and never looking back. What, exactly, had he done in the Marines? How had he hurt his leg? She'd frozen him in time, the boy who broke her heart, but a man stood in front of her. As familiar as he felt, she really didn't know him at all.

"How're Cassie and Madi? You three still close?" Knox freed one hand from his pocket to absently stroke the top of Sarge's head.

Another wound, another memory. "No. Cassie went to NYU and never came back. Madi's in Texas now, I think." The three of them, best friends since fourth grade, had had such big plans. At least Cassie and Madi had followed their dreams. "Madi came through town a few years ago." Ten years ago. "We had lunch. She loves teaching high school." At least, that was what her social media posts were mostly about. That and her family, a handsome-enough husband and twin girls. Danielle didn't think of it as stalking so much as checking in on an old friend without all the awkwardness of actual contact.

"That's a shame." Knox's gaze searched her face, like he knew something was off but couldn't quite figure out what. Sarge bumped his hand when the petting slowed.

"A shame she's doing what she loves?" Danielle envied Madi her focus. She'd wanted to be a teacher and a mom, and she went out into the world and did it. Not that Danielle didn't love her own dual career as greyhound rescuer and vet tech, but it wasn't what she'd envisioned for herself at eighteen. No, that vision was standing right in front of her, squinting like the light hurt his eyes even though the sun was behind him.

"A shame the three of you aren't tight anymore." Knox's squint relaxed, and the corner of his mouth hitched up in a half smile. "You used to have a lot of fun together. Remember Senior Ditch Day?"

"We were kids. Now we're not." Danielle shrugged her shoulders, trying to appear philosophical. People drifted apart. It was a fact. "Like us. So, unless you're interested in the adoption process, I should really get back to work."

"It was good to see you," Knox bit out and turned sharply on his heel, marching off in the direction of the sweets booth before Danielle could respond. Danielle recognized Sydney manning the booth, her little chihuahua strapped to her front in what could only be called a baby sling. Sarge whimpered and watched Knox go with obvious longing.

"Well, that was awkward, wasn't it?" Danielle squatted, a hand cupped under Sarge's muzzle. "Don't take it personally, Sarge. Trust me when I tell you that man is commitment-phobic. It's him, not you."

Another mantra from the post-breakup months. Flurry nudged her chin, and Danielle turned her head to rest her cheek against the top of Flurry's flat head. Dog snuggles were the best. They could get you through anything, even if that thing was watching the man who broke your heart walk away from you again.

CHAPTER 3

KNOX DIDN'T HAVE AN EXIT STRATEGY, AND HE CURSED THE soreness in his leg that kept him from retreating at full speed. All he knew was that every second he stood in Danielle's presence, another year peeled away until he was once again that raw eighteen-year-old, terrified of ruining her life. He'd almost done it, too, knocking her up right before graduation. He'd tried to make it right. The proposal. The ring. He'd even been happy about it. A lifetime with Danielle by his side? It was a future he hadn't deserved but desperately wanted anyway.

In the end, the literal end, she'd lost the baby, and he'd known this was his one chance to do the right thing and let her go. To not repeat the mistakes of his parents, the mistake his mother reminded him of his entire childhood.

"If not for you" was his mother's most common refrain. If not for him, she'd have moved to New York or LA to act. She would've been a star. TV, movies, the grand stage. The dream changed depending on whatever awards show she'd recently watched. Instead, she'd stayed in Miami and been his mom, a sacrifice she expected him to acknowledge daily. It wasn't an accident that he kept his weekly obligation calls to under ten minutes. No matter where he was in the world, he'd always checked in, but he'd never connected. In his fourteen years in the Corps, she'd become a voice on the phone, a tether to a past he'd rather forget.

Warm weight slammed into his bad leg, and he went down. It wasn't the first time, but it had been a long time since he'd been knocked off-balance. His hours of physical therapy training paid off, and he rolled safely to the right, palm planted in the grass.

"Goodness gracious, I am sorry." A wrinkled hand, pale and small, reached down to help him up.

Knox swallowed a grunt and his pride, a bitter pill, and grasped her wrist, using her slight weight to lever himself to his feet.

"Knox, isn't it?" The older woman dabbed at her neck with a paper napkin before tucking it in her bra strap. "I've seen you around, but I don't think we've officially met. I'm Eliza." She slapped her leg, and the black Lab at her side immediately sank to its haunches. "This is Lady. I'm afraid she can get a bit overexcited around the younger dogs and doesn't know her own strength."

"No harm, no foul." Knox swiped at his pants, more for something to do with his hands than concern for grass stains. "Pleasure to meet you. You're a friend of Riley's, aren't you? Do you live in the building?" He referred to the Dorothy, the aging Art Deco fifty-five-plus building his brother Caleb and his fiancée, Riley, lived in, and his brother Lance and his wife, Carrie, were helping to remodel. Knox helped out whenever he could, which was most days except for his never-ending physical therapy appointments, and he'd begun the research for a new security system for the building. With the attraction of the public dog park, Caleb was worried about the Dorothy's exposure and didn't want any thieves thinking the retirement-aged residents were easy prey.

"No, but I'm planning to move in soon." Eliza's face lit with joy. "My house across the street is up for sale, in case you know anyone who might be interested. Once I've got an offer, I'll start the paperwork to move into one of the new remodeled units. A one-bedroom is too small with a dog like Lady, but I think she'll be comfortable in a two-bedroom, don't you?"

Surprised to be consulted, Knox found his head nodding. "Plenty of room for both you ladies, I imagine. You should let us know if you have any special requests. Easier to make changes now than once everything is done."

"An excellent observation, young man." Eliza reached out the same hand that had helped him up to pat his arm. "I'll put some thought into it and let you know."

Knox didn't typically like to be touched by strangers, but Eliza's open face invited informality. Lady bumped the hand that hung at his side, and he absently fondled the top of her head. Her tongue lolled out in appreciation. Knox thought about Caleb and Riley living in the building, about Lance and Carrie's house a few blocks away. He thought about his lonely rental and how little time he spent there. He thought about how he'd been enjoying helping Lance with the renovation work. Turned out he had a knack for whacking down cabinetry and ripping pipes out of walls.

"How much are you asking for your place?" The words were out before he'd fully thought it through, but it would be convenient to live across the street from the place he was spending most of his waking hours.

Eliza named a price that wasn't cheap but not as high as he'd expected with the apology, "I'm afraid it needs a bit of work. That's why I'm moving. I'm long past the age of fixer-uppers, if you know what I mean."

"Do you think I could see it sometime?" A little fixing up didn't scare him, now that he had some basic skills and his brother's expertise to rely on. Plus, he had plenty of hazard-duty pay stashed away, and there was always the child-support money his mother had cashed to spite his father but put in savings for him. Her alimony checks had been generous enough for them both to live on until he'd joined up. Knox hadn't seen the balance in years, but last time he'd checked, it was surprisingly high. His mother had always called it his college money, and he'd had some idea of saving it for his own kids' college funds. But why not buy a house? Wasn't that what Caleb was always nattering on about, the soundness of real estate as an investment strategy? It wouldn't be a home, of course, any more than his apartment was, but he could stop paying rent, flip the house, and make a profit when he moved on.

"Of course!" Eliza reached into her blouse. Knox averted his eyes so he wouldn't see exactly what was going on. "Here's my card. Give me a call. Maybe we don't even need a real estate agent, eh?" She winked at him.

He held the limp card between his thumb and forefinger, trying not to think about where it'd come from. What else did she have hidden in that bra? Dog treats? Bottle of mace? A snack for later? He tucked the card into his back pocket. "Will do, ma'am."

"Wonderful." She beamed at him. "Lady and I'll be heading home now. Nice to meet you."

"You, too." Knox wished he could follow her to the elevator and make his escape. He'd promised to help out with the grand opening. Riley'd conscripted him for cleanup duty, and her friend Sydney had made him promise to help out at the sweets booth. He headed there now, his head full of possibilities. Buying a house didn't have to mean anything. It was just an investment after all.

His heart said otherwise, though. No doubt about it. Seeing Danielle again had brought up those old longings for home and family, a place to belong. But he wasn't eighteen years old anymore, and he knew better than anyone that wishing didn't make a thing so. Still, a house of his own? It was the first thing he'd been excited about since the doctors broke the news to him that he wouldn't be rejoining his unit.

It was the challenge of it, he was sure, the excitement centered around the chance to flex the new skills he'd learned working with Lance. He'd love to pull off a renovation without his brother telling him how to do every little thing. He'd felt the same in the Marines. Each time he earned a new belt in the MC Martial Arts Program, he doubled down and trained harder, always pushing his skill level. It was why he'd ended up as an instructor—he liked to put what he knew to use. It wasn't like he could throw anyone to the mat anymore, but he could certainly show a bucket of plaster who was boss.

He patted his back pocket and headed to where he saw Sydney bustling about behind a table laden with all things sweet and delicious. A three-tiered cake dominated the table, pink frosting with white piping and tiny, plastic dogs cavorting across the top.

Within moments, he dug into his exorbitantly priced slice of pink cake. If the bubble-gum flavor reminded him of stolen kisses from fifteen years ago, that was between him and his taste buds.

———————

Danielle picked up the lone brochure still left on the table. The sun was setting, turning the early March sky pink and orange. The view from the new dog park was stunning, ocean to the east and the Miami skyline to the west. With the exception of a few high-rises, it was a nearly unobstructed view. Danielle paused to take it all in. The Donovan brothers had a lot to be proud of here.

A long-suffering sigh brought her attention back to her dogs. Luna and Flurry slept under the table, their long legs sticking straight out to the side. Sarge stood at attention, positioned so he could keep an eye both on her and on Knox.

It hadn't escaped her notice that the dog was fascinated by the man he'd met today. Sometimes it was like that with dogs. They knew their people, sometimes even before the people did. It was clear to her Sarge liked her, felt protective even, but he'd decided his person was Knox Donovan. Danielle didn't know how to explain to Sarge not to get his hopes up, that Knox was a heartbreaker through and through.

Sarge shifted, putting more weight on his healing leg, and visibly shuddered at the pain. He immediately corrected his stance, putting as little pressure on the affected foot as possible. Danielle's heart constricted. The poor dog had been through so much. She looked across the rooftop to where Knox helped take down the sweets booth table, folding the legs up and stacking it against the collection of other tables. All around the park, dogs lounged near their owners or ran in groups of three or four. People chipped in to help with packing everything away, all smiles and laughter. But not Knox. He worked alone, face grim as he completed his table-folding task and moved on to racking up a half-dozen chairs.

Danielle looked down at Sarge, at the longing in his eyes. The poor thing had been through so much. Too much. She decided right then and there, if Sarge wanted Knox, then Knox was about to get himself a dog.

She sorted the leftover supplies into tote bags. There wasn't much left. The day had been a success with lots of folks stopping by and a few in-depth conversations she felt sure would lead to adoptions. Packed up, Danielle gathered the three leashes in her left hand, determined to make one more matchmaking attempt before the day was done. "Come on, kids. Let's go make some friends."

Luna and Flurry perked up, tails wagging lazily. Sarge looked concerned, but as soon as she headed in Knox's direction, he strained at the lead.

"Hey." Danielle kept a firm grip on the leashes, stopping a few feet from Knox's chair-folding project. "Need any help?"

Knox turned those blue eyes on her, and she was glad she'd spoken first because anything else she might've said flew out of her mind. A bit of pink frosting clung to the corner of his mouth. She couldn't look away. The urge to brush it with her thumb was nearly irresistible. She could picture it, the slide of her skin against his soft lip. She'd always loved how the lower lip was plumper than the upper one, a permanent pout she'd loved to tease into a smile. She could see that smile now, in her memory, and felt the joy that had coursed through her every time she'd stood on tiptoe to press her mouth to his.

Why did no other boyfriend's kiss linger in her memory the way Knox's did? There'd been a few, after that first year, nothing ever too serious. She'd tried to keep it light, fun. Maybe that was why she couldn't even remember one name, not with Knox standing in front of her. Scowling.

Scowling?

"I can fold a chair or two without any help."

His bitterness cut through all her warm, fuzzy memories and landed her smack-dab in this awkward moment. He clearly wasn't remembering the slide of their lips on each other.

"That's not what I meant." Her grip tightened on the leashes, and Sarge turned his gaze on her, concerned. She consciously relaxed her fingers, one at a time. No need to transmit her distress to the greyhounds.

Knox collapsed a chair with a loud clap of metal on metal and shoved it into the pile with the other chairs.

"Hey, Danielle, good to see you." Caleb approached, pushing a low, flat cart half-full of chairs. "Want to give me a hand loading these up?"

"Sure." She gave the dogs the command for stay and grabbed the chair Knox had just folded.

"I told you I've got this." Knox pulled the chair out of her grasp and loaded it onto the cart. "You can go."

His tone was so military, so dismissive. So not the Knox she'd known. She almost cringed, but then she saw that Sarge was cringing and that made her mad.

"Watch your tone around the dogs." Her voice was low and modulated. "I don't want them triggered by your sour mood."

"Triggered? Dogs?" Knox swung another chair onto the cart while Caleb watched the two of them with open interest. "That's ridiculous."

"It is not ridiculous. They are very sensitive to emotion." Danielle soothed a hand along Sarge's spine. The dog visibly relaxed at her touch, leaning into her with a drafty sigh.

"Sure. Whatever you say." Knox loaded the last two chairs onto the cart. He held out the back of his hand to Sarge, the way she'd told him to early today. "Sorry, big guy."

Sarge's tail thumped against Danielle's leg, and he looked up at Knox with adoring eyes.

"You're a good boy, aren't you?" Knox's hand slipped under Sarge's long jaw for a scratch. Sarge took a hesitant step forward, favoring his back leg. Knox noticed, and his eyes narrowed. "What happened to him?"

"Multiple fractures. He'll heal, but the leg will never be the same."

Something came over Knox then, a grim darkness Danielle recognized from her own dark days. Knox's other hand came around to cup Sarge under the chin. He looked into the dog's eyes. "I know how you feel, buddy."

That was when Danielle knew Sarge's instincts were right. Knox was totally Sarge's human. It was clear they were meant for each other.

"Do you want to hold his leash?" Danielle offered him the black lead, but Knox shook his head.

"I'm not really a dog person."

Sarge's ears drooped like he understood the words.

"Doesn't look that way to me."

"I told you not to get your hopes up about me. Couldn't have a dog if I wanted one. I'm renting right now."

"Oh." Danielle's fist clenched around the rejected leash. "Of course. We should get going, huh?" She forced her voice to a cheerfulness she didn't feel. She turned to Caleb, who'd watched the interaction without saying a word. "Today was lovely. Can you let Riley know I said thank you? I have a feeling your new dog park is going to be wildly popular."

Caleb flashed her a smile. "I hope you're right. Amount of money we sank into this thing? Still, it's a labor of love and those rewards can't be counted in dollar bills. At least that's what Riley tells me."

Danielle rested a hand on Luna's head, and Flurry leaned against her leg. "It's good to see you. Keep me in the dog park loop, will you? I think I got some good prospects today."

"You have excellent recruiters here." Caleb crouched down to give all three dogs a good scratch, then stood and gave her a one-armed hug. "Don't be a stranger, huh? These canine Ferraris love to run, don't they?"

"They do indeed. Don't worry. We'll be back." Danielle looked at Knox as she said the words. Did he actually flinch at the prospect of seeing her again? She returned Caleb's hug, then clicked her tongue for the dogs to follow her, heading for the elevator that would take them to the ground floor of the garage where she'd parked her SUV.

"Danielle?"

"Yeah?" She turned at Knox's call. He stood, arms crossed in such a way that she could see more of his Semper Fidelis tattoo.

"It was good to see you."

The elevator pinged, and she herded the greyhounds into the car without answering. What was she supposed to say? When it came to Knox, she didn't know how she felt. Not anymore.

Sarge whined as the elevator descended.

"Don't worry." She kept her hand in the space between his shoulders, reassuring herself as much as the dog. It wasn't the elevator that made her hands shake. No, it was Knox's eyes on her when she'd looked over her shoulder before following the dogs onto the elevator. Fierce. Hot. Possessive.

She couldn't deny it excited her. And terrified her. What would it be like to have Knox back in her life? His gaze had promised she'd soon find out.

CHAPTER 4

KNOX GRUNTED, PUSHING THE LEG-EXTENSION MACHINE UP with both legs, then slowly controlling the glide back to neutral. It'd been two days since Lady had knocked him down at the dog park, and he was determined to build up more strength so he wouldn't be taken by surprise like that again. He hated not having complete control over his bum leg, and after almost two years of recovery, he wanted to be further along. He wanted to be back to his old self, not easily taken down by a fifty-pound Lab. Weren't they supposed to be the friendliest dogs on the planet? A Doberman or Rottweiler would make a better story, but no, his tale was the age-old felled by friendly fire.

"Eight more." Ana, the physical therapy tech, didn't look like a sadistic witch with her two purple and pink braids twirled high on her head and a face that looked like she'd get carded for an R-rated movie. She patted the top of his shoulder. "You're doing great. Seven more now."

"Increase the weight?" Knox's question came out more pained than he'd intended.

Ana's braids shook their disapproval. "We can't rush things. You know that. We talk about it every time you come in."

Three times per week, Knox showed up at the VA physical therapy center for his PT appointments, and three times per week, he asked when he'd be able to walk without the brace. No one, not a doctor or a physical therapist, would give him a timeline. It was frustrating as hell. So he did what he'd learned in the Marines—push harder, push farther. Pain is only weakness leaving the body.

Knox huffed his way through the remaining set, even though his braced leg burned and, on the last two reps, twitched. He didn't tell Ana. She might not increase the weight on Wednesday if he complained today, and as far as he could tell, increased weight meant increased strength in that leg. Increased strength meant an end to living with the brace. Maybe he was showing off when he did an extra rep while Ana was distracted by something on her tablet.

"All done?" She flashed a perfect smile at him. He imagined the braces came off not too long ago. She didn't look old enough to be out of high school, but she'd assured him in their first session together that she was. She'd also told him that she'd earned her A.A. degree and aced her certification in three years, but she did admit that she couldn't legally drink until her next birthday.

"If you say so." Knox never wanted to call it quits at physical therapy, and he performed his take-home exercises religiously. Zealously. If they told him to do something once per day, he did it twice. "Sure you don't want to give me something else to do?"

"You are determined. I'll give you that." Ana checked his chart on the tablet, tapping the tip of the stylus against her lower lip. "Have it your way then. Let's work on balance."

Knox stifled his groan. Strength training, yes. He could push through anything physical. But the balance exercises killed him. "Sure thing."

"Let's put you on the BAPS board for a bit." She bounced away in her high-tech sneakers.

Knox marched after her, ready to face his blue plastic nemesis. He stepped onto foot outlines on the irregularly shaped disk. He immediately grabbed for the bars on either side to steady himself on the board.

"You wanted more weight? Let's try some here." Ana knelt down to fiddle with the board, a post, and a small weight. "Okay, give it a try. Twenty taps forward, then twenty taps backward. You know the drill."

He did indeed know the drill, and he hated it. Today, he found out he hated it even more with weight added to the board so that it took more effort to keep his balance on the unsteady surface. After the first ten taps, his braced leg started to tremble, but he pushed his awareness of it away and kept tapping.

"Hey, hey, hey. You gotta stop him, Ana." Another physical therapist technician, this one significantly older than Ana with gray in his hipster beard and in the long strands of hair he had pulled back into a ponytail. "Don't you see his leg?"

Knox stilled the board, and Ana and the hipster tech both inspected his braced leg.

"Knox." Ana's voice was schoolteacher stern. "You're supposed to tell me when your leg is stressed."

"I didn't feel it," he lied.

"I'm Luis." The hipster took the tablet from Ana. "And you're lying."

Prove it. Knox didn't say the words, but Luis must've seen them in his expression because he shook his head and said, "Leathernecks. Never know when to stop."

Knox knew enough to stay silent. Luis clicked away on the pad, shifting his gaze from the screen to Knox and back again several times. Finally, he asked, "When was the last time you saw your physical therapist?"

Knox tipped his head at Ana. "She's right here."

"Not a tech. When was your last evaluation?"

Knox lifted a shoulder.

"How's next Tuesday? Eight in the morning good for you?" Luis flipped the tablet so Knox could see a calendar.

It wasn't like Knox had a regular job. He helped out Lance nearly every day, but he could come and go as he pleased. Knox lifted his other shoulder. "Sure."

"Good because you are long overdue. Ana, we need to talk." Luis handed the tablet back to her and whisked himself away.

"Sounds like you're in trouble." Knox carefully stepped off the board. "I hope it's not my fault."

"Luis is so uptight." Ana rolled her eyes. "But he is right about one thing. You shouldn't be pushing yourself so hard that your leg shakes like that. You've got to tell me when you're at your edge."

"I tell you." Knox rubbed his leg, which was still shaking.

Ana shook her head so hard that her right braid unraveled and tumbled down the back of her head. "I know you want everything to hurry up, but that's not how the body works. You have to give it time."

"It's been almost two years." Knox didn't mean to raise his voice.

Ana stepped back, holding up her hand. "And it could take another year. Or two. You don't tell your body what its healing schedule is. It tells you."

Knox narrowed his eyes at her, knowing it wasn't her fault his body was so slow to come back from his IED injury. Knowing it wasn't her fault that he wasn't with his unit. That he was medically separated. Separated, another word for divorce. And it definitely wasn't her fault that he'd probably never be an active Marine again.

"Sorry," he growled, his voice still too loud. It wasn't her fault; it wasn't anyone else's fault but his own. He'd grown too complacent, the sameness of the supply run lulling him into thinking he knew the terrain. If he'd been more vigilant, he might've noticed the fresh dirt on the road a few moments sooner, and then maybe Munoz and Whittier would still be alive, and he'd still have full use of his left leg.

Ana wound her braid back up onto her head and secured it with a bright-blue hair tie. "Keep the faith, Knox. You'll get there."

He grunted his response because her *there* meant regaining strength and stability, but she didn't think—no doctor or physical therapist thought—he'd get full use of his leg back. When the medical team at Lejeune determined he was no longer fit for active duty, that was the end of it, his entire career in the Marines. The longer and harder he worked, the more he wondered if they were right.

"See you next time." He rubbed his left leg, right above the brace, willing the muscles to calm the hell down.

"After your meeting with the doc, okay?" Ana quickly passed him, heading to her next appointment.

Knox limped out to his Range Rover and hauled himself into the driver's seat. If he was lucky, Lance's crew would be doing some demolition at the Dorothy today. He could really get behind a sledgehammer right about now. It was satisfying, the swing and smash of demo work. He shot Lance a text that he was on his way, then scrolled through the rest of his messages.

Danielle's message was the fourth one down, right after an automated text from the pharmacy reminding him to pick up his prescription, a note from his mother asking to reschedule their weekly phone call for an hour later, and yet another text from Morales. Knox deleted the pharmacy reminder, texted his mom a quick affirmative, and let his finger hang over Morales' name before deciding a phone call would be quicker.

"Gunny!" Morales' voice was loud enough that Knox dialed down his volume. Morales had been there when the IED exploded, had been the one to pull Knox away from the wreckage, had been the one to tell him Munoz and Whittier were gone. Yeah, they went way back. "How's life in the Sunshine State?"

"Good." Knox rubbed at the ache in his leg. At least it had finally stopped shaking. "How's Atlanta? The business?"

"Damn paperwork with the city, man. It's killing me." Morales had left the Marines a few months after Knox, at the conclusion of his third tour, and knocked around a bit before settling in Atlanta where he was opening an all-Marine veteran-run security firm. "But we're almost there. Set to open any day now. You given any more thought to joining us? We could use the muscle."

Knox winced, glad they weren't on video so Morales couldn't see how exhausted he was from a mere PT session. "You know I got this family thing. Can't leave until this building's finished up.

Besides, might get a medical clearance by then and I'll be back in the Corps."

"Right. Right." Morales had never been good at lying, so his agreement sounded exactly like what it was—humoring a delusion. Knox knew it, but the hope of getting back to his men was what motivated him through his painful rehabilitation. What would he do without it?

Morales cleared his throat, but his voice was still rough when he said, "If that doesn't work out, or you decide you like being a civvie, my offer's still good. Think about it."

"I will." Knox wasn't ready to think about what would happen once the Dorothy was finished and he had to figure out his next step, especially if he wasn't cleared for reenlistment. He probably would take Morales up on the job offer if it came to that, but he still had time to figure it out. As he did so many times per day, he pushed thoughts of the future out of his mind.

Thoughts of the past crept in, and Knox scrolled right to Danielle's text. He knew it was her because his phone showed him the first line of the text: Hey it's Danielle. He hesitated before clicking on the message, reminding himself that she could've gotten his number from any one of his well-meaning family. Still, his mind raced, trying to think why she'd reach out. It wasn't like he'd left a sparkling impression when they'd parted ways on Saturday. No, he'd pretty much been an asshole, doing his best to cover for the pain in his leg and paying for it by landing on his butt in front of her. He sure wasn't the smooth athlete she'd known in high school, but she was texting him anyway. What could she want?

He finally opened her message and smiled at the brief video of Sarge rolling on his back in the grass. The dog's tongue lolled to the side, and his legs pedaled in the air. Knox watched it a few times, noticing the curve of a bench in the background. He knew that bench. He'd helped install it. They were at Fur Haven. He checked the time stamp on the video. Only ten minutes ago.

He gunned his supercharged engine, the pain in his leg forgotten. If he hurried, he might catch Danielle and the dogs at the park. He didn't question why it was so urgent to see her. He was trained to trust his gut, so he did.

The elevator ride to the top of the parking garage was excruciatingly long. When he lunged out, eyes scanning the rooftop park for three greyhounds and one small woman, he was disappointed to learn he was too late. The only occupants of the park were two women holding hands on one of the bone-shaped benches, a pug planted at their feet, gnawing on a palm frond twice its size.

"Hey, are you okay?" one of the women called to him.

"I'm good. Thanks." He walked backward into the elevator, strangely deflated. What, had he thought Danielle was signaling him to come running to her side? He'd lost that privilege when he'd ignored her messages and calls all those years ago. She was clearly running a campaign to win him over to adopting Sarge, and that was all. She didn't want to spend time with him, and he was deluding himself if he thought otherwise. He'd walked away for all the right reasons fifteen years ago. He shouldn't muck it up now with second-guessing. Regrets didn't bring Munoz and Whittier back to life, and they wouldn't make Danielle forgive him for hurting her. His best course of action was no action, and that was always the hardest action of all to take.

———————

Danielle observed her father's careful probing and prodding with worried eyes. She'd known something was up with Flurry for a few days now, but she'd been hoping it was her imagination. The grim look on her father's face said otherwise. She'd been right to come to the clinic straight from the dog park. Luna and Sarge were well taken care of up front—the receptionists doted on her dogs—and now she'd hopefully get an answer about Flurry's condition and be able to start her on medications or whatever else she needed right away.

"I can't figure out what's wrong with her." Danielle kept her hand on Flurry's side while her father examined the pure-white greyhound on the examining table in room two. "At first, I thought she was putting on weight as a show of dominance. It took a few weeks for her and Sarge to get comfortable sharing food. But now they're good buddies, and she's still putting on the pounds. Plus she's sleeping more than usual, and she doesn't want me to rub her belly anymore."

Dr. Morrow palpated the dog's side and used his stethoscope on several pulse points. "Remember how undernourished Flurry was when you brought her in?"

Danielle winced. She didn't like remembering how emaciated Flurry had been, nothing but a sack of bones, really. "And she was so weak from pneumonia, remember? It took her over a month to shake the infection."

"Right." Dr. Morrow finished his exam and stepped back. "That's why we decided to hold off on spaying her until she was stronger. When did we spay her, Danielle? Do you remember?"

Danielle felt all the color leach from her skin. "We didn't."

"That's right." Dr. Morrow went into teaching mode, a habit he'd started when she was five and had declared her intention to become a veterinarian like him. The fact that her gap year had turned into two and then three, and then when her scholarships were no longer available, forever, hadn't stopped him from quizzing her like a veterinary intern. "If she hasn't been spayed, what do her symptoms point to?"

Danielle's shoulders shook with suppressed laughter. "That she and Sarge are more than good buddies."

"Buddies with benefits perhaps?" Dr. Morrow's eyes twinkled behind his glasses. "Isn't that what the young people are saying these days?"

"No, no, the young people don't say that." Danielle let the laugh out, and Flurry pricked her ears in Danielle's direction. "But with his leg? That can't have been comfortable for him."

"Where there's a will, there's a way." Dr. Morrow chuckled.

Danielle shook her head, bangs tickling her chin. "Boy, do I feel stupid. I can't believe I let her spaying get away from me like that."

"She was so delicate at first. You were right to be cautious. Then Sarge came along just as Flurry was at full strength." Dr. Morrow slung his arm around his daughter's shoulders. "You've had a lot going on. It's understandable."

"And now I'm going to have a lot more going on. Puppies!" Danielle knew she should be worried. With three adult greyhounds, her dad's guesthouse was already at maximum dog capacity. Puppies required a lot of care, and then she'd have to find homes for all of them. She should be freaking out, but instead she was thrilled. "When do you think she'll deliver?"

"Best guess? Another month. You know there could be up to a dozen of them." Dr. Morrow squeezed Danielle's shoulders, and she rested her cheek against his crisp lab coat.

"I know." Danielle clapped her hands together. "A dozen puppies! I can't wait."

"You are definitely your mother's daughter." Dr. Morrow sighed and took one more listen to Flurry's lungs. "She never met a puppy she didn't love."

Danielle's smile quivered at the edges. Losing her mom before she could remember her was rough on her but rougher on her father. It was up to him to keep the memories alive, to help Danielle know a mother who'd died of breast cancer before Danielle's third birthday. He'd done a great job. Sometimes, the memories he mentioned were so vivid in Danielle's mind that she felt like they were hers. She swiped at her wet eyes and moved so that she was at Flurry's head.

"You're going to be a great mama, Flurry. And Dad?"

Dr. Morrow turned to catch his daughter's gaze. "Yes?"

"Cast or no cast, I'll be bringing Sarge in tomorrow to be neutered."

Dr. Morrow chuckled. "A bit late to close the barn door now, pumpkin."

Danielle let the nickname slide. "Better late than never."

"Dr. Morrow?" the receptionist's voice came over the room intercom. "Your three o'clock is here."

Dr. Morrow pressed down the button on the ancient com system. "I'll be right there, Bridget. Thank you."

Danielle gave her dad a hug and helped Flurry off the table. She felt her phone ring in her back pocket, but she let it go to voice-mail. She had a lot of planning to do.

CHAPTER 5

KNOX STOOD AT THE SLIDING GLASS DOOR THAT LED OUT ONTO a spacious backyard, especially by Miami Beach standards. Heck, there was enough room to put in a pool and a swing set if a man were family-minded, which he wasn't. Or at least he hadn't been for fifteen years. The fact that he couldn't get Danielle out of his mind since seeing her last weekend at the Fur Haven Dog Park grand opening did not bode well, particularly when the next thought was always *What if*. What if she hadn't lost the baby? What if they had gotten married at the tender age of eighteen? Would they still be together? Would she have followed him around the world, living on bases, or would she have insisted on staying in Florida to finish her veterinary degree? His no-action plan hadn't stopped his mind from playing out all the possibilities, and he'd spent half a dozen restless nights remembering things that were better forgotten.

Lady nudged his hand with her nose, and he obliged her by scratching behind her ears. That was a good thing about dogs, how they were always in the present. He could use a reminder to stay the hell out of his own head and live in the moment. Hadn't he seen enough evidence during his years of service that sometimes the moment was all you had? Images of orphaned children roaming wide-eyed with shock between burned-out buildings overtook his mind, and when he blinked rapidly to clear his inner vision, he saw Munoz and Whittier on the ground with far more than bits of their leg blown off by the IED. Lady whined and pushed into his good leg, breaking the spell of his past, and he used both hands to give her an energetic rubdown. "You're a good dog, aren't you?"

Lady preened at the praise, and he kept up a steady stream of chatter. "That's a fine backyard you have there, Lady. Lots of room, yeah?" Her weight against him was steadying, and it made him think again of how having a dog might be a good thing for him. Sarge flashed through his mind. He'd like it here, wouldn't he? What wasn't to like about that big backyard with so many trees to pee on?

"Pretty, isn't it?" Eliza stayed back, out of his line of vision. "I have a man comes around every other week to keep it tidy. Not too expensive. If you decide to buy the place, I'll give you his info."

"Thanks." His response was as absentminded as his dog petting. In his mind's eye, a new vision emerged. He pictured the swing set, a little girl sliding down the plastic ramp with Danielle's hair and his eyes. He shook his head. That wasn't right. Their daughter would be almost fourteen years old by now. If the baby had been a girl. It struck him that he didn't know, and he likely never would. It wasn't a question he could ever ask Danielle. But he could put a swing set in the backyard. Sell the house to a new family, one with young kids who could grow up playing outside.

Keep the past in the past. Really, he should get the phrase tattooed on his arm right under his *Semper Fi.* Life would be a lot simpler if he could heed his own advice. Truth was, he'd snagged one of Danielle's flyers and kept it on him all week. Her number was on the brochure. Or at least a number that would reach her. It didn't match the one she'd texted him the dog park video from, but he'd use the business number first. He'd ask about Sarge, his second-most obsessive thought of the week. He couldn't get the big dog out of his head, either. Maybe it was the cast on his leg that made Knox feel like they were kindred spirits, but each night in his nearly empty apartment, he thought about how nice it would be to have a dog excited to see him when he walked in the door. He couldn't keep a dog in that tiny place, though, so that led him to only one conclusion.

"I'll take it." Knox gave Lady an extra pat on the head before turning his attention to Eliza hovering near her oak dining table.

"You will?" Eliza's hand flew to her chest, like he'd surprised the breath out of her. "Just like that?"

"It's a good yard. Plenty of room for a dog." He took the few strides to the table and pulled out a chair for himself.

"Sure. Always had big dogs myself. A Rottweiler, then a Great Dane mix. Now her Ladyship here." Eliza made herself comfortable across from him. "Are you sure you don't want to think about it first? Maybe take a few days to mull it over? I hate it when buyers get cold feet at the last minute. Waste of paperwork."

"If you insist, but my feet are plenty warm." Knox raised one shoulder. From what he'd seen so far, the interior hadn't been updated in decades, and that was exactly the kind of project he was looking for—a distraction that would also help him strengthen his leg. If he made a few bucks when he resold it in three or four months? Win-win. "Let's settle terms first, though. No real estate agents, you said? Should I get my brother Caleb to do the paperwork?"

"No need. I was a real estate lawyer most of my legal career. I'll draw everything up." She pulled a yellow legal pad toward her from the middle of the table and produced a pen out of her bra. "How're you planning to finance it?"

Knox took a long blink. "Cash, of course. I don't do debt."

Eliza cackled. "You Donovans. Must be nice."

The comment irked Knox, and though he knew she meant no harm, his voice was still a bit sharp when he said, "It's not family money. I've been living simply for a long time."

"I'm sorry. I forgot for a moment." Eliza reached across the table to pat his hand. "Thank you for your service."

Knox nodded curtly, still unused to civilian reactions to the mention of his time in the Corps. He could never tell if they really meant it or if it was just a thing people said, like saying, "How are you?" and not waiting long enough for a person to respond.

"Then make your offer." Eliza scooted the pad over to him. "We'll take it from there."

Knox took her pen and wrote down her asking price. He wasn't a businessman like Caleb, and he wanted the house. His gut told him this project was what he needed to keep busy in all the hours he wasn't working at the Dorothy. He'd hit the bed every night physically and mentally exhausted, an excellent remedy for clearing his mind of thoughts of the past and the uncertain future. Besides, he wasn't going to try to cheat an elderly woman out of what appeared to him to be a very fair value for the home she'd spent a lifetime in.

When she saw the large number, a smile spread across her face, deepening the wrinkles around her eyes. "You're not much of a negotiator, are you? Sold."

"Don't you want me to think about it for a few days?"

"At that price, I'm not letting you get away." She stuck her hand out across the table. "I'll have the paperwork ready in no time."

Knox took her hand in his, noting the thinness of her skin and the arthritic knobs on her knuckles that must cause her pain. "Good doing business with you, ma'am. If you and Lady ever get homesick, you just walk across the street to say hi."

Eliza's hand trembled in his. "You're a dear boy, Knox Donovan. You take good care of my house. That's an order, young man."

Knox's mouth twitched, but he didn't quite smile. "Yes, ma'am."

———

It was funny how imminent homeownership changed the way Knox viewed the world. When Lance and Carrie moved into the house a few streets over from the Dorothy with their son, Oliver, and their Jack Russell terrier, Beckham, they raved about the "good bones" of the house, and Knox had spent many an evening unwinding after a hard day on the construction site in their hot tub on the back patio. It was a nice place. Comfortable, airy. But he couldn't say why, and suddenly that bothered him.

"How do you do it?" Knox leaned his head back in the hot tub, inching a bit to the right so the jets could hit his lower back right where the muscles were tightest. Carrie and Lance sat across from him, their bodies obscured by bubbles.

"Do what?" Carrie sipped from a crystal champagne flute. She made what she called a "signature cocktail" for hot-tub time, some kind of prosecco-berry mix that tickled his nose until he'd sneezed right into his first glass. Tonight, he stuck with ice water while he was soaking his bones.

"Make everything so…I don't know…homey?" Knox rolled his head to one side and then the other. There was definitely room in Eliza's backyard for a hot tub. Maybe that would be his first home improvement. For the rest, he was going to need Carrie's help. She'd be able to add that special something that would make potential buyers pay top dollar.

"It's my job." Carrie giggled and sipped from her champagne flute. She was on her second one, which made her eyes sparkle and her hands wander. Knox kept his eyes above water level. He did not want to see or even think about what Carrie and his brother did under the cover of bubbles.

"Right. But how do you know what goes with what? Like colors and pillows and stuff." Above him, the stars shone hazy through a thin layer of clouds. "I've lived in my place longer than you've been in this house. Yet mine looks like I moved in last week, and yours looks like you've been here for years."

"I hope you're not saying my décor is dated!" Carrie pointed her champagne flute at him. "That would be very ungrateful, seeing as how you treat this hot tub like it's a job perk."

"It isn't?" Knox raised an eyebrow at her, and Lance chuckled.

"Help him out, Carrie." Lance sipped from his own champagne flute. Lance could throw down scotch with Grandpa William like it was nobody's business, but around Carrie, he tended to drink whatever she was having. Knox didn't know if it was cute or sickening. Both, he decided. Lance set his glass on the outer lip of the hot tub. "He's been in military housing his entire adult life. This is his first apartment. Treat him like one of your client's kids going off to college for the first time."

"A dorm room makeover!" Carrie clapped her hands together, which had the unfortunate side effect of spilling her cocktail into the tub. "Oh no! I'll be right back with another one, and then we'll talk budget. Okay, Knox?"

"Sure thing." He closed his eyes, figuring it would be a while before she came back. The water whirled around him, chlorine wafting up his nostrils, the pump whirring in the background in an even rhythm.

"You really going to decorate your apartment? You're hardly ever there." Lance's voice cut through Knox's relaxation daze.

"Thinking about a few options. I've been back a year. Gets old, living out of boxes." He opened his eyes but didn't look Lance's way. Didn't want to see the pity. Nor did he want to let on that he wasn't really talking about the apartment. Eliza's house had a lot of rooms, and all of them would need furniture and stuff. He could get by with a bed, a couch, and a TV, but he figured he'd need more to stage the house for selling.

"I'm sure it does. Have you given any thought to sticking around? You know, even after the Dorothy's done?" Lance floated his hands on the surface, bubbles popping up between his fingers.

"You'll be plenty sick of me by then." Knox's skin itched where the jet hit him in his lower back, but he didn't move. The pressure felt too good. "You'll be glad to see me go, I'm sure."

"You're wrong, man. I've gotten used to having your ugly mug around." Lance scissored his fingers, bubbles jumping. "Besides, you staying would be excellent for my business. You're a good guy to have on the job, Knox, and adding security systems to what I offer, well, *ka-ching, ka-ching*, hear those coconuts ring." Lance chuckled at his own rhyme, demonstrating that Carrie's signature cocktail had a serious kick even if it was difficult to take anything served in a champagne flute seriously.

Knox reluctantly smiled. "There are worse things than moving back home."

Lance gasped so loudly that Knox was forced to look at him. Lance held his hands to his cheeks, *Home Alone*–style, his mouth open comically wide. "Did Knox Donovan just admit to liking civilian life?"

"I wouldn't go that far." Knox stretched out his left leg, so light without the brace that always weighed it down. Another reason he loved the hot tub—a reason to go without his hobble. "But I'm thinking about it, whether to stay or go. A buddy of mine from the Corps reached out to see if I was interested in coming on board his new security firm, but I told him I have to stay down here until the Dorothy is finished. After that? I really don't know."

"All joking and other job offers aside"—Lance's hand landed on Knox's shoulder—"I'd be happy if you stuck around even longer. I'll miss you if you go away again."

It went unspoken that they hadn't missed each other the first time. Aside from the few occasions every year that Caleb's mom insisted the brothers get together, they'd barely known each other. But Lance was right. If Knox reenlisted and left on another tour now, he would miss his brothers. A year of working together to build up the Dorothy had gone by so quickly, he hadn't noticed how attached he'd gotten to the project, the crew, his brothers.

It would all be ending soon. They had another three, maybe four months left of renovation work. He'd install the new security system, and then it would be over. What was next for any of them? What if they all went their separate ways once they'd fulfilled the terms of the Dorothy contract? Had he been an idiot to buy the house across the street from the Dorothy? He'd been hesitant to bring up his upcoming homeowner status, but now he decided definitely to keep it to himself for a while longer. No need to pressure Lance into hiring him on or anything. Knox didn't need charity. He had options and months before he had to make any real decisions about the future. Buying the house was a practical investment of time and money, not permanent.

"Incoming!" Carrie called from the sliding glass door. Beckham came barreling out, barking his head off at something on the far side of the yard. He sprinted to the fence and back, then hopped up on the hot-tub edge, circling until he was behind Knox.

Knox felt the wet slop of dog tongue on his neck, but he didn't brush the dog away. Lance and Carrie weren't the only people he'd miss if he re-upped or moved to Atlanta. There were Caleb and Riley to consider, and the construction foreman, Mendo, had become a friend. Hell, he'd even miss this wacko dog that loved the taste of chlorinated skin.

Carrie slid her slim body back into the water, sipping her cocktail. "Now, Knox, let's talk vibes. Do you think of your home as a refuge from the world? When you walk in, do you want to be energized? Or calmed?"

Knox groaned and leaned his head back. No way was he telling Carrie he had an entire house to worry about staging. It wasn't like he was really putting down roots, not like Lance and Carrie were doing. Knox ducked his head under the water, disappointing Beckham for a half second before he switched his attention to Lance. Holding his breath, Knox thought about his new home and wondered, if asked, how Danielle would answer Carrie's questions.

"If only our father could see us now, huh?" Lance raised his champagne flute, tipping it against Knox's water glass in a one-sided toast. "He wanted us all in the business, and here we are. It makes me mad sometimes, thinking I might actually be doing what he wanted me to do."

"All I ever wanted was to get away from him." Knox picked up his glass, fingers slipping in the condensation, and took a long swallow of what had become room-temperature water. Still, room temperature felt cool when compared to hot-tub temps, and it tasted good sliding down his throat. He wiped his mouth with the back of his hand, like he'd downed a frothy one, and carefully set the glass back on the edge of the hot tub. Beckham immediately stuck his nose in the top, sniffing loudly.

"Preaching to the choir." Lance shooed Beckham off with a gentle nudge. "At least we're doing things on our own terms. I thought him going to prison would be bad for my business. Now that all the media frenzy is over, no one seems to care what my last name is. And I have to admit it's kind of a relief, having him tucked safely away where I don't have to worry about running into him."

"Can you believe Caleb's mom thought we'd want to visit him?" Knox snorted and leaned back to watch as clouds drifted by, blocking his view of the stars. "She still texts me, like, once a month."

"I finally filled out that stupid visitors' form just so she'd stop bugging me about it." Lance draped an arm over Carrie's shoulders, and she snuggled in to his side.

"Me too." Knox heaved a sigh, recognizing the signs that it was time to leave. Carrie and Lance needed their newlywed time. "Never planning to set foot in the prison, though. I told Christine it was simply a formality, but she insisted. For emergencies, she said. For when hell ices over, I said."

"But you still signed the papers." Lance traced lazy patterns on Carrie's arm with his fingertip. "She's persistent. I'll give her that."

Knox boosted himself out of the hot tub, water sluicing down his body, and grabbed the towel Carrie always put out for him. It was bright purple with a cartoon kid wearing a stethoscope on it. He suspected when he wasn't around, it was his nephew's towel. He padded toward the house, Beckham following hopefully on his heels.

"I'm not going to the kitchen, you greedy mutt." Knox finished drying off outside the sliding back door before stepping inside. Beckham cocked his head left, then right, as if he couldn't possibly have heard Knox correctly.

"Fine." Knox couldn't take the cuteness. "One treat, and that's it."

Beckham yipped his agreement with the deal, and Knox led the way to the kitchen. Beckham stood expectantly in front of the stainless-steel refrigerator door.

"I wonder where the dog treats are?" Knox craned his head, pretending to look for the plastic container Carrie kept filled with tiny pieces of dried liver. "Up here?" He gazed at the ceiling.

Beckham yipped once and danced in front of the fridge, toenails tip-tapping on the tile floor, tail wagging so fast it was a blur.

"Oh, should I look in here?" Knox opened the door, and Beckham stood on his hind legs. His front paws pushed up, like he was raising the roof at some 1990s dance club. Knox found the container and tossed the dog his treat. Beckham caught it, raced out of the kitchen, and launched himself onto the living room couch. It was so easy to make dogs happy. For a minute, Knox indulged in the fantasy that this was his house, Beckham his dog, and Danielle was waiting for him in the hot tub.

Like that was ever going to happen. He needed to move on from this obsession. He pushed thoughts of Danielle in a very skimpy bikini out of his mind and plopped onto the couch next to Beckham. "You've got it good, dog. You know that, right?"

Beckham climbed onto his lap, and Knox decided that refastening the brace and heading back to his lonely apartment could wait a little longer.

CHAPTER 6

THE ELEVATOR DOORS SLID OPEN TO REVEAL THE GREEN expanse of the new Fur Haven Dog Park. A few small dogs romped on the other side of the park. Danielle held her three greyhounds in check, making them wait for her signal to leave the elevator. The garage roof was edged in shrubbery, obscuring the high fence surrounding the park. Above it, the dawn light turned the sky pink. Danielle let out a long breath and gave the signal for the dogs to follow her into the park.

Sight hounds could be tricky to train. As much as they wanted to be good dogs, if they could see something in the distance, their instinct was to go for it. Danielle was glad for the hedges that hid the roof edge from sight. What a greyhound couldn't see, they wouldn't chase. She kept the dogs on their martingales until she'd closed the gate separating the big dogs from the little ones. She knew Luna and Flurry were over their desire to chase small fluffy creatures, but Sarge was new to civilian life. Though well behaved in all the training exercises she'd done with him, this was one of his first real-world tests.

Happily, he ignored the small dogs on the other side of the fence and spent a good amount of time sniffing the base of a palm tree. Although his inclination was to balance on the bad leg and lift the good one, he'd learned to lift the cast. He didn't like it—she could tell from the way he flattened his ears—but a dog had to do what a dog had to do. At his last checkup, her dad estimated that the cast would be ready to come off in another two weeks.

"Good morning." Eliza let her black Lab into the big-dog side of the park. "It's been a while, hasn't it, Danielle? Don't think I've seen you since the grand opening."

"Must mean Lady's in perfect health. That's a good thing, Eliza." Danielle smiled at the older woman she'd known her whole life. Eliza took a seat next to her on the bone-shaped bench. A pile of dog leashes sat between them.

"Fit as a fiddle, that old girl, but she's slowing down these days. I've been giving her some glucosamine for her joints. Seems to be helping." Eliza kept an eye on her dog as Lady politely exchanged sniff greetings with the three greyhounds. "Quite a collection you've got there. I thought you were only fostering the one in a cast, not adding him to your menagerie."

"Sarge *is* a foster. He needs a little more recovery time is all." Danielle felt her face heat at the words, figuring teasing was inevitable.

"Weren't the other two as well?" Eliza asked, a twinkle in her eye. Danielle wished people didn't take such delight in pointing out how bad she was at personally fostering dogs. She found lots of dogs homes. Lots of them. Besides, the goal of fostering was to find the dogs loving homes, and no one could love Luna and Flurry more than she did.

"Too true. You got me there." Danielle watched Sarge stride toward her, his leg cast awkward but no longer slowing him down. "But I won't have a choice with this one. Flurry's pregnant. Once she has the puppies, it's going to be chaos at my place. I'm hoping to place Sarge soon, before he and I get too much more attached."

Her words were slightly negated by Sarge plunking his head in her lap and looking up at her with those big, adoring eyes of his. She knew it was all about the treats in her pocket, but she liked to pretend he was grateful to her for the medical care and steady meals. He rolled his head to the side, watching Eliza, and she obliged him by petting under his long jaw. He let out a contended sigh that made Eliza chuckle.

"Might be a little late for not getting attached." Eliza stood and stretched her back. "We're going to head on out."

"So soon?" Danielle loved her dogs, but human company was nice sometimes, too.

"Big day today. Signing papers on my house."

"You're not moving, are you? You've been in that house, well, all my life at least."

Eliza pulled a napkin out of her bra strap and dabbed at her hairline. "I'm moving into the Dorothy, and I couldn't be more pleased. That house is too big for me. Plus all the projects it's going to need—a new roof in the next year or so, at the very least. A freshly renovated condo sounds absolutely lovely these days. Headache free."

"Of course." Danielle stood to give Eliza a hug, wondering if her dad felt the same way about his home. No, if her dad wanted to downsize, he would've told her. Wouldn't he?

Eliza returned her hug with a squeeze. "My buyer's an early riser, so we're meeting soon to sign the paperwork. I'm lucky to have found someone so quickly, plus he didn't blink at the asking price. Paying all cash, too."

"Good for you, nabbing a big spender. I hope it all goes smoothly."

"Why wouldn't it? I reckon the Donovans know a thing or two about real estate."

"Caleb's buying it?"

"No, Knox. You two had a chance to catch up yet?" Eliza gave her a knowing look. She had a long memory, and Knox and Danielle had not been discreet about where they made out when they were teens.

"Not really." Danielle sank back down onto the bench. "Can't believe he's buying a house here. Your house." Did that mean Knox was staying in Miami Beach for good? The day suddenly felt a lot brighter, the humid air lighter. Not for herself, oh no. She was thinking of Sarge. She vowed to up her adopt-Sarge campaign. That was a happily-ever-after she could root for.

Eliza called Lady to her and hooked up her leash. "Feel free to stop by for coffee when you're done here. I can never drink a whole pot by myself."

Danielle folded her hands in her lap. "Thanks. I might take you up on that." For Sarge's sake, of course.

"I hope you do."

———————

Knox signed the papers in the folder Eliza'd given him with a flourish. He was a homeowner now. Or at least he would be as soon as escrow closed. That cement block of pressure in his chest was not a heart attack at agreeing to spend more money at once than he'd ever spent. The pressure increased, and he resisted the urge to clutch at his chest. Maybe he was wrong. Could be a heart attack after all.

The smile stretching his lips, though, made him wonder if it was true that real estate ran in the Donovan veins. He felt a rightness that he hadn't felt since, well, ever. He gazed around the dining room with new eyes, owner's eyes. And immediately noticed the burned-out bulb in the overhead light fixture would need changing before its buddy also went out and left them sitting in darkness. He was sure many more such delights awaited him, and he couldn't wait.

Eliza sipped a cup of coffee, a small smile playing at her lips. "I hope you're as happy here as I was."

Knox froze for a second. Happy. He hadn't really thought of that emotion in a long time. He was content enough, he supposed, when he felt useful. But he wasn't really the happy type. Could it be happiness and not a heart attack after all? He hoped so.

"How long until I can move in, do you think?" he asked instead of responding to the whole happiness thing. It would take some getting used to, the idea of being happy with his life.

"With a cash deal, could close within the month. You could host a big Easter banquet here."

He shook his head. "Riley and Grams handle all the holiday stuff, thank God."

"Best not to count on it, though. Closings are slippery things and hard to predict." The doorbell interrupted Eliza's lengthy explanation of all the things that could happen to delay an escrow. Lady barked and ran to the front.

"Maybe that's Danielle." Eliza shuffled toward the door. "I asked her to stop by. She's such a nice girl, isn't she?"

"Uh, yeah." Knox rubbed the back of his neck, feeling the prickle of heat that raised the tiny follicles at his hairline. "We went to high school together."

"I remember. You two were quite the couple." Eliza looked at him like he'd disappointed her somehow, which she shouldn't be able to do. He barely knew her. But she did know Danielle, and that made him wonder what Eliza knew that he didn't.

Knox shook off the paranoid thought. "It was a long time ago."

"Live long enough and the years get shorter." Eliza stared pointedly at him.

"Yes, ma'am." Knox nodded solemnly, and that seemed to appease her.

Eliza opened the door with a hard yank. "Why, hello! Bring those three mammoths right in, Danielle."

Danielle entered on a wave of apologies and excuses. She was short, the dogs were tall, and the leashes were tangled around her wrist and with each other. She spun around, untangling herself with a laugh, her short hair whipping in an arc around her head. "These dogs! Sometimes I think they mean to kill me." She unclipped Luna and Flurry, who dropped to their bellies when she gave them the down signal. Then, she set their leashes on a side table near the front door, looking so adorably flushed and rumpled that Knox resisted the urge to launch over the table just to be near her. She nudged Sarge's side with her knee. "Hey, look who's here."

Sarge pricked up his ears and made a beeline straight for Knox. He hit the end of his leash, turning his head to look accusingly at Danielle. She took a few hesitant steps forward, just enough space that Sarge could get his nose in Knox's crotch.

"Oh, sorry about that." Danielle pulled at the lead, but Sarge kept straining forward anyway.

"Don't worry about it." Knox dropped onto his good knee and roughed up Sarge's coat, petting the hair along his spine in the opposite direction. Sarge sighed and rolled onto his back, lolling his head to the side to watch Knox with adoration shining in his eyes. Knox didn't hate that look. Didn't hate it at all.

"Why don't we let the dogs out back, and we can all have a nice cup of coffee? Or tea? I have a kettle around somewhere." Eliza slid open the back door.

"Coffee sounds perfect." Danielle let Sarge off the leash, and Knox echoed her desire for coffee.

Lady led the way out onto the grass, Luna and Flurry right behind her. Sarge didn't budge.

"I think we have a love match." Eliza chuckled, pulling two mugs out of an overhead cabinet.

"Someone's in love, that's for sure." Danielle turned a shade of red Knox hadn't seen since the time they'd fallen asleep on the beach and she had woken up lobster-colored. She'd been so sunburned, she couldn't bend her elbows for almost two days. Funny, he'd forgotten that weekend. He'd been mad at himself for letting her get burned, but he hadn't minded at all spreading aloe vera gel all over her skin. No, that had been a real thrill for his eighteen-year-old libido. She'd had such soft skin. He found himself wondering if she was still as soft, as delicate, as she'd been back then. The flame on her cheeks let him know she was just as sensitive. Would she still suck in her breath in that way he'd loved if he nibbled on her earlobe?

Knox shut down that line of thought as quickly as it popped up and poured his concentration into a thorough rubdown of the dog in front of him.

"A dog knows." Eliza nodded, agreeing with herself, and bustled around in the kitchen until a fresh pot had brewed. She set the coffee mugs on the table.

"The dog made up his mind at first sight." Danielle sat and grabbed a red mug with a Lab head outline, cupping her hands around it. "It's the human who hasn't come around yet."

Knox covered Sarge's ears with his palms. "I told you that I can't have a dog right now."

Eliza cleared her throat and looked pointedly at the stack of papers on her counter.

Knox rocked back on his heels. She was right. Signing the papers meant things weren't theoretical any more. He could adopt a dog, a big one even. This dog. Not right now, but soon. He looked down at the greyhound at his feet, stretched out so that his bad leg with the cast stuck out at the same angle Knox was currently holding his own leg. *A dog knows.* And sometimes a man does, too.

CHAPTER 7

DANIELLE DIDN'T UNDERSTAND THE LOOK THAT PASSED between Eliza and Knox, but when Sarge's tail began to beat against the floor, she knew she wasn't imagining the changed energy in the room. Sarge pushed himself to his feet, a process of keeping weight off the leg in the cast that he'd pretty much mastered but that Eliza's Mexican tile floors challenged. His nails scrabbled for a moment before he was on all fours, head plopped in Knox's lap.

Knox rubbed the spot between Sarge's eyes, and Danielle could swear she saw the dog's eyes roll back in his head.

"How does one go about adopting one of these guys?" Knox played it cool, all his attention on the dog, but Danielle saw the tenseness in the way he held his shoulders, the clench of his jaw.

"One of these guys or *this* guy?" Danielle didn't mean to tease, but it was so obvious that Sarge and Gunnery Sergeant Knox Donovan were meant to be.

Knox grunted in response. Eliza slid a hand over her lips to cover a smile.

Danielle gamely soldiered on. "There's an online application to fill out. I check your references and do a home visit. From there, we decide what's best for the dog." It was clear by Sarge's adoring eyes that he'd already decided what was best for him, and Danielle did feel a little guilty about putting Knox through the adoption paces. A system was a system, though, and she couldn't cut corners, not even for her high-school sweetheart.

"A home visit?" Knox looked around him. "You're in it."

"That's right. You're Eliza's big spender."

Eliza's hand dropped to her side, and she laughed out loud. Even Lady seemed smug, watching them through the glass sliding door.

"Forget coffee. I'm breaking out the champagne. Mimosas to celebrate! Danielle, we signed papers today, and I am officially moving into the Dorothy as soon as we can close escrow." Eliza made good on her promise, opening the refrigerator to reveal a door filled with champagne bottles instead of the usual assortment of condiments most people kept in refrigerator doors.

"That's wonderful!" Now Danielle looked around, too, wondering how the place would be different once Knox moved in. She couldn't imagine him with that rocking chair that looked as old as Eliza or hanging on to the various protest signs stacked in the living room. *The Future Is Female, Fight for Equality, My Arms Are Tired From Holding This Sign Since the 1960s,* and Danielle's favorite, *There's No Excuse for Animal Abuse.* She remembered standing next to Eliza at the animal rights march last year with her own sign, *Kindness Over Killing,* held high. A sudden sadness enveloped Danielle. She'd known Eliza all her life, had attended her first protest at her side as an idealistic thirteen-year-old. Now, Eliza was moving out of the home that Danielle associated with her—the best place to trick-or-treat, the most amazing light display at Christmas, the fake snowman she left in her front yard until March even though Miami Beach never got snow.

"Where will you put your giant Christmas tree?" Danielle looked to the spot where Eliza erected her work of art every holiday season. One year, it'd been so tall that the star scraped the ceiling. Danielle could still see the mark it left.

Eliza rubbed her thumbs against the ceramic mug in her hand. "Truth is, I'll be glad to scale back on all that. I don't suppose you'd be interested in some holiday décor, young man?"

"Couldn't hurt to take a look." Knox clearly didn't know what he was getting himself into, but the alarm on his face when Eliza grabbed his elbow and said, "No time like the present!" and dragged him toward the garage indicated he was about to.

Danielle opened the sliding back door so the dogs could come and go as they pleased, then trailed Eliza and Knox into Eliza's immaculately kept garage. It was like something out of an organization magazine, with matching shelves and cabinets for storage.

"I didn't even know this was here," Knox marveled from the doorway of the one-car garage.

"You bought a house without checking it out first?" Danielle shook her head, sure now that the purchase was a whim. Maybe he and his brothers were flipping properties these days. Danielle's gynecologist always had HGTV on in the waiting room, so Danielle had seen her fair share of shows about the process over the years and could imagine how the whole thing would go. Knox would live here while they worked on it, then resell it quickly for a huge profit. They'd knock out a wall or two, bring Carrie in to stage the whole thing, and voilà! Money in the bank. At least Eliza was happy with the deal.

Knox lifted one shoulder. "I just knew. Besides, I saw the inside. The yard. Figured a garage was just a garage."

A breathless laugh escaped Danielle. "Eliza's garage is magical. Wait 'til you see what she's got."

"Let me move the Jag." Eliza walked up to her dark-green convertible, the *click-click* of the locks greeting her. She climbed in, hit the garage door opener, and backed out in slow motion.

"I'm really hoping that car comes with the place." Knox watched the car with the kind of appreciation Luna showed in looking at barbecue.

"Yeah, right." Danielle snorted. "Eliza loves that car. She buys the new model every year, though, so maybe you can talk her out of this one when next year's model comes out."

"Every year?" Knox whistled. "She's loaded or what?"

"Or what." Danielle pushed back the blockade that was Knox's body and entered the empty garage. "She was a big deal in Miami real estate for a long time, and she's a smart cookie with her money."

"And here I thought I was being so nice, paying an old woman full asking price for her house so she'd have a little nest egg to help her get by."

Danielle laughed. "I'm glad you did, though. Eliza's good people."

Knox took the one large step down into the garage, letting his eyes trail over every nook and cranny. "This will make an excellent workshop."

"For what?" Danielle couldn't remember Knox being very handy. Handsy, yes, but he wasn't the kind of guy who grew up fixing cars with his dad or fiddling with old radios.

Knox did his one-shoulder shrug again. "I've been enjoying helping out Lance with the renovations across the street. Planning to try my hand at fixing this place up myself."

"You and your brothers are like your own *Property Brothers* show." Danielle could picture him being like one of the HGTV contractors, hammer hanging from his belt, pointing out to a work crew which wall needed to come down.

Knox scratched the back of his head. "I suppose."

Not exactly the answer of a home-flipping TV host, but maybe he simply didn't have it all planned out yet. How would Sarge feel if he and Knox were constantly on the move? Back in high school, when Knox talked about wanting to go places like Paris or Tokyo, she'd always imagined herself with him. But he hadn't wanted to take her along—him running off at the first chance proved that. Would he want to take Sarge? Her sudden trepidation about placing Sarge with Knox made her glad for the adoption process. He wouldn't get a dog without being fully vetted, and by then, she'd have figured out his motives for wanting Sarge. And if they weren't pure? No dog for Knox.

Eliza joined him in the center of her garage, beaming with pride. "I do love this garage." She spun to the west wall. "Now over here is where I keep my holiday decorations."

The entire wall was floor-to-ceiling boxes in colors that matched the holiday. A full third of them were green and red for Christmas, and another third were orange and black for Halloween.

"Pink and purple?" Knox asked like he couldn't figure out a holiday to match.

"Valentine's Day, of course. And the yellow ones are for Easter." The wrinkles in Eliza's forehead deepened. "Are you Christian? I should've asked that first. I'm afraid I don't have much in the way of Jewish or Muslim decorations. Or whatever you may be. I'm so sorry. I didn't mean to assume."

"I'm not particularly anything." Knox crossed his muscled arms over his muscled chest, and Danielle couldn't look away from all the muscly muscles and the ways in which they flexed as he moved. "Never been one to celebrate much anyway."

Danielle's heart sank at his words. She remembered their graduation, how her dad had gone all out, renting the clubhouse at his golf course, how they'd worked together choosing decorations and the menu so everything would be just right. She remembered, too, how even though Knox's family showed up for the ceremony, they hadn't done anything special for him, just handed him a couple envelopes of cash.

"The gift for all occasions," Knox had smirked when she'd asked to see his cards. He'd stuffed the envelopes into his pocket and spun her onto the dance floor. She'd been easily distracted by him back then, the feel of his hand on her back, how good he was at dancing when most of the guys in their class couldn't do more than shuffle around to a slow song.

Danielle remembered Knox's mother had come to the clubhouse and stayed an hour or so before rushing off but he'd stayed the entire time, never leaving Danielle's side. That night was one of her happiest memories. For the first time, she wondered if he remembered it in the same way. While her memories were filled with friends and family and their good wishes, were his filled with disappointment that his own family hadn't stuck around to celebrate with him?

"It's not too long before Easter." Danielle forced cheerfulness into her voice. "I'm surprised you don't have your decorations up already, Eliza."

Eliza waved her hand at the expanse of boxes. "Didn't want to go through the hassle if I was selling the place, you know?"

"And we might close before Easter." Knox tilted his head back, examining the overhead storage racks.

"Maybe, maybe not." Eliza drifted toward the yellow boxes. "It's always odd when Easter falls early in the year, isn't it? Can't trust Easter, can you, with the way it moves around on the calendar? I like a holiday that stays fixed in place, reliable, you know?"

"I guess I do." Danielle'd never thought of holidays as being shifty before, but now she was suspicious of Easter. And Thanksgiving, too. "Still, you don't want to let the neighborhood down. And how can Knox know if he wants to buy your decorations if he doesn't know what they look like?"

Eliza cackled. "He didn't even see every room in the house before making an offer."

"I saw enough." Knox spun in a circle like he expected to see the rest of the house from inside the garage.

"Didn't even go in my crafting room."

"Crafts?" Knox said the word like it was from another language, and he wasn't sure how to pronounce it.

"She means her campaign headquarters. You saw all those protest posters in the living room?" Danielle nodded back toward the door into the kitchen. "Tip of the iceberg. She's got a whole room dedicated to rabble-rousing."

Eliza's face fell. "Oh, I'll miss that room. Where will I put all my supplies?"

Danielle curved an arm around the older woman's shoulders. "You'll figure it out."

Eliza gave Danielle a squeeze before pulling away. "That I will. Now, let's crack open some boxes, shall we?"

Knox scanned the wall of boxes. "I really don't need to see—"

"I insist." Danielle put her foot down, both literally and metaphorically. "Let's get these Easter decorations down. I'm happy to help."

"Sounds great." Eliza's agreement was so fast, it surprised Danielle. "Why not put them all out, too? No sense disappointing the neighborhood, is there?"

Danielle planted her hands on her hips. "This'll be fun."

"It will?" Knox scratched at the scruff on his chin, still eyeing the boxes suspiciously.

Eliza's eyes moved from Danielle to Knox, a slow smile spreading across her face. "Why don't I go make some lemonade while you two get all those boxes open?"

"Why do I feel like we were just conned?" Knox asked after Eliza closed the garage door behind her.

Danielle lifted a heavy box off the shelf and grinned. "Because we were."

CHAPTER 8

"WHAT IS THIS?" KNOX HELD UP AN EGG-SHAPED MAGIC EIGHT Ball the size of a bowling ball, periwinkle blue with crack lines indicating the imminent arrival of a chick. Eliza's front yard was most of the way to becoming an egg-hunt obstacle course, filled with colored eggs the size of small children, bunnies dressed in their Easter finest, and Danielle's favorite, a giant Easter basket filled with fake, brightly colored grasses and glass eggs that glittered in the sunlight.

"The Magic Eight Ball!" Danielle swiped bangs out of her face and behind her ear. "Eliza always had that on the patio for kids who weren't allowed any sugar."

"Eggs aren't made of sugar." Knox stared into the eight ball as though it might contradict him.

"Eliza's are." Danielle opened up the last of the yellow bins, revealing a stash of small plastic eggs in every color of the pastel rainbow, plus a small stash of bright-red ones. "She fills these with candy and hides them in her yard. I remember it being such a thrill to find one. I'd plop right down and stuff chocolates in my mouth as fast as I could."

"What kind of parent sends kids who can't have sugar on a candy hunt?" Knox shook the ball, and words whirled in the window.

"The kind who knew Eliza had this." Danielle grabbed it from him. "It's so much smaller than I remember. She eventually found a sugar-free treat to put in the plastic eggs, but by then the Magic Eight Ball Easter Egg was a holiday tradition."

"It's enormous. Aren't those things supposed to be the size of a pool ball?"

"Where's the fun in that?" Danielle wiped dust off the ball with the bottom of her T-shirt. "And this was a lot of fun. Every day, I'd come by after school to ask it questions."

"Every day for your entire childhood? How did I not know about this?" Knox pulled a net of cottony fake grass out of a yellow bin. It stuck to his skin, outlining every contour of his muscled arms, clinging to his tattoo.

"Not *every* day. Eliza usually put the directions out a few weeks before Easter." Danielle tore her gaze away from the inked lettering and gave Knox a wry smile. "And it was mostly a middle-school thing for me. Eliza's house was on my walk home, so I stopped by any day it was out in the yard." Danielle shook the ball. *Reply hazy, try again.* "Then, freshman year of high school, Kenny Rossi saw me playing with it and laughed. Said he couldn't believe I was still such a little kid. That ended my Magic Eight Ball days, I'm afraid."

"What an idiot." Knox's voice was gruff as he picked individual strands of sticky grass off his skin.

"I sure was, letting someone else shame me for some harmless fun." Danielle shook the ball harder than she needed to. Stupid Kenny Rossi. He'd cheated off her in Algebra I, too, and almost made her fail the midterm because he couldn't keep his eyes on his own exam.

"Not you. Him." Knox strung his collection of clingy strings onto the Japanese boxwood shrub along the front of the house. The plastic grass was supposed to go in one of the small baskets Eliza used to line her walkway, but Danielle liked Knox taking decorative initiative so she let him string the grass along the hedge. She also liked him sticking up for her. She probably could've told him more in high school, but he was so popular and she was so... not. It had made her self-conscious, sometimes, wondering what he saw in her.

"I guess we don't know as much about each other as I thought." Knox frowned at the bushes, picking strings out from between his fingers.

Danielle stared at him, hand frozen in mid-eight-ball shake. It hadn't occurred to her that he'd had secrets in high school, too, but of course he had. He'd never wanted to talk about his family, especially his mother, deflecting questions with hot kisses that left her unable to remember her own name, much less any topic of conversation. She gave the eight ball a half-hearted shake to avoid responding. What was there to say anyway, especially after all this time?

Knox nodded at the eight ball. "What's it say?"

Danielle showed him the result—*concentrate and ask again.* "I didn't ask a question, so it makes sense that the eight ball has no wisdom for me."

"What kinds of things did you ask as a kid?" Knox stood back from the bushes, head cocked, then stepped forward to flick a few strands so they draped on the leaves evenly.

Danielle plopped onto the front step and shook the ball again, still no question in mind. "Will there be a math quiz tomorrow? Does Tommy Peralta like me? Will I get Ms. Kandice for homeroom next year? You know, kid stuff."

"Did it answer you?" Knox took a break from hedge decorating and sat a careful few inches away from Danielle, close enough that she could imagine leaning against him but far enough away that she didn't. Not that she would, she reminded herself. It wasn't like that with Knox, not anymore.

She handed him the ball. "Sure. It's what kept me coming back."

"And did Tommy Peralta like you?"

Danielle folded her hands in her lap, fiddling with the nail on her thumb. "I believe the most common reply was *Don't count on it.* Sometimes I got *Ask again later,* which I liked better. More hopeful."

Knox gave the ball a hard shake. "Was Tommy Peralta a complete idiot?"

Without a doubt.

"See?" Knox held the response so she could see it. "You weren't asking the right questions. And there seems to be an abnormal amount of idiotic guys at your middle school."

"I'd say it was a normal amount of idiotic guys." Danielle laughed, comfortable with Knox in a way she usually wasn't with new people. But Knox wasn't really new, was he? Just different. Older, more mature. And certainly more built. The width of his thigh next to hers made her feel small. When he laughed, too, she found herself inching toward him on the tiled step.

"What questions should I have asked?" Danielle caught her lower lip in her teeth, but it was too late to stop the words before they escaped. It wasn't so much the words themselves as the way she'd said them. Low, breathy. Was she really sitting on Eliza's front porch flirting with her ex-boyfriend? She was.

Knox's eyes locked onto her lower lip, and he took a long blink. "You should've asked—" He coughed and started over, this time in a high-pitched cartoon voice, "Will I grow up to be the fairest of them all?"

Danielle laughed at the question and his poor acting skills.

"Here." He handed her the ball after shaking it.

She hefted the weight of it in her palms, turning the plastic window toward her.

It is certain.

Danielle blushed. She felt the heat rise, knew it made her freckles blend together until she was one red-faced mess. She ducked her head, letting her bangs swing forward to cover her cheek while she pretended to study the ball.

"Two for two. Guess that thing *is* pretty accurate." Knox closed the remaining inches between them, and their hips touched.

Danielle's breath caught in her throat. She shook the ball idly to cover her intense reaction to Knox's nearness.

"I always thought so," she said once she'd coached her breathing back to normal. "It made me sad when Eliza packed it up for the year."

"Ask it something now." Knox nudged her with his knee.

Danielle slanted a glance at him under her eyelashes. She couldn't shake the rightness she felt in Knox's presence. The awareness of him, the longing for him. Did he feel the same pull? She asked the question in her mind and shook the ball.

Better not tell you now.

The breath rushed out of her. Had she really thought the Magic Eight Ball would add clarity? A kid's toy? She deserved the disappointment that flooded her, bowing her spine so that she curled into the ball on her lap.

Knox tipped the ball his way with a finger. "A secret question, huh? That's not playing fair. You have to ask it aloud. That's the rule."

"You didn't even know how to play this game five minutes ago."

"Now I do. Only questions asked out loud get real answers. Go ahead, ask it what you really want to know." His blue eyes dared her.

Her heart sped. They might've had their secrets back then, but he'd always helped her feel braver than she really was. His eyes traced her face, the crinkles around his eyes tightening like he wanted to smile. His gaze landed on her lips and stayed there. "Go on. Ask."

Danielle licked her suddenly dry lips, and Knox's breath hitched.

"Does Knox Donovan want to kiss me?" Danielle closed her eyes and shook the ball.

The lightest of touches brushed across her lips. Her eyelids fluttered open at Knox's gentle kiss. His lips pressed against hers for the briefest moment, his blue eyes intent on hers. Her own lips curled into a smile, and she leaned into the kiss, exerting her own pressure. He pulled back a fraction of an inch, then returned for another caress. It was simple and innocent, the tickle of their lips against each other, but her heart pounded like she was in the middle of a particularly brutal spin class.

Or a rough few laps during PE. Danielle closed her eyes, savoring the feel of Knox against her and the memory of their first kiss, as soft and innocent as this one. She'd just come from fourth period, still in the gym shorts that rode up her butt and the T-shirt that turned her breasts into one big camel hump. She'd often thought PE uniforms were specifically designed to humiliate D-cup girls. She'd ducked to the side of the gym, into an open-air hallway that didn't get much use, to wait for the bell. She didn't like changing in front of the other girls, not since the sixth grade when Andrea and Alyson had hidden her regular clothes while she was in the shower.

Now a junior, Danielle had learned to request fourth period PE so she could use the first few minutes of her lunch break to freshen up and change back into street clothes. The trick was staying out of the way so that no one knew what she was doing.

"I thought I saw you duck back here." Knox Donovan had followed her that day. She'd spun, ponytail whacking her cheek like a whip, and taken a quick step backward.

"Just getting an, uh, drink." She sidled over to the ancient water fountain and pushed on the bar. No water came out. Water hadn't come out of that fountain in her lifetime. Still, she put on a show for Knox, wrinkling her brow. "Weird, right?"

Knox stood so the sun was behind him, his broad shoulders blocking the light. "Coach was in a mood today, huh? How many laps did you end up running?"

"Too many." Danielle's chest still heaved from the effort. She knew because Knox's gaze locked there, and his next words were addressed directly to her breasts.

"I see you sneak out here every day. Why?" He forced his eyes back up to hers. "It's not for the water."

A high-pitched giggle escaped her. She sounded like a birthday balloon losing all its air at once. She slapped a hand over her mouth. Guys like Knox Donovan didn't talk to her. She wasn't an athlete like him, with his triple letters in football, basketball, and swim. She was just a science geek, keeping her head down and her grades up.

Knox stepped closer to her, peeling her fingers away from her mouth, one by one. One. By. One. Danielle didn't know if he actually moved in slow motion or if her brain was seizing or something, but his large fingers engulfed her smaller ones. When he was done, they stood across from each other, somehow holding hands. She tugged at their entwined hands, but he hadn't let go.

"I wanted to ask you something." Knox pulled her a little closer. She let him. "What?" Her heart pounded hard enough that she felt it in her throat even though she knew he was likely about to ask her for her bio notes.

His jaw thrust forward and his lower teeth pulled his perfect cupid's bow of an upper lip down, gnawing on it like he was nervous. Ridiculous. She was not the kind of girl who made a guy like Knox Donovan nervous.

He released his tortured lip with a wet pop. Danielle couldn't look away from how it glistened, couldn't shake the desire to reach up and run her thumb along its plumpness.

"Do you want to go to homecoming with me?"

All Danielle's attention was on Knox's mouth, so she saw him form each word with his perfect lips. Heard them with her ears. It was her brain where the breakdown happened because she simply couldn't process the question.

"Homecoming?" She tried to look away from his lips and failed. Those lips curled into a smile. "The dance? It's in two weeks?"

"Oh, that homecoming." Her neurons were firing a million miles per minute; they simply weren't all that concerned with language.

"Yeah, there are signs everywhere? It's in the announcements every day?" He sounded amused and that lightness in his voice finally allowed her gaze to travel up to his.

"Seriously?" Danielle wanted to run away, but his grip on her hand kept her in place. She should say yes. Why didn't she say yes?

Knox opened his mouth, but before he could say something about it all being a joke, Danielle blurted out, "Yes!" It came out too loud, so she said it again, "Yes," but softer.

"Yes?" He echoed, bending toward her.

"Yes." She whispered.

He brought those lips of his closer and closer to her face until he was only a breath away. "And if I wanted to kiss you right now?"

Her "yes" came out on a breath that he caught between them, pressing his lips to hers in a kiss so soft and sweet that her bones melted. Right there in the hallway, with her hideous PE uniform on, still sweaty from the laps from hell she'd run, she kissed Knox Donovan back. The bell rang, but they didn't stop. He deepened the kiss, and she reached up to wrap her hand around the back of his neck. His palm cupped her hip, and she leaned into him.

A catcall finally broke them apart, but he pulled away, smiling. "I don't think I can wait two weeks. Can you hang out after school today?"

Danielle nodded, and he said, "I'll wait for you at your locker."

"You know where it is?" It wasn't false modesty. She honestly thought Knox hadn't known who she was before today.

"Of course I do." He walked away from her, backward like he didn't want to let her out of his sight. And he didn't. Not for almost two years. They'd been *that* couple in high school, always together, always looking for a moment to sneak away and make out. She'd thought they'd be that way forever, but she'd been very, very wrong.

Now, Danielle sucked in a deep breath at the memories. Even the good ones hurt in their own way. Knox pulled away from her, inhaling deeply, then tipped his forehead against hers. They sat that way for a long moment, breath slowing, the scent of him filling her lungs. Earthy, a little salty, and so very Knox. It flooded her, the reality and the memory of him both at once.

"Look," he whispered, directing her gaze to the eight ball in her lap. "The eight ball knew how much I needed to kiss you."

The words *Without a doubt* floated in the square.

"Three for three." Danielle twirled the ball until the words disappeared, trying to act like her whole world hadn't just shifted on its axis. Playing it off like she kissed ex-boyfriends on the street every day.

"Ready for a break?" Eliza's bright voice jolted them both.

Danielle was the first to her feet, brushing at the back of her jeans like maybe some of those sticky grass strands were giving her trouble.

Knox was slower to rise, favoring the braced leg, but he gallantly took the heavy tray with a pitcher of lemonade and three glasses on it from Eliza. "You bet. Decorating's sweaty work."

"Isn't it, though? Looks like you found my sticky grass. Troublesome lot, aren't they?" Eliza sat on the porch swing anchored to the right of her front door. She pushed off with a toe while Knox settled the tray on the bistro table in the far corner.

"Thought I'd never get them untangled." Knox poured lemonade and offered it to Danielle.

She downed half the glass in one gulp. "We were just playing with the Magic Eight Ball. Can't believe you still have that thing."

"I saw you two…playing." Eliza gave them both a wink. "I was planning to keep it. Plenty of room for a few knickknacks in my new condo. But I'm willing to part with it for the right price."

"Name it." Knox gave the next glass to Eliza and then knocked one back himself.

"You both come and help me stuff the plastic eggs with candy the day before Easter. I get quite a crowd, you know. Considering you might be the new owner by then, you bring the candy, and I'll show you the ropes."

"Sold." Knox held out his hand to shake on it. "I like doing business with you, Eliza."

Eliza shook his hand. "Likewise, young man, likewise."

Danielle sipped her lemonade. Eliza loved preparing for her famous Easter egg hunt. She created a new costume every year, usually some version of a rabbit, although there had been a giant carrot one year and a chick popping out of a cracked egg, too. What was she up to, enlisting their help?

Watching Knox relax on the porch, trading quips with Eliza, while remembering the butterfly touch of his lips on hers, Danielle didn't care. Any excuse to see Knox again was good enough for her.

CHAPTER 9

Puffs of clouds drifted lazily by, and Knox let out a long breath he hadn't even realized he was holding. In the Marines, time on the water was not leisurely. It was training for life-and-death situations or an actual life-and-death situation. Kicking back in a low-slung deck chair, nursing a cold longneck, was as foreign to him as attending an opera. But he could get used to it.

He could get used to the brisk air brushing the scalp of his freshly shorn hair, the gleam of the teak deck in the sun, the roll of the small yacht as it motored out to sea. Even the company wasn't half-bad. Lance, Caleb, Grandpa William and his dog, Pops, and for reasons he wasn't completely clear about, Mr. Cardoza, one of the long-time residents of the Dorothy who had appointed himself the unofficial consultant on all the changes at the Dorothy. He also seemed to be on good terms with both Caleb and Grandpa William.

"Another one?" Lance asked, one hand in the cooler, the other with three beers hanging from between his fingers like some kind of beer-juggling genius. He handed the short, fat bottle to Caleb, who loved his weird Belgium ale like their grandfather loved his scotch.

Grandpa William stood at the wheel. Not that he was driving. No, he had a sophisticated navigation system doing that for him. He rested his short glass of the aforementioned scotch on the wheel and stared out over the horizon, looking for all the world like a commercial for men's cologne for the senior set, complete with noble greyhound lounging at his feet. Or on his feet. Pops was all about close contact.

Knox took the second beer out of Lance's outstretched hand

and twisted off the top. He'd always been more of a pop-top guy, but his brothers had their own tastes and Knox wasn't one to complain. Cold beer was cold beer as far as he was concerned. He drained this one as quickly as the first, leaned back his head, and listened to his brothers talk about Caleb's upcoming wedding and when Grandpa William would be setting the date for his own wedding to his ex-first-wife and current girlfriend, who also happened to be Caleb's soon-to-be grandmother-in-law. So much drama, Knox thought, though it wasn't lost on him that between Grandpa William's and Lance's remarriages to exes, his current obsession with Danielle was apparently a manifestation of the Donovans' inability to let go.

"You are a lucky man." Mr. Cardoza wobbled to the deck bar to pour himself a half glass of red wine. Then he bent down to the mini fridge and pulled out a can of San Pellegrino Limonata. The top opened with a hiss, and he filled up the rest of the glass with soda. Knox's service had taken him to Thailand and Japan, and he thought he'd seen some unusual drinks there, but he'd never seen anyone pour soda into wine before.

Since it was unclear who the lucky man was, the three Donovans were forced to wait for Mr. Cardoza to taste his concoction. Apparently, it met with his satisfaction, because he raised it in a toast. "To William and the return of his first love."

Caleb, Lance, and Grandpa William raised their drinks, but Knox was left the odd man out. Mr. Cardoza noticed his empty bottle. "You want me to make a *tinto de verano* for you?"

"Uh." Knox searched his beer bottle for even a drop he could use for the toast. "No, thank you."

"It is very refreshing. In Spain, we drink it in the summer, but here, I can drink it year round. I am a happy man." He ignored Knox's polite refusal and poured a second glass, holding it up for Knox to fetch himself.

"Thank you?" Knox took the cue and hauled himself out of the low-slung chair and over to Mr. Cardoza. Near the bar, a canopy stretched overhead, providing shade and a slight drop in temperature. Knox sniffed the drink first. He'd never been a huge fan of wine. The carbonated fizz tickled his nostrils. He took a sip.

"Well?" Mr. Cardoza leaned a hip against the bar's low counter. "You are refreshed?"

Knox swallowed, pleasantly surprised by the mix of flavors. "I am." He raised his glass.

"Very good." Mr. Cardoza raised his glass again. "The toast, then, for William and the return of love lost."

Caleb raised his glass high. "Let's not forget Lance's recent marriage to his first wife."

"Hey." Lance clicked his bottle against Caleb's. "I only had the one wife. It's not as dramatic as Grandpa William's and Grams' story."

"Only because you haven't lived as long." Caleb smirked at his brother.

"Besides." Lance pointedly ignored the smirk. "This is Caleb's bachelor party. We should be toasting him."

"We will." Mr. Cardoza clinked his glass against Knox's. "First, though, to the lost loves who came back. I got an email." Mr. Cardoza's jaw clicked shut like he hadn't meant to say that last bit.

"An email from who?" Grandpa William gave up on holding his scotch high and sipped at the rim.

"My daughter." Mr. Cardoza gulped his fizzy drink. "She says Isabella is moving to Miami. She gave her the Dorothy information. Caleb, you will sell her one of the new units? The best unit?"

"Sure, Mr. Cardoza. Any friend of yours is welcome. What's her last name? I'll keep an eye out for any communications from her."

"Isabella Arcia." Mr. Cardoza's voice softened on the syllables. "No, her married name is Lucero." The wrinkles in Mr. Cardoza's forehead grew deeper. "My daughter says she is a widow now. She has been a Lucero for over thirty-five years, but in my heart, she is still Isabella Arcia. That is how I knew her."

"Ah." Grandpa William tipped his scotch glass toward Mr. Cardoza. "Your first love?"

Mr. Cardoza nodded, downing the rest of his *tinto de verano* in a few short swallows.

"I'll look out for her," Caleb promised, crossing to the cooler for another of his Belgian ales.

"You." Mr. Cardoza pointed at Caleb. "Learn a lesson from all these men. Don't let go of your Riley. No matter what."

"Don't worry." Caleb apparently had second thoughts about another drink and let the ale slip back into its bed of ice. "I'm never letting go."

The older men chuckled at his vehemence, but Knox stared overhead, silent. The awning undulated in the breeze, even though the navigation system had steered them to a stop just off one of the barrier islands. They could see land, but it would be a long, hard swim to get there on their own.

Lance came up beside him. "Pretty mushy stuff for a bachelor party, huh?" He nudged Knox's shoulder with his own.

But Knox *was* feeling mushy, so he didn't respond to Lance's attempts to talk about how the Heat were doing this season. Knox glared at the nearly empty glass in his hand. Perhaps the *tinto de verano* had a secret punch to it. He couldn't stop thinking about how he should've been more like Caleb and less like the rest of the Donovans. It seemed that even though he'd left his family and crossed the world several times over to change himself, back home, he was just another Donovan, disappointed by love.

Grandpa William and Lance gave him hope, though. Maybe he could earn a second chance with Danielle. She certainly didn't mind his kisses. His body stirred at the memory, so he walked to the railing. No need for his brothers to see the physical evidence of where his mind wandered on this sunny day.

"In my time," Grandpa William was saying from his position at the wheel, "a bachelor party meant strip clubs and lap dances.

I can't believe this is all you've planned. What kind of best men are you?"

"The kind who did what I asked." Caleb defended his brothers. Knox liked the sound of it. He'd never spent much time around Caleb before he'd left for the Marines. What he mostly remembered was how quiet Caleb had been at the few family gatherings they'd both attended, like he was afraid to call attention to himself. Standing at the prow now, his hair windswept, his tanned bare feet planted on the deck, he looked like a confident king of the sea. He didn't need the wheel as a prop to look like he was in charge. He naturally took over wherever he went. It would annoy Knox more if he'd wanted to be in charge. Luckily, he didn't.

Grandpa William snorted. "Well, boys, when it's my turn, I want strippers. In the plural. You got that?"

"Like Grams will allow it." Caleb sounded like he was joking, but he definitely wasn't. His soon-to-be grandmother-in-law was a force of nature, and neither Caleb nor Grandpa William wanted to be on her bad side. She'd always been nice enough to Knox, so he didn't get why they seemed so afraid of her. If she were Caleb's grandmother-in-law, what did that make her to Knox? It made his head hurt to puzzle it out, so he decided the word *family* covered all the bases.

"Did you bring the snorkel gear?" Caleb turned his back on the railing and leaned against it, the sun behind his head like a halo.

"Of course." Lance used his glass to point at the gear bag on the deck. "Let me know when you want to go in."

"Now is good." Caleb crossed to the bag and rifled through it, pulling out flippers, mask, and snorkel. "There's an artificial reef not too far from here."

The yacht pitched, and Caleb tossed snorkel gear to Lance and Knox. "Grandpa William? Mr. Cardoza?"

"Not me." Grandpa William raised his scotch in a toast. "I'll man the decks."

"I'll man the William." Mr. Cardoza grabbed another San Pellegrino from the fridge.

Knox didn't like the idea of Grandpa William and Mr. Cardoza alone and likely drunk on a ship, especially when that ship was their only ride home. "I'll man the grandpa and the Spaniard."

Caleb laughed. "Have it your way. Lance, you ready?"

Lance gave a thumbs-up, and the two splashed into the ocean.

"Scotch?" Grandpa William offered, descending the two stairs to the outdoor bar, Pops padding along behind him.

"Sure." Knox set his glass on the counter by the sink and took the tumbler Grandpa William poured for him. Perhaps the scotch would counteract the mushiness inspired by the *tinto de verano*. Lord knew Grandpa William wasn't known for his gentler emotions. They knocked glasses in a silent toast, and Grandpa William gestured him to sit in the banquette across from the bar. Mr. Cardoza finished pouring his third drink of the afternoon and sat beside Knox.

"Hear you and Dr. Morrow's girl have been seeing each other again." Grandpa William's blue eyes gleamed in a way that Knox suspected meant trouble.

"I wouldn't say 'seeing each other.'"

"Would you say 'sucking face'? Because apparently you put on quite a show for the Dorothy. Patty told us you made out for, like, an hour."

"Yes, she called me over to her place to watch you put out Eliza's decorations last week." Mr. Cardoza huffed in amusement. "We got more of an eyeful than we bargained for."

"It was only a minute. Or two." Knox shifted, for all the world feeling like a recruit being called to the deck. He expected Grandpa William to yell at him to drop and give him fifty at any moment.

"Some minute." Grandpa William whistled. "She's a pretty girl."

Knox couldn't argue with such an objective truth. He nodded, sipping the scotch, waiting for the other shoe to drop.

"Heard you broke her heart. Back in high school." Mr. Cardoza was the shoe dropper. He said the words kindly, but they still pricked along Knox's skin like tiny needles.

Knox choked on an ice cube. "I didn't mean to. I was trying to do what was best."

"Noble, huh?" Grandpa William tsked. "Sounds like you."

Normally, if someone called him noble, Knox would take it as a compliment, but Grandpa William managed to make it sound like an insult. Knox reined in the automatic anger.

"What're you going to do now?" Grandpa William swirled the ice cubes in his glass, eyeing Knox over the rim. "You got a plan? Or you're just mucking around with her feelings again?"

"Because that would not be nice. Everyone likes Danielle very much." Mr. Cardoza held his glass away from Pops' nosy inspection. The greyhound sniffed, then settled back down, draping himself across the tops of Grandpa William's feet.

"I'm not mucking around." Knox knew that much at least. But a plan? He didn't really have one. It was why a whole week had gone by, and all he'd done was respond to her texted pictures of Sarge with smiley faces.

"Then what are you doing?" Both Grandpa William and Pops looked at him with questions in their eyes, heads cocked to one side. Knox imagined Pops' question was more like, "When will you give me a treat?" which was a much easier answer to come up with than trying to answer Grandpa William's question, one he'd asked himself at least a hundred times since kissing Danielle. A question he still couldn't answer.

Knox and Grandpa William both sipped their scotch, staring into the empty space between them. Mr. Cardoza delighted Pops by producing a dog biscuit from his trouser pocket.

Pops was munching on his third treat before Knox finally admitted the truth. "I don't know."

"Better figure it out." Grandpa William poured himself another finger from the bottle. "She's not a girl anymore. You piss off a woman, you pay for that shit the rest of your life."

"You'd know." Knox grinned, feeling the loosening of his tongue that came with the right amount of alcohol.

"You bet I do." Grandpa William pointed a finger at him. "Don't be stupid this time around. Put a ring on her finger as soon as you can. You'll be happier for it."

"M-m-marriage?" Knox sputtered, spewing scotch onto the blue-and-white-striped cushions of the banquette. "We're not talking marriage yet. We kissed. Once." Okay, it was twice, maybe three times—it wasn't like he'd been counting how many times their lips parted and came back together again—but that information was private.

Mr. Cardoza shook his head. "Young people today. Where do you think it's going with a girl like that?"

"A girl like that needs a secure future. What am I even doing with my life?" The right amount of alcohol was apparently dangerous if a man wanted to keep secrets. "Once the Dorothy is done, then what?"

"You buy another building. You do it again." Grandpa William thumped his drink, and the ice cubes rattled against the glass. "That's how you rebuild the family business."

"I never wanted to be part of the family business."

Grandpa William narrowed his eyes. "Why'd you come back then? Nowhere else to go now that the Marines won't have you?"

It was too close to the truth. Knox flinched. "I've got a job offer in Atlanta. With some guys I served with."

"Oh, some guys. Well, by all means, abandon your brothers to go help some guys." Grandpa William was looking like he hadn't taken his blood pressure medication today. A vein pulsed in his neck. "What is wrong with you boys that you don't see what a good thing you have together?"

Knox knew it was pointless to remind him that he was only

here because of Grandpa William's stipulations. After their father lost everything and landed himself in prison, Grandpa William had held out his ownership of the Dorothy like a carrot on a stick, promising to hand it over to Caleb if the brothers worked together. Knox stepped up to do his duty because Caleb needed him, but when the Dorothy was done, all that would be over. And then what? He sometimes felt itchy, like he needed more than plastering walls and researching security systems to fill his days.

Grandpa William and Mr. Cardoza wanted him to propose, but Knox and Danielle barely knew each other. Not anymore. So what did he want? It wasn't a question he'd asked himself in a very long time, not since he'd enlisted. After the IED, he'd been surviving, doing what was necessary, what was in front of him, one foot in front of the other, thinking that once he got full use of his leg back, things would be different. Two years was a long time to live in limbo, and somehow seeing Danielle again, kissing Danielle again, had him longing for things he couldn't even name.

Instead of answering his grandfather, Knox took another drink and walked over to the railing to stare out at the horizon. Man, the *tinto de verano* came with a dose of philosophical angst, no doubt about it. One light shone out in the dark ramble of his thoughts. He wanted more time with Danielle. Maybe even a lifetime. And for sure at least one night. He'd start there. A conversation, a date. How hard could it be?

"You really going to walk away again?" Mr. Cardoza came up beside him and rested his elbows on the teak rail, eyes tracing the line between sea and sky.

Knox hung his head, gazing into the glass he held in both hands. The ice cubes had melted, turning the scotch a watery gold. Walk away from Danielle again? He couldn't imagine it. Her walking away from him? Now that was no stretch of the imagination at all.

CHAPTER 10

"IT'S SUCH A PLEASURE TO SEE THEM RUN, ISN'T IT?" ELIZA shifted forward in her seat on the bone-shaped bench, watching Luna and Flurry lap the large-dog section of Fur Haven. Persistent Lady galloped along behind them, optimistic that she'd catch them. Luna slowed down enough to ignite Lady's hope, and then, just as Lady was close enough to touch her hind leg, Luna sprinted off, leaving the black Lab in the proverbial dust. Eliza chuckled at their antics, but Danielle was on her phone and missed the whole thing.

"I'm sorry. What did you say?" Danielle turned her phone facedown, all the better to stay in the moment. Because pondering what Knox's *Can we talk? I'm almost there* text might mean wouldn't get her anywhere good. Almost where? Did he expect her to be at home? What else could he mean? And needing to talk was almost never a good thing. Was she in trouble for texting him too many adorable photos of Sarge in the past week? The dog was photogenic, and Knox hadn't yet filled out the online application so she'd thought it best to keep him in the loop of Sarge's progress. Or maybe he wanted to talk about The Kiss. Then what would she do? Admit that the barrage of photos was because she couldn't wait until their day-before-Easter date with Eliza to see him again? People talked about how great being young was, but being suddenly thrust back into her teenage emotions was not great, not great at all. This time around, she couldn't even blame fluctuating hormones. So yeah, they could talk, if she got her butt in gear to meet up with him at home. Except her butt stayed put. "About the dogs, was it?"

"All the running." Eliza pointed out their dogs, still tearing up the soft sod. Chunks flew out from under Luna's feet and smacked Lady in the face. From under the bench, Sarge let out a soft woof.

"You're right, Sarge. That is dirty pool." Eliza bent over so she could give Sarge a pat.

Danielle could feel the dog's heat against her bare ankle. He'd seemed thrilled to ride the elevator up to the park and had really enjoyed a nice roll in the grass, but as soon as Luna and Flurry had started running, Sarge hid under the bench. Danielle was more than a little worried. He'd been walking around her place just fine, putting more weight on the bad leg as it healed. She could always hear him coming, the way his cast thumped on the tile floor. She'd thought he'd enjoy the park, but instead she was worried that she'd somehow retraumatized him.

They should go home. Not because she thought that was where Knox was heading but because Sarge could use the safety and security of a familiar place to boost his confidence. That Knox might be there soon was simply a bonus. Danielle slipped off the bench and squatted in front of Sarge.

"You ready to go?"

Sarge perked up his head at her words, one of his ears rotating forward while the other stayed flat against his head.

"You're not leaving so soon, are you?" Sydney, dressed as always like she was on her way somewhere more important, joined them at the bench. Her chihuahua, Chewy, squirmed in her arms to be let down. Sydney set him on the grass, and he took off as fast as his little legs would carry him. Danielle kept an eye on her greyhounds, but their reconditioning held, as she'd known it would. They might've been trained to chase small, fluffy things around a track, but they were well aware that their racing days were over. They'd gladly traded their racing instincts for a loving home. At least, that was how Danielle explained it to prospective new owners.

Chewy leapt at Luna's front leg, enticing her to play. She shot off, and he chased her, the distance between them widening with every step. Chewy dug in, determined, his short legs churning so fast they were a blur.

"We have enough time to stay and wear your little guy out." Danielle leaned back on the bench, and Sarge plopped his head in her lap. His pleading eyes seemed to say, "Didn't you say we were going?"

"Here, for being so good." She covertly offered him a bit of freeze-dried sweet potato, his favorite treat. But not covertly enough. Luna's and Flurry's muzzles were in her business before Sarge had even finished swallowing. Chewy bounced against her leg like the ground was a trampoline and her knee was a wall he wanted to vault. Lady waited patiently while the other dogs scarfed down their treats, then raised her paw like she wanted to shake hands.

"It's alright?" Danielle asked Eliza and Sydney, aware that no matter how much dogs thought it fine to take food whenever and wherever offered, owners preferred to have the last say.

"Go right ahead." Eliza crinkled the plastic bag at her side. "She'll mope if she feels left out."

Lady lipped the treat out of Danielle's outstretched palm and carried it away to eat on the other side of Eliza. Sydney nodded her approval, and Chewy dashed off with his prize.

While the greyhounds nuzzled Danielle's pockets for more, Eliza asked Sydney, "How go all the preparations?"

"For which event?" Sydney laughed happily, crossing one leg over the other in a stance that looked like she was ready for a fashion shoot. Her body-skimming black jeans ended in ankle boots with spiky heels that slowly sank into the sod the longer she stood in place. "The Easter Bonnet Parade is going to be a blast. Twice as many vendors as for our Valentine's Day fair! Fur Haven is really getting a reputation in the area. The event calendar on the website is filling up quickly."

Sydney lived down the street and was a dog park regular long before the dog park even officially existed. Danielle wasn't exactly sure how it had happened, but Sydney was in charge of Fur Haven's website, especially booking and organizing events.

"And the wedding?" Eliza prompted, a gleam in her eye. "Everything set for the big day?"

"Definitely. Now that Riley and Caleb finally picked a date, we are good to go. I even have my bridesmaid's dress. Want to see?" Sydney whipped out her phone and swiped through her photos before Eliza or Danielle could respond.

Danielle's own phone felt heavy in her pocket. Should she respond to Knox's text? They hadn't spoken since their afternoon decorating Eliza's front yard. Since The Kiss. *I'm almost there.* If she sat here looking at wedding prep photos, would she miss him? Her feet bounced like they were ready to take off no matter what her brain said.

She quieted her fidgets and made appropriate sounds of approval at the sight of Sydney in an off-the-shoulder coral dress with so much lace it should've looked fussy but somehow on Sydney looked perfect. Sydney launched into a long story about how difficult it'd been to find a dress that both she and Riley liked, ending in a recommendation for a local tailor who had made alterations at a very reasonable price.

Sarge rescued Danielle from more wedding talk with a whine and nudge of her hand. She stood with a stretch and reached down to clip leads on the greyhounds. "We better hit the road. I have the late shift at the clinic tonight."

"It's always good to see you." Eliza lifted her cheek, and Danielle dipped down to kiss it.

"We're on our way, too. Got a client meeting soon." Sydney offered a little wave. "I've never seen Chewy run as much as he did today, Danielle." Sydney scooped up the Chihuahua and placed him back in the doggy sling. "Look how pooped he is! With any luck, he'll let me sleep past 5:00 a.m. tomorrow."

"Anytime. The girls love to run." Danielle walked toward the elevator and the dogs followed obediently, none of them pulling or straining at the leash. It wasn't easy for three large dogs to make space for each other, and she was happy that they'd figured it out among them.

"I do hope we'll see you here more often." Sydney kept up a steady chatter, waiting at the elevator. "It's such a beautiful space now, isn't it?"

"It is. See you this weekend." Danielle turned to wave one last time at Eliza. Eliza didn't see her, busy as she was rustling around in the tote bag at her feet. She pulled out a paperback novel, and Lady took off to inspect the park's perimeter, one careful sniff at a time.

"Riley told me your dad is a veterinarian." Sydney stepped into the elevator first, then held the door for Danielle. "I've been thinking of switching. The vet I take Chewy to retired, and I'm not sure I like the new vet. He always seems in such a rush."

"Sure. Give me a second, and I'll give you a card for the clinic." Danielle loaded the dogs into the large elevator and pushed the button for the ground floor. She reached into her bag for a card.

"Thanks." Sydney tucked it into her back pocket and asked a few questions about how things worked at the clinic that Danielle answered with half her attention. The other half was busy wondering if the buzz in her pocket was Knox.

Danielle ended the suspense by checking her texts again. It was merely her cell carrier, acknowledging her auto-payment had gone through. She couldn't help but reread Knox's text. Was he already at her house? No, he'd text when he was outside, wouldn't he? If she wasn't there, would he wait for her? She was so engrossed in reading his message for the fifteenth time that she didn't notice when the elevator doors opened.

"I sent the text so you'd wait for me, not run away." Knox stood in the opening, hands casually planted in his back pockets. His charcoal USMC T-shirt stretched tight against his chest, and Danielle couldn't look away.

"Hey, Knox." Sydney exited the elevator first with a friendly smile for Knox. "How's the Dorothy coming along?"

"It's coming. Slower going than anybody likes, but Lance says that's normal." Knox's gruff voice raised the flesh on Danielle's arms.

Danielle wrenched her gaze from Knox's pecs and looked at Sydney. How was she so unaffected by him? Sydney chatted about renovation plans and the wedding schedule for a few moments before heading out with a careless wave. Danielle envied Sydney her poise, her style, her made-for-fashion body.

Self-consciously, Danielle tugged at her old pineapple T-shirt. It'd been cute when she bought it, but many years and many washings later, it was definitely a going-to-the-dog-park shirt, not a run-into-your-ex-who-you're-hoping-to-kiss-again shirt.

Knox's gaze followed her fidgety hands, and he cleared his throat. "I like your, uh, pineapples. I mean, pineapple."

There was only one on her shirt, but the heat in his eyes made her think he wasn't talking about the T-shirt design at all. The urge to cross her arms, to hide in some way, was strong, but her hands were full of dog leashes. She shoved one in his direction.

"Want to walk him?"

"Sure." Knox accepted the leash, a move that made Sarge's tail beat against Danielle's leg at full force. "Where are we going?"

The dogs didn't need a walk, not after their run at Fur Haven. Sarge plopped onto his haunches and craned his neck so that his nose pointed straight in the air, all the better to keep his eyes on Knox.

"I was heading home." Danielle switched both Luna's and Flurry's leads into her left hand.

"Didn't want to wait for me, huh?" Knox absently patted Sarge's head.

"Actually, I was trying to get there before you. But you were coming here?"

A slow smile spread across Knox's face. "So you weren't trying to avoid me?"

She ducked her head so her bangs covered her face. She straightened Luna's perfectly straight collar. "How'd you know I was at Fur Haven?"

"Recognized the bench. From the last photo of Sarge you sent. Plus the time stamp. I was only a few minutes away."

"I was confused by your text." Danielle's fingers squeezed around the embroidered martingale. She forced herself to look up at Knox. "I thought you were avoiding me."

"No. I wouldn't do that."

"But I haven't seen you—"

"Right." He cut her off. "Maybe I would do that. A little bit. But only because I was so damn nervous."

"You? Nervous? I find that hard to believe, Mr. Marine."

"What can I say?" He held a hand out to her, palm up. "You still give me butterflies."

Danielle swallowed so hard she almost choked. "Me?"

"You." His hand remained in the air between them. Open, inviting.

"Me too." She reached out and placed her palm on top of his, a light brush of skin on skin, but she felt the heat all the way to her toes.

His fingers curled around hers, but she was the one who tugged him closer. He took a step, then two, in her direction. All three dog heads swiveled to watch his next move.

He didn't make one. Instead, his mouth quirked in a half smile. "Where's a Magic Eight Ball when you need one?"

"What do you want to know?" Was that breathless voice hers? Made sense, though. Her lungs felt tight, her whole body poised on the brink of flight.

"Does Danielle Morrow want to kiss me?"

Flurry stretched out her long, white neck and nudged their hands. Danielle was pretty sure Flurry's intent was to get them to pet her, but it felt more like a benediction. Permission. Danielle stepped in toward Knox, until her, uh, pineapples pressed into his chest.

Breath escaped in a loud whoosh, and his free hand curled around her waist. He watched her with lowered lids, nostrils slightly flared.

Danielle reached up, sliding her fingers into the short hair over his ears. She pressed with the pads of her fingers, letting them glide across his scalp to the back of his head.

Knox's eyes closed all the way, and he leaned in to her touch. "You can do that all day."

"I'd rather do this," she said in that breathless voice she hardly recognized as her own. Then she pressed her lips to his, nudging into him, testing the fullness of his bottom lip with her tongue.

He moaned, deep and low in his throat, and his lips parted slightly. She swooped in at the opening, and his tongue met hers in a fierce dance. She pressed herself closer to him, and his arm banded around her, his palm in the small of her back, to draw her more forcefully against him.

Danielle lost herself in Knox. Not in the memory of him. No, she'd spent too many nights after their breakup recalling every detail. This was much better than her memories. He was so warm, so solid, and every stroke of his tongue pulled her in more. She could kiss him forever, here on the first floor of a parking garage, in plain view of anyone who might walk by.

The thought brought her back to reality with a crash. Both her hands were cupped around Knox's head, the leashes dropped to the ground.

"The dogs." She pulled back, breath hitched in her chest.

Knox pressed his lips to her forehead, and she looked down, inhaling deeply. Beside them, Sarge sat, still keeping all his attention on Knox.

The girls, on the other hand, were nowhere in sight.

CHAPTER 11

IT WAS DAMN HARD TO STEP AWAY FROM THE SOFT EMBRACE OF Danielle's body, but there was no denying the tension that stiffened her small frame. Reluctantly, Knox let his arms fall to his sides.

"They can't have gone too far." He scanned the garage, filled with older Toyotas and other economy cars in bleached-by-the-sun colors. The Dorothy residents parked on the first floor. The second floor was open to the public, a source of income for both the building and the City of Miami Beach. He didn't see any long-muzzled hounds, but then, as big as they were, they were smaller than any of the cars they might be hidden behind.

"Are you kidding me?" Danielle's agitation was contagious. At least Sarge caught it, whining low in his throat. Danielle shoved a hand through her hair, bangs flying every which way. "In three strides, they can make thirty miles per hour. Top speed is forty-five. They could be *anywhere* by now."

Danielle spun in a distracted circle.

"That is really fast." Knox couldn't stand the distraught look on her face. His fingers itched to reach for her, to smooth back the fly-away bangs, to hold her close so that nothing bad could get to her.

As a Marine, he'd dedicated his life to protecting his country, his fellow Marines, and the objects of his missions, and he'd been good at it. Dedicated. Willing to die to make sure the rest of his men made it out. Heartbroken when he wasn't able to prevent the tragedy of a lost Marine. What was coursing through his veins right now was familiar in some ways. The adrenaline heightening his senses, the drill-and-kill commands echoing in his head, the flex of his fingers reaching for a rifle that was no longer there.

But in other ways, he felt out of his element. How could he stop the tears glistening in Danielle's eyes that she refused to let fall? How could he execute a search-and-rescue mission but without leaving her side? She exerted a gravitational pull on him that made it hard to keep what little distance there was between them.

"Flurry! Luna!" Danielle visibly rallied. Sucked in large breaths that stretched the pineapple on her T-shirt. Whoa, that pineapple. It was going to star in his dreams for many nights to come. He'd always had a thing for Danielle's breasts, but he told himself his horny teenage memories were what made it impossible for any other woman to outshine Danielle in his memory. Yet somehow, those breasts had gotten even better with time, and here he was, staring at her chest while she was freaking out about her dogs.

Knox shook his head, turning abruptly at a shadow that flashed across his peripheral vision.

"Over there," he said in a low voice, pointing with his chin. A white nose, tipped in black, stuck out from under a blue Sebring convertible.

Danielle rushed to the car. "Flurry, you crazy girl. What're you doing down there?"

Flurry belly crawled out from under the car, her tail wagging timidly. She rolled, exposing her chubby tummy for Danielle to pet.

Danielle squatted and smoothed a hand over Flurry's rib cage, her pregnancy evident in the rounded curve of her belly. "Where's Luna, huh? Do you know?"

Flurry blinked up, all innocence, and Knox began a car-by-car search for the other dog. "You didn't tell me your dogs like to play hide-and-seek."

"It's new to me, too." Danielle stood, wrapping the long lead around her wrist. She headed for the opposite side of the garage, Flurry's nails clicking behind her on the concrete floor. "I have to say, I'm not a fan. Not a fan at all."

At Danielle's disapproving tone, Flurry's tail drooped.

Knox slapped his thigh for Sarge to follow him. After the third car that Knox dropped onto his good knee to look under, Sarge adopted a search-and-rescue protocol of his own. At each new car, he'd drop his front half, butt raised in the air. Knox couldn't help but smile at the sight. Then, Sarge swept his muzzle from side to side in a one-eighty arc. When he didn't find anything, he'd return to his full height and stare up at Knox.

Knox had no trouble imagining Sarge in the field, shouting, "Clear!" after he checked out the undercarriage of each car.

"Do you think Sarge knows we're looking for Luna?" Knox called loudly, hoping it would carry to Danielle's position.

Danielle popped up from behind an old Camry. "Probably? It's hard to know for sure what goes through their quarter-pound brains."

Sarge yipped, pulling on his leash so hard that Knox lost his balance and had to brace himself on the nearest car to keep from landing too hard on his bad leg.

"What is it?" Knox reoriented himself and let the leash out a bit to give Sarge his head. The dog pulled him toward the garage exit.

"Oh no, oh no." Danielle followed Flurry's lead in the same direction. "Luna's out on the street." Danielle broke into a jog, Flurry keeping pace beside her. They reached the exit before Knox and Sarge.

"This looks like one of yours." The voice was deep, amused.

Knox wasn't sure who it was, though the voice sounded familiar, but he already didn't like the guy.

"Thank God." Danielle's voice was as breathless as if she'd run laps around the garage. As breathless as if he'd just kissed her.

When Knox finally got outside, he found Danielle kneeling in the grass, both arms around Luna's neck. Above her, way above her, stood Adam St. John, hands clasped around Luna's leash like he was the owner taking his pup out for a stroll.

"You look good with a greyhound."

Knox did not like the way she eyed the handsome architect. Adam had designed the new Dorothy, the parking garage, even the new Fur Haven Dog Park, and as a result, Knox had spent more than a few days working alongside him. He was the kind of architect who liked to be on-site and would pitch in when he could, even if it meant plaster dust on his expensive trousers. So Knox knew Adam wasn't a bad guy. He was maybe even a good guy. He was just standing too close to Danielle, that was all.

Adam handed the leash over to Danielle. "Don't look at me like that. I am not in the market for a runaway greyhound. Or any greyhound for that matter."

The speculative gleam didn't leave Danielle's eye. "Luna's mine, but I have a few dogs in foster care you might really love."

Adam chuckled. "I was warned about your persistence. And I see you've already roped Knox in with your wiles, but with the hours I work, it wouldn't be fair to bring a dog into my home."

Danielle admitted defeat with a regal nod. "You make a good point. If your work schedule changes, let me know."

Adam cocked his head. "You know what? I don't think I will." He stuffed his hands in his pockets and continued into the garage.

"Well, that was rude." Danielle watched the door swing closed behind Adam. Knox had noticed that Riley and Carrie liked to watch the man walk away, too.

"You did try to force a dog on him."

"I don't force dogs on people." Danielle huffed, still crouched down but no longer clinging to Luna. Flurry stood next to Luna, their muzzles crossed in greeting, while Danielle took turns petting them.

Knox exchanged a look with Sarge, who looked like he was grinning. Knox might have a hard time understanding dog language, but Sarge could clearly read him.

"I'm a matchmaker." Danielle filled the silence with chatter, a habit he'd loved in high school when he'd felt so awkward around everyone. Everyone but her. "Everyone has a match. Some people just need more encouragement than others."

Sarge nudged Knox's good leg, and he scratched the dog behind his ears. "You really believe that?"

"I really do. There's a perfect match for everyone." Danielle stood. "Look at you and Sarge."

Knox's gut clenched at her words. He believed her. Believed *in* her. But it wasn't Sarge who was his perfect match. No, his perfect match was smiling up at him, eyes shining with relief at finding her runaway dogs, completely oblivious to the rioting emotions ricocheting through his body. He wasn't falling in love with Danielle Morrow all over again. He didn't have to, because he'd never stopped loving her in the first place.

He reached out a hand. She accepted his help, and as soon as she was on her feet, he pulled her against his chest, capturing his mouth with hers in a kiss so hungry it even surprised him.

She jerked from shock, then kissed him right back. His lips never leaving hers, he gathered up the three leashes and wrapped them around her waist. This time, the dogs weren't going anywhere. And neither was he.

Eventually, the dogs lost patience with them, and the combined weight of three greyhounds leaning on them finally got Knox's attention, especially when accompanied by an investigative snout in his crotch.

"What is it you wanted to talk about?" Danielle smiled while he batted Sarge's nose into a less personal area.

Knox looked into her eyes, sure he'd had some pressing issue to discuss with her but unable to think past the overwhelming desire to kiss her. Could she read the desire on his face?

Her dark eyes softened in a way that made him think maybe she did, but "Was it about helping Eliza next weekend?" was all she said, breaking eye contact with him.

Her prompt made him nod his head, but lying wasn't his nature, so he admitted, "Hell if I know, but it sounds good."

Danielle nodded and got out her phone. "Eliza's still up top at the park. Let me text her." Her fingers flew, and within a few minutes, they had a plan. How was it that he'd agreed to go ten whole days without seeing Danielle again? He liked it better when they were kissing. Things were clearer. He was clearer. In the face of her efficient scheduling and dog handling, he found he couldn't interrupt her to demand what she felt about him. If she thought they could make it work as adults.

This was how adults do it, he supposed. One careful step at a time. He liked it about as much as when they made him slow down at physical therapy. Knox was not a man who liked to tread lightly. Once an objective was fixed, why waver?

Danielle sent him a shy smile. "Do you mind the pictures of Sarge?"

Mind having her name pop on his phone several times a day? But he couldn't tell her how much he looked forward to any communication from her. "It's fine."

"Good, good." Danielle's color heightened, her freckles blending together, and he realized she was uncomfortable. Maybe even embarrassed. With him.

"I'm sorry." The words were out before he knew what he was apologizing for.

Danielle's face went from pink to white in a flash. "You're apologizing for the kiss?"

He tried to read her. Failed. "Yes?"

"Typical Knox. What did I expect?" Danielle lunged toward her car, dogs in tow. Sarge trailed reluctantly and, with even more reluctance, allowed her to boost him into the back of her SUV.

Knox caught up, grabbing her elbow to spin her toward him. "What does that mean?"

"It's all old memories to you, isn't it? But I can't go there again, Knox. We're not eighteen anymore." She yanked out of his grasp.

He didn't like it, how she avoided his touch. He shoved his hands in his pockets. "I take it back then. I'm not sorry."

Danielle's eyes raked him, head to foot. "Geez, make up your mind already." She climbed into the driver's seat and slammed the door.

Knox watched her red taillights until she turned onto the street and out of sight, not sure what exactly had just happened but glad he knew Danielle well enough to know that even if she was mad at him, he'd still see her for Easter egg stuffing next Saturday. Maybe by then he'd have figured out what exactly just went wrong.

CHAPTER 12

KNOX KNELT ON HIS GOOD KNEE AND OPENED HIS ARMS WIDE for his nephew, who was barreling full speed up Eliza's front walkway, an excited Beckham jumping along beside him. An empty basket swung on his arm, and when he launched himself into Knox's hug, the basket whacked Knox upside the head.

"Buddy, you gotta keep your gear in check." Knox rubbed his noggin and exaggerated his wince of pain to make his point.

"K-nox, I'm going to get candy today." Oliver grinned up at him, completely oblivious to the important life lesson Knox was attempting to impart. What did Knox expect with the prospect of sugar rush on Oliver's mind?

Over a dozen children scrambled around Eliza's front yard, shouting to their parents whenever they found a plastic egg. One boy ran past, his cargo-shorts pockets bulging, singing a song he was clearly making up on the fly. "Hippity hippity, hoppity hoppity," he sang loud enough that the residents at the Dorothy across the street could probably hear him.

Knox kept one arm around his nephew and used his other hand to scratch Beckham, who stood on his hind legs, front legs planted on Knox's thigh. "You only get candy if you can find it. You got your X-ray vision on today?"

"You bet, K-nox!" Oliver bounced on the balls of his feet as if in addition to X-ray vision, he could also launch himself into space with the sheer force of his excitement. "K-nox, did you find any yet?"

Knox shook his head and stood, taking Oliver's hand. Once Oliver started learning to read, he'd insisted on pronouncing the K in Knox. At first, it was super cute, but it'd been a few months now and Knox was over it. Sadly, Oliver was not. Knox was afraid he was going to be Uncle K-nox for the rest of his life.

"Sorry!" Carrie hustled up the walkway, hair in a loose bun with long strands framing her features. "I had trouble finding parking, and as soon as he saw you out the window, Oliver couldn't wait. Looks like you guys are ready to start."

"We are. Into the fray?" He offered his arm to his sister-in-law, and she took it with a laugh. Oliver sprinted ahead of them, stopping every few feet to admire Eliza's bunnies and baskets and weird egg-themed lawn stakes. While Oliver scanned the yard for plastic eggs, Knox scanned the area for any sign of Danielle. She'd said she'd stop by this morning before she set up for the Fur Haven Easter Bonnet Parade, but so far, he hadn't seen her short bob of brown hair anywhere.

Yesterday, they'd spent the afternoon in Eliza's—soon to be his—living room, stuffing hundreds of plastic eggs with candy. The red ones had sugar-free, dairy-free, gluten-free treats in them, and it had been Knox's job all day to let parents know so they could direct their kids toward or away from the red eggs, depending on the kid.

The plastic-egg-stuffing process had been surprisingly relaxing, kicked back on the sofa with his bad leg propped on a stuffed ottoman that Lady had gnawed the fringe off of when she was a puppy, listening to Eliza rant about an interview she'd heard on NPR earlier in the day. Danielle had listened, agreeing with Eliza's points, while Knox stayed out of it, stuffing as much candy in each egg as he could. Only an occasional mini-Tootsie Roll made it to his mouth. When Eliza had exhausted her outrage, at least momentarily, she made them coffee and brought out a plate of yellow, pink, and purple Peeps. Danielle had actually squealed at the sight. Knox could eat his own weight in cupcakes given the chance, but he wasn't a fan of the sticky Peeps. He did, however, become a big fan of watching Danielle enjoy them. He found they tasted better after witnessing Danielle's delight.

They'd gone back to egg prep after the snack, filling large baskets with eggs in every color of the rainbow and then some. Danielle had been relaxed, chatting with Eliza about people and pets they knew. Eliza showed them pictures on her phone of her new place across the street.

"Wow, that's practically a palace. You and Lady will be so happy there!" Danielle's finger had swiped through the photos slowly, commenting on each room with such enthusiasm that Knox felt a surge of pride swell through him. He'd helped with the renovation, and it was beyond satisfying to hear it praised. Especially by Danielle.

After the first hour, Knox hadn't had to put much thought into the egg business. Open egg, shove candy inside, close egg, and put in a basket. Repeat, repeat, repeat. Once he had the hang of it, he had a lot of time for his mind to wander, and it wandered to its favorite subject lately: Danielle. Her small hands were engaged in the same task, prying open plastic eggs and sorting through heaps of candy. She occasionally chewed at the chipped polish on her thumbnail, and he noticed a scar across the back of her left hand that hadn't been there in high school. He had questions, a lot of them. Like what happened to make that scar? And why hadn't she become a vet like she'd planned? And most importantly, did she regret kissing him, or would she like to do it again?

Because he would like to do it again, but he was afraid his apology had somehow made everything worse between them. Not as bad as fifteen years of no contact, he consoled himself, but bad enough that he might actually have to engage in a conversation about *feelings* to sort it out, and he'd quite frankly rather kiss her and see where it went than try to untangle their past and present. Where was that Magic Eight Ball egg when a guy needed one?

As if she felt his eyes on her, Danielle had looked up and smiled. He'd smiled back, and her cheeks had gotten as pink as the plastic egg in her hand. *A good start.* As soon as the last egg was filled, Eliza had asked for help hiding them around the yard.

"They'll be okay overnight?" Knox had been skeptical, but Eliza assured him that in the twenty years she'd been hiding eggs, only once had raccoons figured out how to crack them open.

"But they only ate a dozen or so. It worked out fine." Eliza marshaled them out the front door. "The hunt starts at sunrise and is over by noon. I can't get up much earlier than the crack of dawn, not these days anyway, so it's best to get it done now." Eliza shoved a basket of eggs into his arms and pointed to the far end of the yard. "Make some easy to find for the littlest ones and make some hard to find for the ones who think they're so smart."

"Hey, I used to love finding the out-of-the-way eggs!" Danielle hugged a basket to her chest.

"And weren't you a smarty-pants back then? Nose always in a book, using words no child your age should know." Eliza placed an egg on the edge of the step.

"She had a real potty mouth, huh?" Knox swung the basket into one hand, and the plastic weave brushed against his brace. He shifted it to his other hand.

"Oh yeah, always going on about occiputs and prosterna. Your father should've washed your mouth out with soap, no doubt about it." Eliza clucked her tongue in feigned disapproval.

Danielle busied her hands in the basket. "Fine, I get it. I was a pretentious kid."

"Oooh," Eliza wiggled her fingers like a magician conjuring a rabbit out of a hat. "Look at you, still using the big words."

Danielle had forced a laugh. Knox knew it was forced because it didn't reach her eyes. In fact, her eyes were sad when she said, "Well, I learned about the real world soon enough, didn't I? Come on. These eggs won't hide themselves."

Danielle had stayed on the other side of the yard, placing eggs with a focused determination that got the job done quickly. She'd called her goodbyes from the sidewalk, and Eliza had yelled, "See you tomorrow?"

"I've got the Easter Bonnet Parade in the afternoon, but I'll swing by early!" Danielle's brake lights were halfway down the street before Knox could ask her to pin down a more specific timetable.

Eliza had propped a hand on her hip. "That one's always been touchy, but don't worry about her. She's sensitive, but she's tough. She's had to be. See you tomorrow?"

Knox had agreed, his eyes still on the brake lights pulling farther and farther away from him. He thought he recognized Danielle's behavior, and he didn't like where his thoughts took him. Danielle had a secret, a big one. A painful one. One that explained why she'd never gone to college. And as long as she was intent on keeping it, she'd keep running away from him. No wonder she loved greyhounds. Their speed was probably her inspiration.

Eliza told him to come back at an ungodly hour, but it was fine with Knox. He was usually up then anyway. He set a timer on his phone, just in case, and headed for his truck. He followed the path Danielle's brake lights had taken but turned left where she'd turned right. Driving over the Julia Tuttle Causeway into Miami, he felt the tautness of invisible strings pulling him back toward the Beach. He'd floored the accelerator toward his lonely apartment. Tomorrow, he'd vowed, he'd fill out the online application to adopt Sarge. He needed one uncomplicated relationship in his life.

Now, standing in full sunlight, not a cloud in the sky and the temperature already over eighty degrees, Knox found himself getting angry that Danielle hadn't yet arrived. The sun had been up for over two hours. She'd roped him into helping Eliza; she'd agreed to be here. Several families had already come and gone. Where was she?

"A red one!" Oliver held up the egg in triumph.

"You don't want that one." Knox held out his hand. "Let's leave that for other kids."

"No!" Oliver hugged it to his chest. "Red is my favorite color!"

"Trust me, buddy. It is not filled with your favorite candy." Knox knew a lot of ways to disarm an enemy but that seemed extreme for dealing with a stubborn five-year-old. He settled for keeping his hand held out.

Oliver shook his head. "I'll love it, whatever it is, because it's red."

"You're not going to win." Carrie's lowered voice caught Knox's attention. "Our best bet is to hope he gets distracted by another red egg."

"All the red eggs are the same. No dairy, no sugar, no gluten. It's really not the candy experience he's looking for."

"I'm going to find all the red eggs!" Oliver clutched the red egg to his chest, a determined look on his sharp features.

"Go ahead!" Carrie waved him on and tipped her head up toward Knox. "What's in them, then?"

"Near as I could tell? Sticks?" One corner of his mouth lifted in a smile. "Or maybe they were more like twigs?"

"Okay, okay. New plan." Carrie unhooked her arm from his and trotted after Oliver who had decided to crawl on hands and knees and sniff out the red eggs like a dog. Beckham thought this was a great idea, bounding around Oliver with unrestrained glee.

"You're good with him, your nephew." Danielle's voice surprised Knox into stumbling backward a step.

"When did you get here?" He regained his balance, reluctantly grateful for his time on the torture device that improved his stability. He crossed his arms over his chest.

Danielle's eyes traced his tattoo. He felt her gaze like a caress on his skin. He swallowed down the instinct to crowd her, to back her up against the tree only a few feet behind her and kiss her like he'd been wanting to since, well, the first time he'd seen her in high school. It had been at the end of their sophomore year, and he'd had to enter the science fair as a last-ditch attempt to get extra credit for his bio class.

Danielle's project had been on dog behavior, specifically the ways in which they use barks to communicate. She'd re-created a set of tests she'd read about in an article using volunteers from her dad's veterinary clinic. She didn't just have a board, like his stupid presentation on the impact of music on mood—a poorly thought-out experiment he'd conducted the night before with exactly one test subject: himself—she also had a video playing clips from her research process. A fluffy poof of a dog stood on her table, a Pomeranian she'd somehow gotten permission from both the owner and the school to use as a visual aid.

Knox had stood to the side as she'd explained her experiment to the judging panel who consisted of his bio teacher, the principal, and a science teacher from the middle school. The Pomeranian had barked on command, and the judges had watched the entire video. Danielle didn't win the science fair—an injustice, he'd thought at the time. How could they not have been wowed by her enthusiasm and fierce determination? He certainly had been. In fact, he'd found himself thinking about her off and on all that summer, especially whenever he saw a dog.

Danielle had been awarded a runner-up, and he'd gotten his extra credit. But the real prize for him had been learning Danielle's name. School had ended a few days later, but he'd made it his business to find her when the new school year started that August. She'd agreed to go to homecoming with him, when he'd finally worked up the nerve to ask her. And she'd kissed him that day, too, like she never wanted to stop.

He still didn't want to stop. Even with a crowd of toddlers and kids romping around them, shouting out every time they found an egg, he wanted to kiss her. And now he'd been staring at her, at her lips, for too long. What had they been talking about again?

"An emergency came up at the clinic. My dad needed me. He tries to give the staff holidays off." Danielle had clearly been explaining for a while. Her hands were rolling in that way she had when she got going, explaining some kind of complicated surgery her dad had performed.

"Of course you had to help him." Knox said when she ran out of steam. What else could he say? That he'd been disappointed she wasn't here? That he'd thought about her science experiment, years later, when he'd learned to discern the subtle differences in the varying barks of his commanding officers? "You missed some pretty happy little kids. They all seem so excited. I can see why Eliza keeps up the tradition every year."

As if on cue, a kid with a big rubber duck on his little T-shirt plopped onto the ground between Knox and Danielle, bawling his lungs out. The hoodie pulled up over his head sported a duck bill that jutted out from his forehead, and he cried so hard the bill vibrated.

"So excited." Danielle raised an eyebrow at him.

"Hey there." Knox squatted, angling his braced leg out of the way, then gave up the balancing game and sat on his butt, too. "What's wrong?"

"No eggs! No eggs for me!" Snot dripped from the kid's nose, and he wiped it on the sleeve of his hoodie.

Knox took a moment to see if any parents were coming to the rescue, but no one seemed to notice the ducky meltdown. Many of the adults were helping themselves to the make-your-own mimosa station on the front patio, and a few older kids played with the Magic Eight Ball in the corner. Eliza, dressed in a fluffy white bunny suit that could double for the abominable snowman, sat in a giant wicker chair, a line of about three kids in front of her. While the children took pictures with the Easter Bunny, parents opened the eggs, dumped the candy into their baskets, and placed the empty plastic eggs in a giant receptacle by the front door. It surprised Knox what an efficient system it was, and he figured the crying kid's mom or dad would realize soon enough that their darling child needed them. In the meantime, Knox didn't want to leave the kid in meltdown mode while he searched out a responsible adult to handle the situation.

His lookout did reveal one thing, though. There was an egg right behind Danielle's heel. A yellow one. If she stepped backward, she'd crack it wide open.

"No eggs, huh? That's terrible." Knox sat with the kid. "You came for eggs. You should get some eggs. If only we knew where to look."

The kid's lower lip trembled. "I looked everywhere."

"Did you look, say, over there?" Knox pointed to the egg behind Danielle. She turned, saw it, and stepped aside so the kid had a clearer view.

"I did!" The kid sniffled again. "No eggs."

"Are you sure?" Knox pointed again. It was yellow, for God's sake.

The kid squinted. "No eggs! No eggs for me!"

Okay then. New plan.

Before he could think of one, Oliver crawled up, still in dog mode, and scooped up the egg. "Another one!" he crowed and held it up for Carrie to put in his basket.

"At least it's not red." Carrie added it to a stash of about fifteen others. "Hey, Danielle."

"Hey." Danielle dutifully admired Oliver's finds. "Oliver's killing it, huh?"

Before Carrie could reply, the duck-clad kid wailed, "No eggs! He took my egg!" and pointed at Oliver.

Oliver was stunned by the accusation. "I found it!" Beckham came to attention, standing between the two boys. "That makes it mine."

"My egg!" The kid was a few years younger than Oliver. After his claim of ownership, he blubbered until more snot strung out of his nose. He wiped it on his already wet sleeve. Oliver studied him for a moment.

"Mom?" Oliver stood up and reached for his basket. "I think I made a mistake. This one belongs to him." Oliver took out his most recent find. "Here." He placed it in the boy's hand. "This one is yours."

"Mine?" The kid blinked tear-spiked eyelashes at Oliver. A smile trembled on his lips.

"This one, too." Oliver took another egg out of his basket, then another. "And this one."

The kid let out a screech loud enough that all the adults on the porch looked their way.

"Lincoln!" A young mother with an infant on her hip rushed up to them. "Are you okay?"

"Look at my eggs!" He held them up like jewels for his mother to inspect.

"How clever you are." She beamed at him and tucked the eggs into a small, green basket. "You ready to go home?"

"Wait!" Oliver called as they walked away. He reached into his basket and pulled out the red egg. "This one is for his brother. Or sister." He held it up to the baby, but the baby was sound asleep.

The woman smiled and nudged the basket Oliver's way. Oliver dropped the egg in, then spun and ran to his mom.

Carrie's eyes were filled with tears. "That was very generous, Oli. You're a good boy."

"I know." He tugged on her hand. "Come on! There are even more to find!" He dragged her away, leaving Knox and Danielle by the tree.

"I can't think of a better kid to get a red egg." Knox grinned at Danielle. "I wish Oliver'd given him all his red eggs."

She sent a wobbly smile back. "You were so good with him."

"Oli? He's an easy kid."

"No, the other one. The not easy one."

"Aw, no worse than the new recruits I dealt with during my tour at Parris Island. Lots of blubbering there, too." His smile invited her to share in the joke, but she shook her head.

"I mean it. You're going to be a great dad." Her lower lip trembled, alarmingly like the snot-soaked kid's. "You always wanted a lot of kids."

Not if talking about it made her this emotional. Was she thinking of the baby she'd—they'd—lost? How could she not be? He certainly was, especially now. He remembered their whispered conversations in the back seat of his old Acura, how they'd planned the number of kids they'd have, even named them. He winced, remembering how his contributions had been mostly based on Transformers characters. She had rightly shot them all down.

"You too," he reminded her. He'd never thought about kids before being with her, but more kids equaled more sex in his teenage brain, so he'd been all for however many she wanted. "Although I have to admit I was more interested in the idea of making them than anything else."

He'd meant the comment to be teasing, but her whole face colored until she had only one freckle stretching across the bridge of her nose from cheek to cheek. Embarrassed? Angry? He couldn't tell. Should he apologize again? But that had backfired last time, so he did what he'd learned was often the best course of action in the Corps—he kept his mouth shut.

"You deserve those kids, Knox. Kids that you help make." She placed a hand on his forearm and squeezed. "I better get back to the clinic and check on our new patient. Then I really need to get over to Fur Haven. Big day ahead." She reached up on her toes and kissed him on the cheek.

It felt strangely like goodbye. Like goodbye forever. He replayed the last few moments in his head, looking for a clue, but she was walking away so he blurted out, "I'll be filling out the application to adopt Sarge today."

She spun on her heel, wiping at her eyes. "Excellent. He deserves to be with the human he loves."

"He loves you, too." He couldn't stand to see her so sad, especially when he wasn't sure why. Probably that damn secret, but they weren't exactly standing in a secret-sharing friendly venue. "Maybe I should get another dog. Maybe he'd rather stay with you."

"No, you're perfect for him. Besides, I'm about to have a full house." She kept walking, only backward. He took a few steps to keep the distance between them from growing. "Flurry's pregnant."

"Congratulations?" Again, he wasn't sure what the right response was.

She laughed and swiped at her eyes again. "Indeed. Guess I'll see you at the Easter Bonnet Parade later?" Then she did that thing he was getting real tired of. She walked away.

"Yeah," he said, but she was already gone.

CHAPTER 13

DANIELLE SOMETIMES WISHED GREYHOUNDS WERE MORE OF A working breed and less of an eye-on-the-horizon-keep-the-leash-tight breed. She could use one of those little dog carts she'd seen videos of Rottweilers pulling to load up her Homestretch table and props. Table skirt, brochures, greyhound swag like branded tennis balls and notepads. Not to mention Luna, Flurry, Sarge, and all the accessories involved in traveling with dogs—collapsible water bottles, first aid kit because you never know at these events, treats, toys, and in Sarge's case, his midday medication. Poor guy. Her dad had taken off the cast a few days ago, but it was looking like the leg hadn't healed completely right. Sarge would walk with a bit of a limp the rest of his life. On the bright side—for her, not Sarge—her dad had declared him strong enough to go ahead with the neutering. That meant Sarge would be ready for adoption sooner rather than later. And with the way Flurry was putting on the pounds, that was a good thing.

The three dogs had adjusted well to the single leash with three-way coupler, so Danielle wasn't juggling three separate leashes. Still, it was no small feat, wrangling all three big dogs, her canvas totes of supplies, and the fold-up table onto the elevator.

"Need a hand?" Knox's voice was as familiar to her as her own. It shouldn't be after so many years, but it'd taken only that one encounter at the grand opening, and she knew she'd recognize his raspy baritone anywhere. Anytime. Like now. Especially when she was expecting to run into him, just not so soon. She thought she'd be behind the safety of her table before she'd have to confront Knox and make some excuse for why she was so squirrelly lately. Some excuse that wasn't *I want to jump your bones every time I see you, but then I remember how we can't have a future and I want to run away*. In this case, honesty was not her best policy.

"Yes, please." Danielle spun and, there was no other word for it, drank him in. It was as though her senses were starved for the sight of him, in spite of having seen him a mere few hours ago, like she was trying to make up for all the years she hadn't seen him. It was hard to focus when her brain short-circuited every time she saw him. When would this reaction wear off? She suspected never. Knox would always be the one who might have been, and having him around again was only making everything she couldn't have that much clearer.

Knox favored the braced leg, holding most of his weight on the good leg, so she handed the dog leash over to him. "If you can corral my wild beasts, the rest is a cinch."

"What have you done to these poor animals?" Knox's voice was a mix of horror and on the verge of laughing. "You sad things."

"It's an Easter bonnet parade. The dogs are supposed to have hats."

"These are not hats. They are crimes against dogmanity."

"They aren't that bad." She looked down at the homemade Easter bonnets. Okay, they were pretty bad. She'd gotten the idea because Sarge had been wearing an e-collar, otherwise known as the cone of shame, for a few days, ever since the cast had come off. He'd had a few spots rubbed raw by the cast, and Danielle was keeping an ointment on them that Sarge found delicious. The e-collar was to stop him from licking at the healing abrasions. Thus her inspiration—a few minutes on Pinterest, and she'd found her solution. She'd used two more recycled e-collars from the clinic, painting each one like a different flower—daisy for Luna, mum for Flurry, and a happy sunflower for Sarge. They weren't exactly pin-worthy, but they weren't terrible. "You have something against flowers?"

"Those are flowers?" Knox squinted like he was having trouble believing his eyes. "Were you going for an abstract interpretation?"

"They are obviously flowers. Petals, etc. What more is there to a flower?" Danielle held back a giggle. She'd painted the cones late last night and had gone to bed feeling pretty good about her bonnet plan. In the light of day, however, it was clear she didn't have much to be proud of. They were, in fact, terrible.

"It's funny really." Knox bent down to scratch Sarge under the ruff of his costume. "All brains and beauty, no artistic talent whatsoever."

"What're you talking about?" Danielle gestured at the dogs, who wagged their tails at the energy in her voice. "That is talent, mister. Three masterpieces on display."

Knox laughed so loud that Sarge jumped and so hard that Danielle had no choice but to join in.

"Maybe you can say they're mutant plant hybrids caused by climate change?" Knox cracked himself up. Sarge wagged his tail in enthusiastic agreement.

Danielle leaned against the cold cinder-block wall of the garage. "Is it really that bad?"

"What's bad?" Adam joined them, a copy of the *New Times* rolled and tucked into one armpit. He wore gray slacks and a navy sweater vest, dressed like he was attending a board meeting, not a dog park event. "Are you going up to the Easter parade?"

"We are, but I'm surprised you are." Danielle fanned her face with her hand to calm down.

"Caleb and Lance insisted. They said I should see how my design is used." Adam craned his neck as if he could stare through the layers of concrete between him and the park. "They're not wrong. I've gotten two more requests for similar garages. People love their dogs, I guess."

"They sure do." Danielle rubbed the back of Flurry's head, under the e-collar. "You know what they don't like? To have those dogs mocked. Can you believe Knox was making fun of my dog-costuming skills?"

Adam crouched and inspected the dogs. "The costumes are lovely, Danielle. Not many people understand modern art, that's all."

"What do you think the dogs' bonnets are based on?" Knox took two tote bags and slung them over his shoulder and somehow commandeered the table, leaving Danielle with four small totes, one chair, and zero dogs.

"Jackson Pollock paintings, of course. Perhaps a reimagining of his *War*?"

Knox dropped the table from laughing so hard. When he finally caught his breath, he said, "They're flowers, Adam. Flowers." Then he was laughing again.

Adam's dark eyes widened, then he covered his reaction with a smile. "Ah, yes, I see it now. Lovely flowers. Nicely done, Danielle." He straightened and surveyed the pile of stuff. "Looks like you're planning to camp up there. Need some help?"

"Thank you, Adam. It's nice to know a real gentleman." Danielle handed him the lightest bag, the one filled with bouncy tennis balls, and a cushion for the folding chair.

"Happy to assist." He reached for the rest of the bags she'd been carrying, easily holding all the straps in his wide palms. He dropped his newspaper into one of the totes and took her folding chair as well.

"Hey." Knox rearranged his hold on the table, bags, and dogs. "I offered to help first. Who's the real gentleman?"

Danielle looked from the tall, elegant Adam to Knox in his battered *First To Fight* T-shirt and scuffed work boots. Her heart beat triple time, thinking about tracing the ink of Knox's tattoo wherever it might lead. Tracing any part of his muscled anatomy, really. With three greyhounds at his feet, the picture he made was nearly irresistible. But resist him she did.

"Adam, obviously." Danielle grinned at both men, but only Adam grinned back. Now empty-handed, she pushed the elevator button.

"Flattery appreciated, but you're not talking me into adopting a dog. I've been warned about you, you know." Adam's light teasing accompanied her into the elevator where she held the door until both men had lugged all her stuff inside.

"A dog, maybe not. But how do you feel about puppies?" She bobbed her eyebrows at Adam. "Flurry's expecting. They'll be ready to adopt in three to four months."

"And now I know the warnings were accurate." Adam used his elbow to push the button for the roof. "Puppies need even more attention than a dog. Afraid you're barking up the wrong tree."

"We'll see." Danielle tried to make her voice ominous but a giggle spoiled her attempt.

"Leave the poor guy alone." Knox finally reentered the conversation, earning a grateful smile from Adam, and Danielle relaxed with relief. Knox might be hard to read sometimes, but at least he wasn't acting like her hightailing it away from Eliza's earlier today made anything awkward between them. Maybe he was used to squirrelly girls. Her lips twitched, wanting to smile. *Brains and beauty*, he'd said. Who needed artistic talent?

"Clever." Sydney approached Danielle's table, her tiny Chihuahua in a baby sling across her front. His ears perked forward and his head swiveled from side to side, taking in all the sights and sounds of the Easter parade preparations as the rooftop dog park slowly but surely filled to capacity. "Can I take a guess?"

"Of course." Danielle pushed a Homestretch logo sticky pad her way. Knox had somehow produced a giant fishbowl for her, and she'd carefully lettered a sign that said, *Guess the greyhounds' bonnet theme correctly and be entered to win a free annual exam at Dr. Morrow's Animal Hospital. $1 per guess.* Her dad wouldn't mind. Anything for the animals.

"Does it include the yearly shots?" Sydney asked, scribbling her guess on the pad.

"Absolutely." Danielle hadn't thought that far ahead. Why not? Only one person would win, so the prize should be a good one.

Sydney dipped a finger into the front pocket of her skinny jeans and produced a five-dollar bill. "In that case, Chewy and I have a few ideas." She dipped her head, pretending to listen to the Chihuahua's input.

Danielle watched with a fond smile while Sydney finished her guesses, reminding her to write her name and number on each entry.

"Let's make this interesting." Knox slapped a ten-dollar bill on the table.

"You already know what the costumes are." Danielle tsked at him.

"I bet you ten dollars no one guesses flowers, and I bet you twenty if someone does guess flowers, that they don't guess *which* flowers." He slammed an Andrew Jackson next to the Alexander Hamilton and met her raised eyebrows with a smug grin.

"And I bet you"—Danielle narrowed her eyes, thinking—"that if someone does guess correctly, you take Sarge for a whole day."

"Not fair. I'm offering cold, hard cash, and you're offering emotional blackmail. I told you, I'm going to fill out the application." He hadn't yet, though. Danielle had eased up on the video clips and photo texts, figuring Knox might need some space. Some time to think about what taking on a dog really meant for his lifestyle. Maybe she should've kept it up after all.

Sarge whined at the words like he understood them. Danielle comforted him with a few pats to his head. "And I bet that spending some time with him will speed up the process."

"What about his leg?" Knox rubbed his own bad leg. "I thought he couldn't be adopted until he's off the meds and cleared by your dad. And after that? What will his life be like?"

"He'll be fine. What about yours?"

"What do you mean?" Knox snapped, sounding for all the world like a pissed-off drill sergeant.

Danielle fought the urge to shrink back. "Does your leg keep you from enjoying life? Doing work you find meaningful? Spending time with people you love?"

"Of course not."

Danielle nodded. "Exactly. His injury isn't holding him back. Heck, he's going to be a daddy soon."

This time, it was Knox's eyes that narrowed. "I see your game."

"You started the game." Danielle wished she could take back her words. She didn't like to think about Knox and the word *daddy* together. Her stomach clenched, but she held her ground. This was about Sarge, not her and her dashed dreams. Sarge was going to get his happily-ever-after if she had to sacrifice every ounce of her pride.

They stared across the table at each other for a long moment. Danielle's pulse picked up, pounding loud enough she could hear the blood rush in her ears.

"I accept your terms." Knox held out his hand to shake.

Their fingers met, and Danielle felt it all the way to her bones. The warmth and strength of him, the old feelings battling to come to the front. She beat them back down, like she had so many times before, and smiled. "You're on."

Knox walked away, and Danielle knelt down on the ground so she could talk to the dogs face-to-face.

"Look like flowers, okay? Happy, beautiful, flowering, uh, flowers. Okay? You understand."

Luna licked her hand. Of course they didn't understand. For Sarge's sake, she wished she'd brought the paints with her. Perhaps with a bit of a touch-up, she could make the petals more petal-like. She took realistic inventory of the three cones. No, Sarge's fate was in the hands of destiny. Or perhaps an elementary-school teacher who might recognize the intent behind the actual creation.

Teacher? That gave her an idea. She pulled out her phone and made a call.

———————

Danielle stayed at the table all day, delighted that she had to empty the fishbowl into one of her empty totes twice. Her first priority was always finding good forever homes for the foster dogs, but a close second was raising enough money to keep Homestretch operating. Not having a facility kept costs way down, but there was still a lot of medical care involved in the rescue line of work. Her dad couldn't work for free all the time.

Sydney used a bullhorn to announce the beginning of the Easter Bonnet Parade, a loose gathering of dogs and owners who wanted to be considered for the Best Bonnet contest. Danielle was under no illusions that she and her dogs could hope to top the dachshund with an elaborate spray of spring flowers orbiting her head like a crown or the corgi outfitted like a very short cherry tree. A few people had a similar idea to hers, repurposing old surgical cones but with far more creativity than she'd used. One golden retriever's cone turned him into a bowl of Froot Loops, and a Doberman's martini glass even sported a long stick spearing two balls painted to look like olives. Well, she'd tried. It was the spirit of the thing that counted, right? Still, no sense in subjecting her 'hounds to the parade. Someone needed to be the audience. She used the time to sort through the fishbowl guesses, watching as roughly fifty dogs paraded by.

Abstract painting got the most votes, but there were five people who guessed flowers. Danielle separated those into two categories. Three wrote "flowers." That should be enough to win the ten dollars from Knox. Two guessed at species. One wrote "tulip," a good guess and certainly closer than the person who'd guessed "roadkill," but the winner was the person who wrote "sunflower."

"Take that, Knox." Danielle smoothed the sticky note out on the table, eager to show him. She didn't need the sticky for the person's number—it was Lauren's guess. It wasn't cheating to call on an old friend who just happened to teach art classes to kids at the Police Athletic League on Saturdays. Anything for the dogs. Anything to get Sarge what he so desperately wanted: time with Knox.

"I've come to collect my winnings." Knox's limp was more pronounced later in the day.

"Read 'em and weep." She fanned the correct guesses out on the table like a spread of cards.

"Huh." He picked up each sticky note and inspected it. "I guess people have more imagination than I gave them credit for."

Danielle held out her hand. "Time to pay up."

Knox pulled the wrinkled bills out of the front pocket of his jeans. "I don't mind losing to a good cause."

Danielle smiled while he placed the bills in her hand. Her fingers curled over, catching his. Knox's eyes widened in surprise.

"I'll drop Sarge off tomorrow then?"

"I really can't. Not at my apartment. There are rules and things."

Danielle bit her lower lip. "So you're going to back out on the terms of the bet?"

"Dammit, that's not what I said." Knox's fingers tightened on hers. "Can you bring him to the Dorothy? I'll be working there most of the day."

"Sure." Danielle let his hand go, surprised at the reluctance she felt. "Meet you up here at six?"

"In the morning?" he groaned, like that was early, but she knew he'd been up even earlier today to help with Eliza's egg hunt. She suspected he was teasing, so she teased right back.

"Some of us have to go to work."

"Hey, I work."

"When you feel like it."

Knox raised a shoulder. "Ownership has its privileges."

"Six thirty?" Danielle collected the leftover brochures off the table, giving her hands something to do besides miss Knox's touch. She was pleased by how many brochures were gone. She had high hopes for two families that had stopped to talk for a long time, spending time with Luna, Flurry, and Sarge. She was hoping they'd call tomorrow. She had a few fosters in mind for them or, if they were patient, maybe a puppy. Maybe two puppies. She eyed Flurry's ever-expanding belly.

"Six thirty." Knox helped her close down the table, packing totes and folding up the table while she folded the chair.

Once there was nothing left to do, Danielle pretended interest in the parade results.

"Riley and LouLou!" Sydney proclaimed into the bullhorn. Riley and LouLou took a victory lap in their matching Easter bonnets, elaborate concoctions of flowers sticking out in every direction and held together by what Danielle imagined to be about a pound of hot glue.

"Something tells me the voting was rigged. Riley's grandmother was one of the judges." Knox ran a hand through his short hair, the flex of his muscle drawing attention to the Semper Fi scripted on his arm.

"Love her or fear her, no one argues with Gloria."

"True that." Knox lifted tote bags onto his shoulders. "Let me help you to your car."

"Thanks."

"See, I'm still a gentleman. Adam didn't even last an hour up here."

Danielle smiled and collected the dogs for one last lap of the park to say their goodbyes. Knox hefted his load toward the elevator. The sun set slowly in the west, painting the sky in peach and orange. Danielle congratulated Riley and chatted with Eliza for a moment before catching the elevator herself.

By all accounts, it was a success of a day. Potential leads for new homes for her fosters. Money raised for Homestretch. Sarge exhibited no signs of distress from all the socialization. Even her terrible dog bonnets had ultimately been vindicated. Why, then, did she feel so sad, heading home alone?

Alone. She wasn't really, not with her dogs, and she hadn't felt lonely in a long time. But she couldn't help but wish Knox wasn't just packing up her SUV and sending her on her way. She imagined loading up the dogs and climbing into the passenger seat while Knox drove them all home. Not to his place. Obviously, she couldn't live in an apartment that didn't allow dogs. Not her place. The guest cottage was barely big enough for her and three dogs. No way it could accommodate another permanent resident. If this were a fantasy, why not imagine a house with a large yard? Sure, that was where they were going. Home.

CHAPTER 14

KNOX SCRATCHED THE PERPETUALLY ITCHY SPOT AT THE TOP of his leg brace, trying to look casual and not at all like a suspicious stalker dude hanging out at a dog park without a dog. Five minutes wasn't *that* late, but he'd been fifteen minutes early, which made twenty minutes of awkwardly nodding at people while walking the edge of the rooftop park like he was checking out the view or something. For six thirty in the morning, the park was astonishingly busy. Before-work crowd, he supposed, and imagined what it'd be like to join their ranks.

The views were spectacular, with the Atlantic Ocean shimmering in the distance off the east side and views of Biscayne Bay and the Miami skyline off to the west. He could see why Caleb and Riley planned to say their vows up here. Knox checked his phone again. Seven minutes late.

The elevator dinged and a flustered Danielle emerged. At first, he thought the dark circles under her eyes depicted a sleepless night, but as she drew closer, two dogs on her left and Sarge on her right, he saw that it was smeared mascara. Had she been crying?

"Everything okay?" He met her halfway across the park, greeting each of the dogs with a scratch under the chin. Sarge wiggled from head to tail, his skin rippling as if he were made of Jell-O.

"Didn't sleep." Danielle handed him Sarge's leash and used her now-free hand to swipe through her disheveled hair. "Dad got a call after midnight. Hit and run left a poor little terrier with a crushed pelvis. I went into the clinic to assist him, and before I knew it, six hours had passed."

"How's the terrier?"

Danielle's brilliant smile lit up her tired face, dazzling him more than the sun's morning rays bouncing off the ocean. "He made it. It'll be a rough go at first, but he's going to live."

"You're amazing." The words slipped out, unpoliced, but he wasn't sorry for them. He'd watched from afar yesterday as she charmed people into taking her brochures, advocating for the dogs who'd been abandoned by a cruel racing system that didn't care about them now that they couldn't make money off the breed. She was relentless, definitely a good person to have on your side during a fight. Or anytime, really.

She swiped her hand through her hair again, the silky strands clinging to her fingers. "An amazing mess, you mean. But I wanted to get here before you gave up on us. As you can see, Sarge was eager to see you."

Sarge sat at Knox's feet, head tilted straight up to stare at him with adoration.

"I don't know what I've done to deserve this kind of attention." Knox reached down to unclip Sarge's leash. The dog stood and gave himself a full body shake before trotting off to inspect the nearest palm tree.

Danielle let Flurry and Luna off their leads, too, watching as they loped off to the other side of the roof. "That's the thing about dogs. They don't need a reason to love you. They just do."

The softness and longing in Danielle's voice caused an ache in his chest that he absently rubbed with the heel of his hand. "Unconditional love is a rare thing these days."

"Isn't it? You shouldn't take Sarge's devotion for granted. Sometimes dogs know better than we do where they belong."

There was that relentlessness again, but he had to admit it worked for him. "I hear you. I'll fill out the app as soon as escrow closes on the house." He'd taken a look at the application last night, and it was surprisingly long and thorough, not something he could dash off as an afterthought.

"Don't wait. He'll get the all clear from my dad soon, and then

I'll have to treat him like a regular foster. We had a number of families interested in adopting yesterday. I'm supposed to follow up with two of them later today." She smothered a yawn with her hand. "Maybe after a nap, though."

"They were interested in Sarge?" Knox didn't like the jealousy that rose in him at the thought that Danielle might give Sarge to someone else.

"Adoption in general. But he is one of the fosters, and I do need to find him a home."

"How many fosters do you have?"

"Personally? Just Sarge. We have another four with foster families in the area."

Knox's shoulders relaxed. There were plenty of dogs to adopt. Danielle didn't need to start with Sarge. He still had time. Time for what? He shook his head at his own thoughts. He wasn't ready for a dog, was he? Not until he had the house. Another thought occurred to him. It was no big deal to put the house up for sale, but what would he do with Sarge if he reenlisted? It was a long shot, his dream of returning to active duty. Getting a dog meant admitting his days as a gunnery sergeant were well and truly over. Was he ready to accept what the doctors had been telling him all along?

Sarge trotted back to him, collapsing on the ground in such a way that he curled around Knox's feet. Knox might not be ready for a dog, but the dog was clearly ready for him. Like he had with the house, Knox pushed aside concerns about the future and followed his gut instinct. Sarge needed him now. The Marines didn't need him at all. At the end of the day, it was some pretty simple math.

"About the bet?" Danielle was doing something with her short hair, scraping it back and twisting it into a messy knot that she attempted to secure with a tiny scrunchie. Some hair stayed back, but most of it fell forward again, brushing her cheeks. "If it's not safe to have Sarge on-site today, we can reschedule your day with him. I was caught up in the moment yesterday and didn't think about the possible problems of having a dog in the middle of a construction site."

"We'll be fine. I'm helping out today with painting trim in one of the finished units. It'll just be me and Sarge, a bucket of white paint, and a teeny-tiny paintbrush." Knox patted his thigh, and Sarge stood, seemingly eager to have his leash clipped back on. "Speaking of, we should probably get going."

"The paint fumes might not be good for him." Danielle chewed her lower lip in worry.

Knox immediately shut down the image of chewing on her lip for her. His teeth, her plump lower lip. Memories pushed to be let out, but he kept that door slammed shut. "It's a simple trim and touch-up today, and I'll open all the windows."

Danielle squatted down and took Sarge's muzzle into her palms. "Be good. I'll miss you." She kissed the tip of his nose, and Sarge nudged her hand. Luna and Flurry showed up, ready for affection, which Danielle offered through long strokes along their backs.

"Do you want me to bring him to your place tonight?" For some reason, it felt like a cheesy pickup line. He hoped she didn't hear it that way. "To save you a trip, I mean. I can drop him off. It's not a problem. I have a big truck." Why couldn't he stop talking? His men would laugh to hear him fumbling around like this. He bit back the next words that wanted to tumble out of his mouth.

Danielle's raccoon-ringed eyes crinkled in amusement. "The girls love Fur Haven. I'm happy to come back this evening to get Sarge. Shall we say five?"

"Sure." He forced himself to answer with one word. He checked Sarge's leash and led him toward the exit.

"See you later." Danielle's voice followed him into the elevator. Sarge's ears perked, but he didn't look back. Knox envied him. It seemed anytime he was around Danielle, all he wanted was to look back into a past he had no business remembering.

"Good Lord, Knox, what is going on here?" Adam's deep voice made Sarge pick up his head from where it currently rested on a rolled-up tarp. Knox set the small trim brush on the rim of his paint can and descended the two steps of the ladder he was standing on. He'd completed the bottom of the window trim and was nearly done with the top.

"Trim." Knox inspected his work. Darn professional looking if you asked him. "What're you doing skulking around the place?"

"None of your business." Adam strolled in on long legs until he was in the center of the empty living room. He swiveled his head, taking in all the decorative touches—mosaic tiles on the island that separated the living area from the kitchen, the arched opening into the short hallway that led to the two bedrooms. "Carrie told me these pendants would work. Hate to say it, but she was right." He pointed to the ceiling where a brass fixture managed to look both modern and classic Art Deco.

"Above my pay grade." Knox didn't hate the light fixtures, but he didn't love them, either.

Adam disappeared down the hallway, and when he returned, he seemed to notice Sarge for the first time.

"Hey, you can't bring a dog on-site." Adam crossed his arms over yet another sweater vest, this one in dark green. "Not even when a pretty girl asks you to. So you've already adopted the dog, huh?"

"No, not yet." Knox propped himself against the ladder. "I lost a bet is all. Dog spends the day with me, but he goes back to Danielle tonight."

"She's wily." Adam toured the newly renovated living room, stopping every so often to double-check details that even Knox couldn't see. "I've heard that when she decides someone needs a dog, they get a dog."

"It's just for today." Knox intended to adopt Sarge; he simply didn't like the implication that he'd somehow been manipulated into it.

"Mmm-hmm." Adam bent down from his over six-foot height and ran a finger along a baseboard. "These could use another sanding before being painted. Want me to tell Lance to get one of the guys on it? Last I saw, he was out in the lobby."

"I can do it."

Adam looked pointedly at Knox's leg. "You sure you should be crawling around the floor like that?"

"I said I could do it."

Adam straightened, tugging at the bottom band of his vest. "I'm sure you can. You don't have to is what I'm saying."

They stared at each other long enough that Sarge clambered to his feet to stand between them. The defensive posturing made Adam smile. "Not your dog, huh? Want to put some money where your mouth is?"

Knox looked from Sarge to Adam and back again. "Not really."

Adam laughed. "You're smarter than you look, you know?"

"I hear that a lot." Knox picked up the paintbrush. "Can I get back to work?"

"Yes, let the man work." Mr. Cardoza entered the room, his hair wet and carefully combed straight back from his face. "Caleb says this is the one my Isabella can rent. I've come to make sure it's suitable."

"Your girlfriend from Spain?" Knox's tone was light, teasing, but Mr. Cardoza's shoulders stiffened.

"She is an old friend. A widow. I'm only trying to help her with her transition in a new country." He smoothed back his already smooth hair.

"Of course." Adam gestured Mr. Cardoza further into the room. "Let me give you the tour and tell you what finishes Carrie picked out for this unit."

Sarge settled back onto the tarp with a huff, and Knox balanced himself on the ladder again. He had to admit, he liked Sarge's company better than most humans'.

———————

Sarge acted thrilled to see Luna and Flurry, as if they'd been separated for weeks instead of a handful of hours. The three-way sniff went on and on while Danielle looked on fondly.

"He doesn't seem the worse for wear. Perhaps painting agrees with him." Danielle's hair was clean and tamed, falling straight to her chin, and her eyes were covered in oversized blue sunglasses.

"Spent the day napping while I did all the work." Knox tried to sound indignant, but it came out more amused. It was easy to imagine Sarge keeping him company while he worked on his own house, sticking his nose in cans of things he shouldn't and napping on the drop cloths.

Danielle took off the sunglasses, revealing a complete lack of raccoon ring under her eyes. Knox kind of missed it. She'd looked adorable this morning, all ruffled like she'd just woken up. That was one of the regrets he'd had, thinking of her after the breakup. They'd never woken up together. He'd always had to return her home by curfew, and although they'd been late more than a few times, they'd never stayed out all night.

Danielle took a seat on the nearest bone-shaped bench. They were alone on the big-dog side of the park, although two Yorkies and a small mutt of many breeds enjoyed the small-dog side. Knox limped over and took a seat beside her, rubbing above the brace.

"Did you overdo it today?"

"Why?" He flattened his hand against his thigh.

"I noticed—" Her face flushed, and she tucked her bangs behind her ear. "Sorry, it's none of my business."

"It hurts all the time." Knox surprised himself with the

confession. He hadn't even told his physical therapist about the constant pain. Maybe it was time. Acknowledging he wasn't reenlisting also meant acknowledging the reality of his leg. And the reality was it freaking hurt.

"I thought so." She placed her hand on top of his. His thigh quivered, and not from pain. "Dogs can't tell us how they feel, so I have to read their body language. You're good at hiding it, but it's in the way you walk, the way you hold your mouth. Have you talked to your doctor about upping your pain meds?"

"I don't take pain meds." Knox's fingers curled into a fist under hers.

Danielle wrapped her palm around his knuckles. "It wouldn't be the end of the world to have some time free of pain."

Knox lifted a shoulder. "I'm used to it."

"I'm not." Danielle's hand lifted, and he immediately missed it. She folded her fingers in her lap. "It's hard to see you in pain. Anyone, I mean. It's hard to see anyone in pain."

"Then don't look." He didn't mean to be touchy. He didn't mean to scare her off, but apparently those few curt words were all it took.

Danielle stood. "It's been a long day. I should take the dogs home."

"Sure."

She hooked them up with that weird three-way leash. Luna and Flurry paced beside her, but Sarge sat and refused to move.

"Come on, boy," she coaxed, but Sarge wasn't having it. He turned his head, his liquid brown eyes pleading with Knox.

"I can't have a dog, big guy, not yet. My landlord would kick me out."

Sarge sighed and dropped his chin to his chest. Knox hated the feeling that rose in his chest, that protective urge reserved for new Marines too stupid to know what's good for them. Like he'd been too stupid to listen to his doctors, but he'd lacked the imagination to picture a life outside the Corps. For the first time, though, the thought of never again being on active duty didn't depress the hell out of him. It was time to face facts. Be realistic. Adopt this dog, flip his house, and figure out how to live as a civilian for the rest of his life.

"I'll walk you to the car." Knox patted his leg, and Sarge's head popped up. His tail gave a hesitant wag. Danielle wasn't obvious about it, but he saw her hide a smile by ducking her head. Yeah, yeah, yeah, he was a sucker. It didn't stop him from petting Sarge's head and walking beside him all the way to Danielle's SUV.

CHAPTER 15

No doubt about it. It felt right to have Danielle in his new house. Although all his belongings didn't fill enough boxes to even pack the small sitting room at the front, Danielle's presence somehow made the house feel full. It'd been difficult, only seeing her at the dog park for the past two weeks. He'd finally turned in the application, and adoption was pending Sarge's health clearance from Dr. Morrow and Knox taking up residence in his house.

In the meantime, he'd met up with Danielle and the dogs every evening. Danielle had taught Knox the basic commands Sarge knew, and they'd practiced, sometimes until the park went dark. Danielle was all business. No matter how he'd tried to thaw things between them, she kept her distance. Still, she showed up every night with her dogs, and he took that as a good sign. When he'd gotten the news that he could move into his house, his first text had been to her.

Now she was at his house, dressed the part of rescue-agency volunteer in her Homestretch V-necked T-shirt that was supposed to be all-business but outlined her breasts so nicely that it was difficult to tear his eyes away from her.

"I can't believe you really bought it." Danielle propped her hands on her hips, further straining the thin shirt fabric over her chest, and gazed around the room. "It's not Eliza's place anymore. It's yours."

His house. He still wasn't used to the words, but Eliza'd put in a few phone calls to people she knew and the house finally closed. She'd wasted no time moving into her luxury digs across the street and had even hired a cleaning crew to make the place ready for him. It hadn't taken him long to pack a year of his life into boxes Lance and Carrie had helped bring over.

The boxes stood stacked in the front room, a testament to his erroneous belief that his stay in Miami Beach would be a short one. Now, he was a homeowner with an entire wall of his garage dedicated to holiday decorations. The hairs on his neck stood out, like they did in MCMAP training in the rare cases when another Marine had pinned him to the mat. Not that he was *trapped* here. One phone call to Morales up in Atlanta, and he could start a whole new life. Caleb could handle selling this place for him, and Knox could be on the first plane to Georgia.

But as good as Morales had made the offer sound on his follow-up call last week, Knox had still stalled, reminding him he wasn't available until after the Dorothy was scheduled to be done. He'd blamed construction holdups that might keep him in Miami Beach until the end of summer. Morales said he wouldn't wait forever, but for now he had enough guys to get the business up and running. Knox had bought himself a few months. He knew the smart move was to say yes to the job offer, and he would. Probably. Right now, he couldn't think beyond his nervousness about whether or not he'd pass dog-adoption inspection. The place did not exactly scream "good home for a dog." Not yet anyway.

Knox eyed the stack of boxes. Maybe he didn't need to unpack every single one immediately. It wasn't like he was going to live here long. Probation, that was what he'd call it. Do a few flip projects, like new tile for the bathrooms and a kitchen face-lift, and put the house back on the market. He was only a probationary homeowner, not a permanent resident. Although adopting a dog was a serious commitment, it wasn't tied to this house. He and Sarge could live anywhere, even Atlanta. But he wasn't going to tell Danielle that, not yet anyway.

Without Eliza's furniture and knickknacks and stack of protest posters, the house seemed enormous. He needed to project forever-home vibes, which meant he should've unpacked more boxes before Danielle arrived. What had he been thinking, inviting her to a nearly empty house? He shook his head, becoming more sure by the minute that she wouldn't give one of her precious dogs to him. The tile floors and high ceilings combined so that every sound was magnified. Could Danielle hear his pounding heart, or was that sound only amplified in his mind?

Her sneakered feet took her on a tour of the house. Danielle poked her head into each of the three bedrooms and both bathrooms. She trailed a hand along the top of the granite kitchen counters. She stepped over the boxes in the front room, finally deciding to plop onto the floor amid the boxes, cross-legged. She propped her elbows on her knees and looked up at him through her pale lashes. The sunlight pouring from the front window painted her face in streaks, highlighting the freckles across the bridge of her nose. Damn, she was cute.

He propped his hip against a stack of boxes. "What do you think? Dog friendly enough for you?"

"I could hardly say Lady's old house wasn't dog friendly." Danielle's smile brightened the room more than the sunlight. "You seem to be missing some key objects, though. Like a couch. A table." Color bloomed in her cheeks. "Maybe a bed?"

"I have a mattress." A lumpy one that rested on the floor in the master bedroom next to a box he planned to use as a nightstand. It was the same layout he'd used in his apartment, but it somehow looked wrong here.

"A dog bed? Where will Sarge sleep? Those are the kinds of things I need to know during the home visit." Danielle wiggled her butt and pulled a tiny notepad out of her back pocket. She flipped open the cover. "Where will he eat? What will you feed him? How often will he get exercise? How many hours per day will he spend alone?"

"That's a lot of questions." Knox straightened, scanning his boxes like one of them might hold the answers. They didn't. He knew it. He'd never had a dog, not ever. "I don't know the answers, Dani."

The old nickname slipped out. He pretended not to hear the hitch in her breath. God, the memories were killing both of them, if he wasn't mistaken. Why wasn't she married with three kids? If she were unavailable, maybe this constant ache would go away. He doubted it, but maybe.

"I can help." She pushed to her feet, the distance between them so small he could've reached out to brush his fingers over the freckles dancing on her cheeks. Could've. But didn't. Because she wasn't his Dani anymore. She'd given lots of indications that those kisses would not be repeated, which was really too bad but completely her decision to make. He wished he knew why, whether it was something he'd done wrong or that big secret he suspected she had that made her keep her distance.

"I'd like that. Where do we start?" Knox had expected her to bring Sarge with her, but she'd shown up alone. If Sarge were here, then he'd have something to do with his hands. Pet the dog. Hold the leash. For now, he shoved them in his pockets. "A pet store?"

"Sure. There's a Petco down on Fifth Street. Let me know when is good for you."

"Now is good."

Danielle's laugh was nervous, the same giggle she'd get whenever Mr. Leal called on her in trig. "Okay, let's go. I'll drive." Her gaze shot to his leg.

"I can drive."

"That's not what I—"

He waved off her apology and fished keys out of his pocket. "Just tell me what we need."

Danielle ordered a lot of her pet products online. Easier, usually cheaper. But there was no denying the joys of a pet store. She stopped at the three-story cage column of kittens up for adoption and let a young tabby nibble on her finger for a moment.

"Aren't they the sweetest? I'd get a cat except I have so many former racers coming through, and sometimes an adorable ball of fluff like these guys can set them off."

"Set them off?" Knox pushed a shopping cart in front of him, its plastic basket twice the size of a grocery-store cart.

"You know, they're trained to chase a mechanical rabbit? It's frustrating because they can never catch it. Gets their hunting instincts in an uproar. It can take some time to convince them that not all small, fluffy objects are prey."

"Does Sarge have that problem?" Knox clipped out in such a disgruntled tone that Danielle fought the urge to snap to attention. His moods didn't need to impact her, but she got defensive anyway.

"It's not a problem. It's a product of their training. They simply have to be retrained is all."

Knox's lips quirked. "Does Sarge have to be retrained?"

"Um." Danielle caught her bottom lip in her teeth. "You've spent time with him. You know he's making good progress."

"So no cats for me today."

"Afraid not."

Danielle grabbed a second cart and pushed it toward the food aisle. She expounded on the pros and cons of different brands until Knox let out an impatient breath and said, "Tell me what to get and I will."

"It's expensive but really is the best." She pointed out a bag on the bottom shelf, and Knox tossed it into his cart like it weighed four pounds instead of forty.

Next they perused dog beds. Danielle showed him the large pallets Sarge was used to. Knox stacked three of them in his cart and three in hers.

At over two hundred bucks each, they were something of an investment. "How many dogs are you planning to adopt?"

"He'll need one in every room, won't he? Should I get one for outside, too?"

Well, it wasn't her money. She wasn't going to complain if he wanted to spoil Sarge. "How about something weatherproof for the patio?"

Knox eyed the already filled baskets. "We're going to need another cart."

"We haven't even gotten to supplements or dog toys yet. And snacks. You'll want to pick out some treats to use when training him."

"Train him? I thought we already did that. What else were we doing at the dog park every night?" His eyes landed on her lips, and she had to bite them to keep them from tingling at the attention. It'd been like that, night after night, at Fur Haven. The longing looks, the complete focus he gave her. But he'd respected the unspoken boundaries she'd set. Business and dogs.

"He's got to learn you're the new boss." Danielle tightened her grip on the cart's handle to keep herself from reaching out to reassure him. *It's not you; it's me.* It was time to hand over Sarge and relinquish her excuse to see Knox every day, but she couldn't bring herself to fully walk away. Not yet. "I'll keep helping, of course."

Danielle pushed the cart forward, aisle by aisle, through all the products and choices Knox would need to make. Business and dogs. Don't get distracted by the way his jeans pulled across his muscled thighs or how his eyes watched her like her every move was interesting. Which shampoo did he like the smell of? What kind of flea preventive did he want to try? Whenever she gave him options, he picked the first one. Finally, Danielle stopped the cart, right in front of the Easter display. Stuffed carrots and rabbits of all sizes hung from a peg wall, inviting dog owners to pick up seasonal toys for their pets at sixty percent off. Easter baskets wrapped in pink cellophane held giant bones and boxes of treats. The last row was filled with colorful outfits for dogs ranging from tiny to giant.

"Do you think Sarge wants a raincoat for the summer storms or perhaps this dapper sweater for chilly nights?" Danielle held up the two costumes, fully expecting him to choose the first one with the matching plastic booties and keep them moving.

"An outfit? For a dog? You've got to be kidding me." Knox rubbed his hand on the back of his neck. "I mean, a lot of this stuff seems unnecessary to me, but you're the expert here, right? Costumes are where I draw the line, though. My dog is not a costume dog."

"What about the Fur Haven Howling Halloween Party? It's still six months away, but he'll need a costume for that. And what will he wear to next year's Easter Bonnet Parade?" Danielle dangled an oversize straw bonnet with a chin strap in front of him just to see the vein on the side of his neck pulse.

"His dignity." He swiped the costumes from her and slammed them back onto their respective racks, grumbling about the ridiculousness of civilian life.

Danielle couldn't help it; she laughed. "You're so grumpy."

He stopped muttering and gazed at her over the top of Dog Bed Mountain. "And you're elusive."

"What?" Her mouth snapped shut, the urge to laugh completely gone. "What're you talking about?"

"Remember when we kissed?" He didn't move toward her, but she still felt crowded by the intensity of his gaze. The way his eyes held hers hostage. "Because I do. Every day. And every night."

"I—" Danielle cleared her throat and swallowed hard. "Which one?" His heavy-lidded gaze shamed her. It didn't matter if they were talking three weeks ago, a month, or fourteen years. "I remember."

"Good." Knox didn't look away, and Danielle imagined what it would be like to see past the blue irises and into the very workings of his mind. Could she make him happy? Remembering his ease with the kids at the Easter egg hunt, she doubted it. Dogs, not kids, were her future. Not a lot of guys would be on board with that, and he'd said himself he looked forward to fathering his own children. She wouldn't take that from him.

"It's funny, isn't it?" She broke eye contact with him, rubbing a dog-bed tag between her fingers, studying it like it was imperative she know the washing instructions this moment. "How the past sneaks up on us sometimes? But we're not those people anymore, Knox, and we don't want the same things anymore."

"I still want you. Dani, I don't think I've ever stopped." He whispered the words, but she heard them like gongs in her brain. Her skin prickled in the same way as when he used to sneak up behind her in the lunch line and nibble her earlobe.

"But I don't want you." She spoke directly to the dog bed, sure that she couldn't say the lie to his face. His rough intake of breath let her know her shot hit its mark. She regretted hurting him, but better a little hurt now than a big hurt later. "Not like that anyway. I won't say it hasn't been great spending time with you, and I wouldn't let you adopt Sarge if I didn't think you were a good man." She twisted the dog-bed tag into a unicorn horn. "I hope we can be friends, Knox. Do you think that's possible?"

Knox jerked the cart so suddenly that the top dog bed tumbled to the floor. They both reached for it, and their hands brushed. Danielle froze, pulse beating a wild rhythm in her neck.

Knox turned his hand so that their fingers laced together. "Sure, Dani. We can be friends." He let go and reloaded the bed into the cart.

Danielle followed him to check out, disappointed that he'd accepted the friendship boundary so easily. For a moment, she'd thought he'd use her hand to pull her against him and kiss her. For a moment, she'd wanted him to.

They were silent on their drive back to Knox's new house. He waved off her offer to help him carry in all the bags, and Danielle hid her disappointment. Silent or not, there was no denying she liked being around him. Her *friend*. But friends weren't clingy, so she forced a smile and placed a hand on his arm, preventing him from leaving his truck.

"I'll bring Sarge over tomorrow. When's a good time?"

"You tell me." His arm was rock hard under her palm.

"Ten?"

"I'll be here." He slammed out of the truck in a way that Danielle would not describe as friendly.

"Hey." She leapt out of the passenger side and met up with him at the back doors. "I meant it. I don't have a lot of friends, Knox, and I'd like you to be one of them."

Knox's jaw twitched, and he flung open the doors with unexpected force. "I heard you. I just need a minute."

"To decide whether or not you want to be friends?" Danielle couldn't keep the disbelief out of her voice. He shouldn't have to think about it. He'd *left* her during the worst time of her life. She'd forgiven him without even making him apologize. He was *lucky* she wanted to be friends. "You know what? Forget it."

She stomped toward her car. Each step that he didn't catch up with her and beg her forgiveness made her angrier. She slammed her door and tore off, ignoring her phone's text alert.

At a red light, she finally checked.

I still get Sarge, right?

Ugh, that man. She waited until she got home to answer: *See you at ten.*

———

"Are you ready, Sarge? It's your big day!" Danielle forced cheerfulness into her voice, but the dogs weren't fooled. Luna and Flurry nudged her hands while Sarge dropped his head, looking guilty. "It's not your fault, you big lug."

Danielle distributed petting evenly among the three dogs. "Every dog deserves a forever home, and, Sarge, you're getting the absolute best home. Preapproved by Lady herself."

His ears pricked at Lady's name. All the dogs who frequented Fur Haven seemed fond of the old black Lab.

"Yes, Lady will be living right across the street from you. And you'll go to Fur Haven every day."

Sarge whacked his tail against her floor.

She clipped on his leash and made him sit at her side while she kissed Luna and Flurry on the tops of their heads. "You two take care of each other, okay? I'll be back in a while."

The girls licked her hands, and Danielle swallowed hard. It wasn't like the dogs would never see each other again. She'd take her dogs to Fur Haven often, and they'd run into Sarge, she was sure, at least from time to time.

Danielle firmed her resolve. If she kept every foster dog she fell in love with, she wouldn't be able to save as many dogs. It was an important day. Sarge was moving into his new home.

Danielle preferred to bring her foster dogs into their new homes rather than having them taken from hers. That way, she could do one last check of the home and owners, could watch the way the dog was received, and could look for small cues that this was the right—or in some rare cases, wrong—fit. Not that she had any doubts about Sarge and Knox. Sarge had made his choice clear from day one. She knew how he felt, and she tried to take comfort that at least one of them could have what they wanted in life.

Danielle opened up the back of her SUV and lowered the ramp so Sarge could make his way inside independently. Sarge still favored the bad leg and probably always would. Had she told Knox to get a ramp for his vehicle? She couldn't remember, so she added it to the list of instructions she planned to go over with him today.

At every slowdown, every stop sign, every red light—and they seemed to hit them all—Sarge whined in protest from his place in the back. It was like he knew what was going on and was eager to get to his new home. Danielle was happy. She *was*. It was just that she needed to circle the block one more time to make sure that the tears threatening to fall didn't actually make an appearance.

CHAPTER 16

KNOX APPROVED OF WHAT CARRIE'D DONE WITH HIS BEDROOM, and he approved even more of how quickly she'd done it. The rest of his house might look like a storage unit of boxes and mismatched furniture, but his master suite was a true retreat. After nearly two weeks of living in spartan conditions, he and Sarge deserved this bit of luxury.

If offered a hundred bucks, Knox couldn't have named the color on the walls, because gray wasn't quite right, but it was gray enough to give off a misty feeling. The bedding was the girliest he'd ever personally owned—mostly white with silver wisps and navy blobs that may or may not be flowers. He hadn't looked closely enough to tell for sure. He wasn't sure he wanted to know.

He stood near the window on a plush navy rug looking out onto his backyard. Sarge stretched out on the deck, sound asleep, back legs twitching like he was in a race. The giant doggy door Lance installed two weeks ago in the sliding back door ran floor to ceiling and could be taken out during hurricanes, or at least during insurance inspections he had coming up to determine how much he'd be paying in homeowners' insurance. Because he'd paid cash, he wasn't legally obligated to buy an insurance policy, but with hurricane season approaching, he didn't want to take any chances with his investment. The door also guaranteed that Sarge was in charge of his own schedule, and so far, he seemed to appreciate the independence.

As Danielle'd predicted, Sarge's favorite place was the couch. Luckily, he appeared to enjoy the same shows Knox did, so Knox foresaw many happy evenings watching stand-up comics on Netflix. Some of his buddies enjoyed watching any of the many TV series featuring the military, mostly so they could go online and talk about how unrealistic they were. Knox couldn't handle the inaccuracies, though, and stuck strictly to shows that made him laugh. He supposed Lance and Caleb would be surprised by his viewing habits; they often ribbed him about how little he smiled.

Since coming home, he hadn't had a lot to smile about, but he was smiling now. Because Danielle was coming over. Theoretically, it was a home visit to check Sarge's welfare. In practice, he was hoping that she missed him. They'd only run across each other a few times at the dog park, Sarge always out of his mind with delight at the reunion, and he'd texted her a few pictures of Sarge settling in to ease her mind. She'd seemed really freaked out the day she'd brought Sarge to him, and he'd wanted her to know that weird vibe between them or not, Sarge was in good hands. She'd sent the thumbs-up response to every picture, and eventually he'd given up on trying to engage her. Too bad he couldn't give up thinking about her as easily.

Out on the deck, Sarge stretched, ambled to his feet, hopped down the trio of stairs to the grass, and leisurely peed on the steps he'd just walked down. Well, that was unexpected but nothing to worry about. As far as Knox was concerned, the backyard was Sarge's domain, and he could decorate it however he wanted.

Knox's phone vibrated in his pocket, and he pulled it out, expecting Danielle to be texting from the street. Instead it was Christine, Caleb's mom, asking him to go with her to visit his father at the prison this weekend. He was running out of polite ways to say no, but he still typed a careful, noncommittal *Not this time* and hit Send. She sent back her usual *Another time then* with three sets of praying-hand emojis.

In the past year, he'd probably had more contact with Christine than his own mother. That was some of the appeal of the job offer in Atlanta. His mother had remarried a few years back—some guy who'd been an extra on *The Walking Dead* for years—and they lived in a suburb outside the city. If Knox moved up there, he'd know if she needed anything. Their awkward weekly phone calls could turn into awkward dinners. Still, he felt he owed her something. For most of his life, she was the only family he'd had. He really should call Morales and ask a few questions. Get some specifics. After letting Morales know he was interested in the job, he'd deferred any discussion, claiming his obligation at the Dorothy prevented him from making commitments until the work was done. But that window was closing. Then what?

"What do you think, Sarge? You willing to pull up stakes and hit the mean streets of Atlanta with me?"

Sarge thumped his tail agreeably, and Knox smiled. Sarge was the perfect buddy—optimistic and supportive. He'd be fine wherever they ended up. Would it be fair, though, to move the dog so soon after settling in here? Rescues needed stability—that was what Danielle had said when she'd handed him over. Knox didn't want to do anything that would set Sarge back in his recovery.

Where was Danielle anyway? His phone vibrated again, but he ignored it to open the door, figuring she must be parked on the street by now.

No Danielle. On the street or anywhere else he could see. He checked his phone. The message was from Danielle alright, but she wasn't here.

He fought the disappointment that sank his stomach and reread the message. She wanted to reschedule. He wanted to demand why, so he waited a moment before responding.

Sure. Everything ok?

There was a long pause while the dots bounced and bounced some more.

Flurry's having puppies! Like, right now! A full line of smiling faces filled the screen.

His disappointment faded like it had never existed, and a grin broke over Knox's face. *Sarge is having puppies?*

Yes!

We'll be right there!

Dots bounced, then another whole row of happy faces appeared.

It was the most she'd texted him in weeks. Knox strode into the living room where Sarge already waited for him. "Ready to go see your girlfriend?"

Sarge thumped his tail against Knox's leg in agreement. Knox wished he could say the same, that he was rushing to be with his girlfriend. Danielle had made it clear that while she welcomed his friendship, anything else was off the table. Their encounters at the dog park were nice, filled with talk about safe topics like their respective work lives and the weather. If he sometimes wanted to kiss her, he stared out over the ocean until he could think about something other than the feeling of her lips against his. In a way, it was like they were getting to know each other for the first time again. Friends, he reminded himself as he clipped on Sarge's leash. But that was an awful lot of happy faces. He couldn't help if it gave a guy hope.

―――――――

Danielle kept Flurry's head in her lap, whispering words of encouragement while Flurry pushed out her fourth puppy. On the other end, her dad caught the puppy, helping to clean it and giving it a quick health check before settling it with its littermates in a cozy box set up with a heating pad. Behind Danielle, Luna stood, chin propped on Danielle's shoulder, whining anxiously whenever Flurry appeared in distress. Which was often because the puppies were coming hard and fast.

"Number five is on the way!" Dr. Morrow pushed his reading glasses up his nose and smiled at Danielle. "So far, all fat and healthy as can be."

"Of course they are. Flurry is an excellent mother." Danielle stroked the greyhound's long nose before checking her phone one more time.

Here.

Knox never wasted many words.

Let yourself in. We're a little busy. Living room.

Danielle set the phone aside and returned her attention to comforting Flurry and keeping Luna from getting in the way.

"Here it comes!" Dr. Morrow announced, and the little body emerged, covered in goo that he quickly wiped away.

"That's, uh, more graphic than I'd realized." Knox stood in the archway between the dining room and the kitchen.

"The miracle of birth is pretty gross." Danielle smiled up at him from her seat on the floor. She waved him in, promising, "It's less gooey on this end."

Most people might have a couch and TV, and maybe some comfy chairs in their living room, but Danielle used the space as her dog room. Right now, it was set up for Flurry, whelping box and all. Knox's eyes roamed the wall of dog accessories—collars, leads, harnesses, and toys in all sizes and shapes. She'd repurposed an old china cabinet to hold stacks of canned food, and several large airtight barrels lined the wall and housed the dry food she bought in bulk.

In her excitement about the puppies, Danielle'd forgotten that this would be Knox's first visit to her home. What must he think of her? Well, it wasn't like he didn't know her life was dedicated to the dogs. It couldn't be that surprising that her living space was, too.

"Can I do anything to help?" Knox stayed in the archway, Sarge held to his side by his firm grip on the lead. Sarge strained, tail thumping away, clearly intent on getting to Flurry.

Luna handled the situation by padding over to the visitors and giving them both a thorough sniff. She leaned against Knox's leg, looking up at him like she thought he might have a treat handy.

"Dad's got the delivery part under control." Danielle raised her voice above the murmur she'd been using with Flurry. "I'm really just moral support. Maybe you could bring some water from the kitchen? She might be thirsty."

"On it."

Danielle knew it wasn't conscious on his part, but Knox snapped to attention before heading to her kitchen. In a guest cottage comprised entirely of kitchen, living room, bedroom, and bathroom, he shouldn't get lost.

Sure enough, he returned in a moment with a bowl of water filled halfway to the rim. He knelt beside Danielle, the powerful muscles in his thighs pushing against the khaki of his cargo shorts. His good leg took the brunt of his weight while he held the braced leg in an uncomfortable-looking position. Danielle fought the urge to reach for him, to pull him off balance and against her. She could take his weight, hold him in her lap like she held Flurry's head. Run her fingers over the sun creases in his face, trace those eyebrows that gave away more of his thoughts than he realized. She could even picture herself leaning over him, her hair falling forward to brush his skin as she leaned in for a kiss.

The fantasy flashed through her mind in a second, but it was long enough that Knox noticed. His eyes caught hers, and she lowered her lids, worried he'd somehow see her wayward thoughts with his too perceptive eyes. She was the one who insisted on friendship. She couldn't waver. At least not around him. What she thought about as she fell asleep at night was her own business.

"Thanks." She finally got her voice to work and held out a hand for the bowl.

Knox didn't give it to her. Instead, he angled the bowl so Flurry could reach it if she wanted. She craned her neck at an awkward angle and took a few licks before flopping back into Danielle's lap.

"What a good girl." Knox's voice took on a tone she'd never

heard before. So soft she almost missed it, the encouragement and fear all mixed together. "Isn't she a good girl, Sarge?"

Sarge, still held tight against Knox's side, wagged his tail and stretched his neck in Flurry's direction. Flurry raised her head enough, and they bumped noses.

Danielle's heart contracted painfully in her chest. She swallowed hard, lifting her gaze to find Knox staring at her.

"That was about the sweetest thing I've seen in a long, long time." Knox's voice was still soft, reverent even.

The repeated blare of old-fashioned car horns made all the dogs' ears twitch.

"Yes?" Dr. Morrow stood and stepped back from the whelping box, his eyebrows scrunched together in concern. "I'll be in as soon as I can." He slid the phone back into its holster on his belt and squirted some disinfectant onto his hands.

"Emergency?" Danielle recognized the signs. As a sole proprietor, Dr. Morrow was always on call.

"Unfortunately. Someone's brought in a stray that was hit by a car. Bridget says it's real touch and go." Dr. Morrow fumbled keys out of his pocket and shrugged into his tan lightweight jacket. "Flurry's in good shape, and I know you can handle anything that comes up, pumpkin." He kissed the top of Danielle's head and disappeared out her front door.

"You're doing great, Flurry." Danielle soothed a hand over the dog's head and down her neck. "Knox, do you think you can switch places with me? It shouldn't be too long before another puppy pops out."

"I'd definitely rather be at this end." Knox held out his hand, and Danielle grasped it. He hauled her to her feet, and Danielle didn't fight the flash of longing that coursed through her. She loved the feel of his big hand around her smaller one, the way he maneuvered her to standing as if she weighed nothing. Although she knew her dad was right, that she and Flurry had this birthing covered, Danielle was still glad for Knox's steady presence in the room.

Danielle should let go of Knox's hand. She was standing, and Flurry was already whining as another set of contractions started up. But she didn't want to let go. She took an extra few moments to squeeze his hand. To her surprise, he squeezed back.

"You've got this," Knox said like he thought she hesitated out of uncertainty. She swallowed and nodded, not correcting him, because it was one thing to admit in her own head how much she loved being near him and an entirely different thing for him to know it.

Danielle let her fingers slide out of his, one at a time, until only the pads of their fingers touched. In a moment, even that contact was gone, and Danielle settled into place outside the lip of the whelping box. Flurry's body shuddered, and Danielle turned her mind from imagining where else Knox's hands could touch her to the business at hand.

"Number six is on its way." Her hand disappeared into the dog. Danielle laughed when Knox winced. "The miracle of birth isn't so much miracle as it is work."

"And bodily fluids," Knox observed wryly from his position crouched near Flurry's head.

"That, too."

Flurry's sides heaved, and a puppy slid out, as white as its mother.

Danielle stroked Flurry's trembling side. "You're doing beautifully, girl. I think you're almost done."

"How do you know?" Knox asked.

"We did an ultrasound a few days ago. The sonogram showed eight in the litter." Danielle took the puppy from Flurry and placed it with the other six on the heating pad. "There's always room for error in any kind of imaging, but eight is a good-sized litter."

Flurry's heaving turned into panting, and she turned distressed eyes to Danielle.

"You can do it, Flurry." Knox held the dog's muzzle in his palms. "Two more. Then you can rest."

Knox slid onto his butt, braced leg stretched out long and his good leg curled in at the knee. Sarge spread out over his lap, a move that would leave a smaller dog in the triangle created by Knox's legs but that left Sarge draped over Knox in what could only be described as a possessive pin.

Danielle smiled at the sight. She loved to see a happy adoption story play out so well. Knox still had plenty of room to keep his hand on Flurry, who watched him with half-lidded eyes. Luna let out a long sigh and lay down behind Knox, her back to his butt, like she was tired of Flurry getting all the attention. They settled in for the wait. The next puppy might come in half an hour or two hours. Should she warn Knox that it might be a long time? Probably. She didn't.

"It's coming!" Danielle declared only twenty minutes later from her vantage point as the puppy receiver. "Thank goodness. Six hours is a long time to be in labor, isn't it, girl?"

"Six hours?" Knox echoed, one hand on Sarge and the other stroking the top of Flurry's head. "You're a champion, Flurry."

Flurry panted, sides jumping up and down, and let out a long, low whine.

"Here he is," Danielle showered praise on Flurry, offering the puppy to her to lick the sac off like her dad had done for the other puppies. Flurry licked it a few times but stopped with a high-pitched whine. "Another one so soon? That's…unusual."

Danielle finished cleaning the newborn and placed it with its littermates on the heating pad. She checked the temperature— just right—and returned to Flurry. Sure enough, number eight was coming out fast as the others. Without more time between puppies, Flurry could become too exhausted, endangering her and the unborn puppy. Flurry panted, and Danielle watched closely for more signs of distress.

Danielle checked Flurry's heartbeat—accelerated—and sank back on her heels. She rolled her bottom lip between her teeth and listened to Knox whispering words of encouragement to Flurry while he rubbed her neck. She imagined the "good girls" and the "you can do this" were for both her and the dog. Flurry let out a low whine and licked Knox's wrist.

Danielle tried not to let her worry show, not to Flurry or Knox, but Knox picked up on her concern.

"What can I do?"

Danielle raised a helpless shoulder. "Nothing to do but wait and see what happens." Flurry entered another, shortened round of contractions, then flopped her head onto the whelping pen lip, clearly exhausted.

"Almost, almost," Danielle chanted, watching as a dark nose fought its way out of the birth canal. Flurry whimpered and pushed one more time.

Danielle caught the gray puppy, still wrapped in its amniotic sac, and offered it to Flurry for its first tongue bath.

Flurry nosed the tiny puppy half-heartedly, then rolled her head away from it.

"What's wrong?" Knox tensed, like he was ready to spring into action at any moment.

"Oh no." Danielle rubbed at the sac with a washcloth, gentle and steady. "Oh no, oh no. He started breathing before he was out of the sac. His lungs are filled with fluid."

"Should I call your dad?" Knox already had his phone out, but Danielle shook her head.

"I got this." Quick and efficient, she cleaned off the puppy and checked its tongue. Blue. Not good, very not good. She cleared his nostrils, then held him in her hand so that his head rested on her fingers.

She raised her puppy-laden hand to shoulder height, then swung him down at full speed.

"What're you doing?" Knox leapt to his feet.

"Using centrifugal force to clear his lungs." She checked his tongue. Still blue. She gave the little guy another swing, and bits of mucus flew out of his tiny nostrils. "Better, that's better. Come on. Let's get the rest." Another swing while Knox looked on like he couldn't believe what he was seeing.

Danielle pried open the teeny mouth with her thumb and forefinger. "Good, the tongue is pink, and he's breathing on his own." She kissed his head. "You did it, squirt. Good job."

"He's so little. Will he be okay?" Knox's concern made Danielle ache in that same place that seeing Flurry and Sarge touch noses had activated. He reached out a hand like he wanted to touch the runt, but Danielle tucked the puppy next to his siblings.

"Now that he's breathing, yeah." Danielle let out some deep breaths of her own. She'd known what to do, had done it plenty of times helping her dad, but there was always the slight chance that it wouldn't work. She could've lost one of Flurry's puppies. But she hadn't. She beamed at the row of eight perfect puppies on the heating pad.

"He looks exactly like Sarge. Only smaller."

It was true. Although many of the puppies shared some aspects of Sarge's coloring, the runt was a gray brindle exactly like his father.

"Shall we call him Private then?" Danielle's teasing comment made Knox smile.

"Seems awkward. What kind of nickname comes from Private? Privvy. People will think you named him after a toilet." Knox sat back on the floor near Flurry's head, brushing his palm down her neck in long strokes. Sarge immediately planted himself across Knox's lap again, and Luna reclaimed her position at his back.

The sight of Knox surrounded by dogs, her dogs, caused Danielle's heart to thump hard in her chest. She concentrated to remember the thread of their conversation. "I'm sure you Marines have plenty of things you call Privates."

Knox cracked a grin. "And none of them appropriate for a baby."

"Puppy," Danielle corrected, distracting herself with a check of all the puppies. Warm but not too warm? Check. Everyone breathing? Check. "What do you suggest, then, for a name?"

Knox scooted down toward the puppies, not an easy task with seventy pounds of dog weighing him down. His mouth counted off the puppies, one at a time, like he couldn't believe how many of them there were. He turned a smile on her, a smile Danielle knew from experience was a direct result of interacting with puppies. There was no smile in the world like a puppy-induced smile.

"How about Junior?"

"Perfect." Danielle stretched out her legs, preparing to stand. Now that they were sure more puppies weren't on the way, it was time to get Mama and the pups squared away. Knox's hand was there before she could even think of standing on her own.

"Thanks." She used his grip to help herself up, surprised to find that one of her legs was fast asleep. Needles and pins pricked at her as it came to life.

"You okay?"

So observant, her Knox. *Not my Knox*, she corrected herself, no matter how much she enjoyed his attention, the way his eyes tracked her movements, the feel of him. For his own good, she had to stay strong.

She let go of his fingers. "I'm fine. If you want to help, you can refill that water dish and bring it back."

"You got it." When Knox didn't immediately pull on Sarge's leash, Sarge took the opportunity for a quick sniff of Flurry. Luna watched with patient eyes while the two greeted each other before joining in.

"He misses them," Knox observed, brow furrowed.

"They were roommates for several months."

"You'll bring them over? To visit?" Knox pulled up a calendar like he was ready to schedule playdates this very minute.

She arched a brow and pointed at the puppy box with her chin. "Flurry's not going anywhere for a while."

Knox hung his head. "Of course."

"But you two are welcome anytime."

Knox's head snapped up, and his eyes caught hers. In high school, Danielle'd thought they didn't need a lot of words between them, that she could read his emotions as they marched across his face. The years in the military had hardened Knox in a lot of ways, and his emotions were no longer so apparent. But she knew that look in his eye, knew all the way to her bones. He wanted her.

And God help her, she still wanted him, too.

CHAPTER 17

Knox couldn't look away from Danielle's deep, brown eyes. They'd always reminded him of melted caramel, those eyes of hers, and he remembered how they darkened with desire. Darkened like they did just now while she held his stare.

Around them, the dogs stilled, too, as if sensing something in the air. The smell of puppy lingered, and there was plenty of cleanup to do. Changing out the newspapers that lined Flurry's box seemed the most urgent before the smell got any more rank. There were probably a hundred things to do for the puppies.

Still, neither of them moved. He was caught in her gaze as surely as he'd been at eighteen. She was a miracle, this Danielle. She'd always had a big heart and a love for animals, but seeing her so calm and sure, slinging the puppy around with the authority of experience, he'd seen all that promise of her youth come to life. She'd saved that puppy's life, no matter how much she played it off like it was a normal thing to do. He had some field-medic training, but he wouldn't have known what to do with a puppy drowning in its own amniotic fluid.

He'd been so caught up in how they used to be, who they used to be, that he hadn't really stopped to admire who Danielle had become. Sure, he'd noted her curvier curves, had itched to get his fingers on them even. But today he'd seen her in her element, and it broke his heart all over again that she hadn't finished veterinary school. Hell, she hadn't even started it. Why not?

Guilt kept him from asking her, but it didn't stop him from reaching for her. All the restraint of the past few weeks broke, and he circled his fingers around her wrist, tugging gently.

She closed the distance between them willingly, stopping just shy of his body so that he could feel the heat of her through his T-shirt but couldn't actually feel her. His hand landed on the flare of her hip and slipped around to her lower back, pulling her flush against him.

His whole body sighed. Yes. Much better. Her head nestled in the groove under his clavicle that they'd always joked was made especially for her. Her cheek rested there, and he felt the smile as it crept across her face.

"Some things don't change." Danielle's voice was a low rumble. "I missed this spot." She turned and kissed his chest through the T-shirt. "I love that it's still exactly the same shape as my cheek."

"Made for you," Knox replied with the same words he'd used a hundred times when they'd been together. He remembered feeling it, too, how much he'd been made for her and she for him. It'd been powerful, and try as he had over the years to chalk it up to adolescent hormones, he couldn't deny the thunderous possessiveness coursing through his veins right now.

Mine. He didn't say it aloud, knew that it wasn't the right time, that it might never be the right time because he'd blown it so utterly with her—then and, in some way he hadn't figured out yet, now. But he felt it. *Mine.* The word shivered through him, and he pulled her tighter, hugging both arms around her waist.

She snuggled into him, and he felt the tension leave her body, how she softened against him. Sure, he'd been with other women since Danielle, but no one had ever felt like this in his arms, like she could melt through his skin until they were only one person.

His body was on board with the idea of becoming one person with Danielle. He hardened against her, and she was so close that he knew she could feel it. She didn't pull away. Instead, she wrapped her arms around his waist and held him tight.

"This is nice," she murmured.

"Yeah," he choked out, paralyzed by her words, his hands clenched in the fabric of her shirt. Nice? He wasn't feeling nice.

Ravenous. Crazed. About to rip her clothes right off her. An intensity he hadn't felt since the last time he was under fire sharpened all his senses. And she said 'nice'? She was killing him.

He held her, letting his heart thunder under her cheek, his cock swell against her stomach. He held on like he should've fifteen years ago but didn't, like he could crush her into him.

Did he want to kiss her? God, yes. But he was afraid to switch anything about their position for fear she'd step away, shake it off, laugh at how silly they were to let old patterns take over. Insist on that damn word *friend* again.

A snuffle and high-pitched whine took Danielle away from him. She jerked out of his arms and rushed to the small box where the puppies were. He stayed where he was, arms suddenly empty, his whole body tight with the tension that came right before all hell breaks loose on a mission.

"Are you hungry?" she cooed at them, obviously not as affected by their encounter as he was, and one by one moved them into the whelping box with Flurry.

Hungry? He was starving. For her. He watched her every move, ridiculously turned on by her efficiency. She didn't waste any movements, handling each puppy with such loving care that he longed for the same attention to be lavished on him.

Ridiculous. He was not jealous of a litter of puppies. He reached down for Sarge's collar. "This has been—" He cut himself off, not sure where that sentence was going, not sure he could go anywhere until things, well, settled down. There was no delicate way to adjust his crotch so he just did it, glad Danielle's attention was riveted on the puppies. "I guess we should be on our way."

"Oh." Danielle froze, the runt held against her chest. "I have a few things to clean up, and then I was going to make some tea. Would you like to stay for some?"

Knox hated tea. "I'd love to."

He'd drink a hundred cups of tea to see the smile that lit up her face at his answers. "Great. Can you see if the dogs want to go out?" She jerked her chin in the direction of her front door. "The yard is fenced, so they'll be fine."

"Sure." He forced his heavy feet forward. Sarge and Luna followed him. Flurry lifted her head, then let it plunk down. "I guess Mama's too tired."

"Yeah." Danielle patted Flurry's side, then rolled her slightly to pick up some dirtied newspapers. "Eight puppies. It's such a miracle, isn't it?"

Knox wasn't the romantic type, but he couldn't help but think how the puppies weren't the only miraculous thing in the room right now. He shook his head at his own foolishness and let the dogs out to run around the pool. They could all use some fresh air, him most of all.

When he came back inside ten minutes later, he found Danielle in the kitchen sitting on a spindly chair, her cheek flat against the small bistro table under the window. She was sound asleep. It didn't look all that comfortable, but he left her there. He might've hoped things were going in a different direction, but he wasn't going to use her exhaustion and adrenaline to his advantage. A puppy high might not be a federally recognized Schedule II drug, but it was a high—and a crash—all the same. If they were going to move past friends, he wanted her wholehearted, enthusiastic consent. Now was not the time to push the whole friendship thing. He turned off the kettle and employed his stealth training to slip out the door.

———

Danielle hustled down the narrow veterinary clinic hallway, arms full of freshly laundered towels. At the last door on the left, she used her hip to push open the swinging door into the large boarding area at the back of the clinic. Stainless-steel crates were stacked against three walls, with large dog-sized crates on the bottom, medium-sized in the middle, and small-dog crates at the top of each stack. Right now, only half a dozen dogs were in residence, and one very cranky cat howled from her confinement in a mesh-top playpen in the corner.

"I'm here. I'm here." Danielle dropped the bundle of towels on the built-in table that skirted the fourth wall before ending in the door that led outside to the exercise runs. "Everybody hold your horses."

The cat mewled a loud, long protest against any more waiting, so Danielle abandoned her folding duties to squat next to the cage. The cat batted away her proffered finger but then returned a few seconds later to rub her jaw against it.

"Today's your last day, Pepper. I promise."

Pepper seemed moderately placated by the promise and a refill on her kibble. In one of the large crates, a chocolate Lab thumped its tail and watched her with hopeful eyes.

"You're right. Let me get the leashes." Danielle grabbed four leashes off the hanging rack and opened up the Lab's crate. He thanked her with a lick up the side of her neck that left her laughing. "You're such a love, aren't you?" She continued chatting up a stream of small talk while she gathered the Staffordshire terrier, the Rottweiler mix, and the shy Dalmatian for a jaunt outside.

Once they were outside in the warm spring air, she unclipped all the dogs to let them have the run of the outside area. It was no Fur Haven Park, but two large trees on opposite ends of the enclosure provided shade. A squirrel sprinted straight up the trunk of the tree nearest the building, and all four dogs rushed to catch it. They were far too late, but they enjoyed a rousing round of barking and bouncing off the tree in excitement. Even the Dalmatian got in on the fun, sending a few loud yowls in the squirrel's direction.

After determining that the squirrel was suitably intimidated into not coming back down the tree, the hodgepodge pack turned its attention to sniffing the ground and marking territory. The Dalmatian got nervous and came to sit by Danielle on the bench. She idly rubbed its ears while scrolling through her phone with the other hand.

We need you up front.

The text from Gabi, the high-school senior who volunteered her time at the clinic, interrupted Danielle's social media flow, which wasn't the end of the world. The adorable pictures of baby kangaroos at the Australian sanctuary would still be there later. What did alarm her was why she would be specifically requested. Was something wrong with her dad?

She hustled the dogs back inside, locking them inside their crates and distributing a round of treats for all the animals with a sincere "I'll be back to walk the rest of you as soon as I can" before half walking, half jogging to the front of the clinic.

"My dad?" Danielle grabbed Gabi's arm, perhaps a bit too strongly, because Gabi pulled away with an alarmed look, shaking her head.

"No. They were asking for you." Gabi's nod indicated a trio in the waiting room. Carrie, Knox's sister-in-law who Danielle saw often at the dog park; her son, Oliver; and an older woman Danielle had seen around but never met.

"Danielle, thank goodness." Carrie rushed forward as quickly as the startlingly high stilettos she was wearing would let her. She had a small bundle in her arms wrapped in a tea towel. Oliver sucked on his lower lip and held the other woman's hand. "Riley said you were the person to see. We found this little guy when we were walking Beckham, and we didn't know what to do."

Danielle took the warm weight from Carrie and lifted the edge of the towel. Two tiny eyes blinked back at her from a rounded face.

"Hey there." Danielle stroked a finger down the side of the bird's brown and white spotted feathers. "Are you an owlet? Yes, you are." She looked up and met Carrie's eyes. "A burrowing owl, I think. Owls aren't my specialty."

"You already know more than I do." Carrie flipped long, dark hair over her shoulder. "Something's wrong with his wing."

"Will he be okay?" Oliver stepped away from the other woman and frowned worriedly up at Danielle.

"I think so." Danielle squatted and showed Oliver the tiny owl. "You did the right thing bringing him here. We'll call the wildlife center and see what they advise."

Oliver came up on his tiptoes to peer at the bird. "Can I keep him? I promise to take very good care of him."

Danielle didn't miss the way Carrie shook her head back and forth in a frantic "no, no, no" gesture.

"We can't keep wild animals as pets." Danielle tucked the towel around the bird. "The wildlife center will do what they can, and as soon as it's safe, he'll be released."

Oliver's frown showed his disappointment, but he nodded. "To find his mama?"

Danielle thought that unlikely. She smiled softly and let Oliver have one last look at the bird he'd helped rescue. "He'll be happier with other owls."

"I know." Oliver brushed a finger over the edge of the towel. "Bye-bye, bird friend." He watched solemnly as Danielle passed the bird on to Gabi with instructions to take it to the back room.

"You were the right person." Carrie held out her hand. "I'm not sure you've ever formally met the rest of my family. This is my son, Oliver, and my mother, Sherry."

Danielle smiled at the three of them. "I believe you're missing one energetic Jack Russell? I've seen you all at the dog park."

"You have the big greyhounds!" Oliver made the connection quickly.

"I do."

"Can I ride one?"

"No, that would hurt the dogs. But you can watch them run. And I have a new litter of puppies, only three days old. When they're bigger, would you like to come and play with them?"

Oliver nodded and held his mother's hand.

"You're good with kids." Sherry's smile was friendly, but Danielle winced. Soon would come the questions about how many she had of her own and the awkwardness while she debated how much to share. She hated how free people felt to pry into what was private and painful personal business. Still, from manicurists to potential dog adopters, she'd learned to field the questions with a smile and vague answer. But Carrie shook her head at her mom, and Sherry didn't ask.

"What's this about an owl? What do you think I'm running here, some kind of hoot farm?" Danielle's dad emerged from the employees-only door, wiping his hands on the front of his white lab coat.

"They found an injured burrowing owl. Gabi's calling the wild-life center now." Danielle linked her arm through her dad's and pulled him into their little circle.

"Good, good." Dr. Morrow nodded at Carrie. "You're Gloria's new relative. Somehow. Step-half-granddaughter or something?"

Carrie laughed. "Something like that. Riley's my sister-in-law. Or soon to be. You're coming to the wedding?"

"Wouldn't miss it."

"My son, Oliver, and Sherry, my mom." Carrie handled the introductions, and Danielle watched as her father settled into his usual routine of charming people he'd just met. He was good with animals, but the real secret to his success as a veterinarian was how good he was at putting the humans who accompanied his patients at ease. Even if she had her veterinary degree, Danielle wasn't sure she'd ever be able to take his place with the patients.

But he froze when he got to Sherry. She was a few inches shorter than Danielle's dad with a smooth bob of auburn hair and wide, dark eyes that blinked up at him much as the owlet had looked at Danielle.

"I'm Alan. Alan Morrow." He shook her hand.

"Nice to meet you."

Then they stood like that, their hands still joined.

Danielle met Carrie's gaze. Carrie shrugged.

Plenty of women had made eyes at her dad over the years. He was charming, financially stable, even a little bit cute if you liked bald guys and weren't his daughter, but Danielle had never seen him make eyes back.

"Why don't you leave your number, and I'll call you when we have an update on the owl." Danielle tried to ease the awkwardness with some business.

"Yes, please give me your number." Dr. Morrow fished his phone out of the front pocket of his lab coat, pushed a few buttons, and handed it to Sherry.

She entered her information and handed it back to him with a shy smile.

"I'll call you," he said, pocketing the phone.

"Good," she said.

"Oh God," Carrie mumbled loud enough so only Danielle could hear. "Not another wedding."

Danielle's eyes widened. "What do you mean?"

But Carrie just waved and herded her small family out the door. "I have a feeling we'll be seeing a lot more of each other. Soon."

CHAPTER 18

DANIELLE RUBBED HER PALMS TOGETHER AND BLEW WARM breath onto her knuckles. While not technically cold at a few degrees below seventy, the weather had been in the high eighties until yesterday, and the drop in temperature made her think about all the hats and mittens sitting unused in her hallway closet. Across the rooftop expanse, Luna loped in lazy figure eights, apparently running for the sheer joy of it. Danielle didn't much like running herself, but she never tired of watching greyhounds in action. Swift and elegant, they made running appear effortless and appealing.

Poor Flurry probably missed her morning runs, but with eight puppies less than a week old to keep an eye on, Danielle was hesitant to leave them unattended for too long. Flurry was a good mother and didn't seem to mind her narrowed world, but once the puppies were more independent, Danielle looked forward to bringing her back to Fur Haven. No other dog could give Luna the workout she longed for.

A ball of fluff barreled at her from the elevator, and Danielle crouched down to greet LouLou.

"Hey there, cutie pie. How're you feeling today?"

The older dog licked Danielle's hand in response before taking off to join Luna. She couldn't keep up but did seem to enjoy the challenge of it.

"Chilly today, isn't it?" Riley stuffed her hands into the pockets of a fluffy, pink jacket she wore over cutoff jeans and flip-flops.

"Not really, but I wouldn't mind a cup of hot coffee right now." Danielle blew on her knuckles in direct contradiction to her words.

Riley grinned and swung a sparkly fuchsia backpack onto the

bone-shaped bench. "Lucky you." She pulled out a thermos and two travel mugs. "As long as you like it black."

Danielle didn't, but she said, "Black is fine" and accepted the mug in both hands. The warmth seeped into her hands, and she sent Riley a grateful smile.

"Got one for me?" Sydney was huffing from taking the ramp up the side of the parking garage. She let Chewy down from the sling around her neck. He ignored the humans and headed straight for the dogs. A few minutes later, Eliza emerged from the elevator with Lady, who decided to plop down in the middle of all the women rather than join the rambunctious game of chase happening in the middle of the park.

Riley'd brought enough mugs for everyone, and soon there was a companionable silence while the women soaked up their initial burst of caffeine for the day.

Sydney was the first to break the silence. "I've started interviewing for jobs."

"Any place would be lucky to have you." Riley smiled over her mug.

Sydney grimaced. "If only you were the one hiring. After so many years freelancing, I have to admit it's hard to find a good fit. Can you believe the interviewer yesterday said I couldn't bring Chewy with me to work?"

"I believe it." Eliza swiped at the bench with a folded napkin she pulled out of her bra, then took a seat. "Most workplaces frown on rats running around."

"He is not a rat!" Sydney huffed and sipped her coffee. "He's my inspiration. I couldn't possibly work without him."

"Then you might be interviewing for a while." Eliza's words were dry, but her eyes crinkled with amusement. "Unless you set your sights on a rat-catching business."

"Eliza!" Sydney snorted, immediately holding a finger under her nose as if to keep coffee from flying out.

"Take a joke already." Eliza sipped her coffee, looking quite pleased with herself. "How about you, Riley? Wedding planning going smoothly?"

"I wouldn't say smoothly, but it's going." Riley checked her phone and spent a silent moment, thumbs flying. "Speaking of, I better head out. We've got a meeting with the caterer and a potential new buyer doing a walk-through, conveniently scheduled at the same time. Caleb really needs to learn how to use the shared calendar better." Riley called LouLou to her, grumbling about being in two places at once. After LouLou was leashed, Riley waved goodbye, took a few steps, and then turned back to Danielle.

"See you tomorrow? We do this every morning about this time. I bring the coffee. Carrie usually shows up after her run with some fruit slices or something."

Danielle sucked in a surprised breath. "What can I bring?"

Riley tapped a finger to her chin, pretending to ponder. "Sydney either brings delicious muffins or delicious gossip. Eliza brings the snark. What've you got?"

Danielle racked her brain. "Puppy pictures?"

"What? Why didn't you say so?" Riley backtracked, and Sydney and Eliza crowded around. "Show us."

Danielle pulled out her phone and opened up the album she'd dedicated to the puppies. The other women oohed and aahed at all the right moments, so Danielle pulled out the pièce de résistance: videos of a puppy pileup, all wiggly butts and little pink tongues.

Sydney held a hand to her chest. "I'm going to die of cuteness overload. These are on your YouTube channel, right?"

"Channel? Uh, no." Danielle pocketed the phone while Riley apologized for leaving early and dashed out.

"Website?" Sydney thumbed her own phone on. "What's the name of your rescue again?"

"Homestretch."

"It doesn't even come up on a Google search. What're your tags?"

Danielle looked at her blankly.

"How do people find you?" Sydney's finger tapped an impatient beat on her screen.

"Word of mouth?"

"This is worse than I thought." Sydney opened her calendar. "I have an interview today at 1:00 p.m., but after that I'm free. Can I buy you a coffee and tell you how ignoring your web presence is fatal to any business plan?"

Danielle swallowed, fighting that panicked feeling she got in dreams about showing up to a final exam for a class she never took. "That's really nice of you, but I don't actually have a business plan. I don't want to waste your time."

Eliza sputtered on her coffee, and Sydney shook her head sadly. "You should know better than anyone that time spent helping dogs is never wasted, and luckily for you, I'm not afraid of a challenge. Website, YouTube channel, a social media presence. Don't worry. I'll hook you up."

Danielle knew there was more she could be doing to advertise; she simply never had the time to figure it out. Or the budget to hire someone else to do it. "That would be wonderful, but I'm afraid I can't hire you. You could absolutely bring Chewy to work with you, though."

Sydney stuck out her hand. "Alright, my friend, you've got yourself a volunteer. At least until I get a new gig. A paying gig."

"Understood." Danielle shook on it. They finished their coffee before Danielle realized Riley'd left all the mugs behind.

"Don't worry." Eliza held open a tote filled with plastic bags. "I'll take them downstairs. It's quite convenient living at the Dorothy. Almost like living in the dorms back in college. Those were some good times." Eliza told a story about the first protest she attended at UF while she hooked up Lady. Once she was gone, it was only Sydney and Danielle and the three dogs in the park.

"It won't hurt, going digital. I promise." Sydney gathered up Chewy and stuffed him into the sling. "I'll do everything. At first anyway. You'll get the hang of it in no time."

"Thank you." Danielle sat on the bench to watch Luna run, trying to remember the last time she'd had plans with a bunch of girlfriends. High school? Madi, Cassie, and she had spent lots of weekends on Lincoln Road, trying on clothes and sipping smoothies at an outdoor table, people watching. Had it really been that long ago? There'd been occasional happy hours with folks from the clinic, but she'd never ordered more than one drink, self-conscious about being the boss' daughter. She'd usually invent an excuse to leave early, and she'd imagined the others were relieved that they could relax after she'd left. So an open-invitation coffee date was new, but surprisingly, she didn't hate the idea. Carrie rescued owls, and Sydney offered to help Homestretch without any prompting. She'd known Riley and Eliza most of her life. So, friends. She hadn't thought about her lack of them in years, had gotten used to the idea that it was harder to meet new people in adulthood. Maybe it wasn't that hard after all.

What could she bring to the morning coffee-and-dogs get-togethers besides adorable puppy pictures? When it came to baking, her specialty was dog biscuits. A slow smile spread across her face. She might just have found the one batch of friends who would appreciate her narrow culinary expertise. And wait until she broke out the dehydrated sweet potatoes. Fur Haven Dog Park was in for a treat.

CHAPTER 19

KNOX SWUNG THE SLEDGEHAMMER BACK AND LET IT SLAM into the bathroom wall with a satisfying clunk. Maybe because outfitting a bathroom had been his first construction job with Lance, remodeling a former model's downtown penthouse, Knox found bathroom renovations especially satisfying. The crack of old tiles, the way they crumbled to dust at his feet, made him feel like Thor come to life, wielding his mighty hammer.

"Something on your mind?" Lance swung a hammer behind him, his shaggy blond hair making him look more the part of Thor than Knox did. He smiled at the hole he'd punched through the drywall. They were on the last apartment of the remodel, the last demo job. The other units were in various states of completion as the crews made their way through doing their specialized jobs— installing, painting, decorating. Electrical, plumbing. There were a lot of moving parts. Knox didn't know how Lance kept the whole schedule in his head, but somehow it was all coming together.

Knox took another swing. "Just enjoying the destruction. I see why you went into this line of work."

"Fun, isn't it?" Lance set down his sledgehammer to wrestle the sink off the wall. Knox took the other side, lending his strength to breaking the seal that held the porcelain to the tiles.

"Better than the gym." Knox grunted when the sink loosened, and he ended up with the full weight balanced on his thighs.

Lance's eyes widened, and he tugged the sink his way. "Sorry, man. Didn't mean to—"

"My leg is fine." Knox gritted his teeth, willing the words to be true. He didn't like special treatment because of his leg. Just because he wasn't going back to the Corps didn't mean he'd slacked off with his rehab. The leg wouldn't get stronger if he didn't challenge it. And if he didn't get stronger, he wouldn't be comfortable accepting Morales' job offer. Stronger was better, period. He couldn't join a security firm if he couldn't hold his own.

Together, Lance and Knox lowered the orange-swirled Formica monstrosity to the floor. "If you say so. We're due for a break anyway. Can I grab you a water?" Lance dusted his hands on the sides of his jeans, adding to the layers of powder and smears of paint already decorating them.

"Sure. Let me finish up here." Something popped in Knox's leg when he stood. He knew he didn't so much as twitch, but somehow Lance knew and was at his side in a second.

Lance put an arm around Knox's waist. "You okay?"

"I'm okay." Knox ground out the words, but as soon as he put weight on his bad leg, his body proved him to be a liar. His knee gave out, and he fell sideways, only Lance's steady presence beside him keeping him off the floor.

"That is a strange definition of 'okay.'" Lance kept one arm supporting Knox and used his other hand to wrestle his phone out of his pocket. The ridiculously overbuilt phone case made it a tight squeeze.

"Ambulance?" Lance stared at his screen, clearly unsure who to call.

"No. Gotta get to the VA. Help me to my car, and I can drive myself. Don't need my left leg to drive."

"You need it to get out of the car and into the clinic." Lance's fingers danced on the screen. "Don't worry. We've got you."

That was what Knox was afraid of. It was one thing to work side by side for months at a time, to chill in the hot tub, even knock back a few drinks with Grandpa William and Caleb on the regular. Lance at the VA, though? No, no way. He didn't want his worlds overlapping like that, didn't want his brother to see him as anything other than perfectly capable.

The shock of pain zinging up his leg said it didn't matter what he wanted. He pushed knuckles into the injured thigh, gritted his teeth, and nodded. He wasn't used to getting what he wanted anyway.

———————

The *we* turned out to be Carrie. Lance had muscled Knox to his work truck and broken several traffic laws on the way to VA, but he still didn't beat Carrie to the parking lot. She waited for them at the front doors, hands on both her hips, her long, dark ponytail swinging in agitation.

Lance screeched to the curb, and Carrie opened the passenger door. When Knox lifted his foot, she put her hand up.

"Hold it right there, mister. We're getting you a wheelchair." She spun and marched through the doors.

"I don't need a damn—"

"Don't bother arguing." Lance leaned against the open door, watching his wife storm the VA entrance. "She's something, isn't she? Really good in emergencies."

Knox grunted his agreement, but the comment made him think of Danielle. She was good in a crisis, too. The way she'd known what to do with that puppy that couldn't breathe. How calm she was when training her dogs. He couldn't help but wish she were here now. Maybe it wouldn't rankle so much to be in the wheelchair if it were her idea.

A short, round man in pale-green scrubs shot through the doors, wheelchair in front of him. It wasn't fancy. No special features, just a seat, some handles, and two footholds. Knox resigned himself to being manhandled into the contraption.

This wasn't like last time, he reminded himself. He'd be back on his feet before evening, not stuck in a rehab facility for months at a time. He just had to appease the worrywarts all around him for now.

But when Scrubs coached him from the truck down to the chair, his leg completely crumpled under him, and Knox hit the sidewalk. Hard.

Carrie let out a little screech, and Lance lunged to his side a split second too late to catch him.

"*Dios mio.*" Scrubs got hands under him and somehow levered him into the chair.

Knox felt the heat in his skin, the flush of embarrassment. He was fiercely glad that Danielle wasn't here after all. He never wanted her to see him like this, which was why he muttered a few choice curse words of his own when he heard her sweet voice say, "Knox, what happened to you?"

"Nothing," Knox grumbled. "You didn't need to come."

Danielle's face blanched, her freckles standing out in stark relief.

"Of course she should've come. I asked her to." Carrie looped her arm through Danielle's. "I called her because I thought you'd want her here."

"You thought wrong." Knox knew he was being an ass. He heard the assness as it tumbled out of his mouth. Time to suck it up. He shouldn't be such a whiny baby just because a girl he liked saw him with a boo-boo.

"I'll go. Carrie said you needed a friend, but I guess she was wrong." Danielle tried to pull away from Carrie, but Carrie kept a firm hand on her and glared at Knox.

"Danielle rushed here because I asked her to. Take the advice you gave me not too long ago. Don't be an asshole." Carrie's long ponytail lashed behind her, an angry whip.

"You're right." Knox breathed out his anger in short bursts, the same kind of breathing he used for push-ups. *Friends.* The word still rankled, but it wasn't inaccurate. He'd seen her a handful of times in the two weeks since the puppies were born, and she acted like the hug never happened, that she hadn't asked him to stay. So he acted like he didn't remember either. He didn't want to make her uncomfortable. Instead, they'd had more rooftop training sessions with Sarge, had fallen into the habit of sitting on one of the bone-shaped benches afterward and talking about their respective days. They were friends—even if the word made him grit his teeth when applied to her—and friends weren't assholes. "I'm sorry."

"We'll get you inside now." Scrubs pushed the wheelchair toward the building. Knox turned his head, saw how Danielle's eyes darted from the building to her car.

"Come on," he said, giving in to the need to be near her, even in these less-than-ideal circumstances. "If you really don't have anything better to do today than sit in a waiting room with me, I wouldn't mind the company."

A smile trembled on her lips, and he cursed himself for ever making her doubt that he wasn't thrilled to see her. Any time. Anywhere. He wished he could blame his assholeness on the pain from his leg, but he'd grown used to the constant aches and throbs. Sure, today was on the extreme side, but it wasn't anything like waking up after the explosion. Those memories wanted to flood his mind, so he closed his eyes, pushing them back with the memory of standing in his front yard with Danielle's sweet lips on his. That had been a helluva kiss, maybe even worth waiting fifteen years for. He hoped he wouldn't have to wait another fifteen years to try again.

The doors whooshed open. There was paperwork; there were questions. He was whisked away to triage and whisked back almost as quickly. Another thing he'd gotten used to, the slow crawl of time in the VA waiting room. What he wasn't used to, what he could hardly believe, was Danielle sitting next to him, her hand in his while she read a brochure about VA medical benefits. He rested the back of his head against the putty-colored wall and concentrated on the heat of Danielle next to him, the softness of her skin. The doctors could take all day as far as he was concerned.

He hadn't realized it this morning, swinging the sledgehammer with all his might, but this little oasis of calm was exactly what he needed.

Was Knox asleep? Danielle's arm was numb from the awkward angle forced on her by the metal chair arms and her grip on Knox's hand. She didn't want to move, not when his face looked so peaceful. The tension that lined his mouth had softened. His eyes were closed, his dark lashes fanned down, and the sun-squint crinkles around his eyes were relaxed. Head tipped back against the wall, he held so still that she watched carefully for the rise and fall of his chest to prove he was breathing.

When Carrie'd texted her that Knox was hurt, Danielle hadn't thought twice about walking out of her dad's clinic and straight to her car. She knew Bridget could handle the front desk, and it had been a pretty light day anyway. It wouldn't have mattered how many owners and animals filled the waiting room, though. When Carrie said to meet her at the VA, nothing would've stopped Danielle from hopping in her car. Because they were friends, she reminded herself. Good friends.

Poor Knox. He'd been in so much pain, snapping and snarling at everyone around him. He'd reminded her of Sarge when she'd first met him, so used to pain that he couldn't imagine anything better for himself. Like she did with any dog in need, Danielle stayed calm and quiet, giving the animal a chance to acclimate. To understand she wasn't here to hurt it. That she might even be able to help. Knox had responded the same way many dogs did, skeptical and standoffish at first. Then clingy. Not that Knox would ever admit it, but his unrelenting clasp on her hand, even in his relaxed state, told her more than words that he liked having her here.

Danielle turned in the chair, trying to find a better angle to restore blood flow back to her arm. No luck. No luck with maintaining her self-delusion that she was here as a friend, either. Seeing Knox in pain? All she wanted to do was curl up around him and hold on tight. After over two weeks of meeting up at the dog park for morning coffee, Danielle considered Carrie, Riley, Sydney, and Eliza friends, and she'd not once wanted to wrap her arms around any of them and never let go. Her finger traced the veins on the inside of Knox's wrist. Not that they weren't friends, but they were something more. But she kept the friendship shields high because pursuing anything more would end up breaking her heart. Again. Maybe even his, too, and he was already in enough pain. She'd never want to cause him more.

"Hey." Knox's rough voice brought her attention to his face. Eyes closed, his mouth stretching into a lazy smile. "I was thinking."

"Thinking or snoring?" Suddenly, blood flow didn't matter all that much. She was simply happy to feel the heat of his skin against hers.

He ignored her teasing. "Will you go out with me? On a date?"

"A date?" Her fingers curled into his wrist, nails sharp on his skin.

"A real date." He tilted his head in her direction, eyes still closed. "Dinner. Maybe a walk on the beach? Or a movie. Whatever you want."

She took a deep breath, reaching for her calm. He was teasing. She'd started it, so she would tease back. In a *friendly* way. "What if I want flowers?"

"Violets." He cracked open one eye. "I remember."

She remembered, too, the violet corsage the exact shade of her prom dress. How he'd been so nervous, slipping it onto her wrist while her dad took a thousand photos. He'd worn a matching violet pinned to the tux's lapel, and she remembered thinking how unfair it was that the purple made his eyes seem even bluer when her eyes were always brown. Just brown.

"Friends don't date, Knox." But her fingers had uncurled to caress the inside of his wrist, a gentle back-and-forth with the pad of her finger that traced the veins and was also something that friends didn't do. Probably.

"Dani." He tipped his head back, and their eyes met. The tight lines spoke of the pain he was in, but even so, he managed to smile. "One date, that's all. Humor an injured man."

"Playing the wounded-soldier card, huh?" Danielle felt the heat creeping up her neck, into her face, and she felt heat lower down, too, flushing through her body like a wildfire, but she didn't look away. He saw her reaction, and his nostrils flared.

"Marines aren't soldiers. We're Marines." He bopped her nose with the tip of his finger. She resisted the urge to turn her cheek into his palm. "But basically, yeah. Is it working?"

"Only one date?" It was a bad idea. A terrible idea. She was already planning what to wear.

He nodded solemnly. She nodded back.

"We have a deal?" His eyes searched her face like he wasn't sure she'd actually agreed.

"What we have is a date." A giggle skittered out of her, nervous and too high-pitched.

"Good." Knox closed his eyes again, and Danielle closed hers, too, because everything suddenly seemed too much. The lights too bright, the room too warm, Knox too far away. They waited another half an hour, holding hands in the dark they'd created together.

Finally, a nurse opened the door and called his name, then seeing he was in a wheelchair, walked toward them and grabbed the handles. She wheeled him backward through the doors.

He waved at Danielle. "You don't have to wait for me."

I never stopped waiting for you.

The doors closed behind him, and Danielle sank back in her chair. Good thing she hadn't said the words aloud. How pathetic was she? A question she preferred not to contemplate. She took out her phone and opened up her reading app, picking up in her latest romance novel where she'd fallen asleep last night. At least in books, she could believe in happily-ever-after.

CHAPTER 20

Knox kept both hands on the wheel, mostly to keep them from either rubbing his still painful leg or reaching for Danielle, who had dressed like he'd told her: jeans and a T-shirt. But the way the lavender scoop-neck tee outlined her breasts and how those jeans hugged her rounded hips, that was all Danielle. So much for thinking a daytime date would make everything less intense.

"Are you sure you're up for this?" Danielle chewed on her lower lip, her fingers twining and untwining themselves in her lap. "I mean, after yesterday?"

The VA had eventually sent him home after scheduling more tests for the near future. Tests he'd had before and that never came back with the results he desperately wanted. Maybe this time would be different. Maybe not. He needed to plan for bad news, but not today. Today was for Danielle. Thankfully, after a night of rest and alternating heat and ice, his leg was cooperating. Mostly.

"I'm not juggling any bathroom sinks today, so I should be fine." He didn't want to cloud this, their first date in decades, with medical talk. He for sure wasn't going to mention how his leg still hurt like hell, especially if he put all his weight on it. Driving didn't strain his injury, and it wasn't as if he planned to stand around on one leg like a drowsy flamingo.

Knox surreptitiously checked the directions on his phone. He'd propped it on his left thigh, angled slightly toward the door, to keep Danielle from easily seeing their destination. His plan also made it more difficult for him to see the directions, but once they hopped on the extension, it was a fairly straight shot to their location.

"The turnpike?" Danielle swiveled in the passenger seat, point-ing at the overhead sign as they passed under the southbound sign. "We're not going to the Keys, are we? I can't be gone that long. The puppies—"

"You are a difficult woman to surprise." Knox cut across a lane. "There are things south of Miami that are not the Keys."

"Such as?" she asked as if she hadn't grown up here, that teasing smile he adored on her lips.

Lips he was going to kiss today. What was the point of a date if there wasn't any kissing? Wasn't that the difference between plans with a friend and a date? The whole bodily contact thing? If this was the only date she ever agreed to, he planned to get as much of that bodily contact as possible. Starting now. He reached across the center console and grasped her hand. She sighed and flipped her hand so their fingers interlaced.

"Patience. Besides, didn't you tell me Flurry is a good mother?"

"She needs to be let out. And—"

"And don't you live in your father's backyard? He wouldn't let her out if you texted him?"

"Of course he would. So we are going to the Keys?"

He grinned at her tenaciousness. "No, but you can settle in. It's a bit of a drive."

"Mystery man." She thumped back in the seat, his hand still in hers. "How about a clue? Like, how far is a bit?"

"That's too much of a clue. You'll guess in a second." He slanted a glance her way. "Which I'm sure is your intention but will ruin the surprise."

"Fine." Danielle pushed out her lower lip, gnawing on it with her teeth. His groin tightened at the sight. "Will there be food?"

"What kind of date doesn't have food?"

"That's not an answer."

"Yes, there will be food."

"What kind of food?"

"Delicious food."

"Not an answer. You're not very good at this game."

Knox shook his head. "I'm not playing a game. I'm taking this date very seriously, but you are clearly bent on destroying it."

She huffed. "Am not."

"Then stop trying to guess. Enjoy being surprised."

"Fine." She let go of his hand, which was not fine as far as he was concerned, and turned her attention to finding the perfect road-trip music. She rifled through his playlists, trying out a few and snorting in derision. Then she gasped.

"You still have it!"

"What?" An uncomfortable itch rode his spine. What had she found?

She cued it up, and he groaned. "Not that. Anything but that."

"Hey, you're the one who still has it." Danielle turned up the volume. "I loved this song."

"I remember." He remembered every song on the playlist, the one she'd made for him for high-school graduation. She'd called it the Summer of Love, and it included, as far as he could tell, every cheesy love song ever written. That summer, no matter what song came on, she'd scream "That's our song!" and kiss him. So he'd developed a love-hate relationship with the playlist. He hadn't listened to it in over a decade, but he also had never been able to delete it. He'd dutifully transferred it to every new device he bought. And now he knew why. For this moment.

"That's our song!" Danielle screeched with laughter. "God help us both."

"You had terrible taste in music." He turned the music down, but she swatted his hand away.

"Still do. The dogs don't mind." She bounced in her seat, shaking her shoulders as the singer entreated them to never, ever find another.

He smiled. This was already the best date he'd been on in fifteen years, and they weren't even out of Miami yet.

Knox almost missed the turn, but he saw the wooden sign listing farm goods and petting zoo at the last moment. He pulled off the main road and onto a dirt-and-rock path that deteriorated the closer they got to a ramshackle structure made of graying wood. Hand-painted signs advertised canned preserves, goat milk, hand-carved figures, and pies. His mom had brought him here when he was in the first grade and obsessed with goats. He'd read about fainting goats at school, he remembered, and although he'd loved the petting zoo, had been sorely disappointed that none of them had fainted. When planning this day-long date, he'd thought this would be the perfect spot to take Danielle—time with animals she could enjoy but didn't have to rescue herself. It was, however, decidedly shabbier than in his memories. Hopefully, they still had goats, and hopefully they weren't the same ones from when he was six years old.

"What is this place?" Danielle jumped out of the Range Rover before he could round the hood to open the door for her. "Is there really a petting zoo?" She bounced in place, not unlike his nephew when *Meerkat Manor* came on Animal Planet. She already had her purse open, wallet in hand, searching for the five dollars advertised as the entry fee.

"Let me." Knox clamped his hand over her well-worn wallet, pushing it back into her small mesh bag. The cross-body strap nestled between her breasts, outlining them in sharp detail, but he forced his gaze away from the distracting sight and led the way up the weathered steps into the one-room building. Shelves lined every wall, filled with preserves and jars of honey, and a few racks displaying key chains and fake alligator heads dotted the small interior.

An older woman, white hair arranged in tight curls around her face, smiled at them from behind an old-fashioned cash register. "Where you from, folks?" Her smile, though yellowed and crowded, was warm and welcoming.

"Miami Beach," Danielle answered, perusing a card that looked like it had been laminated several decades ago. The edges were jagged and moisture darkened the edges of the paper within. "How much for the petting zoo?"

"You brought your kids? Got a special price for families." The woman's smile widened, and she looked past them as if expecting a troupe of children to come clamoring up the steps.

Knox saw the moment it happened; all the anticipation that animated Danielle's entire body leached from her in the second it took her to inhale sharply and put the card back on the counter. "No. No kids."

The woman looked from Danielle to him and winked. "Don't worry, honey. I'm sure you'll be blessed soon enough."

"No." Danielle stiffened, and then her left leg started to shake. First, it was only a small tremble, but it intensified until her foot tapped against the wooden floorboards like it had to let the energy out somehow. She stared at the woman for a long moment, clearly debating something. Then she spun and darted out the door.

The woman turned confused eyes his way. "What'd I say?"

Knox clamped his jaw shut against the angry words that he wanted to lash at the woman who'd hurt Danielle. He wasn't sure exactly why Danielle had reacted the way she did but standing here wasn't going to help him figure it out. He handed over a twenty-dollar bill. "We'll take two of the bottles."

The woman was too slow, crouching to the level of the small refrigerator behind her. When she finally handed over the bottles with their large plastic nipples, she said, "Tell her I'm sorry."

Knox gave a curt nod. He didn't owe the woman any explanation—not that he could give one—or an apology. She'd started it after all.

He found Danielle, arms folded across the top of a fence

overlooking the petting zoo, gaze on a black dog lounging in the shade of a wild tamarind. She had one of its orb-shaped, sweet-smelling flowers held under her nose.

"It's infuriating." She took a loud sniff. He hoped it was because of the flower and not from crying.

"It is," he agreed, not sure what he was agreeing with.

"I hate it when people ask me about kids." The flower crumbled in her fist, tiny petals drifting to the ground.

Ah, the kids question. He occasionally got asked about them, too, and it always reminded him of her miscarriage. Their miscarriage. Time had dulled the impact for him, although he still felt the sadness each time, but it made sense that each reminder could be a fresh opening of the wound for Danielle.

"Breeders gotta breed," he tried to joke but instantly regretted it. What they were talking about deserved to be ridiculed, but what they weren't talking about—what they hadn't talked about since the day she informed him the baby was gone—was no laughing matter. "What I mean is, they don't mean any harm. She was well intentioned, trying to give us a discount."

"Well intentioned?" Danielle reached up and plucked another flower from the tree, weaving the stem between her fingers. "Where do I even start? First, it's rude. She's essentially commenting on my sex life. How is that even remotely socially acceptable?" The stem tore in two. "How would you like it if people you'd just met asked about your sperm count?"

"I would not like that." He'd never thought about people's questions about kids quite like that before, but she had a valid point. It was a really personal question. "What about people who can't have kids? It could be really painful for them. Or don't want them? Why should they have to explain themselves to strangers?"

Danielle dropped two flower petals and turned a fierce grin on him. "Exactly. But it's rude of me to correct them? I am so tired of this conversation."

He hoped she meant the one about kids and not the one with him. He was afraid to ask directly, so he held out one of the bottles to her. "Here. Wanna go meet some goats? I promise they won't ask any unwelcome questions."

"Thanks." She took the bottle, keeping her head down. Bangs brushed forward, brown hair concealing her face. The rest of the flower floated to the ground, its petals scattering in the light breeze.

"This way." Knox led her around the enclosure. The dog wagged its tail at them before putting its head back on its paws as they passed to the other side of the building where a barn in no better shape than the store leaned in a way that suggested it wouldn't make it through the next hurricane. Another hand-painted sign pointed them behind the barn.

"I'm sorry." Danielle clutched the bottle to her chest. "About back there. I—"

"It's fine. As long as you're fine?"

She nodded.

"Do you want to talk about it some more?"

She shook her head so hard her short hair spun around her head.

Thank God. He tipped the bottle in his hand toward hers in a toast. "Then onward. Baby goats await."

The smile trembling on her lips broke his heart just a little bit. He wanted to go back and give that woman a dressing-down like he would a recruit fumbling his rifle during drills. Instead, he placed his hand between Danielle's shoulder blades, guiding her to the back field where the petting-zoo animals grazed.

Danielle took a deep breath, her back rising and falling under his palm. She tipped her head back, her smile back at full force. "This is heaven."

Heaven seemed a strong word for such a hodgepodge of animals wandering around a half-mud, half-grass pasture, but he remembered his six-year-old self had felt similarly. The baby goats rushed the fence, clearly interested in the bottles. Two potbellied pigs lounged in the shade, and a few newly shorn sheep meandered their way. Chickens pecked away on the grassy side, and in the far corner next to a cement trough, a sway-backed Clydesdale chomped on a mouthful of hay with his giant teeth. One goat pushed his head against the gate, begging for attention. Or a bottle. Probably the bottle.

"Impatient, aren't you?" Danielle reached through the gap in the fence to scratch under the goat's chin while she figured out the latch. After a few fumbles, she got it open, and they slipped in, careful not to let any animals out. Not that any were trying.

Knox shuffled forward, using his knees to move the goats back, bottle held overhead. "They have a good life here, don't they? Strangers coming by to feed them at all hours of the day? We're basically their pizza delivery service."

"It's good to be a goat. They do seem happy to see us." Danielle backed against the fence, a trio of goats clamoring to be first. She lowered the bottle to the gate thumper for a few moments, then transferred to the next goat, and then the next. She bent at the waist, her purse hanging down. A white goat gnawed gently on the strap. Danielle didn't notice, and Knox was pretty sure she wouldn't care if she did.

She petted each goat while it ate, telling them how beautiful they were. Soon, two more goats and a sheep joined the crowd around her. She spoke with each one, praising their friendliness and asking them questions like "Why are you so cute?" that they couldn't answer. He could ask the same thing of her, but he didn't. He leaned against the gate and enjoyed the show.

A bump against his brace made him look down. A brown goat, smaller than the others and with white ears, looked up at him with liquid brown eyes full of hope. Knox had intended to give the second bottle to Danielle when hers ran out, but this little guy was too adorable. Knox offered the nipple and the goat latched on eagerly, sucking half the bottle down with such strength Knox had no idea how Danielle had managed to give her goats turns. In another moment, his entire bottle was empty, and the voracious little beast trotted away to try its luck with Danielle.

"Got it!" Danielle's laugh made the hour drive to Homestead worth it. "The girls are not going to believe it."

"I'm pretty sure anyone will believe goats are greedy little bastards." He set the bottle on the top rail of the fence and brushed his hands on the sides of jeans.

"Knox Donovan, friend to baby goats everywhere." She waded through her sea of admirers, her own bottle empty, too. She showed him her phone, swiping through a burst of photos of him feeding the white-eared goat. "I will definitely be earning my coffee tomorrow morning."

"What do you mean?" He stared at the photos, surprised at how relaxed he looked, like he bottle-fed baby goats every day. The beast really was disgustingly cute with those big eyes and floppy ears.

"Riley brings coffee to Fur Haven in the mornings. Sydney and Carrie usually bring food. Eliza brings the snark, as Riley says." Danielle favorited a few of the photos, then pocketed her phone. "My contribution is usually puppy pictures, but they will love these. You don't mind, do you?"

Mind how happy she looked right now? "Not at all."

Danielle laid a hand on his bicep, covering his Semper Fi tattoo. "This was fun."

"Was? You're not having fun anymore?" He smiled down at her, her big eyes and smattering of freckles making her even cuter than a baby goat. It wasn't the most romantic thought, but he thought she'd appreciate it. He didn't try his luck, though.

She pointed to the empty bottles on the fence rail. "No food, no more love, I'm afraid."

"I'm not so sure about that." His nostrils flared, the scents around them filling his senses. The grass, the goats, Danielle. He couldn't say exactly what it was—soap, shampoo, perfume?—but she always smelled a little bit like coconut, like summers on the beach and tourist drinks.

She licked her lips, and Knox was done for. Her pink tongue, the lushness of her lips. He dipped his head and kissed her, catching her soft gasp in his mouth. Breathing her in.

Danielle relaxed against him, her hand running up his arm to cup his shoulder. Then the best thing happened. She kissed him back.

So much for just friends. Knox didn't have time to feel smug. He tilted his head, slanting his lips against hers. She moaned, leaning against him. He gladly took her weight, wishing there was somewhere they could be less vertical. The barn?

Before he could figure out the logistics, Danielle slipped away from him.

"Oomph." She landed on her hip, sprawled sideways on the ground.

"What happened?" He offered her a hand, but she didn't seem to notice. Possibly because she was covered in baby goats. "What's going on?"

"Off, you wily creatures. I don't have another bottle." Danielle pushed up to sitting, two goats nudging against her chest, another against her back. Two more, the white-eared goat included, watched on. The all-white goat butted its head against her chin, and Danielle's mouth snapped shut.

"Ow! You stinker." Danielle grabbed the goat by the neck and roughed up its hair.

Knox should do something, but it was taking all his discipline not to laugh out loud. He tried offering his hand again, but Danielle was distracted.

"What's this?" She pulled the goat's face closer to hers. "Poor thing, bit of the pink eye, huh? Well, you shouldn't be out here with the others, that's for sure." Danielle used the goat to lever herself to her feet. "Knox? I need to talk to that lady."

"Sure."

She may not have needed his assistance to stand, but he offered his hand again anyway. She took it, and the rightness of that gesture, of her hand in his, helped calm the blood still raging through his veins from their kiss.

Danielle was all business now, and when they reentered the store, she quickly explained about finding pink eye in the white goat and recommended isolating it while it received treatment. She ended her mini lecture with the words, "Pink eye is so contagious."

"Not again." The older woman sighed. "Thought we'd gotten the last of it a few weeks back. Don't worry. I've still got plenty of the medicine." She lifted herself off the stool behind the counter and walked to the front of the store where she flipped the Open sign to Closed. "I'll be right back. You can wash up in the back, if you like?"

"Wash up?" Danielle looked down at her mud-spattered jeans and sneakers, then up at Knox. "Why didn't you tell me I'm such a mess?"

"You always look good to me, Dani." He wiped a smudge off her cheek with the pad of his thumb.

Danielle flushed, freckles merging, and batted his hand away. "It's worse than I thought, isn't it?" She swiped at her face with the edge of her shirt, baring a sliver of belly that made him lose the thread of conversation.

"Knox?" She followed the direction of his gaze and pulled down her shirt with an embarrassed huff. "We should get going. At least it happened at the end of the date."

"End?" Knox shook his head to clear it. That belly. He'd follow it anywhere, including back out to the Range Rover. "This was only Phase One."

"I can't go anywhere like this." She waved down her body. On closer inspection, it appeared the goat at her back hadn't so much been butting her as gnawing on her shirt. The hem was ragged. A small hole gave him a glimpse of the smooth skin over her spine. He calculated the number of minutes and seconds it would take to get Danielle alone behind the barn—not many—and then closed his eyes against the images his mind supplied about what they could do when they got there. A tumble at the petting farm was not part of the romantic date he'd planned so carefully. Time to get back on mission.

"Good thing Phase Two is a change of clothes and checking on the puppies." Knox pulled open the passenger door and resisted offering her a boost up. Touching Danielle right now would definitely spin him off mission, and she'd made it clear earlier that she was perfectly capable of getting in and out of the truck herself. She was so short that it was a bit of a vault for her, but she managed.

She clicked her seat belt in place. "I'm afraid to ask, but what's Phase Three?"

He leaned into the open door with a grin. "Another surprise?"

"Please just tell me." She banged her head against the headrest.

"Dinner."

"Thank God." She motioned for him to close the door. "I'm hungry as a baby goat."

He hopped in the other side and started the engine. "Then how about some cinnamon rolls before we hit the road? There's a famous place a few miles away, and they won't care if you're muddy. I promise."

"Cinnamon rolls?" Danielle bounced in the seat. "This just became the best date of my life."

"Baby goats and pastries? That's all it takes?" He steered them back down the rutted path to the main road, his eyes on the road but his mind on all the other ways he'd like to please her.

"I think," she said, reaching across the console for his hand,

CHAPTER 21

NOTHING LIKE STEPPING DOWN FROM A RANGE ROVER to make a girl feel more like a munchkin than usual. Danielle hid her embarrassment with a smile and accepted Knox's proffered hand to make it safely to the ground. She wobbled on the heels she hadn't worn since Bridget's wedding last year, and he steadied her with a hand between her shoulder blades. She'd curse Sydney for finding them tucked away at the top of her closet and convincing her to wear them, except it was nice to feel the splay of Knox's warm hand against her bare skin. The backless dress was also Sydney's choice, another option Danielle had hesitated over and was now glad she'd embraced.

Yes, Sydney had really come through when Danielle had sent a panicked text from Homestead asking what to wear. Right after Knox drove away with the promise to be back in an hour and a half, Sydney had shown up with two outfit choices and her bag of makeup and hair supplies. Danielle knew she looked good, better than she could have done by herself certainly, and all Sydney had wanted for payment was pictures the next morning at coffee. Danielle wondered if she'd have better high-school dance pictures if she'd had Sydney for a friend back then, but Sydney had laughed and said, "Girl, it has taken me years to get this good. But we're friends now, and I will come running any time you have a grooming emergency." She'd hugged Danielle goodbye, saying Chewy was waiting for her at home, and spritzed Danielle with an expensive perfume before darting away in her yellow Mini Cooper.

Now at Eliza's, or rather Knox's, house, Danielle wobbled up the walkway, still tipsy from the second glass of wine she'd had with dinner. Lights shone in the flanking homes, but Knox's windows were dark. A sheer curtain in the front window shifted, and a dark nose plastered itself to the window.

"I can't keep that window clean." Knox kept his hand between her shoulder blades while they walked to the front door. Heat spread from his fingers, radiating along her nerves. The curtain shifted again, and there was the sound of dog nails scrabbling on the tile and a lone, loud "Woof!"

"Hold on, Sarge!" Knox called through the wood and took his hand off her to find his keys. Her skin felt cold without his touch.

"There are worse problems to have than a greyhound eager for your return." Danielle folded her hands in front of her, pressing the palms together to calm her nerves. The end of their date had been lovely—dinner at Volga followed by a short walk on the beach. She'd rinsed her feet before putting her heels back on, but she still felt sand between her toes. They'd held hands. They'd walked out on the South Pointe Park Pier and watched a cruise ship maneuver into the channel. They'd kissed to the sound of a ship's horn heralding its arrival.

"Will you come home with me tonight?" Knox had pulled back from the kiss, tucking her long bangs behind her ear.

She'd blinked up at him before reaching up on her tiptoes to cup his cheeks in her palms. She was tired of pretending, of passively accepting what could and could not be. Tonight, she was going to follow her heart. "Yes."

He'd been all hustle then, navigating them back to the parking garage and loading her into the passenger seat with so much haste another woman might've found it a little unromantic. But Danielle appreciated the urgency. After fifteen years and their months of careful friendship, a bit of urgency seemed exactly right.

Now, standing on his front step, the motion sensor illuminating them in a circle of light while Sarge woofed his impatience and Knox fumbled the keys, Danielle was way past urgency and right into nervous. If this went where she thought—hoped—it was going, she was about to get naked with Knox Donovan. N.a.k.e.d. No clothes. No bra. No tummy-toning panel to hide behind.

She remembered how much she'd loved his body in high school, the dips and curves of his muscles, his strength when he held her against him. The years apart hadn't dimmed her appreciation for all that taut skin over tight muscle, and if anything, he was more ripped and defined than he'd been at eighteen.

She was not. In spite of staying active, walking dogs and swimming almost daily, the pounds had crept on. She'd never worried much about it. Who was she even trying to impress? Dogs loved her exactly as she was. Her last relationship had fizzled out in her late twenties, and she'd been content enough with her life. She might occasionally envy tall, thin women who didn't need to wear bras with their strapless dresses, but for the most part, she felt like her body expressed who she was. An active, healthy woman who enjoyed a good Netflix binge with all the trimmings—air-popped popcorn, melted butter, Twizzlers, and Milk Duds.

Danielle placed a protective hand over her stomach. Was she really going to be one of those women who worried so much about a few extra pounds that she denied herself the real pleasures in life? She let her gaze swoop from the top of Knox's blond head down to his canvas shoes. Was she going to deny herself all of *that*? She might never have gone to college, but she was no dummy. She sucked in her gut and breathed a sigh of relief when Knox got the door open. She was finally going to see the whole tattoo that scrolled up his arm. Where did it end?

Sarge greeted them by barreling into Knox's good leg. Knox caught him under the chin. "Calm down, boy. I wasn't gone that long."

Sarge's eyes argued that it had been an eternity, but a few moments of ear scratching and all was forgiven. Sarge nudged Danielle's hand with his nose.

"Hey there, remember me?" She dropped into a crouch to give

his neck a good rub. Sarge let out a heavy sigh and rested his chin on her shoulder.

"Can I get you something? Beer? Uh, coffee?" Knox looked from Danielle to the kitchen like he wasn't sure what to do.

"I'm good." Danielle straightened to her feet. "Still full from dinner."

They stood in the entryway, Sarge between them, and suddenly Danielle didn't know what she was doing there. This was a stupid idea. They'd broken up for a reason, and although it had hurt a lot, she'd eventually come to understand that Knox had done the right thing. What would they have done, married at eighteen? It wouldn't have worked out, and breaking up later would've been that much more painful. Sleeping with Knox tonight would be a big mistake. The biggest. It might give them hope that they could recapture their imagined future together, an impossibility now. She should thank him for the date and get out of here. Her muscles tensed for action.

Knox grabbed her around the waist and pulled her against him. All thoughts of running flew from her mind as soon as his mouth touched hers. Hesitant at first, like he somehow knew what she'd been thinking, then more sure when she opened her lips and invited him in. She stretched up onto her toes to thread her fingers behind his neck. They made out. There was no other word for it. Right there by the front door like a couple of teenagers. The thought made her giggle, and the giggle broke them apart.

"What's so funny?" His words were hot breath against her cheek.

"This. Us. We're finally old enough not to have to feel each other up through our clothes, but still we stand in the entryway like my dad's going to walk in on us any minute."

"But your dad's not here." He waggled an eyebrow at her. "It's like all my high-school dreams are coming true at once." He tugged her toward his bedroom.

She followed, her hand in his, feeling both eighteen and her full thirty-three years. Knox stopped at the foot of the bed and pointed at the floor.

Sarge whined and flopped onto a large dog cushion situated under the window.

"He wants to sleep in the bed, but, big guy, there's not room for the two of us." Knox's voice was firm, but his face was guilty. Danielle loved that about him, that he could feel so much for his dog but still hold the disciplinary line.

"I hope there's room for me in this bed." Danielle toed off her heels and stood barefoot on the tile floor. He really needed more than the one throw rug by the window. The tiles were chilly from the AC.

"Let's find out." Knox grabbed her by the waist, lifting her a few inches, and then planted her in the center of the bed. "See? As I suspected, a perfect fit."

Danielle stretched her arms overhead, enjoying how he seemed to appreciate the view of her spread out before him. Then something flashed across his face, a fleeting frown, a crease in his forehead that he smoothed away almost as soon as it appeared.

But she hadn't imagined it. Something was wrong. She saw it in his eyes, the blue that dimmed as they looked everywhere around the bed but not directly at her.

"What is it?" She propped herself up on her elbows. Looking down, she saw how the position pushed her belly together. Not her most flattering angle. She sat all the way up, pulling in her legs so she was cross-legged on his bed. Maybe she'd imagined the appreciation in his eyes. Maybe those extra few pounds had just hit him, and he was wondering what he was doing here with her. Her stomach knotted, so she crossed her arms across her belly to soothe it. "Is it me?"

"No." Knox's eyes finally found hers. He let out an impatient huff. "I just can't—" He palmed the back of his scalp, his olive

T-shirt rising to show an inch of skin. "I haven't yet...you know." He slapped his braced leg. "After this happened, I—"

Danielle's eyebrows tried to rocket off her face. He hadn't had sex since the injury? It made sense, she supposed, at least at first. He'd been hurt, then in recovery. But he'd been home for over a year, and she hadn't imagined how women checked him out whenever he walked by.

"Are you serious?" It probably wasn't the most sensitive thing to say in this moment, but it was all she had. She rose to her knees and knee-walked to the foot of the bed. "That's what you're worried about?"

"Well, yeah." His hands dropped to her waist, cupping her hips and pulling her against him.

She fought his pull, keeping enough distance so she could look into his face. "What exactly are you worried about?"

He swallowed. Hard. "The, uh, mechanics?"

Oh. She chose her next words carefully. "Was more than your leg injured in the attack?"

He saw where she was so delicately heading and shook his head fiercely. "No, nothing like that. I mean, my usual moves are dependent on my legs taking a lot of weight, you know? And I don't know how the bad one will hold up."

"Oh." She licked her lips, hiding a smile. "There are websites, you know. You aren't the first veteran to come home wounded."

"You looked?" His hands slid around, cupping her butt cheeks and pulling her closer. She didn't fight him this time because she could feel her flaming cheeks. She rested one against the soft cotton of his T-shirt.

"Maybe? After our first kiss. I didn't want it to be awkward if we, you know, ended up like this."

"You mean like I've made it awkward?" He spoke the words to the top of her head. "I should've known you would've done your homework. You always were such a nerd."

"A nerd you couldn't keep your hands off of." She tipped her chin up and brushed a soft kiss against his lips.

"True." He whispered against her sensitive lips. "But you didn't seem to mind." He increased the pressure of the kiss, licking the seam of her mouth until she opened for him. Mmm, she could kiss him for hours. But she had other things on her agenda tonight.

"Tell you what." Danielle scooted back. "Why don't you come over here?" She widened the distance between them until she was centered on the bed again. "And lie down?" She waited while he followed her directions, joining her on the mattress flat on his back. She swung one knee over his hips and lowered herself down, her flared skirt billowing around them. "And let me do all the work."

Danielle felt him harden against her, in the spot already hot and wet for him. She leaned forward, kissing her way up his chest as her hands moved the T-shirt up and over his head. The Semper Fi tattoo mystery was finally solved. It tilted up his arm and onto the bicep where a fierce eagle stared her down. She leaned down and kissed the bird's beak, then traced each inked letter with her tongue. Knox sucked in a breath and then seemed to forget to release it. She sat back, pleased with her work. All that skin. All that muscle. All that Knox.

And it was all for her.

———————

Knox didn't know where to look first. As always since what seemed like the beginning of time, his eyes were drawn to her breasts. They strained against the thin fabric of her dress, a peek of her lace bra showing above the purple fabric. Or her eyes, so deeply brown they appeared black in the dim light of his bedroom. Or her face, so pleased with herself. So intent on him that she actually licked her lips, and he didn't think she was aware of how sexy that unconscious gesture was. He'd spent a good portion of their senior year devising ways to get into her pants. He couldn't deny the gratification at watching her plot how to get into his.

But first this dress had to go. He skimmed his hands up her thighs, gathering the material in his fists and urging her to lift her arms. She was so small that he didn't have to lift off the bed much to get the dress over her head. He flung it off the side and lay back to enjoy the view.

And what a view it was. She had the most magnificent breasts. He lifted up, abs tightening, to take one in his mouth. She threw back her head, leaning into the pressure, and with a lift of his hips, he made her moan. And moan again. When she was panting for air, she broke away long enough to skim his dark jeans and skivvies off his body, and then she was back, plumping her breast for his mouth, her knees on either side of his hips.

This time when he lifted up, she arched her back, taking him inside. With her head thrown back, the long column of her neck stretched and exposed, she was the most beautiful thing he'd ever seen.

"I was wrong earlier today." She smiled down at him, placing her palm in the center of his chest.

How could she form words? He was so close. He kept his eyes on her, kept the rhythm going. She closed her eyes, apparently luxuriating in the feel of him, her hips still rolling with every thrust. She bent down and cupped his face in her hands.

"This is the real heaven," she said and kissed him. Her words shuddered through him, and his vision blurred around the edges. She was killing him, but he couldn't stop. She met him stroke for stroke until she was on the edge, and when she came, he went with her.

"Heaven," he agreed when he could finally speak again. She was already asleep.

CHAPTER 22

Shit, shit, shit. What had she done? Danielle couldn't deny that waking up with an eyeful of Knox was no hardship, but she hadn't meant to spend the night. One time, she'd promised herself, one night to remember, and then she'd go back to her perfectly normal, perfectly comfortable life and not worry about any kind of future with Knox Donovan. Who was she trying to fool? This was her pattern—to be good, so good, for so long that when she cracked, it was never in moderation.

In her twenties, she'd tried lots of ways to lose weight, cutting out carbs and sugar for weeks, even months at a time. Hell, she'd been vegan for a whole year, a dietary choice undone by severe abdominal cramps and the belief that a slice of cheesecake would make her feel better. One piece turned into two and two into four, and she'd felt exactly like she was feeling now—out of control. She was old enough to know better now. Starvation always led to binging, and there was no doubt she'd been starving for Knox's touch. If only she'd woken up early enough to sneak out.

But no, she'd overslept, and Knox was looking at her with those midnight-blue eyes in a way that did something to her insides, made them all gooey. She didn't want to starve herself again, but she couldn't have ice cream for dinner every night—not without paying a price. When Knox found out what that price was, he wouldn't look at her like that anymore. She let out a long sigh.

"Good morning." He didn't smile, but he looked happy. Face relaxed, eyes crinkled in amusement. He looked like a man who'd gotten laid, and she probably looked like a raccoon tumbling out of a trash bin.

"Where's my phone? I need to text my dad." Danielle thought

she'd be home by midnight. Flurry and Luna hadn't been out in a very long time. Luckily, her dad was an early riser and hadn't yet left for the clinic. He texted back immediately that he was happy to check on the dogs. He even sent her a winky face. A winky face! From her dad! When had he learned to use emojis?

"Everything okay?" Knox rolled onto his side, propping his head on his hand.

Everything was not okay. Her brain was mush. All she wanted to do was snuggle up to him and go for round three. Or was it four? Last night was one long blur of pleasure. At least it would be a good memory, once she walked out of here. Once she let Knox know they couldn't have anything more than yesterday. And last night. And friendship. Of course, friendship. That had been the deal, right? One date, then back to normal. That was how she remembered it anyway. That the date extended itself into the next day was a mere technicality.

"Looks like you need coffee." He rolled that delicious body away from hers, and she did not—would not—groan at the loss or ogle him as he dressed. Okay, there was a little ogling, but if this was her last memory of him like this, what was the harm in savoring the moment?

She dressed to the sound of him rooting around in his kitchen. In the bathroom, she scrubbed at the raccoon rings under her eyes, vowing to ask Sydney if there were some kind of mascara that didn't eventually migrate off the lashes and into dark circles. She flushed, she brushed, she gave herself a stern look in the mirror. *Do it now before you get too attached.* Oh, who was she kidding? She was already too attached. *Do it now before you can't.*

She entered the kitchen, determined to say the words that would break her heart all over again. Except the look Knox gave her when she walked barefoot into his kitchen, his gray T-shirt reaching to her midthigh, nearly undid her. She had to do it now. Immediately. But first, coffee.

Knox held out a steaming mug to her, and the scent of a fresh brew made her mouth water almost as much as the sight of his tapered abs disappearing into his low-hung camouflage pajama bottoms that weren't camouflaging anything. No doubt about it, topless Knox scrambled her thoughts.

She sipped from the too-hot cup, letting the caffeine reanimate her dormant brain cells. Then, she spoke the death knell of every relationship she'd ever had, including the one with him. "We need to talk."

He took the ceramic mug from her hands and set it on the counter next to his. "We do. One sec, though. I think this is really important." He rested his hands on her hips and pulled her toward him for a kiss. He tasted like how she wanted to start every day for the rest of her life—coffee and heaven and the secret sauce that was all Knox.

What was one more time in the grand scheme of things? Technically, it was still part of the same date. She kissed him back, suddenly frantic for more of him. All of him. He met her kiss for kiss, walking her backward down the hall and into the bedroom until her knees hit the edge of the bed. She tumbled onto the rumpled sheets, Knox's weight bearing down on her. She felt tears rise in her eyes, so she closed them tight. She would be strong later. Do the right thing later. Be sad later.

For now, she gave herself over to Knox's touch, his questing fingers, the desire that thrummed between them. If later all she'd have of him were memories, didn't she deserve to make the best ones possible? At least this kind of binging was calorie-free.

———

Without a puppy, a leash, or a Homestretch brochure in her hand, Danielle wasn't quite sure what to do with the floppy appendages at the ends of her arms. Behind her, two more women arrived at the Dorothy's lobby, bridal-shower-themed gift bags in their grips. Danielle cursed herself for contributing to the honeymoon fund online instead of bringing something tangible to give Riley. Danielle settled for stuffing her fingers into her armpits, freshly showered as she was, and adopted a kind of nodding-bobbing head motion as she stood in the Dorothy's lobby surrounded by more feminine company than she'd had at once since she dropped out of the Brownies in the second grade.

"Danielle!" Carrie held out both her hands, forcing Danielle out of her chosen stance and into the awkward position of deciding if she should offer her armpit-palms to Carrie. Carrie's smile was so wide and welcoming—and it wasn't like Danielle had been hiding where her hands had been—that she threw caution to the wind and let Carrie pull her toward a side table where a few older women were gathered around a centerpiece of pink roses. "So glad you made it! You remember my mom, right?"

Danielle nod-bobbed at Sherry.

"Hi!" Sherry popped out of her chair to give Danielle an unexpected hug. "Don't you look darling! Let's get a selfie for your dad." Sherry held her phone at arm's length and squashed her face next to Danielle's. "If there are two people, it's not really a selfie, is it? What do they call it? An ussie?" Sherry laughed and checked the photo she'd taken. "This is terrible. Carrie, will you take our ussie?"

Carrie took her mom's phone. "I'm pretty sure me taking the shot makes it a plain, old picture, Mom." She snapped a few angles and handed the phone back.

Sherry took a few moments to choose her favorite. "Alan will love this one, don't you think?" She showed it to Danielle for approval.

Alan? Sherry was texting Danielle's dad? Sure enough, there was a whole string of texts, going back for days. Maybe weeks. With winky faces! Was her dad… Were they…? Her brain stuttered to a halt.

"Looks great!" Carrie grabbed Danielle's arm and dragged her away. "Come on. There are more people to meet." Once they were out of earshot, Carrie whispered, "You look stunned. Didn't you know they were dating?"

"I did not."

"Mom's really happy. I hope you don't mind?" Carrie pushed a stray hair back into the loose bun at the base of her neck.

Danielle looked back at Sherry, who was showing the pictures to the woman next to her. "I don't."

"Good." Balloon strings dangled from white and iridescent balloons, catching in Carrie's hair. She shoved them out of the way with good humor. "And where were you this morning, huh? Sydney showed us some pictures of your outfit last night. You looked amazing."

"I, uh, overslept." Danielle felt heat rush her face. She was probably pinker than the balloons floating overhead. "We had a nice time."

Carrie frowned. "Nice? With those heels? What is wrong with my brother-in-law?"

"Nothing!" Danielle's vehemence took both women by surprise. Danielle toned it down a notch. "It was a perfect date. I can't believe Sydney dropped everything to help me out. And how did she even have dresses in my size?"

Carrie took the distraction bait. "Sydney's condo is better stocked than most boutiques with loans from all the designers she works with."

Danielle relaxed now that the subject was no longer her date with Knox. Her mind lingered on her morning rather than the small talk Carrie kept up as they headed back toward the large, circular table in the center of the lobby. One more time had turned into two more times, and she'd had to sneak out on a sleeping Knox in order to dash home to get ready for the bridal shower. So they hadn't had The Talk yet, which meant she was technically still free to fantasize.

She imagined that yesterday's date could turn into another, then another, until they were spending most nights together. Eventually, they'd skip the going-out part of dates to enjoy staying home to watch movies and eat popcorn together on a couch she'd help him pick out. He'd keep her favorite orange blossom tea on hand, and she'd have her own toothbrush in his bathroom. She could picture Luna and Flurry lounging in the backyard with Sarge while the puppies scampered in the grass.

It was scary how easy it was to imagine her life with Knox in it again, the new fantasies layered over the old ones, twining together to show her a future she desperately wanted. She couldn't have that future, but she could enjoy today, heavy with the possibilities, before facing the reality of her situation once again. Forcing Knox to face it, watching his expression dim as she killed all those lovely possibilities. The sadness, a long-time friend, knocked threateningly on the mental door she kept it locked behind, but she reinforced those mental dead bolts. A bridal party was no place to melt down.

Carrie plowed a path through a gaggle of guests toward where Riley sat at the main table with her Grams beside her. More pink roses sat in a glass vase, and petals were scattered across the cream linen tablecloth like confetti.

"Thanks for inviting me," Danielle said when she got to Riley, a bit unsure why she'd been included in the prewedding festivities. Morning coffee at the dog park was one thing, but wedding events were a whole other level of friendship. She suspected that it had something to do with Knox, but no one knew about last night. Not all of last night, anyway. Besides, she'd been invited long before their date.

So she wasn't officially here as Knox's...whatever they were at the moment. Maybe it was that the morning coffee talk so often centered around wedding preparations that Riley thought it would be rude not to invite her. Maybe she was a pity guest. Her hands

crept back toward her armpits, but she detoured them to the pockets in her navy slacks instead.

"We girls have to stick together against all that Donovan male
posturing." Carrie laughed, and Danielle blushed. So she *was* here
as Knox's…whatever. Carrie introduced her around the table, and
Danielle nod-bobbed some more, relieved when they got to two
familiar faces.

"You're Princess Pugsley's moms, right?" Danielle recognized
them from Fur Haven. They were often there in the evenings
when she and Knox had their training sessions with Sarge.

"I'm Kiki." The taller one reached out to squeeze Danielle's
hand in greeting. "This is my wife, Paula." The plumper woman
gave Danielle a friendly smile. "And you're the greyhound lady.
Have you thought about offering regular training classes at Fur
Haven? Lord knows our Princess could stand to learn a few
manners."

Danielle nod-bobbed, suddenly nervous again. "No, I hadn't.
I'm not really a dog trainer."

"Could've fooled us. Talk to Riley or Sydney. We'll be the first
to sign up!" Kiki and Paula both looked so hopeful that all Danielle
could do was smile weakly back at them.

"Come on, Danielle. There are a few more people to meet."
Carrie rescued her from having to commit on the spot to a community dog-training schedule, bringing her around full circle to
end on the other side of Riley. "You know Riley's Grams, right?"

Although Grams was Riley's grandmother, most people called
her Grams. Danielle had been doing so for years, whenever Grams
brought her cat to the clinic. Danielle rounded the table and kissed
her cheek.

"Hello. Thank you for including me." Her remark was for both
Grams and Riley, who looked lovely in a floaty pink dress with
straps so tiny she couldn't possibly be wearing a bra. "I hardly recognize the lobby."

Carrie beamed. "Thank you. It only took a few hours."

Riley tugged at a balloon string floating overhead. "Don't be modest. You've been planning for weeks."

"It's true. I have. And do we have some surprises in store for you."

"I hope that means strippers. I haven't seen a good stripper in years." Grams sipped something bubbly from a clear, plastic cup. "They're mostly gay, you know. That's what I hear. But who cares? Eye candy is eye candy, am I right, ladies?"

Riley snatched the cup from her grandmother's grasp. "I'm cutting you off, Grams. The guests aren't even all here yet and look at you."

"Give that ginger ale back, young lady. A little caffeine is good for my blood pressure." She punctuated her claim by snatching her cup and finishing off the drink.

"You are impossible. Ginger ale doesn't even have caffeine." Riley stood, stretching her back. "Danielle, you must think we're heathens. Can I get you a drink? Ginger ale, obviously, or a diet soda of some kind? I'm afraid the champagne hasn't arrived yet."

"Am I early?" Danielle fought the impulse to check her evite. She hadn't wanted to be late, but she also didn't want to be so early that she inconvenienced her hosts. On the other hand, half the seats scattered around the room at tables of various sizes were already filled.

"No, no, no." Sydney's voice rose above the chitchat filling the air. "It's me. I'm late."

"Always late," Riley said fondly and gave Sydney a hug.

"My fairy godmother." Danielle nod-bobbed, unable to stop the nervous gesture. "How's Chewy?" she asked before Sydney opened the obvious conversational door of how the date had gone. Danielle wasn't ready to discuss it, not until she and Knox had The Talk, and certainly not in front of all these people. Until then, was it so wrong to coast on their assumptions? To imagine she belonged?

Sydney sighed dramatically. "My Chewy, the love of my life,

is in big trouble. He ate my Dolce & Gabbana sneakers. Both of them." Sydney held a hand to her heart. "What am I going to do with that little monster?"

"Spoil him? Not leave shoes on the floor?" Danielle's head finally stopped nod-bobbing now that they were on the safe subject of dog behavior. Her manners kicked in, and she gestured at Sydney's bags. "Need any help?"

"Please, that would be wonderful." Sydney hefted a canvas tote in one hand. "Give me a second, and I'll get the champagne punch set up. It's a family recipe." She winked at Danielle. "Not my family. They're useless when it comes to recipes. I found it online. Still, it's going to be yummy. Come with me. I've been researching a bunch of animal rescues, checking out their online presences, and I have a ton of questions for you."

"Sure. What do you need to know?" Danielle followed Sydney to the refreshment table set up near the mailboxes at the back of the lobby. Sydney asked so many questions about Homestretch that Danielle barely had time to answer one before the next one landed. In no time, they'd assembled the punch, complete with fresh fruit floating in a lemon-lime soda and champagne mixture.

Sydney poured two cups and handed one to Danielle. "To the amazing YouTube channel I'm going to help you set up for Homestretch so we can find those puppies their forever homes."

"Thank you." Danielle tilted her cup toward Sydney and took a sip. Her eyes widened. "This is delicious."

"Told you." Sydney used the punch-bowl ladle to fill a line of glasses. "Let's get these to the troops ASAP. Riley's going to need a lot of booze when she finds out all the games Carrie and I have planned for this afternoon."

"Games?" Danielle's throat was suddenly so dry it took two long pulls of punch before she could talk again. "Like Bunco or something?" Grams often talked about her Bunco group while waiting with her cat to see Dr. Morrow at the clinic.

CHAPTER 23

Danielle wasn't sure how it happened or how exactly her current predicament counted as Sydney having her back, but it was many glasses of champagne punch later, and Danielle hobbled down the makeshift runway in her wedding gown.

Wedding gown in a very loose sense of the words because it was made out of toilet paper. Hobbled because the skirt—constructed by wrapping toilet paper around her legs in a binding tight enough that she could only move a few inches at a time—ripped a tiny bit with every step. If it ripped all the way up the leg, Danielle would be parading down the runway in her underwear and bra. How exactly had she ended up as the model again?

"I love it!" Riley stood at the end of the runway, a score sheet in her hand. Grams was the other judge. Two weddings in the near future equaled two brides-to-be. "Very elegant."

Compared to the first wedding dress to come down the aisle, a risqué number that Carrie and her mother had called "worthy of Cher," Danielle supposed hers was elegant. Sydney and Eliza had been the designers of her mermaid-inspired style. Toilet paper crisscrossed her breasts then wrapped around her hips, leaving a small swath of belly exposed. Toilet paper also wrapped around her arms, down to her wrists, and plunged down her back, stopping just above the bra strap. Danielle had never worn anything like it—not in real fabric or toilet paper—and she was no fashion model, but she did feel a tiny bit sexy in the concoction.

Wedding gown number three made Patty, who slowly made her way down the runway with her walker, look more like a mummy than a bride. Kiki and Paula, the designers, cheered Patty when she executed a twirl inside the confines of the walker. When Patty reached the judges, there was applause for all three dresses, and then Sydney declared, "Fashion shoot," and before Danielle knew what was happening, cameras were out and this weird-ass afternoon was immortalized for the ages.

"I knew we shouldn't have left you ladies alone for so long." Caleb didn't even try to hide the laughter in his voice. Danielle's hand automatically went to hide the swath of stomach revealed by her toilet-paper dress, but Caleb's eyes were only for Riley. He strode toward her from the direction of their apartment down the hall, LouLou the poodle trotting beside him in a high-stepping prance.

"You're not supposed to be here at all." Riley lifted her face for his kiss.

"I couldn't stay away." He dipped down to brush his lips across hers, then pulled away with a smile. "Or rather, LouLou couldn't stay away. From the dog park. You know how she gets."

Riley's eyes narrowed, but her matching smile belied her attempts to look annoyed. "Admit you were being nosy."

Caleb touched his nose like he'd never noticed it before. "Me? No, Knox asked me to meet him. He's got to run that beast of his." Caleb's eyes flicked Danielle's way.

Danielle sucked in her stomach and studied the intricate way Sydney had tucked the toilet paper into a string belt to hold up the skirt. She missed whatever he said next, and then he was gone and Grams cleared her throat.

"I'm proud to announce that Sydney, Eliza, and Danielle are the winners!"

The assembled women clapped, and Sydney curtsied. "What did we win?"

"The best of prizes," Grams intoned gravely. "The greatest of honors."

"Spit it out already," Eliza griped. "And it better be good."

Riley and Grams exchanged a look that even Danielle could tell meant trouble.

"You three"—Riley paused, milking the moment every bit as much as her Grams would have—"get to plan our bachelorette party!"

Danielle shook her head, sure she hadn't heard correctly, but Sydney was already accepting with "How fun! You knew I'd do it anyway, right? Like you could stop me."

Riley smiled. "I'd hoped so. But I wanted to make it official." Sydney hurried to her for a hug.

Eliza bumped Danielle's elbow with her own. "Strangest bridal shower I've ever been to, but thank goodness for Sydney. Looks like you and I are off the hook."

"Oh no, you're not." Sydney waggled her finger in their direction. "I'm deputizing you. Phones out, everyone. Time to set up the group chat."

"Penises." Grams' voice cut through the tip-tap of Sydney setting up the chat. "Penises on everything. The cake. The tiaras."

"Tiaras?" Danielle whispered to Eliza.

"Penis tiaras," Eliza whispered back.

"The tablecloths. The napkins." Grams continued her list.

Danielle typed fast to keep up with the requests.

"The strippers!" Grams surveyed the group triumphantly. "The strippers should definitely have penises. Big ones, if you know what I mean."

"You're not being subtle. And there will not be strippers." Riley made the slashing sign at her throat. "Got that, ladies? No strippers."

Danielle erased the line item.

Grams stuck out her lower lip. "Sometimes, Riley, I wonder who raised you."

"The best grandmother ever, that's who." Riley slung an arm around her Grams' shoulders, and Grams blushed prettily at the compliment.

"But for real, ladies." Riley made eye contact with Sydney, then Eliza, then Danielle. "No strippers."

"Strippers it is." Eliza cackled, and only Grams joined in on the laugh.

Knox had seen some strange things during his days in the Corps, but he'd never seen anyone dressed completely in toilet paper before, and here he was staring at three of them.

"What is going on?" he whispered to Caleb, hand tight on Sarge's leash. The dog somehow knew Danielle was inside and was straining to get closer to her, a sentiment Knox well understood. He couldn't be mad that she'd gone on with her day like last night was a regular, not-at-all-life-changing night. Except he kind of was. He'd liked her in his bed. Liked it so much he wished they were both still there.

He peered through the glass doors at the front of the Dorothy, noting the abundance of pink and the too-loud laughter. That punch bowl was undoubtedly spiked. He couldn't imagine any other way someone had convinced Danielle to be draped in toilet paper. Not that she wasn't rocking the look. She totally was. And it was easy to imagine how quickly the toilet paper layers would rip away with one firm tug of his hand.

Caleb held LouLou under his arm and joined him at the glass door. "It's the bridal shower. Some game or something. We can go around the back if you want to avoid it."

Sarge whined as if he understood the suggestion and disagreed.

"Into the fray?" Caleb pushed open the door before Knox decided the best course of action. He'd woken to an empty bed, a disappointment so acute he'd lain on his back for a full minute, staring at the ceiling, before deciding she'd probably gotten anxious about her dogs and the puppies. He'd shot her a good-morning text. She'd not returned it. He'd followed up an hour later with a picture of Sarge lounging in the sun. Still no response.

Restless, he'd asked Caleb to meet him at the dog park. He might not be able to run three miles in twenty-five minutes anymore, but it sure was a joy to watch Sarge work off his injury. While the weak leg was still a challenge for the dog, he'd taken to trying out short bursts of speed, especially when they first arrived at the park.

"Knox?" Caleb held the door open, and the sounds of women's laughter drifted out.

Riley's and Grams' bridal shower was a perfectly good reason for Danielle to turn off her phone. Knox ignored the restlessness in his stomach. Everything was fine with Danielle. She'd had an obligation. She wasn't ignoring him.

Except she did. Or at least tried to. She saw him across the lobby and quickly looked away. Sarge led the way through the clumps of women, and Knox nodded greetings to the women who called out to him but didn't stop to chat. Danielle was heading toward the women's bathroom as fast as she could hobble in the whatever-it-was she was wearing, and lucky for him, that wasn't very fast.

"Hey." He let out the leash a bit, and Sarge got to her first.

Predictably, she slowed for the dog. "Hey." She petted the top of Sarge's head while he gave her toilet-paper outfit a thorough sniffing.

It wasn't an outfit, though. Knox's gaze traveled hungrily down her body, catching on a strip of belly visible between the layers of toilet paper. It was a wedding dress.

Intellectually, he understood it was some girly bridal-shower joke, this odd contraption of a dress made out of the flimsiest material possible. But it was Danielle. In a wedding dress. And it made him a little dizzy on his feet. He braced a hand against the wall for support. "Marry me."

"What? You didn't just say that." Danielle's eyes darted from him to the bathroom like she wanted to escape. Why? Last night, and this morning, had been perfect. Hadn't it?

"Dani, I'm serious. You're dressed for it and everything." The *marry me* had slipped out without conscious decision, but his gut reactions had saved his life in many situations. He trusted his gut now. There was something so right about Danielle in a wedding gown that it made his insides clench with need just looking at her.

"Stop teasing." She glared at him, then led him past the bathroom, down the hallway to Caleb and Riley's place, and out a side door. They stood on the top of a three-step stoop he'd watched Mendo and Lance retile with a mosaic pattern Carrie'd picked out. It was a warm day, but Danielle wrapped her arms around her waist, hiding the sexy patch of belly playing peekaboo with him. "Knox, I—"

And suddenly he knew. She was going to end it, end it before they even really got started. He felt the same panic crawl up his throat he'd felt when the doctor first told him about the medical separation paperwork making its way through the correct channels. As close as they'd been last night, today she was going to separate herself from him.

"Wait, let me—" Knox scrambled for the words that would stop it from happening. Sarge leaned against his leg, and Knox gave him the signal to lie down. The big dog sighed and stretched himself out, effectively blocking anyone else from using the door. If only Danielle were as eager to please, but she wasn't one of the Marines under his command or a rescue in need of some structure in a loving home. She was Danielle Morrow, and she was about to rip the heart out of his chest and crush it in her small hand. He couldn't let that happen.

Knox's grasp tore the toilet paper at her waist. He slid his palm over the curve of her hip and lowered his face to hers, sliding his lips from her ear, along her jaw, until he could press them softly against her mouth. Soft, so soft. He nuzzled his nose against hers. "Is it so crazy that I want to wake up with you every morning?"

"You're not being fair." Danielle pulled away from his kiss, the back of her hand against her mouth as if to ward him off. Knox reached to bring her against his body, but she took a step away from him, teetering on the edge of the step. "I can't do this with you. Not again."

"Do what?" Knox worried about the stubborn tilt of her chin, the hard gleam in her eyes. "This?" He ignored her body language and hauled her in, flush against him.

"Stop it." Her voice shook as much as the body pressed to his.

Shit. She was scared. This time, he was the one to step back. He held up his hands. "I'm sorry. Please, talk to me."

Her brown eyes were so wide, and they shimmered with unshed tears. He fought back the instinct to take charge, to command the next action, to demand her surrender.

Danielle clasped her hands in front of her. "I don't know what we're doing. What you want from me. But we can't have a future together, so we should end it now. Go back to being friends."

"I've been pretty clear what I want. And friendship is not it." Knox tracked every twitch of her muscles, so he didn't miss the way she winced at his words. "What?"

"This." She waved a hand between them. "Yeah, it feels good, but if we go down this road again, what happens?"

Knox blinked. He could think of a hundred things, no a thousand things, that could happen. That he'd make happen. Between them. In bed. His bed. Not her point, though, and he couldn't blame her. Last time, he'd knocked her up, thrown her life a real curveball. She was right to be skittish.

"I'll be careful. We'll use protection." He gentled his voice, meaning to reassure her that he wasn't as careless as he'd been when they were teens. He'd take care of her this time. Except he hadn't, had he? He'd been careless with her once again. No wonder she was upset.

Danielle made a sound he'd never heard before, a low keen that suddenly erupted into a choking sob. She wrapped both hands around her stomach and bowed her head, long bangs sweeping forward so he couldn't see her face. He took a hesitant step forward, but she—there was no other word for it—growled at him.

He held up his hands where she could see them, the universal sign of surrender. "What's wrong?"

"I told you, I can't do this." She ripped off some of her toilet-paper sleeve to dab at her wet eyes.

"So don't marry me. That was a stupid thing to say. We've only been on one date. But at least let me take you out a second time. Give us a chance, Dani. The chance we didn't have before." Knox could actually feel the adrenaline ramming through his body, putting every nerve ending on high alert.

Danielle hid her face in the crook of her elbow, shoulders shaking. When she finally dropped her arm to look at him, her eyes were puffy with tears.

"We had our chance. You walked away." Her voice didn't accuse, not exactly, but he felt the slap of her words.

"I thought a clean break was best." He ducked his head, unable to look at her while he uttered the mantra that had gotten him through boot camp, had helped him stay strong against the temptation of reaching out to her.

"Best for you maybe." She swiped at the tears already drying on her cheeks.

"Best for you." That had always been his reasoning. "I didn't want to ruin your life. Keep you from achieving all your dreams."

Danielle stomped her foot. "Your mom is such a bitch."

"What?" Knox's head snapped up.

"You heard me. I don't like to talk bad about another woman, but she really did a number on you, acting like having you was the end of her life. You bought it, too, hook, line, and sinker. All that guilt over something you had no control over. And look what it did to us." She gestured between them like it was an insurmountable chasm.

He blinked, the familiar guilt rising, bitter in his mouth. "She could've been a star."

Danielle snorted. "Plenty of stars have kids. Open your eyes, Knox. Your mom was miserable, and she took it out on you. But you're a grown-up now. See the situation for what it really was."

Knox's head shook and shook. Danielle was right. If he were honest, he'd known for years that his mom didn't really have what it took to be an actor. Although she did love drama, she loved her leisurely lifestyle living off her generous alimony checks from Robert Donovan more. In his entire life, she'd never done one thing—taken an acting or singing class, auditioned for a local theater group, nothing—to get her closer to her dream.

Still, he felt the need to defend her, his mother, the only person in his family who hadn't mocked him for enlisting. "She did her best, in spite of everything."

"Did you know she told me I was lucky to lose the baby? Lucky." Danielle's eyes filled with tears again, and her breath hitched. "If that's her best—" She sucked in a sob, heel of her palm to her mouth to hold it in.

"Dani, I—"

She shook her head hard enough that the toilet-paper train tumbled to the floor. She kicked it out of the way and said something softly to Sarge. The dog leapt to his feet and moved out of her way. She wrenched open the door, then looked back over her shoulder before stepping into the building.

"This time, I'm the one doing the walking. Let's see how you like it."

He watched her blurry white form float down the hallway. He didn't like it, not at all. He plopped onto the top step and slung an arm over Sarge's shoulder, chest heaving like he'd completed an obstacle course. He took a moment to calm his breathing and squelch the impulse to hunt her down. She wouldn't thank him for running her to ground, and he didn't know what he'd say when he caught up with her anyway. "It's just you and me, big guy. What do you think of that?"

CHAPTER 24

"SUCH A WASTE." DR. MORROW STOOD IN THE DOOR OF THE exam room, observing while Danielle calmed down the frantic kitten on the stainless-steel table. She held it close to her chest so it could hear the steady beat of her heart, its front paws in the circle of her fingers to keep it from scratching her. The kitten's tail swished angrily, but the yowling had calmed to mewling.

"Almost ready for you." Danielle ignored her father's comment. It was one he made regularly, at least once per week, since she'd announced that she would not be attending college. You'd think a decade would dull his disappointment, but no. This was the one bridge they couldn't seem to cross. "Give me a few more minutes."

"We could sedate him."

"Not necessary," Danielle cooed in her cat-calming voice. The kitten wriggled and butted its head against her.

Dr. Morrow stood beside her, a heavy hand on her shoulder. "You really are magic with the animals, pumpkin. I wish you'd rethink becoming a vet. Someday I'll retire and then what will happen to my clinic?"

"You're a long way from retirement." She gave her standard answer to his standard guilt trip. It wouldn't always be true, but she figured she had another twenty or so years before his concerns were actually valid. "And I'm happy as I am."

Another standard answer and one that had been true, mostly, for a long time. But today it felt wrong on her tongue. She wasn't unhappy, but happy wasn't the right word, either. Not since her fight with Knox. What had she thought would happen with Knox Donovan? That they'd somehow forget years of silence and separation to live happily ever after? She'd set herself up for that fall, and fall she had. The only thing she was proud of was that she'd put an end to it last week before things got any worse.

"What if I'm not?" Her dad readjusted the stethoscope around his neck.

"Not what? Happy with how my life is going?" Danielle didn't remember her mother who had died of cancer while she was still a baby. For as long as she could remember, it was her and her dad. The upside was that he'd always been there for her. The downside was how much of a say he felt he should have with her decisions. She was so tired of this conversation.

"Happy with how *my* life is going." He fidgeted with the stethoscope some more and then buttoned and unbuttoned his lab coat. "Sherry says I work too much. She says I should take some time to enjoy life. You know, before it's too late."

Sherry. Danielle resisted the urge to roll her eyes. Five minutes in her dad's life, and Sherry was already interfering in their business? Danielle and Carrie had spoken just this morning at Fur Haven about their concern that their parents were spending too much time together. They both knew what the winky face meant. Danielle was worried that after so many years of staying off the dating market, her dad was making up too quickly for lost time.

"So take a vacation. I can hold the fort down here for a few days." She snuggled her face into the kitten's soft fur, hiding her face from her dad because he read her so easily.

"What if I wanted to take a few days per week off? A semiretirement, if you will? Then what? Without your degree, I can't leave the clinic in your hands. Danielle, if you won't do it for yourself, do it for me." His fidgety hands finally rested on his little chub of a belly.

"Why don't you understand that at a certain age, it's simply too embarrassing to go back to school? The ship sailed, Dad. Get used to it. I have." She settled the kitten on the table, gesturing for her dad to take a look.

Instead, he pulled out his phone. "Look at this article. An eighty-year old woman just got her A.A. Don't talk to me about too old. It's never too late to chase a dream."

She traded him the phone for the kitten, glancing at the article. "Some people win the lottery, too. Doesn't mean it's a good investment."

Dr. Morrow kept one hand on the kitten and placed the other on his daughter's shoulder. "Pumpkin, you are always a good investment. Can't you even try?"

Danielle placed her hand over her father's and summoned a wobbly smile. "Dad, don't worry about me. I'm good."

He didn't smile back. Instead, he tugged on his stethoscope in that nervous way he had when he had to deliver bad news to a client.

"What? Spit it out. I have feline leukemia, don't I? Is it too late for treatment?" She tried to joke it out of him, but he didn't crack a smile.

"You're fired."

At first, she was sure she'd misheard. "Can't fire a volunteer." She tried another joke, but this one fell as flat as the first. She squeezed his hand and kept a firm grip on the kitten.

"You're not a volunteer, although the way you come and go as you please, I'm sure my other employees must think you are." Dr. Morrow didn't return the squeeze. Didn't look at her but studied the shiny surface of the exam table like he could see microscopic germs with his bare eyes. "But I do pay you a salary. And room and board, I might add. So I can fire you. I am firing you. I should've fired you a long time ago."

Danielle snatched her hand back and cradled it against her chest. *Fire, firing, fired.* She was definitely not mishearing him. "Why?"

"Sherry says—" He sucked in a breath and started over. "Sherry pointed out something I've known for a few years now. I've made it too easy for you to coast through life without having to make any real decisions. You're not living up to your potential."

"My potential?" Danielle parroted, looking around her for clues this was some kind of surreal dream. "My potential is fine. I help animals every day. You like having me here."

"I do." Dr. Morrow landed a heavy hand on her shoulder. "You're my daughter, and I love you. Helping out when you were a kid? Good preparation for becoming a vet. Sticking around after you decided not to go to college? Necessary at first. I know that. But you've been fine for years, and you're still in the job I gave you so I could keep an eye on you, back when things were so bad for you. Remember?"

Remember the worst years of her life? No, thank you. They sat with her, though, lurking in the dark corners. She'd banished them to the far recesses of her mind. Being around Knox made her want to remember some of the better times, before the doctors and treatments and her so-called cure, but she wasn't willing to do it—not at the cost of returning to the depression that colored her early twenties.

"I'm sorry, Dad." She pushed back memories of the days she couldn't get out of bed, the days she could eat entire sleeves of Oreos and still feel hungry, the days that turned into weeks and months while she figured out how to live with her condition. "Sorry I've disappointed you. I thought we had a good thing here. I guess I was wrong."

"We do have a good thing. Can you blame me for wanting more for you than good? I want the best for you, pumpkin. I always have." He patted her shoulder and used both hands to position the cat on the table. "That's why I'm also giving you thirty days' notice that you'll need to move out of the guest cottage. It's time to choose your own life."

"What?" Danielle swallowed hard. "You don't think that's a little harsh? Firing me and making me homeless all on the same day?" Tears threatened to blind her, but they weren't sad. No, she was furious. This whole conversation was nothing like her father. Sherry was behind this. Her daddy would never kick her out.

"Like this little one"—her dad tickled the kitten's chin, and the tabby purred loudly—"I'm sure you'll land on your feet."

Danielle's mind ran on unfamiliar tracks. Without her job at the clinic, how would she support Homestretch? Without the guest cottage, where would she live? How would she pay for it? She couldn't simply get a job at another veterinary clinic. She wasn't a certified vet tech; she was trained by her father, not licensed by the state. Out on the job market with only her high-school diploma? She'd never be able to afford living on the Beach on minimum wage.

"Fine. I'll apply to a couple of schools. Is that what you want to hear?" Anger made her voice shake, and the kitten shied away from her. Animals never shied away from her. The kitten's fear hurt her almost as much as her father abandoning her for his new girlfriend.

"That's my girl." Her father beamed at her. "Now, can you help me get this little one's temperature?"

Great, a stick up the butt. Always a favorite with the animals. She got the kitten in position, getting the task over with as soon as possible. The kitten's eyes were wide with shock, but it was done before she had time to protest too much. The kitten mewled accusingly while Dr. Morrow continued the examination.

"Believe me, sweetie, I know how you feel." Danielle kept hold of the kitten's head, thinking how she wanted to research colleges about as much as she wanted a thermometer up her butt. A few rejection letters should get her dad off her back. It'd be worth the time just to prove her dad wrong, and then he wouldn't have the heart to kick her out. She hoped. Because if she didn't have her dad and her cottage and the clinic, what did she have?

You could have Knox an evil voice in her brain whispered. He'd looked so sucker punched last week when she'd walked away from him, the toilet-paper gown in shreds by the time she locked herself in the stall in the lobby bathroom. She'd done it to spare him, but he'd never know why. She hoped he'd move on now, go out and find the life he deserved. She supposed that was all her dad wanted for her, too. Why did doing the right thing have to suck so much?

―――――――

It was too late to back out now. Sydney's Mini was parked near the curb, and she and Carrie were climbing out, loaded down with bags. Danielle had cleaned up her place as best she could with eight puppies underfoot, but it still looked like what it was: a dog-house. These were her dog park friends, though, so maybe they'd understand. Sydney needed some pictures for the website she was building and some footage of the puppies for the first video post on the new Homestretch YouTube channel. It wasn't like Danielle was asking for the cottage to be considered for an historic home tour or anything.

"Come on back." Danielle waved them through the side wrought-iron gate that led past her dad's house and the pool and to her cottage.

"Are you so excited about the bachelorette next Thursday? I can hardly wait." Sydney squeezed by the recycling bin and ducked under a low-hanging palm frond.

"It'll be interesting, that's for sure." Carrie's dry delivery let Danielle know she was not alone in dreading what Sydney had cooked up for the party, and somehow she'd convinced Lance and Knox to go along with it.

"I've never been to a bachelor and bachelorette party." Danielle kept her comment neutral. Sydney had put a lot of time and effort into the planning, and all Danielle had had to do was say yes to the many texts Sydney sent.

Sydney clapped her hands together, and the stack of bracelets on her left wrist jangled. "It's going to be epic." Sydney's eyebrows jumped up and down.

Instead of responding, Danielle waggled her eyebrows back, and Sydney cracked up. Danielle held the gate open so Sydney and Carrie could enter the backyard. It wasn't Carrie's fault Danielle's days at the cottage were numbered. In spite of her promise to her dad last week, she had yet to fill out a college application. Or look for another place to live. Although no longer going to the clinic freed up large chunks of her day, she had puppies to care for. Who had time to scour the internet for job leads and college-essay writing advice when she could spend her time picking out perfect names for each puppy? Not this girl.

"You're on a canal!" Sydney spun in a circle, taking it all in, her ankle-length skirt floating around her like a balloon. "And what a gorgeous pool!"

"Thanks. It's my dad's, really. I'm just staying here." Danielle gave her standard line, but she heard the falseness of it even if her friends didn't. *Just staying here* implied she'd eventually move out, but so far, she'd spent her entire adult life living on her dad's property. Right after high school, she'd stayed in her childhood bedroom. When it became clear she was never leaving for college, she'd moved into the guest cottage. Temporarily, she and her father had agreed. Temporary turned out to be over a decade. On some level, she knew her dad—or rather, Sherry—was right. She had to stop pretending things were temporary and acknowledge that this was her life. She hadn't consciously chosen this life, but it suited her. Why did her dad have to go and fire her and shake everything up?

"Lucky." Sydney swept her blond hair over one shoulder and pulled a professional-looking camera out of the tote bag dangling from her crooked elbow. "My rent went up again last month. That's why I've been going on all these interviews. I love having my own styling business, but a steady paycheck would make me sleep a lot better at night."

"Still having insomnia?" Carrie walked back from where she'd been inspecting the small dock over the canal, her high-tech sneakers smacking on the concrete. With her hair pulled into a high bun and her body encased in tight workout wear, it appeared she'd come straight from one of her runs. "That sucks."

"Doesn't it?" Sydney snapped a few shots. "Light's good. Maybe we can take some photos with the dogs out here."

"Sure." Danielle led her friends into her place, warning them to watch their step as they entered. Carrie was a parent's dream come true. Smart, successful, beautiful. Happily married with an adorable child. No wonder Sherry thought Danielle's life needed an overhaul. Compared to Carrie…well, there was no comparison. Not really. Her life was literally going to the dogs.

"Oh. My. Goodness." Sydney started shooting photos right away, keeping up a stream of steady commentary on the adorableness of each puppy. She paused to switch to a video camera, cooing at the puppies the whole time.

Sweet Pea and Tilly put on quite a show for her, tumbling over each other and chewing on each other's tails. Daisy, Pinto, and Monki scampered around Carrie's feet, and Junior, the runt and puppy who looked most like Sarge, made a beeline straight for Danielle. Danielle didn't want to commit yet, but she was fairly sure he was about to become her third dog. In a small cottage. It was insane. She should find him a better home. She reached down and scooped him up, nuzzling into his puppy-smelling fur. Just not yet.

Flurry and Luna eventually ambled over to greet the visitors while the rest of the puppies slept on, oblivious to the chaos around them.

"Do you mind if I give myself a tour?" Carrie eyed the living-room-turned-puppy-room with some distress. "To see where the people live?"

"Make yourself at home." Danielle moved into the kitchen. "Tea?"

"No, thanks. I'm ready to work." Sydney plopped onto the floor, taking more photos with every breath. Roxy gnawed gently on her outstretched foot.

Danielle put the kettle on, more to soothe herself than anything. Carrie came back in, flowered notebook open and in hand. Her eyes visibly measured the kitchen, and she jotted down a few notes.

"What're you doing?" Danielle lifted the kettle as soon as the water bubbled. She didn't like to wait for the whistle.

"Don't mind me. I'm just doodling." Carrie sat on the one kitchen chair at the bistro table, so Danielle leaned her hip against the counter and held her mug in both hands. "This place is quite a challenge, even for one person. But you've got ten dogs, Danielle. In what? Seven hundred square feet, give or take? That's seventy square feet per being. You really need to zone better."

"Sure. I'll get on that." Danielle smiled over her cup. "Zoning."

"Are you laughing at me? You know people pay for my interior design advice." Carrie shut her notebook and clipped the pen to the cover.

Danielle's smile grew. "Not dog people."

"I'm a dog person!" Carrie lunged to her feet. "Those are fighting words. Beckham is a part of the family!"

"Sorry." Danielle held up one hand. "Thanks for the advice."

"My mom told me to come with Sydney today. She's worried about you living out here all by yourself." Carrie's return smile invited Danielle in on the joke.

But Danielle didn't think it was funny. "Translation: she wants to turn my home into her crafting cottage or something?"

"My mom? Crafting!" Carrie laughed so hard she had trouble catching her breath. She bent at the waist like she was getting a cramp.

"Then what? A she shed?" Danielle could picture it—Sherry moving in and rearranging everything, including Danielle's space.

There'd be a couch and a TV in the living room in no time, and then where would the puppies live? Where would she live? "I know Sherry's behind my eviction notice, but I still have two weeks, so I'd appreciate you backing off the redecorating on her behalf until I actually move my stuff, and my dogs, out." So much for keeping her anger focused on Sherry. It spilled out of Danielle's mouth and all over Carrie.

Carrie hugged her notebook to her chest, looking chastised. "She really is worried about you. She said something about you applying to colleges?"

Danielle groaned. "The two of them won't leave it alone, will they? I told Dad that to get some peace, but I'm too old to start over. What school wants a thirty-three-year-old freshman?"

"Any school would be lucky to have you!" Sydney called from the puppy room, proving how small Danielle's place really was.

Carrie scooped up a puppy that had escaped into the kitchen and kissed its domed little head. "Community colleges are open access."

"What does that mean?" Danielle sipped her tea, glad to see Tilly having no trouble with socialization. Carrie's arms were getting a thorough licking.

Carrie didn't seem to mind and beamed in delight at Tilly. "It means if you have a high-school diploma or GED, they have to accept you. You could take one class at a time, and you wouldn't have to move out. It's a way to ease into college, if you want, and maybe keep your place."

"Did Sherry send you here to say that?" Danielle eyed Carrie suspiciously over the top of her mug.

Carrie shrugged. "It may have come up in conversation."

"You can tell them I said I'll look into it." Danielle sipped her tea one last time and set it on the counter. "And now I know why I was lucky not to have a little sister."

"The way our parents are carrying on? You may end up with

one anyway." Carrie set the puppy down, and Tilly scampered back to her littermates. "Be glad I ran interference for you on all the questions about Knox."

"What?" Danielle hadn't told her dad anything. But perhaps Knox told Lance who told Carrie who told Sherry who told her dad. Goodness, Miami Beach was a small town sometimes. "Nothing is happening with Knox. We're not even speaking right now." She timed her visits to Fur Haven to catch the coffee klatch, but she'd stopped going in the evenings because that was when Knox and Sarge were there. It was better if they didn't have contact, easier for him to move on. Problem was, her no-contact rule was backfiring. She could feel the deprivation building up, the binge on the horizon. If only he were as easy to get over as a half-gallon carton of ice cream. She was afraid, though, that if she gave in again, she wouldn't be able to walk away. Not a second time.

Carrie made a hmmming sound and said, "If you say so," while doodling in her notebook. "Would it be so bad if there were, though? You two seem good together, you know?"

"Danielle!" Sydney's voice saved Danielle from having to answer and pulled both Danielle and Carrie into the puppy room. Sydney knelt by Flurry's water bowl. "Is that normal?"

Sweet Pea was facedown in the water, not moving.

"No, definitely not." Danielle was on it, scooping up the puppy with one hand while she grabbed a spare stethoscope off the cabinet. "Strong heartbeat but not conscious. He must've inhaled some water." She used a finger to gently push on Sweet Pea's chest. A few drops of water dribbled out of his mouth, and then his chest rose and fell on its own. Danielle's shoulder slumped from relief.

"What do we do?" Carrie had her phone out, ready to dial.

"Let's get him to the clinic. He's already breathing on his own again, but I want him checked out."

"Let's go." Sydney was already scooping up her things. "I've got enough material to keep me busy for days."

"Please lock the door behind you." Danielle didn't want to wait for Sydney and Carrie to gather all the bags and pack up the camera. She was already out by the pool when she heard Carrie's voice call after her.

"Just think. If you were a vet, you could handle this yourself."

Smart-ass little sisters were definitely the worst. Especially when they weren't wrong.

CHAPTER 25

KNOX KEYED IN THE CODE ON THE NEW VIDEO INTERCOM panel he'd had installed outside the front door of the Dorothy. Security cameras in the common areas and outside the exterior doors would come later in the week, but for now, he enjoyed the satisfaction of a plan coming together. Knox followed the screen prompts and was pleased to see the current list of Dorothy residents scroll by in alphabetical order. He'd been looking for top-of-the-line security systems, of course, but ease of use was also an important factor. Nothing too complicated or time consuming. Pleased, he tried dialing Caleb's extension.

"What?" Caleb's voice was clipped and irritable.

"It's working!" Knox's glee was disproportionate to the task at hand, but he was pleased. The intercom installation was the first thing that had gone right since Danielle literally slammed the door on him and walked away. His garage-door opener had stopped working, and the repairman talked him into putting in a new system with better sensors. The ice dispenser in the fridge clunked its last, leaving the appliance sitting in a pool of water, and when he'd decided it was better to simply replace the whole thing, the delivery guy had banged a huge gouge in his front door bringing in the new refrigerator. No, homeownership was not agreeing with him, not at all. Each problem seemed to lead to a new problem, and before he knew it, he'd dropped five grand on his so-called investment and hadn't even started his renovation projects yet. Perhaps his estimate that four months was plenty of time to flip a house was overly optimistic.

"What's working?" Caleb's voice was clipped, but Knox didn't take it personally. He knew Caleb had attended a city council meeting earlier in the day, and he was never in a good mood after those.

"The call box." The Dorothy's old security box had been a relic from several decades past, and the residents had gotten in the habit of propping the doors open rather than dealing with the hit-or-miss security box. It made him feel good, keeping people safe. "My work here is nearly done! I'll be a free man once again."

Caleb's guffaw came through the speaker loud and clear. "Keep thinking that, but we both know you'll find more reasons to stick around. There's no denying you're settling in."

Knox leaned a forearm against the wall, bringing his mouth close to the box. "I am not."

Caleb's only response was to laugh harder.

Knox ended the call. The box was good and checked. No need to keep talking on it when Caleb was only a few hundred feet away. Besides, his know-it-all littlest brother was wrong. Sure, following his gut had led to some hasty decisions that looked like settling down, but he wasn't settled. Not by a long shot. He could walk away anytime.

Knox's phone buzzed in his pocket. Thinking it was Caleb, he picked up. "What?"

"Gunny!" Morales' voice lifted Knox's mood. A move to Atlanta was looking better by the minute. The Dorothy was nearly done—or at least his part in it was. Danielle wanted nothing to do with him. His house was a money pit. His leg seemed to be getting stronger. Maybe the universe was telling him it was time to make a choice. Maybe it was time he said yes to Morales.

"Yes." Knox interrupted Morales' detailed report on the state of downtown traffic to give his answer. *Take that, Caleb. No settling happening here.*

"Yes what?" Morales chuckled, the bastard. He knew exactly what Knox was talking about, but Morales was going to make Knox say it.

"Yes, I'll come up to Atlanta. That's why you're calling, isn't it?" He'd be letting down Lance, but his mother would be happy. As happy as she was capable of being anyway.

"Finally!" Morales bellowed into the phone. "I was starting to think you were going to stay down there forever."

"Naw, my family thing is wrapping up. I should be able to head up after my brother's wedding." He should've finished out his current round of physical therapy by then, too, and heard back about the tests they'd run on him at the VA. Morales didn't need to know about all that, not yet anyway. As long as he continued to heal, slow going as it was, he should be able to handle routine security details.

"Good news, Gunny. That's good news. We could really use a man like you up here. You'll make the clients feel safe, no doubt about it."

"That's the point of a security firm, isn't it?"

"True that." Morales filled him in on the setup, told him he'd have his own office. Knox nodded, even though Morales couldn't see him. It felt familiar, this style of briefing, the knowledge he'd be picking up stakes and moving soon. Familiar was good. He rubbed his thigh above the brace. Familiar was safe.

"So you're going. Just like that?" Caleb stood in the open door, having clearly been eavesdropping the past few minutes.

Knox was really off his game if he hadn't heard Caleb walk up behind him. "Not immediately. But once you've tied the knot, yeah. Why not?"

Caleb stepped all the way outside, and the door swished shut behind him. "Lance thinks you're staying on to open the security side of his business. You bought a house."

"I never promised Lance anything, and I've said from the beginning the house was just a side project, an investment." Knox felt an itch between his shoulder blades that in the field meant he might be in someone's sights, but here in civilian life, it meant something was off, really off, but he couldn't figure out what it was.

"You got a dog." Caleb arched an eyebrow and bounced it for emphasis.

"Sarge will go with me. I'm not abandoning my dog."

"No, just your family." Caleb's blue eyes were icy with accusation. Knox wondered if his own eyes pulled the same trick. It was eerie, sometimes, how looking at Caleb or Lance was like looking in a distorted mirror.

"What family? My mom's in Atlanta. Dad's in jail." He tried to make his eyes icy, but he couldn't tell if it was working.

Caleb rocked on his heels. "We built this together." He waved behind him at the Dorothy. "We're a good team. Don't you want to stick around and find out what else we can build together?"

"Spoken like a Donovan."

Caleb's eyes narrowed. "And like a Donovan, I'll buy your house and raze it to the ground if you leave. I'll build a sewage plant over it."

"No, you won't. Not so close to your beloved Dorothy."

"You're right. Teeny, tiny little apartments then." Caleb's gaze challenged him. "How do you like that?"

Knox didn't like the idea of his house being torn down. It was a money pit, but it was salvageable. What was Carrie always going on about? It had good bones. He couldn't admit that, though, so he flipped his hand. "I don't care, as long as you pay market value when you buy it from me."

"Oh, I'll get your market value and then some." Caleb sounded like an actor in a mobster movie. "You won't believe how much I'll rent those teeny, tiny apartments for when I'm done with it."

Knox laughed. "Are you trying to threaten me by telling me you're going to make a lot of money? I'm not sure you understand how threats work."

Caleb cracked a smile. "Yeah, I heard it as it came out. I don't think I'll ever be the crime boss our father was."

"Thank God." Knox offered his fist for a knuckle bump.

Caleb reciprocated. "Thank God. For real, though, Knox, don't leave yet."

"Of course not." Knox repeated the fist bump. "We've still got work to do. I won't leave until everything's tied up tight."

Caleb refused the second bump and offered his hand to shake instead. "You've got yourself a deal, brother."

Caleb walked away, toward the garage where his beloved Porsche was parked, and Knox stayed planted outside the front doors. He still had a few tests to run on the security box and an unsettled feeling in his stomach. Knox owed Morales his loyalty after everything they'd been through together, but he was starting to think he might owe Caleb and Lance some. He'd thought of his fellow Marines as his brothers for so long that it hadn't occurred to him that his actual brothers might start to feel like family, too.

———

Danielle sat in her usual place on the stool at her father's breakfast island. As he'd done every Sunday she could remember, her dad stood at the induction cooktop flipping chocolate-chip pancakes. As was also their tradition, she had three flavors of syrup lined up in front of her, one for each pancake she would eat—maple, blueberry, and butter pecan.

What was new today was an extra body at the breakfast bar. Sherry's, to be exact, and it wasn't like she'd come over for an early-morning sugar hit. Her blue terry-cloth robe and memory-foam slippers declared that she'd been here all night. No, it was Danielle who was the visitor this morning, interrupting their intimate weekend.

Sherry propped her chin on her hand and turned her attention to Danielle. "How's the job hunt going? Your father said you've sent out some résumés."

Danielle kicked at the counter with her bare toes. "No

interviews yet, but I do have a few leads on a possible new place to live."

Her dad stiffened at the stove for a moment before plating the first pancake. He brought it to the breakfast bar and placed it in front of Sherry, which was fine with Danielle. The first pancake was never quite right. Sherry beamed at him like he'd handed her a plate of diamonds and said, "Oh, this looks delicious!"

"It is," he assured her and poured out another helping of batter into the pan.

Sherry spread butter on her pancake and took her time examining each of the syrup bottles. "I'm so pleased you've taken up the challenge your father gave you. I think you'll really like being out on your own."

"I'm pretty sure it wasn't my father's challenge," Danielle said low enough that she hoped her father couldn't hear. "But don't worry. I'll be out of the cottage by my eviction deadline, and you can turn it into whatever you've got your heart set on. Just know that if you hurt my dad, I will come for you."

Sherry's eyes widened and she put down the syrup bottle with a loud thud. "I think we've gotten off to a bad start."

"You think?" Danielle knew she was acting like a teenager, so she went all in and rolled her eyes.

Sherry swiveled her stool in Danielle's direction. "It's not like that at all. I have no designs on the cottage. Your dad is worried about you. He's done his best for you, and he doesn't understand why you aren't happy."

"I am happy," Danielle said in a voice that admittedly wasn't very happy sounding. "Or I was. Until you butted in. Do you know that most apartments want a security deposit for pets? Per pet?"

Sherry kept her voice low and soothing. "I didn't butt in. I was invited in. By your father. I told him a little bit about how lost I was at your age. I was so angry at my ex-husband that I let that anger make all my decisions, and the only way I could escape was into a bottle. There are large chunks of Carrie's childhood I don't even remember. And I am deeply sorry for all that I missed." Sherry stopped and took a deep breath. She reached for Danielle's hand. "Carrie cut me out of her life. Didn't want me near her son. It was a wake-up call, a wake-up call I wish I'd heard years before. I've been sober almost six years now. I didn't want you to be like me, regretting what should be some of the best years of your life."

"I'm not an alcoholic. I've never done drugs." Danielle thought for a moment. The doctors had sure put her on plenty. "No illegal ones, anyway. I'm not some out-of-control mess that needs saving. In fact, I save lives. Or I did, before my dad fired me." She glared at Sherry. Intellectually, she knew Sherry wasn't evil. Emotionally? Totally different story. Like Cinderella's evil-stepmother story. Except stepmother wasn't the right word. Dad's-step-girlfriend didn't sound nearly ominous enough, though.

"I'm not saying you are. But you are letting opportunities pass you by. Why don't you reach out and grab some of them before it's too late?" Emotion shone in Sherry's eyes so brightly it looked like she might cry.

"Pumpkin, here you go." Dad slid a pancake in front of her. "Are my girls having a nice chat?"

"The nicest." Danielle bared her teeth at her dad in what she hoped passed for a smile. Sherry lifted herself off the stool to share a kiss with her dad. Over the pancake. In front of Danielle. Maybe she really did need to move out.

Danielle focused on her pancake, slathering it in butter, then the maple syrup. She cut it into tiny bites, reminding herself that her dad deserved to be loved for the very cool guy that he was.

Mercifully, the kiss ended and he set up the next pancake.

"I haven't always had the best taste in men," Sherry confided like they were now girlfriends or something.

"My dad is great." Danielle knew it would make her dad happy if it seemed like the two of them were getting along so she raised her voice. "I guess your luck has changed."

Sherry's eyes followed Danielle's dad's every move and gasped in surprise when he used the pan to single-handedly flip a pancake without a spatula. "Hasn't it? I can't believe a man like him is into someone like me."

Danielle stuffed her mouth with four squares of pancake, declining to comment, because *me either* seemed mean when all Sherry'd been doing was trying to help. She was obviously terrible at helping, but one thing this breakfast cleared up was that it was well-intentioned meddling.

A group text from Sydney gave her reason to disengage, and she took her sweet time replying. Sherry stood and made her way into the kitchen, reaching up to peck Danielle's dad on the cheek.

Do I have to? She texted Sydney.

Invite them! They're so cute together was Sydney's reply, and Carrie jumped in to say Mom will love it!

Fine, Danielle texted back, *but I'm finishing my pancakes first.*

CHAPTER 26

THE CROWD OUTSIDE THE WYNWOOD HOT-SPOT RESTAURANT made Knox nervous, even if he was related to most of them. When Sydney proposed combining the bachelor and bachelorette parties, Knox's relief was only outshone by his gratitude for not having to handle any details. The last thing he could imagine was hitting the strip clubs with his grandfather. The horror. But that was what Grandpa William had insisted he wanted, and not even Caleb with his bargaining expertise could sway him. So dinner and a show on a less-crowded Thursday evening was a godsend, honestly, and his only part in planning had been to send Sydney a thumbs-up whenever she'd run details through the group text.

Danielle was in the group text, too, so he knew she was alive at least. He'd taken Sarge to Dr. Morrow's clinic for a checkup because he was worried about Sarge's limp, not to see Danielle. Still, he'd been disappointed that she wasn't there and even more surprised to learn she didn't work for her dad anymore. How was she spending her time? Because it sure wasn't with him.

Patty, out on the town in a yellow paisley housedress, and Eliza, wearing Crocs with her dark pantsuit, were making their excuses, saying, "We'll catch a Lyft back to the Dorothy." Patty did look tired, and Eliza had been skeptical about the show part of dinner and a show since the first group text. Their imminent departure opened the bailing floodgates, and soon Danielle's dad and Carrie's mom, who appeared to be together now, were calling a car, too, claiming to also be too tired to go on. However, their long kiss at the curb indicated they might have other plans tonight. Next to make excuses were Lance and Carrie, claiming they needed to get home because their babysitter had texted them that Oliver wasn't feeling well.

"I hate to be that party planner"—now Sydney was jumping on the bandwagon, hands flying fast enough to make her bracelets jingle—"but I have to get up early for a photo shoot tomorrow. It's a last-minute gig, and I couldn't turn it down. Rent's due, no matter who's getting married." She kissed Riley on the cheek. "I know you will have the best time. Enjoy!" She headed over to the next block to catch a ride on a busier street.

So that left the grooms-to-be, Grandpa William and Caleb, and the brides-to-be, Grams and Riley. And him. And Danielle. Who wouldn't look at him, not even when he stepped aside so she could enter the rented limo ahead of him.

"Where are we going?" Grams knocked on the glass divider between the driver and the roomy back seat. "I demand to know our destination!"

"Should we tell?" Knox asked Danielle. They were currently the only two people in the back seat who knew the plan. Sydney maintained that given the older couple's insistence on strippers and the younger couple's insistence on no strippers, the best course of action was silence. Let them be surprised! she'd texted. They're going to love it! We just have to get them in the door.

Danielle shook her head and pulled the strap of her purple dress toward her neck to cover the half inch of bra that peeked out. He'd tried not to watch her all night, but his eyes strayed back to her again and again. In the close confines of the limo, he could smell her perfume, a light scent with a hint of vanilla that made him think of candy. And licking.

"Sorry." He cleared his throat when the word came out gravelly. "Sydney swore us to secrecy."

"Sydney's not here," Riley pointed out.

Caleb pulled her hand into his lap and said, "Let's all relax and enjoy the experience, shall we? Surprises can be fun."

Grandpa William harrumphed. Riley turned the conversation to a discussion about two potential buyers she and Caleb met with earlier that day and whether they'd make an offer on one of the newly renovated two-bedroom units at the Dorothy. Danielle stared out the dark window, and Knox stared at her. Covertly, of course. He was trained in stealth after all.

The limo pulled up in front of a dance studio in a neighborhood on the outskirts of Miami gentrification, and doubts assailed him, doubts that multiplied once he stepped inside. Floor-to-ceiling mirrors covered three walls, and the fourth wall was painted a dark red. Inspirational sayings like *Just Get Up and Dance* and *Enjoy Every Step* scrawled across the wall in black, painted in swirls and whorls like the words themselves were dancing.

Who was he to even think about taking a dance class, especially this kind of dance? His leg was still sore from the workout he'd given it earlier today, and he had no desire to make a fool of himself in front of his brother and his fiancée. Or Grandpa William and Grams. Or Danielle, especially not Danielle. She used to love to dance with him, and he hadn't even tried after the IED exploded his life. At least he had a life, he reminded himself, sending silent apologies to Munoz and Whittier for the millionth time.

"Over here!" Riley snapped him out of his memories and motioned him over to a seat in a row of folding plastic chairs against one of the mirrored walls. He took the last open seat, the one on the end and next to Danielle. One good thing about everyone bailing on them. She couldn't avoid him, like she'd been doing all night.

The lights dimmed, and a woman emerged from a door camouflaged in the red wall. She was dressed as a flapper—a knee-length number with swinging fringe and gloves all the way up to her elbows. She struck a pose in the doorway, the light behind creating a silhouette. Music blared from overhead speakers.

The song sounded familiar—swinging and heavy on the

saxophone. The dancer walked, slinky and smooth, to the center of the studio. She started to dance, an old-fashioned burlesque style, that might have been sexy if he weren't sitting next to Danielle, hyperaware of her body heat and how if he reached out only a few inches, he could touch her.

When the dancer whipped out two large feather fans and used them to play peekaboo with her body parts as pieces of clothing flew out from behind the fans, Grandpa William let out a long, loud wolf whistle. Grams smacked him on the arm. When he repeated the whistle, Grams grabbed him by the arm and hustled him out the door with a loud "Billy, the only peekaboo you're getting tonight is from me."

Certainly more information than Knox was comfortable having about his grandfather's private life, and now they were down two more people in what was supposed to be a big, fun group outing. The dancer kept up the waving fans, ignoring the older couple's sudden departure.

When the song ended, the dancer was lying on the floor, fans coyly positioned so it appeared she was completely naked behind them.

The lights brightened, and the dancer popped up from the floor, fans discarded behind her. She wasn't naked at all, but a nude body suit certainly hinted at it. Her body was strong, with thick thighs and enough flesh on her bones that when she did a body roll as she walked toward them, all the right parts jiggled. She was older, with a few streaks of gray in her dark hair, and she held her arms out to the sides like she was fluffing an imaginary cape.

"What did you think? Burlesque is something else, isn't it?" She approached their line of chairs, confidence in every line of her body.

"Amazing!" Riley held hands with Caleb. "Will you be doing another dance for us?"

"Not exactly." The dancer extended her hand to Riley. "I'm Monica. Come with me."

Riley took the hand with a backward glance at Caleb, and Monica picked up Riley's chair and plunked it in the center of the dance floor. "Take a seat."

Riley did, eyes wide with excitement. "Are you going to dance for me?"

"No." Monica swept her right hand out in a wide sweeping gesture. "You will dance for us."

"Oh no, I couldn't possibly," Riley protested, but the look in her eyes said well, she might. Then they flickered to where Danielle and Knox sat, and Knox very much felt like a third wheel. He recounted the number of people in the room. Make that fifth wheel. He was about to suggest to Danielle that they make tracks like everyone else and leave Riley and Caleb to a more, um, intimate lesson, but she ignored his attempts to subtly get her attention.

"In fact, if the other lady will bring her chair to the center?" Monica extended her left arm in an exaggerated flourish. "Let's get your lesson started."

Danielle stood slowly, gaze darting from her chair to Riley and back again. Finally, she sighed and moved her chair, a vote for not using subtlety with her. Noted. She blinked too fast, a sure sign she was nervous. Knox understood how she felt. He wouldn't want to be out there, either, even if it was just a lesson. She was a good sport to go along with Sydney's plan—a classy nod to Grams' and Grandpa William's respective requests for strippers. Danielle really had nothing to worry about. She'd always been a good dancer—not in any kind of trained way, but what she lacked in knowledge, she'd always made up for in enthusiasm. And Knox had to admit, he was really looking forward to watching Danielle strut her stuff.

"Now, ladies, please stand behind your chairs. Gentlemen, you will come here." Monica pointed to the seats.

Knox and Caleb exchanged a look. It appeared it wasn't a lesson only for the ladies. Monica shuffled across the floor and grabbed Caleb's and Knox's hands, dragging them to their feet. "Burlesque is for everyone, my friends. And the chair dance is very easy. You will see. No problem for the leg." She grinned at him charmingly, but Knox still felt shame ripple through him. She thought he was afraid because of his leg.

Danielle patted the back of her chair. "Looks like it's me and you, friend."

Ouch. Her first words said directly to him all night, and they were boundary setters. He still was unsure exactly why she'd ended it with him. Up until they'd slept together, she'd seemed to forgive him his idiotic decisions in the past. But now he was unforgiven. Unforgiven was a whole lot of no fun. Still, the least he could do was sit his ass in Danielle's chair and give this burlesque thing a shot.

"You got it, friend." He planted his butt and stretched out his braced leg. "Although, in my experience, friends don't ignore each other's texts."

Danielle mumbled something about puppies and job hunting, and Knox nodded like he believed her reasons why in the past weeks, he'd been unable to get her to respond to anything other than pictures of Sarge. Even then, all he got were thumbs-up responses.

The chairs were placed a few feet apart, and the first thing Monica did was teach the women how to walk around the chair. Eight steps around. It shouldn't be sexy, simply walking, but watching Danielle concentrate, lower lip caught in her teeth as she emulated Monica's moves, was definitely doing it for him.

This lesson wouldn't be so bad if his role was to sit in the chair and appreciate Danielle. In fact, he owed Sydney a huge thank-you for this opportunity. He and Danielle needed to talk, really talk. He didn't know what he'd say, exactly, that would make up for leaving all those years ago, for buying into his mom's worldview instead of building his own. He just knew he had to try. But he couldn't try if they weren't in the same room, and now they were.

If he could get her to agree to talk to him, any embarrassment he was about to suffer during the dance lesson would be worth it.

Danielle walked around him again, and this time, Monica added a body roll at the end. It happened behind his left shoulder, but he could see Danielle in the mirror. Her roll wasn't as smooth as Monica's, but those magnificent breasts of hers made it more dramatic. Monica instructed the women to repeat the move, eight steps, body roll. Riley was copying Monica, too, but he couldn't take his eyes off Danielle. With each repetition, she gained a bit more confidence, a bit more attitude. She was into it, and that made him into it, too.

"Guys, sit up straight." Monica grabbed another chair and set it across from them. Knox scooted his butt back and lifted his chin, hoping that whatever came next involved touching Danielle.

"This is the man's part." Monica demonstrated—stick one leg out, bend over it, look up. Knox's braced leg was already stretched in front of him, and the move seemed easy enough. Except it wasn't. Man, his hamstrings were tight. He gritted his teeth and met his own gaze in the mirror. If Danielle could body roll, he could handle bending over and looking up. Monica had the guys repeat the move three times.

Next, she showed them how to straighten the spine, hand on knees, and then flash the mirror. Not really flash, but it felt like it. Feet on the ground, hip width apart, splay the knees. Then snap the knees together.

"Just a sneaky-peeky!" Monica demonstrated one more time, then had Knox and Caleb repeat it three times.

"Together now!" Monica snapped her fingers, pointed Danielle and Riley into position behind the chairs, and the music came on. "Listen to the beat. Ladies, you start." Etta James crooned something bluesy about wanting to make love, and Danielle stepped around him.

"Gentlemen, do your thing." Monica kicked out her leg, and

the men followed suit. Danielle was forced to step over his leg, and Knox started to understand how the dance would come together. He saw his own fierce grin in the mirror when he looked up. By the time Danielle was doing her body roll, he was on to the knee move.

"Good, good. One more time." Monica counted out the beat, and they put all the moves together again. This time, Knox was free to watch Danielle, her face a mask of concentration. She stepped over his leg, and he looked up fast so he wouldn't miss the body roll.

Monica took Caleb's hand and tugged him up and over to her chair. She used a hand in the center of his chest to push him into a seated position.

"Hey, that's my man!" Riley laughed, no real alarm in her tone. "You can't take him."

"For the demo only. You can still marry him." Monica tapped Caleb on the shoulder, taking her place behind him. "You remember your moves?"

Caleb nodded and grinned at Riley the whole time Monica circled him. After the body roll, she stepped to the side and slid backward into Caleb's lap, kicking out one leg. "This is next! Now, gentlemen, you have to catch your ladies."

"I'm not sure how this is going to work." Danielle raised her hand like she was in elementary school, but she didn't wait for the teacher to call on her. "It's some kind of trust fall, isn't it?"

Monica held up a finger. "Let me show the hold." She placed Caleb's hands on her waist and said, "Now push, like so," and she was back to standing. "See, very trustworthy. Now, go to your bride and show her how it's done."

"Whatever you say." Caleb returned to his own chair, and Riley placed her hand on the back of his neck. She was always doing that, touching him in some small way whenever they were near each other. Knox envied them that, their physical ease with one another. They didn't have to wait for the strangest bachelor party ever for an excuse to touch each other.

Monica clapped her hands together. "Let's try the new move. One, two, three."

Riley collapsed onto Caleb's lap, and he pushed her up with a laugh.

Danielle didn't fall. Instead, she eyed Knox's lap suspiciously. "I liked the walking part better. You sure you can hold my weight?"

He bristled, hairs on the back of his neck standing on end like Sarge when a squirrel dared to invade his backyard. "I'm not incapacitated." *Not yet* whispered in his mind but he pushed away the depressing thought. "I can certainly sit in a chair without hurting you or me."

"I didn't—" Danielle brushed her bangs behind her ear. "I meant I'm not as light as I used to be. You know, in high school."

Knox remembered the mornings when he'd find Danielle at her locker, how his whole day felt brighter because she was there, and how he'd scoop her up from behind and swing her around. She'd always beat at his arms and demanded to be put down, and he'd always said, "The ransom for release is one kiss," and she'd always paid. Happily, as he recalled.

His gaze ran over her, comparing the Danielle in his memory to the woman standing before him. "Believe me, it's in all the right places."

She blushed. One moment, she was normal-Danielle color, the next flushed like they'd been dancing for hours instead of a sedate twenty minutes of walking around a chair a few times. He raised his arm and brushed his knuckle against her heated cheek. "Let's practice."

She visibly swallowed and turned her back to him. "I'm coming now."

"You don't usually announce it." He chuckled at his own joke. She turned her head to glare at him.

"Fine, no more warnings." She bent her knees and fell.

It was only a few inches, but to Knox, it seemed to happen in slow motion. Her body moving closer and closer to his until finally she was on his lap, her world-class ass on his thighs. He put his hands around her waist, and his fingers tightened like they didn't want to let her go.

She scrambled off his lap and spun around. "You're supposed to push me back up, not take advantage of the situation."

"Sorry." He hung his head, not sorry at all. "You're just so soft."

"I told you I was too heavy." Danielle crossed her arms over her stomach.

"That is not what I said." He grabbed her hand and tugged her back onto his lap. "You can stay here all day if you like. All night." His breath hit her neck, and he saw the goose bumps that rose on her skin. She might not think they could have a future, but they could certainly have a now. And wasn't today the beginning of tomorrow anyway?

She tipped her head back so their eyes met. "Knox, we can't."

"But think, if you give me a second chance, you can make me pay for what I did our entire lives. Wouldn't that be satisfying?"

Danielle's long bangs brushed against his cheek. "It's not about that. We'll have to break up eventually. It's better to do it now."

There were so many things wrong with what she'd just said, he didn't know where to start. Before he could decide, Monica showed them a new move where Danielle spun around in front of him and repeated the sit, stand, kick on the other side. Another march around the chair, and the dance ended with Danielle straddling him, their faces inches from each other.

He owed Sydney. Big time. Like a million dollars.

Monica made them practice three more times, then she put the music back on.

Etta James' emotional voice, the bluesy song, the repeated references to making love. Knox was transfixed by how Danielle took it all in, performing her walk, her rolls, with a sensuality that heated his blood and sent it pumping to the place she would be in one, two, three…

She landed on his lap, and he used her waist to boost her back up. He watched her spin, her short hair spinning around her, then she repeated the move on his other side. He wanted to pull her in his lap and keep her there until both of them were breathless. But they weren't alone, so he pushed her back up and she disappeared behind his chair. He forgot his next move, and then Danielle was back, leg sliding over his thighs, across his straining fly, down his hip. His breath caught.

Danielle sat, her softness against his tense thighs. Her breath came hard and fast, more than their short dance warranted. Her hands were supposed to land on his shoulders, and she was supposed to arch backward. Instead, she cupped his cheeks in her palms, her eyes dark with desire.

"Come home with me." His words came out so rough he wasn't sure she understood him.

Smiling, she arched back, giving him the best view in the room. His heart couldn't decide if it wanted to stop or beat itself out of his chest. The combination made him breathless, or maybe it was simply Danielle. She smiled at him upside down in the mirror, and that did it. His heart stopped cold, and he probably died, because the next thing she said was, "No. But you can buy me a coffee tomorrow."

Somehow, they got through the last few minutes of class. Said their goodbyes. Even though they'd already given Sydney money for a generous tip that she'd prepaid online, he slipped Monica another twenty. She winked at him and said, "Go get her, *Papi.*"

If only it were that simple. But coffee was a start.

CHAPTER 27

IT WAS HARD TO BE UNHAPPY WITH A PILE OF PUPPIES IN HER lap. As soon as she'd gotten home from the dance studio, Danielle had sat cross-legged on the floor of her dining-room-turned-puppy-pen and let Flurry's brood clamber over her like she was nothing more than a mountain that needed climbing. She had no idea how long she'd been in her puppy bubble, but she was no closer to sleep than before. Images of Knox in that chair, watching her every move with such intensity, burned in her mind.

Who was she kidding? It wasn't her mind that was burning. No, other parts of her burned, too, and the memory of straddling Knox and holding his face in her hands didn't do anything to put out the flames. She'd come so close to kissing him, under the bright lights of the studio, in front of Riley, Caleb, and Monica. She'd come so close to going home with him. Her older self would thank her for keeping a clear head during this whole debacle. No binging, no regret later. Her present self, though, was sad.

Junior, the one who most looked like his papa Sarge, sprawled across the top of her thigh with a sigh that shook his whole body.

Danielle tipped a finger under his chin. "I know how you feel, squirt." It had been a long week with no fewer than three meetings with potential landlords who sent her on her way as soon as they heard how many dogs she had. Plus, there was her round-the-clock puppy-watching schedule. At nearly seven weeks old, they didn't need the constant care of the first month, but there was still a lot to do with eight puppies. Staying out late for the burlesque lesson tonight had been fun, but the strain of seeing Knox, and feeling Knox, and thinking about Knox had made her too jittery to sleep even though she was exhausted to the bone.

"Get it? Bone." She flipped one of the puppy's ears. "Aren't I hilarious?" Tilly agreed by using needlelike puppy teeth to nibble on her thumb.

Flurry and Luna lay on big dog beds under the window, both fast asleep. It was past midnight, and a sliver of moon shone through the glass. As they often did, and more intensely since their night together, Danielle's thoughts drifted into memories of Knox. Not the hazy, gilded memories she'd carried for over a decade, replaying in her mind to figure out what she'd done wrong, which *exact* moment was the one when she should've seen that the forever she and Knox so often talked about wouldn't last even three months after their high-school graduation.

When had he stopped loving her the way she'd loved him— with all the earnest passion of her eighteen-year-old heart? It didn't matter how many times she replayed their time together, she never found the moment. The ending always came out of nowhere, always hit her with the force of a hit-and-run accident where she was a scooter and he was a Mack truck.

No, these days her mind drifted to the kiss on Eliza's lawn. The smoldering looks at the dog park. The awe on his face when the puppies were born. The rightness of sitting next to him in the VA waiting room, like time hadn't passed and she was still his go-to person. The night she spent in his bed. She wished she knew what she was feeling now, if it was real or just old memories influencing her present behavior. Was she overthinking things? Was there a way they could be together that wouldn't end in heartache? She wished she could talk to him. Well, she would. Tomorrow. She'd promised. But after weeks of avoiding him, afraid she wouldn't stick to her resolve to spare them both more pain, tomorrow seemed too far away.

Danielle picked up her phone, and one of the puppies bumped its nose against the back. The time flashed at her. Too late to call. Wasn't it?

But one thing they'd always shared was their love of the night. If she was still up, her bet was that he was, too. She took a chance.

Pretty moon tonight, right?

She held her breath while puppies climbed her belly like a mountain. Gizmo stuck his nose into her armpit and immediately fell asleep. Junior sprawled across her collarbone, nuzzling his face into the side of her neck.

Her phone dinged, and she let out her breath. Not a text, though. A picture.

An old picture. Back-to-school dance, senior year. Knox wore dark-wash jeans and a crisp button-down. She smiled up at him in her peach lace sundress with the high-low hem, her hair pulled up in a sparkling barrette, wisps framing her face. A yellow crescent moon hung in the background, a cutout taller than the both of them, against a black backdrop with twinkling lights for stars.

I loved that dress, she typed. She'd loved him, too, but when it came to confessions, she figured better to start small.

The dots bounced. And bounced. The puppies settled around her, falling asleep one at a time until she was the only one awake in the room.

I loved you in that dress.

Her heart raced at the reply, enough so that Junior lifted his head and darted out his tongue in a quick lick before settling back down again. Was she brave enough to do it? To admit what she was feeling and damn the consequences?

I loved you in those jeans. I loved you. Period.

She'd done it. Not that it was such a big revelation. She hadn't been shy about telling him back then. But now? Now she was one letter away from admitting how she really felt. Sure, she'd loved him back then, but did that equal loving him now? Danielle was afraid it might. She was afraid that once again, she felt more for him than he felt for her and that once again, he'd break her heart. Tonight had proved that like last time, she couldn't stop herself from falling. But did her feelings—then or now—even matter? Like the old song said, sometimes love's just not enough.

I loved you, too.

His response was quick. She wanted to hit FaceTime, to see him in real time, to judge his expression. Was his admission simply acknowledging the past or was he, like Danielle, springboarding from the old emotions to new ones?

It killed her that the only way to find out was to trust him. It killed her to know that she couldn't.

Now what? Knox stared at his phone, both thrilled and appalled that he and Danielle were batting the L-word around again. Sure, they were using the past tense, but it must mean more than that, right? Why else dredge up the old feelings? For his part, he'd done his best to ignore them, especially the first few years in the Corps. But now that he'd seen her again, tasted her again, he couldn't imagine how he'd ever walked away in the first place.

Stupidity. It was the best answer he could give. It was the only answer he had. Well, that wasn't true. Stupidity and pride and his mom cheering him on every step he took away from Miami Beach and Danielle Morrow. Wouldn't it be funny if he moved to Atlanta *with* Danielle? His mom would keel over. His mom. He still couldn't get over what she'd said to Danielle, how those words still haunted Danielle—and now him. Lucky? They hadn't been lucky.

How different would his years in the service have been if he'd known Danielle was at home waiting for him? Or if she'd moved with him from base to base? If they'd had kids? Would he have re-upped as many times? It was too late to think about those things, to wallow in regret. What was done was done.

His phone dinged, and his heart pounded in response. Would she move from the past tense to the present? Was this how dating worked now? Everything done by text? It was both safer and scarier at the same time. He wished he could see her face. He wished she'd come home with him, and they could've had their own private burlesque show in his bedroom.

But she hadn't, and the notification wasn't a text. It was a photo of the puppies, all snuggled against her side. He could see the curve of her waist and the slight rise of her belly in the photo.

Ding. Good night.

Sleep well, he texted back, strangely deflated. He'd thought they were working up to something, but like so many things with Danielle, he had no idea what was actually going on. *See you tomorrow.*

She didn't reassure him with so much as a thumbs-up. He stared at his phone for a long time, and he woke up with it still in his hand.

The Coffee Pot Spot probably wasn't the best place to fill out college applications, but she didn't actually expect to finish them today anyway. She was only using the soul-sucking activity as a way to kill time until Knox showed up. The coffee shop was loud and crowded, and she was on her second round of the Beatles covers playlist blasting down from the speakers in the ceiling. But there was coffee and a definitive lack of puppies being too adorable to concentrate, so Danielle took a long sip of her latte and read the directions one more time.

High-school transcripts? She knew it wasn't an unreasonable demand for a college to make, but humiliation swamped her nonetheless. She was thirty-three years old. What was she thinking, applying to the local community college? The first time she'd applied to colleges, her high school had taken care of anything. It was so long ago, and there'd been a counselor to help her.

Even if she did somehow get in—an outcome she doubted not because she thought an open-access school would reject her but because she wasn't sure she'd ever correctly complete the online application—she'd be over a decade older than her classmates. She'd be the old lady.

If she waited, she'd be even older. And homeless. If her dad was the only landlord who'd tolerate her running a rescue on his property, then she had to earn the right to stay. She needed an acceptance letter in less than two weeks. There was only one way to get it.

She took a deep breath and opened up a new browser window. Her high school had to have some kind of website, right? If nineteen-year-olds could figure this out, so could she. A handful of clicks and a few bucks later, her transcripts were on the way. Feeling quite accomplished, she ordered a second latte, this time with mocha because she deserved it, and moved on to the next session.

Personal essay. God, she'd worked so hard on her first one, back in high school. It'd been a thing of beauty, filled with all her passion and focus. The years working at her dad's clinic, the summer she'd interned at the wildlife sanctuary, her lifelong, unwavering goal to become a veterinarian.

The latte arrived, via a gangly but friendly young man who was smart enough to set the drink down out of the spill range of her computer, and Danielle savored the dark sweetness. Hopefully, the additional caffeine would get a few extra brain cells firing. What happened to the girl she used to be? Her life didn't lack passion and focus, as her father had implied. Homestretch was everything to her. Even now, she missed the comfort of a large dog leaning on her leg.

The difference was ambition, she supposed. After the miscarriage, the diagnosis, the rounds of unsuccessful attempts to control her condition, her focus shifted inward. Understandably so, she reminded herself. She'd been right to delay college admission. What kind of a roommate would she have been, crying all the time? What kind of student would she have been, too depressed to get out of bed for days at a time? No, she'd done the right thing. She had nothing to be ashamed of. If anything, she should be proud. She could've stayed that girl forever, but then Florida outlawed greyhound racing and she'd found a new passion—her greyhounds.

That sounded like it could be a personal essay. Danielle typed the word *ambition* at the top of her page and jotted down a few notes. Took a couple sips of latte. Checked her phone, which she had on silent.

Busy? Knox's text asked. Ready for that coffee?

Danielle gulped down more caffeine. They hadn't talked, really talked, since the bridal shower. That should've been the end. But distance plus burlesque lessons plus their late night texts equaled an unsolved, and possibly unsolvable, problem. Could she be with Knox, even for a short while, to explore their undeniable attraction without wanting too much from him? They weren't kids anymore. The thirties were not about messing around. Knox needed someone he could spend his life with, and she, well, she was damaged goods. Literally missing pieces of herself. When he looked at her like he had last night—as if she wasn't merely a snack but an entire buffet, and he was a starving man—she felt whole in a way she hadn't since she was eighteen. What if she told him, and he didn't leave? Could she take the risk? She shouldn't hope, but hope swelled in her anyway, a balloon without a tether threatening to pull her too high.

Her hand shook as she opened up her phone. The extra caffeine, no doubt.

Sure. She could waffle about college-essay topics later. *Already at the Coffee Pot Spot.*

Be there in a few. Wait for me?

Danielle's pulse sped so abruptly that it had to be the caffeine hitting her system. Wasn't that her problem? Always waiting for him? Her fingers hovered over the keys, typed: *Sure.*

A happy face? Danielle stared at the screen for a long time. Of all the strange things between her and Knox the last few weeks, the happy face might be the strangest. She sent one back to him so he could enjoy the weirdness. They were not happy-face people.

In her own texts, Danielle preferred to use the dogs or the occasional holiday emoji. What was next? The blowing-kisses face? She shook her head at the absurdity.

A few terrible paragraphs of her personal statement later, Knox slid into the chair across the round table from her.

"How're the puppies? Did they get a good night's sleep?" His smile took over his face, all those teeth and, God help her, dimpled groove lines.

Danielle took the last gulp of her latte. Puppies she could talk about for days. "Great. Lively. Adorable. Honestly? It's hard to be away from them."

"I can imagine." Knox's eyes searched her face. For what? She wasn't sure. She attempted to project cool competence, a cautious friendliness. Not a desperate longing and wish to launch herself across the table at him. How many more nights might they have had together if she hadn't pushed him away so soon?

The waiter showed up and Knox ordered an Americano. "For you?"

She held her hand over the top of her empty mug. "Better cut me off. I may not sleep tonight as it is."

"Decaf?" The gangly waiter's Adam's apple bobbed on the word.

"God forbid." Danielle laughed at how she and Knox said the same thing at the same time.

"Jinx," Knox said before she could. "Now you owe me a kiss."

Danielle felt the flush rise on her skin, so she busied herself with saving the document on her laptop to cover the memories flooding her mind.

———————

Homecoming banners decorated the high-school hallways, and for the first time in three years, Danielle was excited about it—all of it. The game, where she'd get to watch her boyfriend play. The dance, where she'd get to dance with her boyfriend. The drive home, where she'd get to make out with her boyfriend. Yeah, Danielle was into the whole boyfriend thing. *My boyfriend.* It'd been three weeks since their first kiss, and she still wasn't used to the words. She whispered them to herself, holding her calculus textbook against her chest while trying to remember her Spanish vocabulary words for the quiz she had right before lunch.

"Watch it!" Angela Bowers plowed into Danielle, a full body slam that sent Danielle to the floor in a sprawl of limbs and scattered papers from her notebook.

"Sorry, I—"

"You have nothing to be sorry for." Suddenly, Knox was there, looming over her in all his tallness and winning-football-team swagger. He dropped into a squat to help her gather her things. "Angela's just—"

"Your ex." Danielle knew more about Knox's past than he knew about hers. She didn't hold it against him. Between his family and his athletic prowess, he was often the subject of gossip. Between her studies and her time at her dad's clinic, she was not. It was how things were.

Knox snorted and swiped a hand through his already tousled hair. "She's not quite over it yet."

"And are you? Over it?"

His blue eyes collided with her brown ones. "Of course I am. I would never have asked you out if I still had a thing for someone else."

Danielle's breath rushed from her lungs, and she closed her eyes. Knox really did say the sweetest things sometimes.

"Now my thing is all for you." Knox lowered his voice so only she could hear him.

Danielle's eyes popped open, and a blush crept up her neck. She didn't mean to eye his crotch; she really didn't. But she did, and he caught her.

His cheeks flamed brighter than hers. "That's not what I meant."

A strangled giggle escaped her. He watched her warily, then joined in with a chuckle. "Although I suppose that interpretation isn't entirely inaccurate."

She laughed harder, dropping her textbook in the process, then laughing more when they bumped heads trying to grab it at the same time.

"Knox—"

"Danielle—"

"I'm crazy about you." The words came out at the same time, both of them a little breathless from laughter.

"Jinx," they said together, then "Jinx" again and again until Danielle was laughing too hard to keep up, and Knox got in a "Jinx" without her.

"Finally." Knox tipped her head up toward him with a finger under her chin. "Whoever wins a jinx gets a kiss. You know those are the rules, right?"

Danielle'd never heard any such thing, but she nodded solemnly. "Right."

His lips brushed hers lightly, a kiss appropriate for being in public. But Danielle was seized by a feeling she'd never had before, so bright and strong it felt like her chest might crack open from the pressure of it. So she used both her hands to pull him down toward her, stepped into his body, and made the kiss hers. Students streamed around them on their way to class, but Danielle wouldn't break the kiss. The bell rang, and still they were kissing.

"Break it up." A teacher leaned out her classroom door. "And get to class, you two."

Danielle stood in the hallway, feeling like the walls were spinning. She kept her hand on the center of Knox's chest, his heartbeat under her palm. His breath came quick and hard, and for a moment, she thought they both swayed on their feet. Maybe it was a lack of oxygen. That had been one long kiss. Maybe it was the disorientation of moving from their own private world and back into school mode. Or maybe it was love.

Maybe it *was* love. Danielle wasn't sure. She'd never felt it before. But what else could it be?

"Danielle—"

"Knox—"

"I love you."

Knox's hand cupped her face, his thumb tracing her bottom lip like he was hypnotized.

"Jinx," Danielle said, leaning into his touch. "You owe me a kiss."

Knox dropped his forehead against hers. "Dani, my love, let's get out of here."

And that was the first time, but not the last, that Danielle skipped class.

———————

Now, fifteen years later in the coffee shop, with a smiling Knox sitting across from her, Danielle couldn't string two words together to save her life. *Jinx* had been their code word for "I love you," a shortcut when they were in public, a demand for a kiss, an inside joke not because it was funny but because it was theirs.

"Jinx?" Danielle stuttered the word, then tried to cover by gulping her latte, but every last sip of it was gone.

"Yeah, jinx." Knox's gaze pinned her in place. "Our jinx. Remember?"

Like she could forget. The tremble started in her belly but moved quickly to her limbs. The hell with being careful; the hell with anything that kept them from being together even one more minute. She reached a hand across the table, and he caught it in his. "Come here."

Knox half stood, and she tugged on their joined hands. He leaned across the table until their mouths were a breath apart.

"Jinx," she whispered and closed the distance, heart hammering like she was eighteen years old again, until their lips touched. That same urgency from so long ago overtook her, and she grabbed onto the back of his head with her free hand. "Knox, let's get out of here."

"Thank God I live nearby." Knox pulled her to her feet and threw money on the table.

She followed him out the door, the jangle of the door less jangly than her nerves. They stopped at her car, and Danielle found herself pressed against the driver's door. "Five minutes, okay? That's how long it should take to get to my place."

"See you in five." Danielle slid into her car, jumping when Knox tapped on the window. She rolled it down. "Yes."

He leaned in and kissed her again. "Jinx."

"But I didn't say anything."

"Jinx, jinx, jinx. Now drive, woman. I'm right behind you."

Danielle laughed and gunned the engine. The material for her personal essay was certainly getting a lot more interesting now.

CHAPTER 28

CHECK YOUR EMAIL. DANIELLE GROANED AND FLIPPED HER phone facedown. Couldn't she ignore the outside world for one more day? The phone vibrated, and Danielle debated stuffing it under her pillow to suffocate it.

"Who is it?" Knox's arm snaked over her waist and pulled her flush against him. She loved how warm he was, even naked, how the heat radiated off him like her own personal furnace. She snuggled into him, squinting her eyes against the sun slanting in through her cottage window. One bonus of being fired was that she could sleep in as late as she wanted. And boy had she wanted to this week.

"Don't know. Don't care." She tipped her chin back, and Knox obligingly nuzzled into her neck. The hand on her belly slid upward, and Danielle hummed her approval for starting her fourth day in a row with Knox covering her in kisses.

"That's my Dani," Knox whispered into her neck. "Cold, heartless. Uncaring. You're famous for it, really, that no-can-do attitude of yours."

"Hey." Danielle maneuvered herself around to face him. "You really want me to check my phone now?" She trailed her finger down the center of his chest, then lower. And lower.

Knox's nostrils flared, and his eyes got a little unfocused when she circled her fingers around him in one long, slow stroke.

"Well?" She paused at the top of the caress. "Should I stop to read my texts?"

"Maybe not. Right. Now." His words came out in short pants of breath.

"Good answer. Guess what you win?" She ducked her head under her paisley comforter and made him moan.

The text was from Sydney. Danielle had missed morning coffee again. She couldn't help it if staying in bed had suddenly become a lot more alluring. Knox did eventually dress and head over to the Dorothy. Now that the last unit was coming together, the brothers seemed in a hurry to get all the finishing touches done. Danielle sleepwalked through her morning routine, letting out Flurry and Luna, then feeding the puppies and changing the cedar chips in their playpen. Sweet Pea immediately plopped his head in the water bowl, apparently not traumatized by his near-drowning experience from exactly the same thing only a few weeks ago.

Once she had her tea brewed, Danielle checked her phone. The number of emails was higher than usual, so she tracked down her laptop where she'd left it in the puppy room and opened it up outside on one of the poolside lounge chairs.

"What is this?" Danielle clicked on the first email. Adoption application. So was the second email and third. She scrolled down the list. By her count, there were over twenty adoption applications filling her inbox.

She pulled out her phone to text Sydney back. *What is going on?*

Check the comments section on the YT channel.

Danielle opened up the Homestretch YouTube channel where Sydney had posted three videos of the puppies. They each had over a thousand likes. So many comments! A brief skim showed that people really loved the puppies. Sydney had linked to the Homestretch website, and people in the comments claimed to have already filled out an application. Based on the volume in her inbox, they weren't lying.

Are the puppies YouTube famous?!

It would take a couple hundred thousand more views for that to be true, but it's a strong start. Are they really filling out the adoption apps?

Danielle read through the first app, a couple in Gainesville who wanted to come down and meet the puppies. *They really are*, she texted back.

Sydney's response was an incomprehensible string of emojis, but Danielle got the general gist—excitement.

Thank you. Danielle sipped her tea, a bit stunned. She'd never had more applications than dogs available for adoption before, and all it had taken was a couple of videos. She scrolled through her email again, looking for any responses to the résumés she'd been sending out. Nothing. Maybe she needed to post cute videos of herself to get people to hire her.

Or maybe she already had a job. She'd told Sydney she'd never had time to figure out all the social media and website stuff. She'd been focused on the dogs and her work at the clinic, but she had lots of time now. If this little bit of effort yielded such an enthusiastic response, what would happen to Homestretch if she went full-time with it?

She placed her mug of tea on the table beside the lounge chair and got to googling. Luna and Flurry stretched out on the concrete pool deck on either side of her. A full hour passed while she researched and researched some more. Applied to attend a rescue alliance fair in Orlando. Downloaded forms. Watched a few tutorials.

"I can do this," she told the dogs. "It doesn't have to be a money-losing hobby. It can be a money-losing business!"

Luna perked an ear, and Flurry let out a sigh. Neither seemed all that impressed with her new plan.

"What business?" Her dad's shadow blocked the sun, casting a shadow over her laptop screen.

Danielle jackknifed into a seated position. "I think I figured out what I can do!"

Her dad rubbed a palm over his bald head and took a seat on the lounge chair on the other side of the small table. "I haven't seen you this excited in a long time. Tell me."

She showed him the YouTube channel, the adoption applications, a lot of her research, ending with, "It's not a nine-to-five job, but I think it could work."

"You've never been a nine-to-five person." Dr. Morrow crossed an ankle on his knee and leaned forward. "It makes sense for you is what I'm saying. But what about school?"

Danielle's excitement deflated like a balloon three days after the birthday party. "About that." She turned her computer toward him. "There's an email from the community college. I've been afraid to open it."

"It's not like they can turn you down."

Intellectually, she knew he was right. Emotionally, it still felt like a lot to open that particular email. "But they can give me more paperwork."

"Is it even paperwork if it's all online?" Her dad winked at her. "Open it, pumpkin. Today seems like a day for good news."

She closed her eyes and clicked on the email. "What does it say?"

"Bad news, I'm afraid." Her dad's jolly tone belied his actual words.

Her eyes popped open. "What is it?"

"You're going to have to register for classes, and that means more paperwork." He turned the screen toward her. "How about starting with one class to see how it goes? You don't want to take on too much while you're scaling up your rescue work."

"Seriously?" It was a day for miracles, it seemed. She couldn't wait to tell Knox.

"I'm proud of you, pumpkin." Her dad stood and kissed the top of her head. "I really need to get to the clinic. I'm already late."

Could she squeeze in one more miracle? "Daddy?"

"Yes?" His response was cautious, probably because she sounded like her ten-year-old self begging to stay up a few hours past bedtime.

"No one is going to rent to me while I have ten dogs." She

opened one of her rental rejections to show him as proof. "Now that I have all these adoption applications to sort through, check references, interview—that sort of thing—do you think I could get an eviction extension? At least until the puppies are old enough to go to their new homes? I promise to look for my own place after that."

A wide smile took over Dr. Morrow's face. "Of course. That sounds quite reasonable." He kissed her head again and walked to the main house whistling.

"I like Sherry!" she called after him, feeling magnanimous. He raised his hand and wiggled his fingers at her. Danielle went back to work. The dogs settled in for a long wait.

———

Knox stood back to admire the new bathroom. It still needed work—like tiles and, oh yeah, fixtures. His part, though, was done. The room had been taken down to the studs, the plumbers had done their part, and Knox had put in the new walls. It was the first time he'd done it on his own with only occasional supervision from Mendo, the construction manager, and Lance.

"It's not exactly ready to show." Caleb studied the small room like he was cramming for a test. "I can't believe we're on the last unit. It's been a crazy project, hasn't it?"

Knox grunted. He wasn't going to get all emotional about a building, even if that building had brought his brothers back into his life. It was a moment in time, and like every other moment, it would end. His brain flashed to Danielle wrapped in her comforter, staring up at him with her cheeks flushed from her most recent orgasm. Except that moment—that moment he intended to draw out for as long as possible.

Lance crammed himself into a bathroom meant for one, possibly two people, at a time. "Little crowded, huh? Maybe we should've taken out more walls. Want to start over, guys? I'm sure Adam could draw us up some new plans in no time."

Caleb groaned. "Absolutely not. I'm ready for this to be done. If I have to go to one more zoning meeting…"

"Did I hear someone take my name in vain?" Adam crowded into the small room, and Knox started to feel like one of those clowns in a VW Bug whirling around a circus tent at full speed. Adam stood a good half foot taller than the three brothers, which gave him an excellent view of the ceiling when he craned his neck. "Is that a leak?"

"Son of a—" Lance planted his fists on his hips and looked straight up.

"Gotcha!" Adam laughed. "Everything's perfect. Like I'd design a leaking building."

"Anything can happen in an old building," Caleb said, his tone resigned. He'd be living in the Dorothy for the foreseeable future, so all upcoming issues would be his to handle.

"Speaking of." Knox stepped into the hallway, a clown escaping the car, and motioned Adam to follow him. "Can you take a look at my back deck? I'm hoping a few new boards will fix it, but I'm afraid it might be structural."

"Probably is." Adam ran his finger down the new trim on the door. "You need to learn an important lesson about homeownership. Whatever the worst-case scenario is? That's the answer. However much money you think it's going to cost? Multiply that by three, and you'll probably still be lowballing it." He laughed at his own joke.

"So you'll take a look?" Knox didn't laugh. Adam was no stand-up comedian, and the truth of what he was saying hit a little too close to home. Still, he wanted to do as much as he could before he left to increase the resale value when he put it on the market.

Adam checked the time on his phone. "I've got a few minutes. Want to head across the street?"

Knox answered by leading the way out. Adam followed, and Caleb caught up with them.

"Thought you were taking that job in Atlanta after the wedding."

Knox's jaw clenched. He still owed Morales a text with all the details of his move, but the details were more complicated now. There was Sarge to consider. His leg and how it didn't seem to be getting better no matter how many PT exercises he forced himself to do every day. And Danielle. Would she pick up everything to live in Atlanta? He couldn't imagine her leaving her dad, Homestretch, her morning coffee club at Fur Haven. Could he even ask that of her? On the other hand, she was looking to move, to find a new job. Maybe now was the perfect time to ask her.

Caleb stopped, effectively blocking Knox from continuing down the hallway. "Unless you're having second thoughts?"

Nosy little brothers. "Nothing has changed." Except everything had. He still had some time to figure it out. Caleb's wedding was in a couple of days, and the finishing work on the last unit would be done a few weeks later. Would that be enough time to get Danielle on board with Atlanta? How bad could a ten-hour drive with eleven dogs possibly be?

"Oh yeah." A few minutes later, after Sarge had checked everyone out and collected a round of petting, Adam surveyed Knox's back deck with a grimace. "Whole thing's rotting. Better to rip it out and start over."

"Before or after you sell it?" Like the annoying little brother he was, Caleb had trailed after them. Sarge stood at his side, levering Caleb's hand for more pats.

"Maybe I'll keep it. As an investment. You know, wait until the market's better." Knox settled into the idea. If he didn't sell, he could come back anytime. He hated to admit it, but he'd miss Caleb and Lance in a way he never would've believed when he'd taken off for the Marines all those years ago. Back then, they'd been reluctant relatives, forced together by Caleb's mom and their dad's negligent attentions. Would he have ever enlisted if he'd had the kind of connection back then that he had with them now? No sense in rewriting history. Lots of mistakes had been made, leaving Danielle his biggest regret, but not knowing his brothers now a close second. The only thing he could control was his future, and he'd promised Morales his future would be in Atlanta. That didn't mean he couldn't have a place on the Beach, too, did it? No, it did not.

Feeling pleased with his new idea, he gave a curt nod to Adam. "Tell me what I have to do."

Adam rubbed his palms together. "There's an idea I've been wanting to try."

"Let's do it." Knox crossed his arms over his chest. "I trust you." He didn't know who was more surprised by the words, him or Adam, but they were true. Sometime in the past year of working together, Knox had gotten attached to the tall guy always poking his nose in the various projects with his predictions of gloom and doom. Knox liked that about him. Caleb and Lance could be painfully optimistic, but Adam told it like it was. A realist. He would've made a good Marine.

"It's going to be expensive," Adam warned, eyes already darting around the yard like he was taking mental measurements.

"What a surprise." Knox clicked his tongue for Sarge to join him.

"He's good for it." Caleb led the way back inside. "Look at all the money he's saving by not having furniture."

"Shut it," Knox grumbled, embarrassed for the first time by his minimal possessions. He'd been spending more time at Danielle's in the past week, and with the upcoming move, it hadn't seemed important to purchase couches and dining room tables and whatever else rooms needed to look lived in. If it were his home away from home, though, Danielle would undoubtedly at least want a sofa to sit on.

CHAPTER 29

Fur Haven Dog Park was transformed. White pillars surrounded the park, some kind of gauzy fabric billowing in the ocean breeze. A gazebo stood at the east end of the rooftop park, the Atlantic Ocean a glittering blue jewel in the distance. Nets of tiny lights illuminated the palm tree trunks, and a long, white carpet made from some kind of fabric that sparkled in the sun ran from the elevator to the gazebo. Hundreds of chairs were arranged, facing east, and freestanding flower arrangements dotted the fairy-tale landscape.

It was, perhaps, the girliest thing Knox had ever seen. He didn't hate it. He did hate the gray suit that in spite of several fittings still managed to make his underarms itch. Could be worse. Could be itchy in the crotch. Could be itchy in the crotch in the Middle East. At least here he had his brothers next to him, and although Lance didn't say anything, he could tell Lance was itchy, too. The clues were in the way he shifted his arms, like he was looking for a comfortable position.

"It's something alright," Lance drawled in his slow way.

Caleb clapped both brothers on the back. "Carrie and Sydney really outdid themselves. Riley and I couldn't be happier."

"Isn't it bad luck to see the venue before the wedding or something?" Knox felt weird standing on the rooftop, all dressed up with only his brothers for company. The ceremony was still hours away, like six hours away. He wasn't even sure why Caleb had insisted on meeting them here, insisted that they wear their matching gray suits. Like uniforms, Knox had thought at the last fitting and hadn't hated the idea of belonging to a unit of brothers, his actual brothers.

He'd been thinking a lot these past few days about family and the future. Perhaps it was waking up with Danielle every morning, whether it was at his house or hers. He'd even joined Danielle two days ago when she met up with the morning coffee gang at Fur Haven. He was starting to see how his life could be, if he let it. If Danielle would agree. He'd have to ask her about Atlanta soon, but he was enjoying the present too much to be overly worried about what came next. He was easily distracted by Danielle's kisses, her teasing glances, the way she'd hum a bar of that Etta James song and crook her finger at him. They had a lot of lost time to make up for, and he didn't want to waste any of it making her uncomfortable.

"I have a limo waiting for us." Caleb shifted, rocking back on his heels.

Knox's suspicions rose. "To whisk you and Riley off on your honeymoon?"

"Eventually." Caleb rolled his neck. "But first, I have a huge favor to ask the both of you."

Dread pricked the skin along Knox's spine. "What kind of favor?"

"I want to go see Dad."

"Our dad?" Lance cracked out an incredulous laugh. "You're kidding, right?"

Caleb grimaced. "Afraid not. If we leave now, we'll be back in time. But we need to leave now."

"I didn't ever see him before he was in prison. Why would I go see him now?" Knox was proud of his clean break. When he thought about family, Robert Donovan never entered his mind. The break was complete, as far as he was concerned, happening long before the investigation, trial, and incarceration.

"I know." Caleb landed a heavy hand on Knox's shoulder. "But it feels like something I need to do. Settle this. Let go of it. So Riley and I have a clear start, you know?"

"Sure. Fine." Lance's foot bounced on the ground to an invisible beat. "What I don't understand is why we have to go with you."

"Exactly." Knox was glad at least one of his brothers hadn't lost his damn mind.

"Knox. Lance." Caleb looked each of them in the eyes. "You're my best men. My brothers. I'm asking you to do this for me, with me. Today."

Caleb'd always been a smooth talker, and Knox saw it working on Lance.

"Okay." Lance swallowed. "I'm in. At least it'll get your mom off my back."

"Why?" Knox barked, unwittingly slipping into Gunny mode.

"The truth?" Caleb shoved his hands in his pockets and rocked forward and back on his heels. "I don't want to go alone. I know Mom made you fill out all the visitation paperwork, so I figured why not take my brothers with me? I sent our names in a few days ago to set up a visit today. We've been okayed, but we have to leave now so I don't miss my own wedding."

Knox looked at Caleb, his little brother. The one raised by their father, always the golden child. Until he wasn't. Until he made the break that he and Lance had made at much earlier ages. How much more difficult must this be for Caleb? The son who thought he'd follow in his father's footsteps until those footsteps led right to federal prison?

Knox nodded, slowly. Deliberately. He didn't want to go, would be fine if he never saw his father again. But one thing he knew for sure. You didn't let a brother go into battle alone.

"I'm in."

―――――――

Knox wished he were more surprised by how prison looked, but he'd seen enough movies and TV shows over the years that it looked like another movie set to him—maybe a little grittier and definitely a lot smellier. Neither the large nor small screen quite captured the mixture of industrial chemical cleaners and human sweat with a hint of rage and despair. It was the same with war zones. Hollywood could show a hundred casualties of war and get every detail right, but the real thing felt different. Smelled different. Knox was good at blocking the memories that wanted to rise to the surface, replacing them with two-dimensional representations. It was a learned coping mechanism that came in handy as he followed his brothers into the room where they'd see their father.

Lance and Caleb had seen their dad prior to his incarceration, but Knox's last memory of him was the day he'd informed their father he was enlisting.

"You want to die in some hellhole halfway across the world?" his dad had spit out, rage making his voice lower and harsher. It would've been better if he'd yelled, but they were at his club, eating Sunday brunch overlooking the eighteenth hole. He tugged on his checked silk tie as if it were choking him.

Knox swallowed his bite of French toast, the house special infused with orange and hibiscus, served with a small side of maple syrup and sprinkled with powdered sugar. The powdered sugar stuck to the roof of his mouth, made his tongue thick. At least, that was what he told himself when he was slow to respond.

"I want to serve my country," he'd said, but of course it was more than that. He wanted to be a different man, a man like his football coach, a former Marine and Gulf War veteran. A good man. An honorable man. A man who wouldn't get a girl knocked up and ruin her life before it'd even really begun. A man the exact opposite of his father. Danielle's miscarriage had been his wake-up call. Wanting to be different from Robert Donovan wasn't enough. He needed something drastic that would force him to change his ways. That would take him far away from Danielle and the temptation her soft body offered him. He'd talked to Coach Suarez, and Coach personally escorted him to the recruiting office. He'd signed papers that day. This conversation with his father was a formality. That was what he should've said.

Instead, he'd stood, cloth napkin dropping to the floor, and walked out.

Today, he hung back as Caleb and Lance cautiously greeted their father, taking seats in the two metal chairs across the small table from Robert. He wasn't handcuffed, but an armed guard stood in the doorway, the position Knox would've preferred. Knox leaned against the cold wall, glad there wasn't a chair for him. He didn't really belong here. He was backup.

But he wasn't invisible. Robert's dry comment was "So you're still alive. That's good to know."

Knox gave him the ten-mile stare in reply.

Lance covered a laugh by coughing into his hand. "Look, Dad, we can't stay long. Caleb's getting married today."

"Thank God." Robert leaned forward on his elbows. "For a minute, I thought my sons had formed a boy band."

Lance didn't hide his laugh this time. "No, these monkey suits are purely Caleb's idea."

"Not purely." Caleb was trying to smile, but it didn't quite reach his eyes. "Riley and I are getting married this afternoon."

"What're you doing here then?" Robert's lip curled in a familiar sneer. "It's not like I was invited."

"You couldn't have come anyway." Lance had no trouble giving their dad hell. Knox envied him. His thoughts weren't coming in words, more like waves of color, reds and oranges, which he was pretty sure meant he was angry. He locked down his muscles and stood at attention. He just had to get through it, for Caleb's sake.

"You didn't give me a chance to find out, did you?" Robert pushed his graying hair back with one hand. "Maybe a judge would've taken pity on me. Given me a release to attend the ceremony."

"I didn't want you there." Caleb had stopped trying to smile, his face now as stone cold as their father's. "But I did want to see you. Mom's been on me to visit, says you have something to say to me. Well, I don't want to start my life with Riley with that hanging over my head. So out with it. What do you want to say so badly that I had to come all the way out here to hear it?"

Robert pushed back in his chair, putting distance between him and the table, between him and his sons. He looked at them. The three of them looked back.

"I'm sorry." The words escaped Robert in a rush. "To all of you." He pushed at his thinning hair, leaning back with his hands behind his head. "I thought I'd apologize one at a time, but seeing as you've banded together, I'll do it all at once. I'm sorry, okay?"

"Sorry for what?" Caleb's expression didn't change, not even to blink.

"For this." Robert waved his hand, encompassing the room, the prison, perhaps even the whole situation. "I didn't mean for it to end up like this."

"You're sorry about how it ended?" Caleb's voice was as tight as his lips. "Not the rest?"

"The rest of what?"

"Enough." Lance pushed his chair back and lurched to his feet. "It's no surprise he's sorry he got caught. What criminal isn't?" He turned his anger on Robert. "If that's all you've got for us, we wasted a drive. Come on, Caleb." Lance brushed past the guard and disappeared into the echoing hallway.

But Caleb didn't move, so Knox stayed sentinel on the back wall. The air was charged, like something was about to go down. Knox's fingers flexed for the rifle that wasn't there.

Caleb planted his palms on the steel table and stared across at their father. "Is that all?"

Robert stood and paced to the corner and back. "I'm sorry I mixed you up in it, Caleb. I almost screwed up your life."

"Almost?" Caleb choked out.

Robert plunked back into his chair. "Fine. I screwed up. I screwed you up. Probably your brothers, too. And I'm sorry." He let out a long breath. "I really am. You have to believe me."

Caleb's chair screeched against the concrete floor as he pushed back. "I do." Caleb turned and grinned at Knox. "See how good I am at those words? Always thought Riley'd be on the receiving end, though."

Knox's lips twitched, but he held back the grin. "I won't tell her she wasn't the first."

"Appreciate it." Caleb laughed, apparently letting go of the tension that had gripped him moments before. He circled the table and clapped their dad on the shoulder. "Thanks. Mom was right. It is cathartic."

"So you'll be back." Robert looked up at him with hope in his eyes.

Caleb blinked suddenly wet-looking eyes. "I don't know. I'll think about it."

"You do that." Robert covered Caleb's fingers on his shoulders with his own. "It was good to see you. Maybe someday you'll bring this Riley to meet me."

"Maybe." Caleb peeled his hand away. "I'll have Mom send you some pictures from today."

Robert smiled. "I'd like that."

Caleb nodded, swallowing hard enough that his Adam's apple bobbed sharply. He exited the room without looking back.

Knox could've followed him, but he didn't.

Robert raised both eyebrows. "Did you want something?"

Knox didn't know where the urge came from, but he crossed the room in quick strides. Robert leapt to his feet, like he didn't want to be taken by surprise. Knox wrapped his arms around the older man's shoulders, giving him a distant but sincere hug. Robert patted Knox's back, hesitation apparent in the tense lines of his body.

Knox stepped back quickly. "It's good to see you, old man."

"Hey, who are you calling old?" Robert chuckled, looking a bit stunned by the turn of events.

Knox smiled. "What're you gonna do about it?"

"Nothing, you big brute. Geez, you really bulked up, huh?"

Knox raised a shoulder in response. "And I know over twenty ways to kill someone with my bare hands." He held his hands out in front of him like they weren't part of him.

"Looks good on you, Knox." Robert shook his head. "But I'm glad you're home."

Strangely, in this bare-walled prison across from the father he'd vilified but who was really just an aging man who missed his family, Knox was glad he was home, too. It hit him, then, that Atlanta wouldn't feel like this, no matter how much he owed Morales. But a commitment was a commitment, and he'd only be a ten-hour drive away.

"I'll be back." Knox pushed the chairs Caleb and Lance sat in under the table.

"To torment me?" Robert cracked a smile.

"Why else?" Knox took another second to take stock of the man his father had become. A bit soft around the middle. A lot sorry about how things turned out. He'd been mad at his father for so long he almost didn't recognize the new feeling. It wasn't exactly pity, but something else. Something that felt a lot like forgiveness.

Knox caught up with Caleb and Lance in the hallway. A guard led them to the exit.

"What was that about?" Lance asked.

Knox raised a shoulder. "I couldn't tell you, but it sure felt good."

"You're crazy, you know that, right?" Lance shook his head. "Let's get this guy back to the Beach. Wedding bells are ringing."

"There aren't going to be bells." Caleb held the door for Lance and Knox.

"Wedding. Bells. Are. Ringing." Lance punched Caleb's arm as he passed.

Knox's cheeks were sore. He touched them with his fingers and realized it was from smiling too wide. He waited until Caleb and Lance took the lead out to the parking lot, falling into his preferred position of bringing up the rear. Covering the exit. Keeping his eyes on his team. Caleb punched Lance back, but Lance dodged with a laugh. Knox let his cheeks ache. He didn't know if he'd trust this much happiness if it didn't hurt a little.

CHAPTER 30

BY PROCESS OF ELIMINATION—THE ELIMINATING FACTOR being that everyone else, including LouLou the poodle, was in the wedding party—Danielle ended up in charge of Pops, Grandpa William's arthritic greyhound. Danielle had arrived early to get her instructions, an ironic twist because Grandpa William had adopted Pops from her. But Danielle respectfully nodded her head while Grandpa William explained about keeping a firm hold on the leash because Pops would want to join the wedding party up front, but Riley and Caleb were insistent that LouLou be the only canine star of the wedding show. Grandpa William had then handed over a Coach travel bag of dog toys, treats, collapsible water bowl, and bottles of both filtered and sparkling water.

"He likes his bubblies." Grandpa William had winked at her when she'd raised an eyebrow at the Perrier.

"Noted." Danielle had stuffed the bottle back in the bag and taken Pops' leash in her hand. "Pops and I will be fine. My father is a vet, you know." She'd felt a twinge of something, a bit of wrongness in the wording. She should be able to say *she* was the veterinarian. One class at a time. She would be doing her first one online, a composition prerequisite, while she sorted out the legalities of turning Homestretch into a fully functioning nonprofit endeavor. She might even take some business classes on her way to her veterinary degree.

"Pops likes you. That's what's important." Grandpa William had spoken some gibberish about being a good dog to Pops and disappeared into the elevator, leaving Danielle alone on the rooftop dog park turned wedding venue.

She wasn't exactly alone. Black-suited employees hustled,

setting up chairs and constructing the gazebo where Riley and Caleb would say their vows. Florists made several trips up and down the elevator, arms and carts overflowing with every kind of flower that came in pink. It looked chaotic, but when they were done, Danielle had to admire how the groupings of flowers did define the spaces.

For her part, she kept Pops to the back, near the wall. He was content to sniff every blade of grass he encountered, a process that would keep him occupied well past the wedding if she let him. Knox and his brothers had appeared for a few moments, but then disappeared just as quickly. Knox hadn't even noticed her in the corner on dog duty, which was probably for the best. The way the light-gray suit outlined the smooth flex of muscle under the fabric was enough to keep her speechless. At some point, her hormones had to calm down, right? But so far, the more time she spent with Knox, the more she craved him.

She didn't regret her to-hell-with-it decision, but she did fear what came next. She knew Knox wanted to talk about it. She also knew she wasn't ready. She didn't want to tell him, didn't want to see the disappointment on his face or hear false words of reassurance. And she for sure didn't want to think about what him walking away again would do to her. The longer she kept her mouth shut, the more memories she could collect before it was all over, this time for good.

She brushed at the semiformal cocktail dress she was recycling from attending Bridget's wedding last year. The neck revealed enough cleavage to feel sexy, and the shimmery bronze material lightened her eyes and inspired her to wear the eye shadow with a bit of sparkle in it. She hadn't been too sure exactly what dog sitting during a wedding ceremony would entail, so she'd considered wearing more practical flats. Instead, she couldn't resist the ridiculously high heels she'd bought with the dress. The hem hit an inch above her knees, and the heels made her calves look amazing.

Besides, how many opportunities did a dog-rescue expert and soon-to-be part-time student get to dress up? Not many.

So far, her decision wasn't disastrous. Her feet were a little achy from standing so long, and she'd only had one instance where the heel had sunk into the damp grass and she'd had to yank it out. She had the hang of it now, how she had to balance her weight as evenly as possible across the shoe's sole, not letting the toe or the heel take too much weight.

"Danielle!"

Danielle turned to see Sydney flagging her down, her formfitting gown even more beautiful on her than in the picture. Danielle tugged on the leash, and a reluctant Pops followed her to the elevator where Sydney stood, hip propped out to hold the edge of her iPad.

"You look lovely." Danielle commanded Pops to sit, and he did, eventually—after a minute of sniffing Sydney's glittery shoes.

"Thanks." Sydney blew a bang out of her face. "Honestly, I feel a bit naked without Chewy's sling. And Chewy."

"No one will know." Danielle would normally have been more reserved around a woman like Sydney, someone who seemed to have everything together, but Sydney was so danged nice. The morning coffee ritual often included her, and Danielle had come to appreciate Sydney's true and deep love for her dog, her quick wit, and her eagerness to help anyone, anytime. Sydney had kicked off the Homestretch YouTube presence like it was nothing, but it was everything to Danielle. Of all the dog park friends, Sydney was the one she felt closest to.

Sydney flipped her iPad around so Danielle could see it. "So far, everything looks great. Only problem? The groom and his brothers took off in the limo."

"Took off?" That sounded bad to Danielle. She didn't have a tremendous amount of experience with weddings, but it seemed like the groom should be nearby during the preparations.

Groomsmen, too. What could possibly be more important than the wedding today?

"Disappeared." Sydney snapped her fingers. "Riley's not worried, but she's overly sappy lately. You know, since she found out." Sydney patted her belly and waggled an eyebrow at Danielle.

Danielle's hands flew to her own belly. "I didn't know!"

"That's what happens when you skip out on the morning meetings." Sydney's disapproving frown didn't reach her eyes. "All the hot gossip that goes with the hot coffee."

"I, uh, overslept." Danielle checked on Pops, sitting attentively at her feet, to make sure he wasn't about to become an emergency. And also so Sydney couldn't see the real reason she'd missed so many mornings this week—her inability to get out of bed when Knox was in it.

"Again, huh?" Sydney grinned at her knowingly. Danielle had mentioned she and Knox were seeing each other, much to the other women's delight, but she hadn't given much detail. Sydney was clearly making up her own, and she probably wasn't wrong. "Well, now you know. Baby on board, though luckily, it's too early to really see. I only had to let her dress out a smidge for today." Sydney held her thumb and forefinger together very closely. "Don't tell anyone. So far, she's keeping it to just us girls."

Us girls? Danielle hadn't had a group of girlfriends since high school—and back then, it'd been Madi, Cassie, and her—but she liked it, the *us* part of us girls. She liked it too much. At the clinic, the front office staff and vet techs were mostly women, but she was the boss' daughter and so never felt quite like part of their crowd. To think here she was now, being caught up on shared secrets and chastised for missing out on a get-together. Danielle's face felt like it would break from the size of her smile.

"So"—Sydney shoved the iPad at Danielle—"Riley's sure Caleb and company will be back in plenty of time, but this wedding planner is one nervous wreck. Can you double-check my day-of list? I'm worried I've forgotten something."

Danielle scanned the multipage document, noting that everything was checked off with a pink rose petal by each completed item. "You forgot one thing."

"I knew it!" Sydney grabbed the iPad back. "It's something big, isn't it? Like the rings or—"

"You're forgetting to enjoy yourself." Danielle reached over and turned the iPad off. "Everything is done, you look amazing, and there's at least another hour before guests start arriving. Don't you have to go take pictures or something?"

Sydney blinked her big, hazel eyes. "Don't make me cry."

"By stating facts? Come on. You're tougher than that. Go enjoy this amazing event you planned."

Pops huffed as if in agreement, and Danielle patted his domed head to let him know she appreciated his support.

"I'm so glad I ran into you. One more minute assuring Riley's mom everything is under control would've driven me insane." Sydney threw her arms around Danielle for a tight hug. "You'll keep an eye on things up here? And text me if any of the groomsmen miraculously appear? And enjoy yourself, too? I'm sorry you got stuck with Pops. Grandpa William was insistent."

Danielle hugged her back, careful of the applique on the front of Sydney's dress. "Honestly, I'm happy to help out in any way I can, and I'm better with dogs than people. Go. I'll be your eyes and ears up here."

Sydney kissed Danielle's cheek, first one and then the other, and fled to the elevator with a backward wave. "You're the best!"

"I am the best." Danielle told an indifferent Pops. He ambled to his feet and followed her to a seat. She chose a spot close to the front but on the outer aisle so Pops would have room to spread out without tripping the wedding party as they made their way down the aisle. She passed a pleasant half hour taking photos of all the preparations and texting with her dad, who was puppy sitting until closer to the wedding. He responded by sending her short videos of the puppies tumbling over one another to get to the water dish. Pinto won the scuffle and launched himself so enthusiastically into the bowl that he landed muzzle first, splashing the others with a tiny tidal wave. Tilly rocked back on her heels, her expression dumbfounded. Danielle laughed out loud.

"Excuse me, ma'am?"

Danielle gritted her teeth. She might be in her thirties but that was still much too young to be ma'ammed in public. She flipped her phone facedown and gave her attention to a young man in a tailored suit. "Yes?"

"Groom's or bride's side?" He held out his arm like she was supposed to take it and wasn't already situated exactly where she wanted to be for the ceremony.

Also, trick question. Technically, she was more Riley's friend than Caleb's. Together, they were two-fifths of Us Girls. On the other hand, she was pretty sure Grandpa William would want Pops on the groom's side. Before she could make up her mind, a voice answered for her.

"Groom."

She craned her neck to find Knox looming over her. She held up her finger in the one-minute gesture. She flipped her phone back over and messaged Sydney.

One groomsman accounted for.

Sydney's response was instant. Thank God. Ask him where the hell Caleb is.

"Where the hell is Caleb?" Danielle was nothing if not literal.

Both Knox and the usher looked shocked at her abrupt descent into harsh language.

"He's back." Knox's brows furrowed. "In plenty of time, I might add."

"Tell that to Sydney."

"I will." He pulled out his own phone and texted. "You know my cousin?"

The usher. Danielle shook her head.

Knox talked and texted at the same time. "This is Danielle. Danielle, my cousin, Sean. Caleb dug up all the relatives for today. Some of them I've never even met before."

"Hey, you know me. Mom showed me pictures of you at my baptism."

"Right. You've gotten a bit taller. And learned to speak. Good for you." Knox still texted, and the corner of his lip lifted like he was amusing himself. "Some relatives I have even less memory of. Mom didn't like to have much to do with the Donovans after the divorce. If not for Caleb's mom insisting on inviting me to every event of Caleb's life, I wouldn't even know my own brothers."

"Hey, man." Sean pretended to wipe a tear from his cheek. "Don't get so emotional. The wedding hasn't even started yet, and I don't want to run out of tissues before I get a chance to hand one to a gorgeous, single lady in distress." Sean flashed the inner pocket of his suit coat to show it stuffed with Kleenex.

"Stay away from this gorgeous, single lady." Knox finally put down his phone and leaned a hand on the back of Danielle's chair. "She bites."

"Knox!" Danielle sprang up for her chair. "What will the children think if you talk like that?"

Knox grinned. "The children should do their jobs and leave the gorgeous ladies to me."

Sean laughed a long, honking laugh that struck Danielle as so funny that she laughed along.

"I'm being serious here." Knox didn't let his face crack, but Danielle could tell he was laughing on the inside. His eyes crinkled ever so slightly at the corners, like they did when he smiled.

"Enough." Sean used one of his hoard of tissues to wipe at his eyes. "The groom's side is over there." Sean offered her his arm. He was taking his usher duties pretty seriously, or maybe it was that she was the only guest to arrive so far and he needed the practice.

"Thanks." She stood, tugging Pops onto his feet.

"Wait." Knox put his hand on her elbow. Sean took the hint and moved over to loiter by the elevator. His day was made when two Dorothy residents emerged, and he was able to escort them to the bride's side.

Danielle led Knox to the groom's side of the chair setup. "What?"

"How are you?" Knox cupped the back of his neck, squinting at her like something wasn't right.

"Why? Do I have something on my face?" Danielle wiped at the corners of her mouth. She'd downed a quick doughnut on her way to Fur Haven. Had she been walking around with vanilla custard on her mouth? Surely, Sydney would've told her. Or Sean would've totally been on it if she'd needed a tissue, right?

"No, you look great. Beautiful." His eyes traveled up and down her shimmery dress, and Danielle was glad she'd gone with the ridiculous heels, because his eyes definitely lingered on her legs for an extra moment. "I–I saw my dad today."

"In prison?" Danielle snapped her jaw shut. Somehow it had been hanging wide open, like she was some cartoon character getting shocking news. "That's where you guys went?"

Knox stuffed his hands in his pockets, straining the tailored lines of the slacks. "Yeah, Caleb had some idea about getting closure before the ceremony."

"How did it feel, seeing him after all this time?"

"I'm not sure. Caleb seemed relieved. Lance got angry." Knox lifted a shoulder. "Me? I mostly felt sorry for him."

"Didn't he bring it all on himself?" Danielle shifted her weight from one foot to the other. The shoes were beautiful but not exactly comfortable. But beautiful. And Knox was looking at her legs again, so she pushed her aching feet out of her mind.

"I know a little bit about regretting past choices and mistakes." Knox's voice grew husky, and Danielle forgot all about her numb toes. "It can be hard to face how much you've hurt someone you love."

Love. Danielle's eyes locked with his. "So you forgave him?"

"I hugged him." His mouth quirked like he couldn't believe it himself.

"How'd that feel?" Danielle stroked a hand down his arm, shoulder to wrist, and entwined her fingers with his.

"It felt good to put the past to rest." Knox inhaled deeply. "It doesn't have to affect me anymore."

Danielle's gut clenched. Was that why he wanted to talk to her now? Did he want to put their past to rest, too? What kind of closure would he ask for? The kind where he gave her a hug and walked away because this week had been fun and all but they couldn't have a future together? Was he figuring on getting all the unpleasant closure tasks behind him before the ceremony? Was she on some kind of wedding-day to-do list where he ticked off his items one by one with a giant X?

Knox pulled at his coat sleeves, even though the suit was perfectly cut to his frame. He fiddled with the cuff links and then let out a long, controlled breath. "It was funny because at first I was so mad, but then looking at him, I couldn't hang on to it. All that anger, years and years of it. Danielle, he's just an old man in a cell. He ruined everything good in his life. I felt nothing but pity." Knox raised his other shoulder. "So I hugged him. And you want to know something really weird?"

Danielle held her own elbows, arms crossed over her stomach, waiting for the punch that was sure to come. "What?"

"On the ride back, all I wanted was to tell you about it. And then you were here, like you were waiting for me." He stopped fidgeting and caught her eyes with his. Those blue tethers kept her from gasping like she'd taken one to the gut. It wasn't the blow she'd expected; no, it was worse. When Knox Donovan looked at her like that, all she could think about was his hands on her body, his mouth on her skin, as quickly as possible, please.

"I'm watching Pops." Danielle didn't want to leak her feelings all over him or admit that she would've waited for him if he'd asked. Their present balanced on a thin line between the past that had hurt them both and the future they didn't talk about. She didn't want to be the one who pushed them too far in either direction. Taking it one day at a time had gotten her through her depression, and it would get her through this, whatever it turned out to be, too.

"But if you *were* waiting for me, then I would've rushed home to tell you. And maybe asked for a hug. Because I really need one."

Well, that broke her. She launched herself at him and wrapped her arms around his waist.

"Yeah, that's the stuff." He tightened his arms around her and held her. Long moments passed. They swayed a little. Pops grumbled and settled at their feet. The hug went on and on, until Danielle lost the sense of her body being separate from his, until their hearts beat in the same cadence.

Until Knox's phone buzzed. He pulled away to check the message. "I'm missing photos. Guess I have to go."

Danielle was the first to step away. "Go."

"Will I see you later? At the reception?" Knox ran the pad of his finger down her cheek. "I need to ask you something."

"At the reception." Danielle stretched up to peck his cheek. Knox turned his head at the last moment to land a sweet kiss on her mouth.

"I'll look for you," he said and was gone.

Pops snorted. Danielle didn't blame him. This back-and-forth was ridiculous. It was time to define what they were doing. He couldn't give her a hug like that and not wonder where this relationship was going. They were definitely more than hooking up. The question that dogged her thoughts as more and more guests arrived was: how much more?

CHAPTER 31

DANIELLE HAD TO ADMIT IT WAS THE LARGEST WEDDING SHE'D ever seen. There were several hundred people in attendance, with chairs stretching as wide and long as most of the dog park. The sprays of flowers festooning every available surface covered up any lingering dog smells, and the groomsmen looked handsome in their gray tuxedos. Caleb, standing on the inside of the gazebo, wore a slightly darker gray than his two brothers and grandfather, who stood beside him in an open V formation.

The wedding started with Oliver, the five-year-old ring bearer, barreling down the aisle at top speed with LouLou loping alongside him on a hot-pink and rhinestone bedazzled leash, tail wagging. At the front, Oliver slammed to a stop in front of his dad. Lance gently coaxed him into place next to him. Oliver clung to his leg, eyes wide as he looked out at the crowd. Caleb took LouLou's leash and faced the aisle, clear expectation on his handsome face.

At some cue Danielle missed, everyone turned to watch the bridesmaids process down the aisle. In contrast to the matched groomsmen, each woman wore a dress of her own choosing, something Riley'd insisted on in spite of Sydney's nearly daily appeals to be more coordinated. Like the riot of loud flowers everywhere, though, Danielle found it charming. First there was Sydney in her stunning gown, then Carrie in an emerald sheath that clung to her and rippled with each step she took. Next, Eliza followed in a flowing silver tunic, and finally Patty came down the aisle, leaning on her yellow walker, her yellow Crocs peeking out from the hem of her floor-length dress festooned with bright sunflowers.

When at last the string quartet played the opening strains of the bridal march, Riley glided down the aisle in the palest of pink wedding gowns, holding hands with her Grams. Both women smiled widely, processing slowly toward the front. Once Grams kissed Riley's cheek and took her seat, Riley handed off her flowers to Sydney, positioned LouLou between her and Caleb, and took Caleb's hand.

The words flowed around Danielle, the descriptions of marriage as a life partnership, the admonition never to give up on each other, the exchanging of simple vows and simple rings. The whole time, Danielle couldn't look away from Knox. The suit was tailored to fit over the brace, so one leg looked bulkier than the other, but he still looked good to Danielle. In her mind, the leg brace only proved his courage and loyalty. No doubt about it, of all the men standing up there, Knox was the real catch, even if his eyebrows were furrowed in that way that let Danielle know his leg was hurting.

He must've felt her stare because he turned his head in her direction. Over the heads of many guests, across the distance between them, Danielle felt the pull. He held himself so still, his complete focus on her. It was physically painful not to go to him. So much undefined between them, but she didn't care. She wanted to be near him, soaking in his heat and that clean smell he carried with him like he'd just scrubbed behind his ears.

Her fingers twitched, alerting Pops to her heightened awareness. He raised his head and plunked it on her knee. She patted him absentmindedly, thoughts whirring in her mind faster than greyhounds around a track. She wanted to be with Knox. One night, one week, one month—whatever time limit she imagined for them—would never be enough for her. But she couldn't give him the family she knew he wanted, and she didn't think she could live with the long-term disappointment that would set in. The eventual resentment. The right thing to do was to walk away, but she wasn't sure she had the strength to do it. Couldn't she keep him for a little while longer and then selflessly give him up to be happy with someone else?

Pops nosed at her wrist, alerting her to how her fingers had fisted in his fur. Poor thing. She relaxed her hand. No, the longer she held on to Knox, the harder it would be when they inevitably parted ways. It would be better to end it now. It would hurt, but not as much as it would hurt later. Not at the reception, though. She couldn't break up with him at his own brother's wedding. No, she'd wait until after, maybe even tomorrow.

Her fingers glided across Pops' scalp, and the old dog leaned heavily against her leg in appreciation. So she could dance with Knox at the reception, could enjoy him at least for today. She smiled at him over the heads of all the guests, and he smiled back, his eyes full of promises she intended to let him keep. At least one more time.

When Riley and Caleb shared their first kiss as a married couple, Danielle swiped away a tear, wishing Sean were nearby with one of his tissues. Her small clutch was useless, only big enough to hold her phone, keys, and a lip gloss. The cheers woke Pops up from his impromptu nap, and he sat up with a low grumble in his throat. The musicians played something lively, and Caleb and Riley led the way to the elevator. They disappeared, waving at their guests, as the doors closed behind them.

The wedding party filled the next elevator, and then the ushers had their hands full, arranging groups of people for the descent. Her dad and Sherry made it into the second elevator, but Danielle hung back with Pops. She wouldn't make him take the ramp, not with his arthritic joints, but she also wouldn't squeeze him into an elevator with a bunch of strangers.

The first to arrive, Danielle was also the last to leave. Alone after even the ushers left, Danielle spun in a slow circle, taking it all in one last time. It had been a perfect wedding, and she was sure that Riley and Caleb were heading right into their perfect happily-ever-after. She took a few more pictures, wanting to remember every moment because she knew she'd never have anything like it for herself.

Knox thanked God for the open bar. The whole ceremony had gotten to him and not in the shed-a-tear-out-of-beauty way but because he kept thinking how it should've been him and Danielle exchanging vows. Not today, obviously, but years ago. He'd asked, and she'd said yes, and then things had fallen apart. Like with his leg, he desperately wanted things to go back to the way they were. Also like his leg, he feared there'd been too much damage for that to ever be possible. Seeing her sitting in the row with her dad, a greyhound at her feet, it had hit him that she wouldn't want to leave her life here. How could he even ask it of her?

Where was she? He scanned the packed lobby of the Dorothy, not finding her by the buffet or on the dance floor. Caleb and Riley had already danced their first dance, joined on the floor by Grams and Grandpa William. And of course, LouLou standing on her hind legs to be included had been so adorable that the photographer had gone wild taking pictures of her. Knox had no doubt there'd be more pictures of the poodle than of him in the couple's wedding album.

He sipped his second drink and walked out the front doors to loiter on the newly landscaped front lawn. Tables and chairs had been set up out here, too, but not many people had come out yet. He found a round table with a pink rose centerpiece and planted himself, stretching out his leg. He felt himself settle into recon mode, the long wait a part of the job, no need to complain or wish it away.

Knox was finally rewarded when Danielle made her way toward him on those tottering heels that made him notice her calves in a way he hadn't fully appreciated before, Pops ambling along beside her like they were old friends. He supposed that they were. She smiled when she saw him, and he gestured for her to take a seat at his pink rose table.

"It was beautiful, wasn't it?" Danielle tucked Pops' leash under her thigh and blinked those big, brown eyes up at him.

He grunted something he hoped sounded affirmative and took another sip of the weird Belgian ale Caleb favored. He'd lost a bet, and his penalty was a month of drinking Caleb's beer. He hated to admit that it was growing on him. A little.

"Your leg hurts?" Danielle folded her hands in her lap, then refolded them. Why would she be nervous? His men had often told him he had a scary-ass resting bastard face. He tried to look some other way, but he didn't know how to change his face. A forced smile would be worse, wouldn't it?

He gave a stiff nod in answer to her question. No use pretending otherwise. The leg was unhappy with him today and letting him know it in no uncertain terms. The over-the-counter painkillers he'd taken before the ceremony weren't cutting it, nor was alcohol doing much to numb it.

"Do you need anything?" Danielle's hand landed on the table like she might reach for him. Instead, it landed palm down on the white linen tablecloth. Her fingers toyed with a fallen rose petal. "Other than someone to teach you how to have a civilized conversation?"

"Sorry." Knox set the drink down. She was right. Get out of his head and into the moment. Ruminating could get a Marine killed. Stay sharp, that was what he needed to do.

And nothing wrong with a little redirection, either. "The ceremony got to me, I guess. I can't believe my little brothers are both married now."

And I'm not. It hung between them, his long-ago proposal that she'd accepted. His more recent one she hadn't taken seriously.

"I'm sad." Danielle shredded the rose petal into smaller and smaller pieces. "I'll never have something like that."

"You could." He willed her to look up, but she didn't. Probably afraid he'd propose again. Who knows? Maybe he would. His gut urged him to pop the question, but his mind warned him to tread lightly.

"It wouldn't be fair to"—she blinked suspiciously wet eyes—"whoever."

That again. Her big secret. "What if whoever didn't care about whatever it is you think is such a big deal?"

"Whoever *would* care. Eventually. Because it is a big deal. Especially for you."

"How can you be so sure? Give me the chance to prove you wrong." He held on to the edge of the table like it was about to take off.

"I'm not wrong." Now she looked at him, and it speared him like a KA-BAR blade to the jugular. Whatever she was holding back, it was big. And painful.

"Maybe you are. Maybe you aren't." He tried to make eye contact, but she was intent on her petal-shredding project. "Try me."

Danielle shook her head. "I thought I could do this, but now's not the time. Not at Riley's wedding. We have to—"

"Dance with me." Knox stood and held out his hand. What was he doing? He didn't dance. Not since the IED. Not for years before that, if he were honest. But the burlesque lesson had gone fine, better than fine. And Danielle liked to dance. It was enough reason to try.

"Your leg hurts."

Somehow, Knox couldn't stand even a minor rejection from her right now. He slammed down the rest of the Belgian ale. "For the pain. I'll be fine. And this is a wedding reception. Aren't we obligated to dance?"

"What about Pops?" She chewed her lip, a sign she was about to agree. He stifled the urge to grab her and make a run for it.

Instead, he remained standing, hand still hanging in the air. Waiting for her. God, how many years had he spent waiting for her? "We'll find my grandfather first. Come on."

Finally, clearly reluctantly, she took his hand and let him pull her to her feet.

It didn't take long to deposit Pops with Grandpa William, who was holding court at the head table with stories about last year's cruise and his plans to book another cruise for the family as soon as Riley and Caleb were back from their honeymoon.

Then Knox and Danielle were on the dance floor, and even though the tempo was too fast for a slow dance, Knox took Danielle in his arms anyway. He curved a hand around her waist and brought her against him. Her right hand curled over his heart, and it settled into a steady if elevated beat for her. They swayed.

Not to the song. They swayed to a long-ago song under a night sky. At least, that was where Knox was in his mind. That night they'd gone to see the holiday lights at the botanical gardens and gotten lost in the rain-forest section. He remembered the humidity and how the stars had peeked down at them from between the wide leaves of the canopy layer. And he remembered how sweet Danielle's kiss had been, still flavored like the ice cream cones they'd eaten earlier. She'd pressed a button on her phone, and a song had played. He couldn't remember it now, but it had been slow and given him a reason to hold her. It was all he'd needed then and apparently all he'd ever needed, because everything in him calmed down now that she was in the cradle of his arms.

She might think they couldn't make this work, but her body betrayed her. It whispered to him how much she wanted to be with him, and he held on to that message. Held on to her. Dipped his forehead to rest against the top of her head. Inhaled her freshly shredded rose petal scent, memorized the way she fit against him. Eventually, the music caught up with them, a slow song with crooning words, and he pulled her tighter.

He took a step back and his damn leg wobbled.

"We should stop." She lifted her head from where it had come to lean against his chest. "Your leg."

"My leg is fine." But another step betrayed him. Not his step, though; a drunken Sean twirled his partner a bit too vigorously, and she knocked into the head table. Pops jumped up at the clear attack on his people and let out a loud "Woof!" before slipping his collar and bolting onto the dance floor.

Sean laughed and caught his dance partner against his chest, but Pops was not deterred from inspecting the people who'd assaulted his table. He headed straight for them, plowing through the crowded dance floor, a dog on a mission. He was unafraid of high heels or long legs. He woofed again and picked up speed, ramming into Knox right at the knee. His left knee.

Knox's leg buckled, and he had only a second to push Danielle to safety before he crashed to the dance floor. But she didn't budge. Instead, she went down with him, and he landed on top of her in an embarrassed heap. The music continued to play, but the dancers backed away, making room for them to recover.

"Pops!" Grandpa William called from his seat, and Pops spun around and loped back to the table, completely unaware of the chaos he'd caused.

"Knox!" Caleb was at his brother's side in seconds. "You okay? Danielle?"

Knox used his arms to lift himself off Danielle. His leg twinged and complained, but the leg could go to hell. He pushed himself to sitting and tried to help Danielle do the same.

Her eyes were wide with fear, and her hand clutched her chest, right above that daring neckline that had been driving him wild earlier. She beat her chest with her fist, mouth opening and closing like a suffocating fish.

"Breath's knocked out of you?"

Her head nodded so vigorously that her hair slipped from unseen pins to tumble into her face.

"Hang on. It takes a moment for it to come back." His training kicked in. He knew how to handle a downed Marine. He talked nonsense to her until the panic faded from her eyes, and she inhaled deeply.

"Should I call 911?" Riley hovered behind Caleb, LouLou clutched under her arm.

"Not necessary," Danielle gasped out. "At least not for me."

"Me either," Knox said before anyone could ask. "I was just clumsy. That ale you drink is stronger than it looks, Caleb."

Caleb and Riley exchanged a look that made Knox think they weren't going to buy his story, but ultimately, Caleb nodded and offered him a hand up. Riley helped Danielle stand, dusting off her dress and helping her slip back on the heel that had fallen off in the fall.

"No dogs!" Grams' voice carried over the music, over the crowd. "There will be no dogs at my wedding, and that's final, William Donovan. You hear me?"

"I hear you." Grandpa William put the collar back on Pops, tightening the martingale loop. "Only Pops and absolutely no other dogs. I am one hundred percent with you on that, my darling."

"No dogs." Grams ran her finger across her throat like she was a mobster ordering a hit.

"No dogs that aren't Pops. I hear you loud and clear." Grandpa William circled the table to take a seat next to Grams, and Pops settled under the table, his head on Grams' mauve shoes. Grandpa William tipped his head to whisper in Grams' ear. She pinkened and said, "Okay, one dog," and giggled.

"You sure you're okay?" Caleb clapped Knox on the back as they headed off the dance floor, the guests already piling back in for some kind of line dance the DJ was hyping to distract from the drama.

Knox rubbed at his damn leg. "Yeah, I'm fine." He looked around, first slowly, then more frantically. "Where's Danielle?"

"Hustled off to the bathroom. I'm sure she'll be back soon." Caleb led Knox off the dance floor and toward the bar. "Let me buy you an ale, and you can tell me what's going on with Danielle. You two looked pretty intimate on the dance floor, especially for a guy about to move to another state."

Knox glared at the bathroom door that had swallowed Danielle up. "Hell if I know."

———————

"You were practically doing it with Knox on the dance floor, and now you want to sneak out the back door? What is going on with you two?" Riley blocked Danielle from exiting the bathroom by shoving LouLou at her.

Danielle accepted the poodle, who licked under her chin in greeting. Danielle felt her panic subside. How smart Riley was to know that she needed a little dog time to settle her nerves. She rubbed LouLou's fur in circles, and LouLou stretched her neck, nose to the air, mouth stretched into what for all the world looked like a smile.

She needed to answer Riley. Riley was her friend, and Danielle was ruining her wedding reception. "You should go back out there."

"Out there can wait. Danielle, I've been worried about you for a while. Tell me what's going on with you." Riley petted LouLou, too, and the joint attention made the poodle shiver in delight.

Danielle felt the same degree of panic as when the wind had been knocked out of her on the dance floor. "Honestly? I have no idea." A sob escaped her, and then she was crying. Crying hard. More than even Sean's tissue stash could've dealt with. She let go of LouLou to pull a long train of towels from the paper-towel holder. She held one to her face, the rest waterfalling to the floor and around her feet, which still hurt like crazy.

"Oh no, oh no, you heard about Knox and Atlanta." Riley wrapped an arm around Danielle and texted with her other hand. In a moment, Carrie and Sydney were in the bathroom, too.

"She knows." Riley lifted towels from the floor until they over-flowed her arms. "We need to get her out of here."

"Wait, what? I don't know anything." Danielle sniffled. God, she felt ten years old, crying because she took a dodgeball to the chest too hard. And darn it, the more she thought about them, the more her feet hurt.

Carrie and Riley looked at each other, then Sydney. Sydney cleared her throat, clearly volunteering to deliver whatever the bad news was. "When the Dorothy is finished, Knox is taking a position at a security outfit in Atlanta."

"He turned down a perfectly good job offer from Lance, too." Carrie's narrowed eyes broadcast how she felt about that decision. "He didn't tell you?"

"No." Danielle pulled in a shuddering breath. "You said he's leaving?"

The three women nodded, and Danielle felt the bathroom walls move toward her. Her vision darkened at the edges. "He's leaving again?"

Carrie took LouLou and handed her off to Sydney. "I've got this. Syd, you get the bride back out there." Then she draped an arm around Danielle's shoulders and pulled her in for a hug. Too stunned to even cry, Danielle stood there, shaking.

Riley's makeup repairs were made from a tiny kit in Sydney's clutch. Riley's dress was straightened. Before Danielle knew what was happening, Riley and Sydney were gone, and she was alone in the bathroom with Carrie.

"He's an asshole." Carrie whispered the words sweetly in Danielle's ear. "He doesn't deserve you. I can't believe he wouldn't tell you. What is wrong with him? Ugh, men." Carrie kept up the trash talk, getting more outrageous as the rant continued until finally Danielle was able to stand on her own. The shaking subsided.

"I want to go home." Danielle rubbed at her newly raccooned eyes.

"Of course you do." Carrie wet a paper towel and dabbed at the smeared mascara on Danielle's face. "Then you need to give Knox what for. I won't even tell him a little hell is coming his way. I wish I could see his face when you lay into him."

"I'm not mad." Danielle tidied her dress, straightening the straps and tugging the neckline a millimeter higher. "I knew it would end. At least now I have a timeline. After the Dorothy is done. That's what? Three weeks out? Maybe a month?"

"Oh no, I'm not doing his dirty work for him. Come on. Let's get you out of here." Carrie hustled Danielle out the side door of the Dorothy. "I'll tell your dad and my mom you weren't feeling well after the fall. Don't be surprised if she comes out and checks on you tonight."

"She doesn't need to." Danielle paused with her hand on the door, ready to push it open and make her escape.

Carrie gave her a one-sided hug. "That's not how family works. Don't sleep naked tonight, okay? They might get home late, and that would lead to all kinds of awkwardness."

"I won't." Danielle mustered a watery smile for Carrie and stepped into the night. Maybe it was cowardly to run away. Maybe it was smart. She'd figure it out tomorrow.

CHAPTER 32

KNOX IGNORED THE BUZZING IN HIS POCKET, CONCEN-trating on creating a perfect line with the trim paint between the baseboard and wall. The edging tool would probably help, but Knox enjoyed the challenge of freehand painting. It required all his focus and freed him from corralling roaming thoughts and run-away emotions, like the ones he was deliberately blocking from yesterday's wedding reception. Of course she'd run off after his fall. Weddings made a person think about forever, and who wanted to spend forever with a guy as broken as he was? He thumped his bum leg with the heel of his hand. Stupid thing was feeling fine today, or at least as fine as it ever felt. A night of tossing and turn-ing, wondering what he could've done differently, said differently, in the past week that might have changed things—might've con-vinced her to run to him instead of away.

Sarge whined and bumped his back pocket, a move that jigged the tiny paintbrush.

"Dammit."

He wasn't cursing at the dog, but Sarge still took it person-ally, drooping his head, tail between his legs. Danielle had told him that greyhounds often carried their tail tucked under—something about aerodynamics and reduced drag while running—and not to take it personally if Sarge walked around that way. Combined with the sad eyes, though, the tucked tail made Knox feel like a jerk. He wiped the errant paint away with a damp towel and deposited his painting supplies onto the drop cloth under his feet.

"Come here, boy." Knox knelt on his good knee and patted his thigh. Sarge slunk over to him, tip of his tail tentatively wagging.

"It wasn't you. You're a good boy, the best boy. I hate the damn phone is all. It's like a needy baby, always wanting me to do something for it. Check this notification, answer this call, return a text. Sometimes a man just wants to be alone with his paintbrush and his dog, you know what I mean, Sarge?"

Sarge's tail thumped full speed by the end of Knox's speech, and Knox took a long moment to rough up the dog's fur, showering him with praise the whole time.

"Now that's something I never thought I'd see," Lance drawled from the doorway. "Guess you have a soft side after all."

Knox pushed to his feet, not deigning to comment. "Almost done here."

"Figured as much. Interested in doing the unit Mr. Cardoza picked out for his friend? He's anxious for it to get the finishing touches. Says she'll be here soon, so we're stepping up the schedule a bit to try to get it done in time."

"Sure thing." Knox wiped his palms on his jeans. "I've probably got an hour, maybe two, left in this unit." His phone buzzed again, and he ignored it. He picked up the paintbrush and dipped it in the paint, ready to resume work. It buzzed again, this time the sound for leaving a voicemail. Who did that these days? He hated voicemail even more than he hated picking up the phone.

"You're not going to check it?" Lance sauntered in to inspect the trim work thus far. "I prefer to know who I'm ignoring when I'm ignoring them."

"Probably a sales call." Knox's phone buzzed again, going through the same cycle that ended in a voicemail.

"Maybe it's important."

Knox couldn't think of anything important enough that it had to be dealt with right away, but then he remembered Danielle had told him a few days ago that she was going on a home visit today to check out a potential new foster home. What if she'd gotten in trouble? What if she needed him? He pulled the phone out of his pocket, then turned the face in Lance's direction. "It's the VA. Probably an appointment reminder or something."

He had the phone out anyway. He clicked on the voicemail and felt the blood drain from his face.

"What is it?" Lance was at his side, hand on his shoulder. "Bad news?"

"My test results are finally back." It'd been so long since they'd been ordered and administered, it was easy to forget. The VA wasn't known for its speed, especially in noncritical situations. "They say I have to come in to discuss them."

"That's normal, right? They don't give results over the phone, do they?"

"They've given me good news over the phone, negative test results and all clears. Calling me in? It must be bad." Knox steadied his breathing before Sarge could pick up on his distress. He didn't want to worry the dog over a phone call.

Lance's grip on his shoulder tightened. "What were you tested for?"

"Honestly? I don't even remember. They're always taking blood and pictures of some kind or another. I don't even know what to be worried about." Just the total loss of his limb. The news that he'd never gain full use of his leg. Infections. Deteriorating mobility. He'd be no good to Morales if the news was bad. No good to anyone, really. His grip tightened on the phone.

"Want me to go with you?" Lance planted his hands on his hips in his classic I'm-the-boss-of-this-job-site stance. "I could hold your hand."

Knox choked out a laugh. "It's fine. I'll call back for an appointment."

Lance clapped him on the back. "I'll leave you to it. Keep me posted, will you?"

Knox gave him a thumbs-up and hit Redial. After a few moments of establishing who he was, he had an appointment for the next day. Another bad sign as far as he was concerned. The VA was never in a hurry. His hands shook a little when he picked up the paintbrush, so he decided to call it a day. Perks of being an owner and not a regular grunt.

"Come on, Sarge. Wanna go to the park?"

Sarge surged to his feet, practically bowling Knox over on his way to the door. Apparently, Sarge did indeed want to go to the park. Knox locked up behind him, trying to shove down the hope that Danielle would already be up on the roof. What were the odds? *Better if you text her*, a little voice whispered in his mind. He obeyed. Might as well use the phone for something good. Exactly like how he'd felt on the drive home from visiting his dad in prison yesterday, Danielle was the only person he wanted to talk to. Would she want to talk to him? He let out a relieved sigh at her reply.

Just got back from the home visit. I'll pick up the girls and head over there now. The dots bounced and then she added, I shouldn't have run off last night. Sorry.

Knox stopped hating his phone. Good little gadget that it was, it was bringing Danielle right to him. He didn't question why he needed to see her so urgently; he just knew that he did. Sarge pulled him toward the front doors, and because they had time, Knox pointed them at the ramp that wound its way up the side of the parking garage to the park. A runner with a Doberman at his side passed Knox and Sarge on their way up the slope. Knox kept his steady pace, even though Sarge wanted to rush ahead. Since getting out of the cast, the dog sometimes forgot his own limits. Knox didn't like to be the one to remind him, but he also didn't want the dog to injure his weakened leg, so he kept a tight hold on the leash and focused on keeping his own weight evenly distributed so his knee stayed stabilized. Ana would be proud of his restraint.

They busted through the door at the top of the ramp,

triumphant. They might both be a bit limpy, but there was nothing holding them back. At least not now. A pit settled in Knox's stomach, a mixture of anxiety and rage. What could be in the test results that couldn't be said over the phone? Nothing good, that was for sure.

———

Danielle found Knox on the far end of the park, overlooking the ocean in the distance. Sarge leaned heavily against Knox's good leg, ignoring Luna's and Flurry's inquisitive sniffs. A bad sign. Danielle approached with caution.

"Knox."

His body flinched like he'd taken a blow. Slowly, he turned his back on the view, keeping a steady hand on Sarge's head. "You came."

"Are you okay?"

Knox didn't look okay. He looked like he hadn't slept well in a week, dark circles under his too-dilated eyes. She should've hashed things out with him last night rather than leaving them both to stew.

"Yeah." He squeezed his eyes shut and opened them again, his face rearranging itself into a stoic mask that Danielle didn't like one bit.

She wanted to rush him, to wrap her arms around him and promise that whatever it was, she'd make it go away. But after a week of the best sex of her life, the most fun she'd ever had with a partner, she'd run off without telling him she knew his secret plan to move in a few weeks. Not that it mattered. Last night, lying in her bed alone, she'd decided his Atlanta job was a blessing. She'd never have to explain why they couldn't stay together because he'd never been planning on staying anyway. She pretended relief was all she felt, but at the base of it all was an emotion she recognized well—fear. She was protecting her heart, but the way it thumped right now, unsteady and hard in her chest, let her know that it wasn't working. Whether they were kissing or not, her heart was involved again.

"I need a favor." He ran a palm down his cheek. "From a *friend*." He stressed the last word like it was foul tasting in his mouth.

"Sure. I'm here." Problem was, he wasn't. Or wouldn't be, not once the work on the Dorothy was finished.

"I've got to go to the VA. For test results."

"You want me to watch Sarge? I'm happy to." Danielle attempted distancing herself. If she started now, she'd be used to it by the time he actually left.

"I want you to come with me."

So much for distance. The starkness of the words, the bleak look he was trying to keep out of his eyes. It was bad. Her gut tightened. Real bad. "Yes." What else could she say? Whatever else was going on between them, he was her Knox. "When is it?"

"Tomorrow." Knox knuckled his bad thigh.

She gathered up all three dogs and herded everyone, including a silent Knox, to the elevator. "How bad is it?"

Knox closed his eyes before answering. "I don't know."

"What do you think it is?"

He quirked one corner of his mouth at her. "Nothing good."

Danielle wrapped the dog leashes around her hand, over and over again. "Okay, game plan. Tomorrow morning, we'll take Sarge to my place, and I'll drive you."

"I can drive." His knuckles were so white against the dark denim of his jeans.

She swiped at her bangs, all the better to glare at him, but they fell in her eyes anyway. "I didn't say you couldn't."

"Fine." He ground out the words.

"Fine." There was no joy in winning. "What time should I pick you both up?"

"Eight."

Danielle wasn't sure why he was mad at her when he was the one not telling her he had one foot out the door this whole time. Mad was better than afraid, though. They rode the elevator in silence, but she didn't think she imagined the soft "thank you" she heard when she stepped into the parking garage.

"See you tomorrow." She practiced walking away from him. No sense making a big scene. He'd tell her when he told her, and she'd take it with grace. Their ending was inevitable, and she should be grateful she wasn't going to have to be the bad guy in their breakup.

Danielle held herself very still in the small chair in the corner of the doctor's office. Knox sat on the edge of the patient table, his braced leg stretched in front of him. On the wall, the doctor was showing them some MRI and X-ray results and saying a lot of words Danielle couldn't process. It wasn't that she didn't understand them. She'd been reading radiology results at her dad's clinic since she was kid. It was that she couldn't match what was being said with Knox. Her Knox. Her strong, capable, active Knox.

"So there's a surgery or something, right?" Knox's eyes were haunted again, and he wasn't trying to hide it.

The doctor, an older man with a ring of white hair circling his otherwise bald scalp, shook his head and laid a hand on Knox's shoulder. "No, but you'll continue the PT, of course. Keeping up the strength and balance is important, but the brace, I'm afraid, is your best option."

"There's nothing else? Really nothing else?"

"You were lucky to keep the leg, Knox. Everything else is a miracle. You know how many guys I've seen with similar wounds that we had to amputate? You should be thanking your lucky stars for all your limbs."

"So I'll never get full mobility back? It's really over."

"You knew that."

"I guess I'd hoped. If I worked hard, if I—" Knox bit his lip and turned his face to the wall.

"Early on, there was hope that the damaged muscle would regrow. It does in some cases, but it's been nearly two years and there's no sign of regeneration. At this point, it's about as good as it's going to get."

"This is it? For the rest of my life?" Knox's hissed words were laced with fury. The doctor took a cautious step back, but Knox stayed on the table, his gaze locked on Danielle. She offered a weak smile that did nothing to relax him.

"I'll be back in a few minutes with some new 'scrips for you that should help with pain management." The doctor walked backward to the door and closed it behind him.

Danielle slipped out of the chair to stand in front of Knox. She put a hand on his thigh, above the brace. "It'll be okay. You'll keep fighting, and you'll prove them wrong."

Knox choked out a mirthless laugh. "That's rich, coming from you."

Danielle snatched her hand back. "Excuse me?"

"You want me to fight? You?" Knox's hands bunched the white paper on the table until it tore. "What do you know about fighting?"

"I know it seems hard right now, but a good night's sleep and you'll be back at your PT, proving them all wrong." She tried to keep her voice upbeat, like she was outlining cancer treatments for an older cat. "It's a harsh blow, but there are options. There are always options."

"Please stop." Knox ripped paper off the table and crumpled it in his fists. "I don't need to hear this from you, especially you."

"What's that supposed to mean?"

"It means you're not a fighter, Danielle."

Danielle straightened her spine. "That's not true, and you asked me to be here."

"My mistake." Knox waved the paper with the test results in front of him, a careless streamer. "Oh, you'll fight for your precious dogs, do whatever it takes to train them and settle them in a good home. You'll give up your whole life to accommodate them, your living space, everything. But you won't fight for yourself. And you sure as hell won't fight for us."

"You know we don't have a future," Danielle said through clenched teeth.

"Because you won't fight for it. Guess you don't really believe there are always options. It's all or nothing, huh? Just like when we were teens."

Danielle's fists clenched at her sides, balled up like she wanted to hit something. And she did want to hit something. Something named Knox. "You. Left. Me."

"You let me leave."

"I *let* you leave? What was I supposed to do that I didn't? I called; I emailed. I talked to your *mother* for God's sake, and for what? For nothing. She told me you were relieved to go, and I should leave you alone."

"She said that to you?" Knox's stare pinned her in place. "When?"

"Back then. I told you." Danielle waved her hand. The past was the past. "My point is that I had to learn what battles to fight, and so do you."

"Mom never told me she talked to you." The paper fell from Knox's hand. "What did she say?"

"After telling me how lucky I was?" Danielle was surprised at how fresh that long ago hurt still was. "She told me to take a hint, that your no response was a response and I needed to move on." Danielle swallowed. "She wasn't wrong."

"Yes, she was. And so was I." Knox pushed himself to standing.

"I'm sorry if me being an asshole back then convinced you not to fight for yourself, but, Danielle, you could have so much more in your life. Why don't you want more?"

"How did this become about me?" Danielle swiped at her suddenly wet eyes. "Of course I want more. But what's the point? You're leaving. I should've known from the start you wouldn't stick around."

"You're the one running from me. I've tried to be understanding, to give you space." Knox's hands fisted in his lap. "But it's clear you don't think of me as long-term material. Is it really about what happened in the past, or is it about my leg? You heard the doc; it's never going to get better."

"You think I care about your leg?" Danielle's voice rose. So much for gratitude. "I love you, you idiot. Including your leg."

"Then what the hell has been going on since the reception?"

"You thought I was avoiding you because of your *leg*?" Danielle closed her eyes, not sure if she should laugh or cry. Or both. At the same time.

Knox raised his hands shoulder-height, palms up. "Why else?"

Then she did laugh, a sound so hard and brittle she didn't recognize it as her own. "Why else? Why else?" She bent over, hands on her knees, wheezing out that hard, brittle laugh until her lungs hurt.

"Why are you laughing?" Knox's voice got very quiet. "Dani, are you okay?"

She straightened. "Why else you ask? Atlanta, Knox. When were you going to tell me? Or were you going to disappear one day, send me a text from the road? What about Sarge? Planning to give him back?"

"I would never leave Sarge behind."

The words were out. Danielle thought she could almost see them hanging in the air. She dropped forward, head to her knees, like the plane she was on was about to crash. If only it were that simple—a machine falling from the sky, oxygen masks deploying to save her life. But nothing dropped from the sky to help her. She gasped for air.

"But you'd leave me. Good to know where I am in your ranking." She sniffed, loud and long, refusing to let the tears out. Not in front of him. Knox didn't deserve them. He'd just admitted his dog, the dog she'd given him, meant more to him than she did. This was why she should've kept her mouth shut, gone along like she didn't know, let him walk away again without a fuss.

"I was going to ask you to come with me."

Danielle didn't want his pity-revisionist history. "Right, that's why you never mentioned the job offer. Your plans. Because you wanted me to know."

"I was going to ask you." Knox knuckled his thigh, squeezed his eyes shut, then opened them again. "I was afraid you'd say no."

Danielle kept her face hidden. "Too late now, I guess. You'll never know what I would've said."

"Dani, come with me to Atlanta. At least consider it, will you?"

Danielle sucked in one long breath and crossed the short distance to where he sat on the table. She placed her palm against his cheek. "No."

"No?"

"You're right to leave, and I'll let you go when it's time. We never had a future." Her hand slid down his neck, down his arm. Her fingers traced the letter of his Semper Fi tattoo. "What I do want is for it not to end until you go. Can we enjoy these last weeks together?"

"Am I allowed to try to change your mind?" He palmed her waist and pulled her toward him.

"You can try. It won't work."

"As long as I can try, we have a deal."

Danielle let her forehead collapse onto Knox's chest, snuggled it right into the dip that fit her cheek so perfectly. "Deal."

He ran his hand down her back. "That's my girl."

And that was her problem, wasn't it? She was his girl, and pretending she could walk away at any time wasn't going to change the basic truth about her universe. At least she'd have more memories of him to revisit once he was gone. She could be mad at him later. For now, it was enough to stand in the circle of his arms.

The doctor cleared his throat, alerting them to his return. "I called in a new med for you to try, and here's a re-up on your PT. I'd like you to try some water therapy."

"Water therapy?" Knox kept his arm around her, and Danielle didn't mind one bit.

"Your physical therapist can show you some things to do in the pool that might help. Do you have access to a pool?"

"He does." Danielle smiled at the doctor for offering an option, for giving her something to do besides worry about a future without Knox in it. She was excellent at rehabilitation programs. Her experience was mostly of the canine variety, but having a patient who could speak would only make things easier, right? "I can help."

Knox's grip on her tightened. "You don't have to."

She tilted her head to meet his gaze. "Let me fight this with you, Knox. We can have this much at least."

"You're dangerous," he said and kissed her forehead. "Okay, Doc, you heard her. Tell us what we need to do."

CHAPTER 33

Danielle felt Knox's gaze burning through the thin material of her bathing suit like the bright hibiscus print wasn't even there and all he could see was her walking toward him naked. The modest one-piece covered all the important bits and had a panel for flattening the jiggly bits, but she still fought the urge to cross her arms protectively over her stomach. The heat in his eyes stopped her. It didn't matter that she didn't look like one of the hordes of wannabe models flocking the South Beach shores. This was Knox, and he loved her body. Always had. Nothing made her feel sexier than the way he looked at her.

So she let her arms hang at her sides, her stomach tightening in anticipation. She was supposed to be helping him with his physical therapy, but heat flushed his cheeks in a way that let her know he was as moved by her as she was by him. His reaction didn't just surprise her. It delighted her. She wanted her body to please him the way his strength pleased her. It was less than three weeks until he started his new job in a new state, and she was all about making the most of the time they had left.

"Shall we?" She brushed by him, preceding him into the pool. She sucked in a sharp breath when the cool water hit her belly. The water was usually warmer this late in June, but overcast weather had cooled the water the past few days. She ignored the cold. Knox needed her. Or at least he needed her dad's pool to stay active and follow his PT schedule in an environment that kept stress off the injury.

Behind her, Danielle felt Knox enter the pool. The water around her seemed to warm at his presence. She stepped farther out, until the water covered her breasts, before turning to him.

"Lie back." Her fingers under the water's surface curled in invitation.

"Thought you'd never ask." He gently kicked off from the bottom and straightened out his body until he was floating less than a foot from her. She stood behind his head, holding her fingers lightly against the back of his neck, digging in where she felt tightness. He groaned, and she dropped her hands.

"Sorry. I didn't mean to hurt you."

"It only hurts that you stopped."

Tentatively, she put her fingers back in place, and he stretched his neck to give her better access.

"Heaven," he rumbled, opening his eyes. "And the view's even better."

Danielle smiled down at him, for once not overly conscious about how her breasts bobbed in the water. Other men commented about her assets in ways that made her feel uncomfortable, but when Knox did it, she felt nothing but appreciated. She was glad someone enjoyed them, given all the trouble they were and the expense of bras up to the challenge of such heavy lifting. She'd miss that about him. Another thing to add to her growing list.

"Join me." He used his big toe to push off the side of the pool, a move that sent him leisurely floating away from her.

Danielle leaned back to float, too. Knox swung an arm out and linked their pinkie fingers.

They floated. She chatted idly about the conference this weekend in Orlando where she was hoping to learn more about running a rescue operation as a business rather than a hobby. He listened, even offered to keep an eye on the puppies for her. It was so normal, so every day, that Danielle couldn't stop smiling. The heat still simmered between them, arcing through the water, but there was a comfort in it. The reliability of it. In the few days after the doctor's appointment, they'd gotten closer—discussing his physical therapy, finishing up the registration and actually hitting Pay for her first college class, playing with the puppies. He'd taken to bringing Sarge over in the evenings and staying the night. It should've felt crowded in her little cottage, but it felt just right.

The dogs paced the poolside, anxious. Eventually, they settled down, collapsing on the covered patio with a loud exhale. White clouds, fluffy and fake-looking as a child's drawing, floated overhead.

"Do you see that one?"

Danielle didn't know which direction to look because Knox hadn't pointed.

"Doesn't it look like a dog?"

Then she saw it. A tall, thin cloud with what looked for all the world like a long muzzle and even longer tail.

"It does." Danielle smiled. "I always see dogs in the clouds."

"You would."

The pool water flowed toward the skimmer, gently pulling them along. They drifted with no effort. It was a metaphor, she thought, for their relationship. Floating along until the drain sucked them in and ripped out her guts.

Knox let out a long sigh, the kind that sounded like months of pent-up feelings being released. "Best PT ever."

"PT hasn't even started yet."

Another sigh, this one softer and more resigned. "A few more minutes."

"A few more minutes." Danielle was in no hurry to go anywhere. The water made her weightless, a sensation she never got tired of. Her free hand flapped occasionally in the water, steering her closer to Knox, and a soft wind pushed the clouds slowly across the sky. Her cloud dog stretched until it looked more like a snake than a hound.

"Hey." Knox's fingers squeezed hers. "This brings back some memories, doesn't it?"

Wet, hot memories flooded her mind. Yeah, eighteen-year-old versions of them had certainly spent some time in this pool.

"I don't recall ever floating calmly, chastely holding hands like this."

"No. My hands were definitely otherwise occupied in those days." He chuckled and tugged her closer so that they floated side by side, their body heat warming the few inches of water between them.

Without warning, her breasts ached, and she knew the only relief they wanted was the pressure of his hands on her. She forced herself to take long, steadying breaths. She was here to help. Physical therapy assistants did not plant their feet on the pool floor and throw themselves at their client for long, soul-drugging kisses. No matter how many times her mind played the image, she would keep her hands to herself. Except the hand he was holding, of course.

"Come on. Let's do the exercises."

Knox's words startled Danielle out of another replay of the time he'd sat on the second step with her in his lap, and they'd kissed until her dad had come out the back door in his droopy swim shorts and scared the bejeezus out of them with a disgruntled "My eyes, my eyes! I'm too young to be a grandfather." Danielle had sunk into the water, quickly tying her bikini top back in place. Knox stayed on the step, his normally fair skin flushed redder than a sunburned Canadian tourist enjoying the beach on Thanksgiving Day.

Today, her dad was at the clinic, and she and Knox were all grown up. She forced her thoughts away from all the carnal possibilities and back to the task at hand. Physical therapy. Helping Knox get stronger. So he could leave her—which is what she wanted, she reminded herself. They'd decided, hadn't they?

Danielle let her feet drop to the pool floor. "Shall we start with the stretches?"

Knox grunted his consent. They braced their hands against the edge of the pool and started the sequence the therapist had made him practice at the VA on his last visit. Danielle kept an eye on him for any signs of distress, but his face was as stoic as ever. Not by a single muscle twitch did he betray even the slightest sign of pain. What a tough job his physical therapist had, trying to figure out how far was too far with men who'd been trained to give everything they had, no matter the personal cost.

"Need a break?" Danielle leaned her head against the pool edge after they'd finished the third set of stretches.

"I'm fine." Knox's face might as well have been carved from the Diamond Brite coating that lined the pool's surface.

"Sorry." Danielle lifted one side of her mouth in a half smile. "Let me rephrase. I need a break."

"Oh." Knox's whole face changed. Gone was the stone-cold Marine. Knox's eyes, bluer than the tile around the edge of the pool, narrowed as he studied her. "You okay?"

"Sure. Just need a breather."

"Why don't you sit on the step?"

Her mind flashed back to that long ago day, and the words popped out without her full consent. "I will if you will."

It didn't seem possible, but Knox's eyes grew darker. Maybe he remembered, too. "Come on, then." He took a seat on the second step and patted his lap.

Danielle settled on his thighs, wiggling into a comfortable position wedged close against his body. She leaned her head back so that it rested on his shoulder. Knox's arms came around her waist and latched in front of her.

"This is nice." She rolled her head, and her neck cracked. She hadn't realized how tense she was. She rolled her head in the other direction, and her neck cracked again.

Knox growled something.

"Pardon?" She twisted her head but found herself staring at the side of his neck, which didn't exactly shed light on his expression.

"It's not nice."

Danielle jackknifed forward. "Sorry." She started to get off his lap, but his grip around her waist kept her in place.

"That's not what I meant. Dani, about this agreement we have—"

"Yeah?" Danielle knew what those words meant. She told her heart not to break, that it would be better to rip the Band-Aid off. It didn't listen to her, and she thought she could actually feel it cracking open. "Coming to your senses already?"

"Stop it." He pulled her against his chest and rested his chin on her shoulder. "What I mean is I can't help but think that this could be our future. Together." He buried his face in her shoulder. "And I can't stop thinking about this." His lips kissed their way up her neck until he could tug at her earlobe with his teeth.

"You think about my ears?" She tilted her head back.

"I think about all of you. About how all of you should come to Atlanta with me." His hands splayed over her belly and inched their way up.

If her breasts could talk, they'd be screaming *Yes!* But they couldn't, so Danielle scooted back another inch to give him better access. She felt his desire for her against her back and she pretty shamelessly rubbed herself against him. He groaned, so she did it again. Then she turned so their mouths were close enough to kiss.

"You know why that's a bad idea."

"I'm going to have to disagree with you on that. I have some thoughts."

"Later?" Danielle was all about putting off the pain and grabbing the pleasure right now. "I'm not exactly in a talking mood right now."

His answer was a fierce kiss, one that sent flames racing through her veins. She was surprised the pool water didn't start boiling around them. She twisted, running her hands down his torso, enjoying the dips and edges of his muscles, the way they tightened and flexed under her touch.

One of his hands slipped over her breast, and the other found its way under the leg of her one-piece suit and cupped her mound. She moaned into his mouth and gave up on any last bit of rational thinking.

"Is this okay?" he broke from their kiss to ask.

"Please." Sentences were beyond her at this point.

"Thank God." The breath whooshed out of him, and she was close enough to breathe him in. Then his mouth was on hers again, and she forgot that they were outside, in the pool, in the middle of the day. It was just Knox and her, and it was perfect.

Danielle melted in his arms. There was no other word for it. Her body relaxed under his touch, giving him full command of her senses. Knox felt eighteen again, a little amazed and a lot turned on that she trusted him to touch her like this. But he also felt his age and experience. He wasn't fumbling around anymore, hoping to get something right. He might've spent over a decade away from her, but he remembered how to touch her. Had spent recent nights studying her every reaction, every sigh, every flex of her muscles. She shifted, restless, and he smiled into her hair. She'd always been so responsive. He was glad that hadn't changed. He changed the rhythm of his stroke, and she arched against him. Yes, she was his.

His. Knox didn't stop to think about it, just let the rightness sink in. Danielle panting under his touch, her body arching with each stroke of his finger, this was what he'd been missing. Now that they were back together, long-dormant feeling sparked to life. To some degree, his years of service had made it necessary to numb his feelings, to not get too attached to people or outcomes, but now he found himself desperately attached. She felt it, too, he could tell. What could he do to convince her to trust him, really trust him again? What would it take to get her to change her mind about Atlanta? He hadn't figured it out yet, but he would.

When Danielle came apart in his arms, he held on tight, waiting while she rode it out. Her body shuddered delicately, and she turned her face into his neck, gasping for breath. If he had his way, she'd never catch her breath again. He liked her like this, warm and pliant and happy.

"I'm feeling pretty jinxed right about now." Danielle's voice was a bit hoarse and a lot amused.

"It's more than the jinx." Knox knew it came out too harsh, but Danielle didn't seem to mind. He was pretty sure she'd purred. "You know I love you, right?"

"For now." She held her arms over her head and looped them around his neck.

"Forever." His campaign to change her mind started now. "Ready to go inside?"

She kissed the tip of his nose. "As soon as I can walk again. You may have to wait a while."

"I can't wait." He stood, picking her up with him.

She smacked his chest. "Put me down!"

"Nope." He hopped up to the pool deck, Danielle clasped against his chest.

"I'm too heavy."

He stopped and glared down at her. "You. Are. Perfect. Now shut up and tell me where you want this to happen. Pool deck? Patio?"

She blinked up at him, a bit dazed. "Cottage."

He strode toward her front door, not letting go of her until he found her small bedroom. The yellow walls and flowered bedspread had become as familiar to him as his own. He bounced her, wet bathing suit and all, into the middle of the bed. It was small, bigger than a twin but not by much. It was a tight fit for the two of them, which was fine with him.

The dogs had followed him to the cottage, and he took a moment to shoo them into the hallway and shut the door.

"At last." He lay down on his side, one hand on her belly. "I have you all to myself."

She smiled up at him, and his heart froze for a second. He wanted to see that smile every morning for the rest of his life. It made sense in some way, though. The last time he'd thought about things like forever had been with Danielle. There was something about her that made him want to lock it all down and never let go.

So he wouldn't. Not this time. Not ever again. Now, all he had to do was convince her to give him another chance to make her happy. To start over in a new town, clean slate. He skimmed the bathing suit off her body, pretty sure he knew where to start the negotiations. Maybe after her third or fourth orgasm, he'd propose. She was always so agreeable while her body rode out the aftershocks. He shucked his own swim trunks and rolled her on top of him. Time to start those negotiations. Luckily for him, he enjoyed negotiating.

CHAPTER 34

KNOX LET HIMSELF INTO DANIELLE'S PLACE WITH THE KEY she'd lent him. Teenage him would've loved to have such easy access to her, and adult him certainly didn't mind, either.

"You're here!" Danielle's voice traveled down the short hallway from the bedroom. "Thank goodness. I was about to roll out." A small suitcase bumped its way along behind her until she finally stood in the dining-room-turned-puppy-room with him. Her hair was loose, the long bangs brushing her jawline, and she wore dark jeans with some kind of drapey blue blouse. Silver bracelets jangled at her wrist, and she fingered a small pearl pendant necklace.

"You said 9:00 a.m." He checked his phone. He was technically two minutes early.

She blew bangs away from her mouth. "I get nervous traveling. Are you sure you're okay to take care of the puppies?"

He shifted his gaze from contemplating the lushness of her lower lip to where the puppies cavorted in their playpen. "They're growing so fast. Pretty soon they'll take over the whole cottage."

"Don't I know it!" She parked the suitcase by the front door and pulled a printed page out of her back pocket. "I've got the instructions we went over here." She handed it to him. "And I'm only in Orlando, so I can be back here in under four hours if you need me."

Of course I need you. He kept the words from tumbling out of his mouth, but just barely. He'd chickened out, not proposing to her last night. Or the night before. Or the night before that. They were in a good place, and truth was, he was afraid to rock their little boat. The last thing he wanted was to send her running from him again. *Tick tock*, though. Morales wanted him in Atlanta as soon as possible, but Knox wasn't going anywhere until he was sure Danielle would follow. He'd told Morales he needed to stay another few weeks to finish out his physical therapy. What could the guy say to that? He'd gotten his extension, but every minute of it felt like a bomb counting down on his relationship with Danielle.

"I can handle the puppies for a weekend. Can't be any worse than wrangling new recruits." He sent her a smile meant to reassure. Instead, her teeth gnawed that lower lip he loved so much. He couldn't help himself. He reached out and slid his thumb along its plump surface. "Don't worry."

She nodded, bangs bobbing. "I'm going to say goodbye." She picked up each puppy for a quick snuggle, promising each one she'd be back in two days.

Two days. They stretched before him like an eternity. He'd gotten so used to seeing her every day, how they met up at Fur Haven in the evenings and headed back to her place for the night. It felt odd to think of going to the dog park without her. But with three adult greyhounds to keep exercised, that was exactly what he'd be doing.

"Go." He waved her out the door. "I've got this."

She hesitated another moment, showering a bit of love on Luna and Flurry before turning to him with a forced smile. "Suddenly, I don't want to go anymore."

"It's a big event. You could find lots of homes for your fosters. Learn more effective fund-raising techniques. Make connections that could help you build the rescue." He reminded her of the reasons she'd given him when they'd been floating in the pool.

She straightened her spine and rolled her shoulders back. "For the dogs."

He toasted her with a pretend glass. "For the dogs."

The door closed behind her. Knox didn't know how long he stood there, watching the space where she'd been, but tiny, needle-like teeth on his ankle shook him out of his daze.

Daisy lolled on the floor, tiny jaw locked onto Knox's sock.

"How'd you escape, huh?"

Flurry snorted like she couldn't believe such a stupid question. Luna circled a dozen times before lying down on her dog bed. Knox picked up Daisy and put her back in the pen. He counted them for good measure and came up short by two.

"Who's missing?" He scanned the pen, the floor, under the cabinet. No puppies. Great. Danielle wasn't gone even half an hour, and he'd already lost two puppies. Not good. So not good.

"You could help." He glared at Flurry, but she huffed and lay down with her back to the playpen, clearly over the whole mothering thing. Who could blame her? The little stinkers were everywhere with their sharp teeth and endless energy. It wouldn't be too long until they'd outgrown their playpen and not too long after that, it'd be hard to imagine all eight of them comfortably residing in this tiny cottage. Danielle needed a bigger place. A place with a yard. Like his place.

It was easy to imagine the puppies scampering in his backyard while Sarge, Luna, and Flurry looked on from the deck. It was even easier to imagine sitting out on the deck with Danielle in some comfortable chairs he had yet to purchase, drinking wine after a long day. It was easy, too easy, to imagine all the ways in which Danielle would so easily fit into his home. Making nachos in the kitchen. Watching TV in the living room. Sleeping in his bed. Hell, he even had entire bedrooms he could give her for puppies. It was a pretty picture, one they could replicate in Atlanta. It was just harder to see because he'd never been there. But they'd find a place. He's spent his adult life moving from base to base, following orders. There was always a new place to land. It would be fine.

Framed photos on the wall of Danielle at different ages caught his attention. In all of them, her wide smile was in place. In three of them, her dad stood beside her, arm around her shoulders, growing progressively balder as the years passed. Some photos were school pictures, ending on a serious one of Danielle posed in her high-school graduation cap and gown, chin propped on her fist, staring at the photographer like she had a secret. She would've been pregnant at that point, and his throat tightened at the memory of their loss.

He returned to his favorite of all the pictures, the one that showed Danielle at about ten years old holding a red Popsicle high in the air while a long-haired dog licked her face. She looked so happy, it damn near broke him. Because it wouldn't be fine.

Danielle's whole life was here. She loved her dad. It would hurt her to move away from him. She was excited about starting her online class, about all her plans for Homestretch, not to mention how the morning coffee crew at the dog park would miss her. His sisters-in-law would blame him for taking Danielle away from them.

What exactly was waiting for him in Atlanta? A job he knew virtually nothing about. A strained relationship with his mother. House hunting that wouldn't end well because he'd never find a house he liked as much as the one he currently owned. Compared to staying here, working with his brothers, living with Danielle? Was he really in such a hurry to give it all up? The ten-year-old Danielle in the framed photo was home. Did he really want to rip her away from it?

He roamed from kitchen to living room to Danielle's bedroom door. One thing in favor of small living spaces was that there couldn't be too many places for puppies to hide. Sure enough, he found Pinto and Monki wrestling in a pile of Danielle's laundry.

"Come on, you scamps." He scooped them up like footballs under each arm. "Let's see what's on our list of things to do today." He dropped them back into the playpen where Sweet Pea and Tilly dogpiled on top of them.

Knox studied the list Danielle had left behind and added a few lines of his own, like calling Morales to figure out some alternatives. Could he be part-time? A consultant? Or if he turned down Morales' offer, was he closing that door forever? It was too much to think about right now. He started on the detailed feeding directions, determined not to let Danielle, or her dogs, down.

Danielle felt like a thief sneaking into her own home. She'd seen Knox's truck in the driveway and wondered why he'd still be at her place so late. She wasn't supposed to come home until Monday, and she hadn't expected him to sleep with the puppies. She'd thought he'd enjoy being back in his own bed for a few nights.

Her pulse picked up, thinking about him asleep in her bed, waiting for her. She was glad the rescue summit had ended early. Danielle was absolutely exhausted from her two days of manning the Homestretch booth, and she'd sorely missed Luna and Flurry. They were such great icebreakers when people came to the table to talk to her. But Luna got carsick easily and Flurry should stay with the puppies, so she'd left them with Knox.

Last night, she'd thought about them all alone in her house. Tonight, driving back to the hotel from the fairgrounds, she'd wanted nothing more than to snuggle up with them and watch some mindless TV. It was only a three-plus-hour drive. She'd packed up the car and headed home, her foot heavy on the gas pedal. Home. It had always meant her dad's place, her dogs. In the darkness of her car's interior, soft music on the stereo, she had to face the fact that she wasn't racing home. She was racing to Knox. While she could, obviously. Why waste another night away from him if she didn't have to? There were plenty of lonely nights to come.

In the puppy room, she found Knox. And the dogs. All the dogs. He was sound asleep on his back, one hand covering his eyes. Sarge lay against one side, and Luna bracketed him on the other. Flurry had the dog bed to herself. Knox's chest rose and fell with each breath, and the puppies sprawled on his chest rose and fell with him. Three puppies covered his torso. Pinto slept in the space between his knees, and the other four slept in a pile at his feet.

What had gone on here that not even one dog rose to greet her? She thumped the suitcase onto the tile floor, and Flurry blinked sleepy eyes at her. A few of the puppies stirred but didn't waken. Danielle coughed, then coughed louder.

"Hey!" Knox jackknifed at the waist, sitting straight up, puppies tumbling off him like leaves off a tree. "You're home. Is it Monday?" He rubbed bleary eyes with the heel of his hands.

"I came back early. It's not quite Monday yet. Close, though." She checked the time on her phone. "Another hour."

He blinked up at her, much like Flurry had, while Sarge and Luna heaved to their feet and trotted over to greet her.

"That's more like it." Danielle rubbed their ears. "I missed you guys."

"I missed you, too." Knox stood, cradling Pinto in his hands. "We need to talk."

Were there four more dreaded words in the English language when it came to relationships? Especially their relationship? Danielle knew she shouldn't be surprised that he'd eventually pin her down with those "thoughts" he'd mentioned last week. The dogs were too much for most guys. It was why she hadn't had a boyfriend in so long. With the puppies, the pressure was eightfold. What guy wouldn't crack under the strain? He'd been passed out from exhaustion mere moments ago. No one wanted to live like that. No one but her.

Danielle shook off the long drive and gathered her courage. "Sure. How about over tea?" She headed into the kitchen and put on the kettle. It gave her restless hands something to do besides grab for Knox the way they wanted to. Why hadn't she lain down on the floor next to him and snuggled up like one of the puppies while she had the chance? Thanks to her slow reaction time, she'd never get the chance again. He was going to say his goodbyes now. She tried not to let the thought get her down while she chose caffeine-free tea bags and placed them in two plain white mugs.

Knox sat in the one chair by the tiny bistro table she used for all her meals, so she leaned back against the edge of the counter, stuffing her hands into the pockets of her baggy jeans.

"The puppies are getting big. I swear they put on two pounds each since yesterday." Knox grinned up at her, and Danielle's heart thumped loudly in her chest. This wasn't the opening line she'd expected. She'd been waiting for something more like "It's been fun, but I'm heading to Atlanta…"

"And they'll only get bigger and bigger." Danielle could get on board with this topic. She could talk dogs all day and all night long. It was certainly better than where she'd thought this conversation was going.

Knox frowned, and Danielle's heart stuttered in her chest. Here it came. The other shoe, dropping.

"Your place is too small. Your two greyhounds alone are enough to crowd it, but now with the puppies? They need more space."

Danielle swallowed hard. "I'm going to find them homes. I know I can't have ten dogs here. Or anywhere really. I'll find a new place once the puppies are adopted."

"They need room to run and play. They need grass and sunlight." Knox continued like she hadn't spoken, like he was getting through some kind of rehearsed speech. "They need a yard. A big one. Like mine."

"Wait." Danielle braced her hands on the counter behind her. "You want me to bring the puppies to your house to play?"

"I have extra rooms. I can turn one into a puppy room, at least until they're too big or adopted out. There's plenty of space." Knox had begun counting points off on his fingers. When he got to his thumb, he looked up at her. "I think it's best. For the puppies."

"If they visit you?" Danielle's breath was tight in her chest, and not in that good, breathless way he often inspired in her. Panic. It was definitely panic stealing her breath.

"To live with me." Knox wiped his palms on his thighs, clearly done with his list ticking.

"You want the puppies?" Danielle's words came out whisper soft. "All of them?"

Knox pushed to his feet. Took a step toward her, then another. "Flurry and Luna, too. They'd like all the space, and Sarge misses them." He stopped with only an inch between them.

Danielle inhaled sharply, past the pain in her chest. He smelled like Knox. And puppies. "You want to take all my dogs?"

Knox shook his head slowly, a smile tugging at the corner of his mouth. "No, I want them to live with me. Because I'm pretty sure that if they move in, so will you."

Danielle slapped a hand against her chest to keep her heart from leaping straight out of it. "What?"

"I'm bungling this, aren't I?" Knox leaned in, dipping his head so that their lips brushed ever so softly. "Move in with me, Dani. Bring the dogs. And the puppies. And all your stuff."

Danielle's hand drifted from her heart to his. She pressed against his chest, felt the strong, steady beat of him. "Why?" she whispered against his lips.

"Logistically, it makes sense."

Logic shouldn't turn her on like this, but it did. "Tell me more about these logistics."

"The yard, the space, Fur Haven across the street. It's ideal for the dogs. And you're ideal for me." Knox dropped his forehead against hers. "Please, Dani."

Danielle looped her arms around his neck. "Until you move to Atlanta?"

"Something like that. I'm working on it." His eyes bored into hers, and he must've liked something he saw there, because he smiled. "Do you trust me?"

She lifted her lips the short distance to his and kissed him, really kissed him, with all the joy crowding her body. He kissed her back, pressing her into the counter until the edge bit into her lower back, but she didn't care.

"We'll figure it out tomorrow. Tonight, let's go to bed."

Danielle followed him to the bedroom, ignoring the kettle's whistle. It would turn itself off in a moment, and she wasn't letting go of Knox for anything. Not tonight. And if she had her way? Not ever again. But when had she ever gotten her way? They were delaying the inevitable, and she planned to enjoy every extra minute he wrangled for them.

CHAPTER 35

CLOUDS PUFFED THEIR WAY SLOWLY ACROSS THE CLEAR BLUE sky. Danielle stepped off the Fur Haven Park elevator, letting Flurry, Luna, and Sarge off their leashes as soon as the doors cracked open. They rolled out into the park, greeting familiar dogs with a sniff and an invitation to run. Soon, they were running laps along the edge of the rooftop park, a small squad of assorted mutts trailing after them, trying to keep up.

"Girl, show us the rock." Riley was the first of the three women gathered at the bone-shaped bench to greet her.

Danielle wiped the stupid grin off her face. She'd had a good morning. A very good morning. One could even say orgasmically good. "Sorry, what?"

"The rock? The ring?" Riley held out her hand like she was showing off an engagement ring, the diamond on her own wedding band sparkling in the sunlight. "Lance already told Carrie, and Carrie—"

"Should probably have kept her mouth shut." Carrie held out a cup of coffee to Danielle. "But Lance could hardly believe it when Knox texted him last night."

"Neither could Caleb. Knox has been so insistent he's not sticking around." Riley lifted a flask and poured a healthy measure of amber liquid into the yellow mug. "We figured we'd celebrate with you this morning. Irish coffee–style."

"Thank you." Danielle sipped at the doctored brew. "It's delicious. But what are we celebrating, exactly?"

"Your engagement!" Riley laughed. "You must really need your caffeine this morning, hmmm?"

"Leave the girl alone." Eliza sat on the bench with a newspaper pulled up on her iPad. "I think we may not have the full story."

Danielle looked at each woman, one at a time. Their indulgent smiles. Eliza's raised eyebrow. "What, exactly, did Knox text his brothers last night?"

"That you were moving in!" Carrie sipped her mug thoughtfully.

"I did." Danielle poured herself another bit of Irish into her half-full mug. "For now. Until he leaves for the new job."

"I knew it." Eliza clucked her tongue and dabbed at her forehead with a tissue. "You all have weddings on the brain. Just because Caleb and Lance were quick to pop the question doesn't mean Knox will. Look how long it took William to get Riley's grandmother back."

"Wait." Maybe the caffeine was helping her think more clearly. "You think Knox wants to marry me?"

Eliza shrugged one shoulder, but the other three heads nodded solemnly.

"That's—" Danielle gulped down the last of her warm coffee, stalling for time. Likely, she had to admit, but not what she wanted to discuss. Luna nuzzled the hand dangling at her side. She placed a steadying hand on the dog's head and took a deep breath. "Ridiculous. He's got Atlanta, and I already told him I won't go with him."

And then she burst into tears.

They came out of nowhere, the tears. She'd been happy, brilliantly so, only moments ago. She'd woken in Knox's arms, the sound of squealing puppies in the next room her alarm clock. She'd checked on them, made sure Luna and Flurry understood the dog door, and tucked herself right back into bed with Knox. He'd been awake by then, too, and they'd started their day with slow kisses and a quiet, intense kind of lovemaking Danielle had never experienced before. Everything was great. Perfect.

"Oh no, oh no." Riley wrapped an arm around Danielle.

"I'll text Knox." Carrie's thumbs were already flying on her phone.

"No!" Danielle sniffled and attempted to pull herself together. "It's nothing. Don't worry. We have an understanding."

"Oh my God." Riley's eyes grew wider and wider. "Are you pregnant?"

Danielle felt the words like a blow to her abdomen. Her stomach physically contracted like it was taking a hit. She doubled over, sobbing so hard she wasn't sure they could understand her denial. "No, no. It's not possible."

"You know." Riley tightened her hold on Danielle. "When two people love each other very much—"

"It's not possible. I had a hysterectomy." She'd avoided the h-word for so long, it felt cathartic to say it. She sucked in a breath before explaining. "Endometriosis. It was bad."

"Oh." Riley sank down to the ground with Danielle, her hold on her shoulders firm. Soon, two greyhounds flanked them, crowding them with warmth and investigating noses. "I'm so sorry, Danielle. I didn't know."

"I'm sorry, too." Carrie plopped on the ground beside them, heedless of the possible grass stains to her linen trousers. "I've heard it's really painful."

"No one knows. Well, my dad and my doctors, but no one else." Danielle ran the back of her hand under her nose. "It's fine. It's just, you have to understand. Knox wants a big family. Always has. So whatever this is we're doing, it's temporary. I'm going to enjoy it, of course, but it won't last. I'm glad that he's leaving. Really. It makes it easier, knowing the expiration date, you know?"

Danielle didn't miss the look that passed between Riley and Carrie. They didn't believe her. But time would prove her right.

"You have to tell him." Carrie added another shot to her Irish coffee.

Riley took the Bailey's and topped off Danielle's mug. "Today."

Danielle took a long drink and nodded. "I know."

You're in trouble.

Lance's text came as Knox was grabbing toast out of the toaster. He'd woken to find Danielle and the big dogs gone. Fur Haven, he'd figured, probably sipping coffee with his sisters-in-law. He knew they all enjoyed the ritual. He just didn't want to wake up that early to join them ever again. He liked Riley and Carrie. They were good people. He could appreciate them later in the day.

I don't actually work for you, you know.

So what if he came in a bit late today? He'd had a late night, moving all the dogs into his home and getting the puppy room set up at 1:00 a.m. Today, they'd need to go back and get Danielle's stuff. He couldn't wait to see Danielle's clothes filling half the closet. She could have more than half, really. It wasn't like his stuff took up much space. In fact, she could have all the closets in the whole house if she wanted. As far as he was concerned, whatever was his was hers now.

Lady trouble. Lance followed up his text with an emoji of a shocked face. Danielle thinks it isn't permanent. I thought you proposed last night?

She moved in with me. Knox munched on his toast without bothering to put anything on it. A man needed sustenance for conversations like these with his brother. Especially with his brother.

She told C & R that it wasn't permanent.

The toast dropped from Knox's hand. Hell no. Maybe he hadn't been specific because he owed Morales a phone call first, but he thought she'd understood. They were building a life together.

Did you say the words Will You Marry Me? Or not? The next emoji from Lance was a confused face and then a diamond ring.

Not in those exact words.

Lance filled Knox's screen with rows of laughing faces, laughing-with-tears faces, rolling and laughing faces. Better get to it then.

Knox stared at the toast on his kitchen floor, thinking how if Danielle were here with the dogs, that bread would be long gone. *I need a ring.*

Forget about that. You need to talk to Danielle ASAP. And that's an order.

Knox shoved his phone in his pocket. Brothers were a pain in the ass. But that didn't mean Lance was wrong. Still, he'd made a commitment to Morales. He owed the man a call. Shit.

"Ready to shake the sand off your feet and get to work?" Morales' cheerful voice boomed in his ear. "You rolling in early or what?"

"About that." Knox rammed shoes on his feet, phone balanced between his ear and shoulder. "I'm gonna need more time."

Morales was silent long enough that Knox checked his bars and hit speaker. A thunk on Morales' end sounded like he'd set something down, hard. "Thought you might say that. Look, I've been patient. How many times have you changed your arrival date now? Twice? Three times? I've lost count. Makes a man think you might not want the job after all. You backing out on me, Gunny?"

"Now's not the best time." Knox tightened his brace and grabbed his keys, his mind so full of Danielle he couldn't handle Morales right now. "Can I call you later?"

Morales cleared his throat. "I've got a business to run here, and if you're not gonna come through, you need to tell me now."

"I don't want to let you down, but I can't live in Atlanta." Knox didn't want to be so blunt, but urgency pushed him to faster, faster. "Maybe we can work something else out."

"It's that girl, isn't it? The one from high school." Morales chuckled. "You never did get over her."

Knox and Morales had knocked back more than a few together over the years, so it didn't surprise Knox that Morales knew about Danielle. He knew he'd talked about her, especially in the early years. He *was* surprised Morales remembered, and Knox figured he deserved the truth. "Yeah, it's her. I can't leave again."

"I knew it." Morales sounded smug, and Knox could imagine the shit-eating grin he must be wearing.

"I swear I will call you back, but right now I've got to ask her a really important question." Knox hung up on his buddy, and it wasn't more than thirty seconds before the first text notification hit his pocket. What now? Did Caleb need to chime in? Maybe his mother wanted to give him more horrible life advice? But it was Morales.

Invite me to the wedding.

Knox choked on a laugh, and he knew he owed his buddy a longer conversation—which he would absolutely initiate. Later. For now, he texted back a thumbs-up. Morales deserved someone all in, and Knox wasn't that guy anymore. Maybe they'd work out a deal where he could consult, maybe they wouldn't. Either way, his life was in Miami Beach now.

Knox paused to send one more text. To his mom: *I'm asking Danielle to marry me.* She replied with an entire row of question marks. He didn't answer, figuring he'd fill her in later, however it turned out. He was done worrying about making her happy; it'd been foolish to ever think he could. She'd chosen her life. Now he would choose his. He tore out of the house, hoping he wasn't too late.

But he was. The elevator doors opened onto the rooftop dog park, and he was met with an angry group of women. Women who were usually quite pleased to see him. Riley shook her head. Carrie and Eliza wore matching expressions of disapproval.

Carrie stepped forward. "You idiot, she's taking the ramp."

He nodded his thanks and took off, ignoring the twinge in his leg and the litany in his head that shouted at him in his old drill instructor's voice that he needed to move, move, move. His whole life depended on it.

CHAPTER 36

DANIELLE SWIPED AT HER EYES WITH THE BACK OF HER hand. Gosh, she'd made such a fool of herself in front of everyone at the dog park. Between Carrie and Riley, Knox was sure to hear about it. She placed one foot in front of the other on the rubberized ramp that wound its way down the side of the parking garage. Most folks took the elevator, but a few hardcore running enthusiasts, like Carrie, took the ramp up and down from the park. This morning, it was empty and Danielle's sneakers squeaked against the ramp's surface. Sarge, Flurry, and Luna trotted along beside her, alternately nudging her in the thigh. They knew she was upset. She needed to get it together. For the dogs.

Look at all the good things in her life. She loved her dogs, the puppies, her new plan for Homestretch. Really, she had nothing to complain about, much less shed tears over. Get a grip already.

A lone tear escaped the corner of her eye and trickled down her cheek, heedless of her mental pep talk. Because deep down, she wanted what Riley and Carrie had—that complete certainty in another person. She thought she'd been happy enough, but these past few weeks had showed her she wasn't. Enough, that is. Yes, she was happy, but waking up with Knox this morning, well, she'd learned she could be happier. And now she wanted that, and she wanted it all the time and forever.

"Dani!"

She spun at the sound of her name, her heel catching on the rubber ramp in exactly the right way for her to lose her balance. She landed on her butt with a *thump*. Luna nosed her chin questioningly, and Flurry flopped down beside her, like it was perfectly natural to take a break on the way down the ramp. Sarge pulled in Knox's direction but sat when he hit the end of his leash.

Knox's hand reached down for her. Danielle gave it a think, but no, there was no graceful way out of this situation. She grasped his hand and levered herself back to her feet.

"Hey." She swiped her bangs out of her face, tucking them behind her ear.

"Hey."

She could tell from the tone of his voice that he already knew. Somehow, Carrie or Riley, or both, had gotten to him.

He tipped her face toward him, finger under her chin. "You know I love you, right?"

Her smile trembled. "Jinx."

"I mean it." His blue eyes searched hers, so worried and shadowed that she forgot her own embarrassment for a moment and reached up to cup his cheek in her palm.

"I love you, too. You know that."

"It's still good to hear."

"Agreed." Standing with Knox so close made her feel even more ridiculous for how she'd acted. Knox was a good guy, and he was here for her. No one could predict the future. Would it be so bad to live in the moment with him, however long that moment lasted? No, no it would not.

"I don't have a ring." Knox's shoulders scrunched forward. "It's why I didn't ask last night. I wanted everything to be perfect. You know, big romantic gesture or whatever. But I couldn't wait for all that, not when you walked through the door and I realized how much I'd missed you. I want to spend my life with you, Dani."

Danielle swallowed hard. "You don't have to say all this. I know Carrie must've told you about my breakdown. It's not your fault. I'm fine with how we are."

"What if I'm not?"

"You're not?"

Knox blew out a frustrated breath. "On some level, I thought living together would prove to you that my leg wouldn't hinder the kind of life we could have together."

"I never thought it would."

"I guess maybe I did. Huh." The finger under her chin slid along her jawline and into her hair. "It's humbling that you have more faith in me than I do."

"That's kind of how these things work, isn't it?"

"What things?"

"Relationships. But, Knox?"

"Yeah?" His other hand had slipped to her nape, and he seemed distracted by the flow of her hair through his fingers.

"I'm not really the forever kind of girl, am I? There's not going to be a picket fences and babies, and I know you want those things. I'll love you for as long as you let me, but I don't want you to tie yourself to a woman who can't give you the future you want."

"You're the only future I want."

Those ridiculous tears started up again. "You mean that now, but I won't hold you to it. Not after you know."

He pulled her against his chest, and she felt the pounding of his heart, the drumbeat to her favorite song. "Know what? What is this big secret?"

———

Clutching her sides as if to hold herself together, face downturned, Danielle uttered words so soft he almost missed them. "I can't get pregnant."

Knox shook his head, sure he'd misheard. "But when we were—"

"It was endometriosis." Danielle sucked in a long breath and slowly straightened until she looked him in the eye. "I didn't know it back then, but that's what caused the miscarriage. By the time

I was diagnosed, the damage was done. Too much scarring, too many fibroids. After years and years of unsuccessful treatment, I finally had to have a hysterectomy."

"No." Knox's head shook back and forth, faster and faster. "You wanted a big family. You'd already picked out names."

The tears spilled from her eyes. "I know."

"I don't understand." Knox blinked his eyes hard, moisture gathering in the corners. After leaving home, leaving Danielle, he hadn't planned on any kind of future. He hadn't really expected to survive too many more tours, but when his mind had wandered to old age, he'd imagined a wife. Kids. Grandkids. If they all happened to look a bit like Danielle, well, they were his fantasies and no one else needed to know about them. "You could've told me."

"When?" Her simple question speared him. He'd shut her out when she'd needed his support. He'd been a selfish Donovan, disguising his decision as some noble sacrifice meant to benefit her. Really, he'd only been running scared.

"I'm sorry." The words weren't enough, but he had to say them. He wasn't running anymore. "I was an idiot back then, probably still am today, and I'll never be able to make up for how I hurt you." He reached for her, but she flinched away. He didn't blame her. He settled for taking Sarge's leash. The dog leaned against his leg, and Knox scratched the top of his head, looking for the right words to say. Or at least better ones. "It was bad, wasn't it?"

"Yeah." Danielle's tortured gaze met his, and he saw how this confession destroyed her. How the past sat right there with her, clouding her vision. "Plus the depression. Afterward. It took a few years for me to—" She swiped at her nose with the back of her hand and stared up at the sky.

So many pieces fell into place. The way she'd reacted at the Easter egg hunt, at the petting farm, probably even why she'd been so hesitant to be with him at all. "Is that why you didn't go to college?"

"At first, yeah, the pain. It was chronic and unpredictable, and none of the treatments we tried lasted for long. I couldn't attend classes like that."

"And after?"

"After? The scholarships expired."

"Your dad has money. Don't tell me he wouldn't have footed the bill."

Danielle smiled. "You sound like him. By then, it felt too late. Everyone I knew had already graduated, and I was still working at my dad's clinic because I couldn't hold down a real job. Depression. It was crippling, more so than even the endometriosis. Honestly, the hysterectomy set me free. It stopped the pain, the worry. Eventually, the depression stopped, too. I started Homestretch a few months after my surgery, and that's what helped the most."

Of course she had. Danielle never thought of herself first. Knox ached to pull her into his arms, but he was afraid she'd pull away again. Instead, he opened his arms wide, inviting her in for a hug.

She let him stand there for a moment, awkward, unsure, hurting for her. Then she threw herself at him, wrapping her arms around his waist and burying her face in his chest.

"This is what's so unfair. Where was this hug when I really needed it?"

Knox was gutted, like an old-fashioned bayonet had skewered him. He'd left her, alone and in pain. Okay, she'd had her father and her friends, but she'd wanted him to stay. She'd never made a secret of that. She'd called and texted for close to six months before giving up on him.

"I'm an asshole." Knox breathed the words into her hair. "A self-centered, know-it-all asshole, and I am so, so sorry that I left you alone to deal with all that."

She sniffed and wiped her nose against his T-shirt. "You are an asshole."

"But, Dani?" He lifted his head and used a finger to tip her face toward his. "This time, I'm not going anywhere."

"Oh God, that's even worse." She backed away from him, fast. "Please, go home."

"If that's what you want." He'd do anything for her. Couldn't she see that? "Will you come with me?"

But apparently, she couldn't. Her shattered eyes met his. "In a while. I need to take a walk."

The thought of leaving it like this between them was too much. He had to make her understand that this time was different; he was different.

"I'm not going to Atlanta. I'm not going anywhere you aren't. For too long, I've been drifting, doing what I felt like, what came easily. But I'm making a choice, Dani, and my choice is you. Forever. What you've told me doesn't change that."

"You say that now. Let it sink in. No kids, not ever. No grand-kids. No family." She shook her head and shuffled down the ramp with Luna and Flurry. He watched until she disappeared down the street. Then he thunked his head against the concrete wall. Sarge nudged his hand with a soft whine.

"I know, big guy. We really screwed this up."

Sarge looked at him with unblinking eyes.

"Sorry, you're right." Knox petted his head. "You didn't do anything wrong. I screwed this up all by myself. What should I do?"

Sarge pawed at Knox's hand and nosed Knox's pockets where there were still two treats.

"Good to know your priorities."

What about his own priorities? Danielle was at the top of the list now, and her running away was no more than he deserved. How could she ever trust him again after what he'd done to her? It was so much worse than she'd ever let on, and he didn't know how to fix it. He'd figure it out, though. *Semper Fidelis* wasn't just a slogan; it was a way of life. And he wanted that life to be with Danielle.

"What is going on?" Danielle stood on the sidewalk facing Knox's house. Granted, her walk had been a long one, but when had he had time to do all this? Red, white, and blue bunting draped the boxwoods and hung from the banister.

He sauntered toward her on the front walkway, Sarge at his side. "Fourth of July is right around the corner."

"But that's not—Wait, what is… What is wrong with you?" Her eyes didn't know where to look next. There was just…so much.

"I'm allowed to be patriotic." His words were flippant, but his hands played in Sarge's fur, betraying his nervousness.

"And the rest of it?" Danielle swept her hand to encompass the entire front yard. "It looks like a holiday décor store exploded out here." In addition to the American flag hanging from the pole on the front porch, the Easter decorations were also back out on the yard. And the Halloween decorations, the Christmas decorations, the Valentine's Day hearts. Reindeer were draped in American flags while tiny Easter bunnies cavorted with skeletons. Fake tombstones that said things like *I Told You I Was Sick*, *Tomb Sweet Tomb*, and Danielle's favorite, *Don't Laugh, You're Next*, sat next to snowmen and four-foot-high glitter hearts. It was possibly the most bizarre thing Danielle had ever seen. Even Luna and Flurry seemed hesitant, standing on either side of her like battle-ready guards.

"I'm here for the duration, Dani. Every month of every year. Every holiday. Our house will be the place to go for Easter egg hunts and trick-or-treating. We'll be a neighborhood institution, buying more and more decorations every year until the entire garage is filled with boxes. That's my plan. My commitment. I'm not going anywhere." He took a few more steps toward her but stopped when she put up her hand.

"That all sounds like family stuff, Knox. Even this grand gesture, isn't it for the benefit of kids? You can't help it. Deep down, you want your own family. What kind of person would I be to deny you that?" Her hand trembled in the air.

"You're the person I love." He stepped into her palm until it rested in the center of his chest. "I never thought of myself as particularly family focused, but you're right about one thing. I want a family with you. But, Dani, a family can be whatever we make it. It can be you and me and a bunch of dogs. And my brothers and their families. And your dad. Don't you see? We already have family."

Her fingers curled in his chest, and she looked up to lock eyes with him. "No kids, Knox. Ever. You can't tell me that's what you really want."

"You know there are other options, right?" He held her gaze, steady and true. "If we want children, they don't have to come out of your body."

She pulled back. "That's a little graphic."

"Adoption, foster care. If we decide to have a family, we've got options. Hell, you're already a proven foster-care expert."

"Dogs and kids are not the same thing." She blinked, tears clinging to her eyelashes, blurring her vision so that he looked like a hazy lump of everything she ever wanted. "You wouldn't mind if our kids weren't yours? Or if there were no kids at all?"

"What's so great about my genetics that I'd be such a snob about it? Biology doesn't make a family. Choice does. We can choose any kind of family we want. Even if it's all dogs. Our family is whatever we make it."

"You've only thought about this for a few hours. You need more time."

"Isn't fifteen years enough wasted time? Dani, we've both been coasting, practically asleep at the wheel. Being with you again has woken me up, and I don't want to go back to being numb." He covered the hand in the center of his chest with both of his. "We can make it work. I know we can."

A round of applause exploded across the street. Danielle turned in Knox's arms. Eliza, Carrie, and Riley stood in front of the Dorothy.

"Say yes!" Riley shouted.

"He hasn't asked me a question yet," Danielle shouted back.

Knox pulled her back against him, positioning her in that way that made it feel like their bodies had been made to fit together. He leaned his head down, bringing his lips close to her ear.

"Do you want to marry me, Danielle Morrow?"

Danielle smiled so wide that the other women started whooping their approval.

"Having trouble deciding?" His breath tickled her ear. "Do you need me to get the Magic Eight Ball egg?"

"There's no mystery here." She leaned into him, cheek nestling into her favorite spot on his chest. "If you're sure, I am too."

"Then say yes."

Danielle stepped away, her palms sliding down his *Semper Fi* tattoo to grasp both his hands in hers. "Yes."

Luna yipped, and all three of the well-trained dogs jumped on them, knocking Knox off his balance. He and Danielle both went down and were soon buried in a pile of wiggling dogs.

"You okay?" Danielle asked after she'd caught her breath and struggled to a sitting position.

"Are you kidding me?" Knox stretched over the top of Sarge's head to kiss her. "This is the best day of my life."

Cheering friends and misbehaving dogs forgotten, Danielle returned the kiss with her whole heart.

ACKNOWLEDGMENTS

To Kait Ballenger, mentor and friend. Thank you isn't big enough for all I owe you. Terry Price and Katy Yocom, thank you for all the hours of dreaming and scheming. You inspire me to keep going. SpLove always.

Jenny Luper, you've been on this journey with me every step of the way. Thank you for the love. For listening. For your valuable insights. And, of course, for the signature hot tub champagne cocktails served in crystal flutes.

With gratitude to Alex Flinn, Curtis Sponslor, and Gaby Triana, who read the first few chapters and helped me craft a stronger vision. Nicole Cabrera, thank you for not letting me get away with "just" anything. Steven Dos Santos, thank you for always being game for a brainstorm and some word play.

Ben Cook, my dear pseudo-sib, thank you for your help filling in so many blanks. Any mistakes are mine alone. This world is a safer, better place because you're in it.

Herman Geerling, who always picks up the tab, whether it's for dinner or an M.F.A. You've given me so much, and I am so grateful that you are my dad.

Nicole Resciniti, you always know the right thing to say. Your optimism and savvy are greatly appreciated.

For help naming the puppies, thank you to Karen Balcanoff, Madison Cabrera, Barbara Cannatella, Angel Conlon, Julie Edelstein, Chris Kirchner, Heather Schwarz, and Carrie Rathel.

As always, a sincere thank you to the Sourcebooks team who put so much into making this series great—my editor Deb Werksman and the dedicated folks behind the scenes: Dawn Adams, Sabrina Baskey, Susie Benton, Rachel Gilmer, Stefani Sloma, Sierra Stovall,

Katie Stutz, Jocelyn Travis, and Cari Zwolinkski. Special thanks to Diane Dannenfeldt and Jessica Smith for your eagle eyes and incredible patience.

ABOUT THE AUTHOR

Mara Wells loves stories, especially stories with kissing. She lives in Hollywood, Florida, with her family and two rescue dogs: a poodle mix named Houdini Beauregarde and Sheba Reba Rita Peanut, a Chihuahua mix. To find out more, you can sign up for her newsletter at marawellsauthor.com.

FUR HAVEN DOG PARK SERIES

Mara Wells brings you the love of an adorable puppy and a forever home in this heartwarming series

Cold Nose, Warm Heart

Caleb Donovan has plans to demolish Riley Carson's beloved building, but she and her fellow neighborhood dog park devotees won't go down without a fight.

A Tail for Two

Lance Donovan agreed to dog sit only to help out his younger brother. Little does he know that an encounter with his ex-wife and their dog at the local dog park is going to turn his life upside down...

Paws for Love

Danielle Morrow works tirelessly for greyhound rescue, though she guards her own heart vigilantly. But now that Knox Donovan is back, she might be ready for her own second chance at love...

"Full of humor and heart."
—*Publishers Weekly* for *Cold Nose, Warm Heart*

For more info about Sourcebooks's books and authors, visit:
sourcebooks.com

WARM NIGHTS IN MAGNOLIA BAY

Welcome to Magnolia Bay, a heartwarming new series
with a Southern flair from author Babette de Jongh

Abby Curtis lands on her Aunt Reva's doorstep at Bayside Barn with
nowhere to go but up. Learning animal communication from her aunt
while taking care of the motley assortment of rescue animals on the farm
is an important part of Abby's healing process. She is eager to begin a new
life on her own, but she isn't prepared for the magnetism between her and
her wildly handsome and distracting new neighbor...

PUPPY KISSES

A heartwarming series by Lucy Gilmore, featuring service puppies who might just be matchmakers in the making...

Dawn Vasquez never takes life too seriously. But when she rescues a golden retriever named Gigi, Dawn begins to imagine what it'd be like to settle down and let someone rely on her for a change. Unfortunately, Adam Dearborn—a handsome, hopelessly buttoned-up cattle rancher in need of a guide dog—has also fallen in love with the little ball of fluff and stubbornly insists that no other animal will do. Adam isn't sure what drives him to fight to keep Gigi for himself, but he suspects it has something to do with his growing—and unfortunate—attachment to Dawn...

"Uplifting, romantic, and heartwarming."
—*Long and Short Reviews* for *Puppy Love*

For more info about Sourcebooks's
books and authors, visit:
sourcebooks.com

RESCUE ME

In this fresh, poignant series about rescue
animals, every heart has a forever home

A New Leash on Love
When Craig Williams arrived at the local no-kill animal
shelter for help, he didn't expect a fiery young woman
to blaze into his life. But the more time he spends with
Megan, the more he realizes it's not just animals she's
adept at saving...

Sit, Stay, Love
For devoted no-kill shelter worker Kelsey Sutton, rehab-
bing a group of rescue dogs is a welcome challenge.
Working with a sexy ex-military dog handler who needs
some TLC himself? That's a whole different story...

My Forever Home
There's no denying Tess Grasso has a way with animals,
but when she helps Mason Redding give a free-spirited
stray a second chance, this husky might teach them a few
things about faith, love, and forgiveness.

"Sexy and fun..."
—*RT Book Reviews* for *A New Leash on Love*,
Top Pick, 4½ Stars

HEAD OVER PAWS

It'll be love at first bark for Debbie Burns's Rescue Me series, featuring an animal shelter and the humans and pets whose lives are transformed there

Olivia Graham isn't in a position to have a dog of her own, but her new role as a volunteer rescue driver for the local animal shelter will keep her close to her four-legged friends. When she's called to transport dogs and cats that have been misplaced by flooding, she doesn't hesitate to help, but her aging car isn't as reliable as she is and sparks fly when she's picked up by veterinarian Gabe Wentworth...

"A lovely, easy, and wholesome story that animal lovers are sure to enjoy."
—*Night Owl Reviews* for *My Forever Home*

For more info about Sourcebooks's books and authors, visit:
sourcebooks.com